Anchored Hearts Vol. 3

Letting Go of Us

International Bestselling Author
J.M. WITT

Acknowledgments

Rick: Thank you for your support and encouragement. It means the world to me that you're proud of me, even if it is smut! Smut to be proud of!

My children: Please get along and play nicely so mommy can keep writing for her fans!

Betsy: Thank you times infinity. You've pulled me back from the ledge more than once. I love you!

Letty: You've held my hand through this process more than you know. Thank you so much!!

All my friends: Thank you for taking a leap of faith on me. Your support means the world to me.

Bloggers: There are so many of you to thank. I can't name names because I'll just shoot myself in the foot. Without your support I wouldn't be here today. Thank you.

Betas: My loves, my bitches. I love you girls. Angela, Tracey, Tami, Jasmine, Elaine, Betsy, Marina, Lisa, Melanie, Letty, Jessica, and Rebecca. THANK YOU! I'm so thankful to have you girls. You'll never know how much your support means to me. The last couple months have been wonderful and I look forward to many more. I can't wait to meet you ALL!

Skye & Tyf: What can I possibly say to thank you? You girls are my rocks and my bff's. I'm so honored and blessed to call you mentors as well as friends. Without you, I'd never be able to shake it off!

My fans: Wow. That never gets old. Your loyalty has blown me away. Thank you a million times over. I hope that my words touch your heart. Remember, nothing is worth having if you're not fighting for it. Anchor your heart!

Letting Go of Us

one

Finished

~ JAMES ~

Rainbow. I couldn't believe she'd said it. We weren't even doing anything. But she meant it. She *knew* that if she said that word, it was done, over, finished, everything we had. Gone. One simple word. I was trying to explain to her, get her to listen, I was getting ready to do anything just to have her back. At least, I wanted to try.

Instead, she crucified my soul with that one word. Now I had a fucking tattoo as a daily reminder of what happens when you let someone capture your heart. FUCK. It was the exact reason I had the no kissing, no emotions rule with all my subs. I was so damn mad. I stormed into the penthouse, a rage fueling every move. Running up the stairs, two at a time, I ran into Melissa in the hallway. It'd been a long time since rage had fueled my desire, except that night at the club with Cassidy a few weeks back. Not my finest moment. My cock twitched as I closed the distance between Melissa and I.

Melissa backed up against the wall shaking her head at me. I wanted to sink my dick into a hot, trembling pussy, but not hers. Growling, I quickly turned from Melissa and made my way to my room. Stripping out of my clothes, I pulled on some shorts and went to my workout room. Taping my hands the best I could I began decimating the bag.

By the time I was done I could barely pick my sorry ass up off the floor. Melissa, nowhere to be found, was either locked in her room or she'd left. I couldn't blame her either way. We'd come to terms with the fact that we weren't good together, not compatible. Melissa and I had attempted a Dom/sub relationship, but it hadn't worked. I was too Dom and she wasn't sub enough.

All I wanted was my bed, and Cassidy. My Blackbird. And I could never have her again. Safe words were there for a reason. They were the 'out' for any sub. Clearly she wanted out.

~ PAUL ~

THINGS HAD BEEN extremely tense around the office. I had been avoiding James at all costs. From what Cassidy had told me, when she wasn't sobbing, they had ended things. Divorce papers were being drawn up. I felt horrible for her, knowing the pain she was going through. But, selfishly, I wanted a second chance with her and it was so close I could almost taste it.

James and I only discussed business and we weren't spending any unnecessary time together. My spare time was spent at the gym, with or without Cal, and my free time with Cassidy. It was Easter weekend and I was spending it alone. Cal, Jane and Cassidy had gone up to their Dad's place for the holiday. My own mom had tried to get me to come home, to Atlanta, but I just wasn't up for a quick trip back. Cassidy was expected home the next day and I was already eager to see her.

My thoughts were consumed with her, just like they had been all those years ago.

Sitting just outside my barracks, I was writing Cassidy a letter. I promised her a letter every day. I hadn't mailed any yet, but I would soon enough. A shadow crept over my letter and I looked up to see Cora's shapely figure. Her hands were perched on her hips as she smiled at me. Looking down, I rolled my eyes and chastised myself for ever sleeping with her. Clearly, my dick had been doing my thinking for too long. Cora was just a soft place to bury my cock, nothing less, nothing more. Even Cal had warned me to steer clear of her.

"Welcome back." When I didn't respond she whined, "Didn't you miss me?"

As I gazed at the letter, I asked her, "What do you want, Cora?"

"You. I missed you."

"Ha! I highly doubt that. Dutch-Boy warms your bed when I'm not in it. Everyone knows that."

Before I could stop her, she snatched the letter from my hand. She looked to the letter, then to me, and back again. "Who's Cassidy?"

"Give it back, Cora."

"Tell me who she is."

She was bound to find out one way or another. I didn't think she'd give two shits so I just told her. "My girl." Reaching my hand out, I ordered, "Now give me back my letter."

Hesitantly, she handed it back. "Since when do you have a girl?"

"Since, I just do. Jealous?" I looked up and saw what looked like worry all over her face. She was jealous. Oh well. She'd get over it.

A couple of days later Cora cornered me as I was headed to mail my stack of letters to Cassidy. I had decided to mail Cassidy several letters at once, rather than one every day. Ok, so part of it was that I was lazy. Cal was still barely talking to me, telling me how I'd better do right by his baby sister. I had every intention of doing just that. Fucking Cora was the only thing standing in my way, literally.

"Paul, we need to talk."

"Cora, there's nothing to talk about. I'm not interested."

"Are you interested if I tell you there's a baby?"

Christ. I hadn't thought about that day in so long. Granted, everything that had gone down between us all never left my mind, but that day in particular…I never allowed myself to think about it. If I could go back, I would've mailed those letters to Cassidy. Instead, I made the worst decision of my life, though at the time I thought I was doing what any good man would do. What Cassidy would expect from a man she loved. Fuck, I was an idiot.

OVER A WEEK LATER, I still hadn't heard from Cassidy. At the gym, with Cal, he'd assured me that she seemed to be fine. That night, after texting Cassidy as I left the gym, I decided to go home and shower. When I got out of the shower and dressed, she still hadn't responded. I hopped in my SUV and made my way to her place. The lights were on and her mustang sat in the driveway. It was a sweet ass ride, but the license plate—MRSJB3—irked the hell out of me. It was a reminder of every obstacle in my way.

I really wasn't trying to encroach on her marriage. She was someone I cared about and so was James. But if he wasn't going to be the man she deserved, then I would be. Walking up the steps to the door, I knocked and waited. I could hear the music blaring, nothing surprising. The girl liked her music and she liked it loud. I couldn't fault her for that.

She probably couldn't even hear me knocking. I banged on the door again and waited before turning the knob. It was unlocked and that annoyed me. She knew better even though Ryan's car was parked out front. Gazing at him he nodded in acknowledgment as I made my way inside.

Closing the door, I stood and took in my surroundings. I could smell cleaning detergent. She must've been cleaning and there was no telling where in the house she was. I let my ears focus on the song playing, immediately recognizing Stabbing Westward. Listening to the lyrics I wondered who she was listening to it for, or if it was just random selection.

When the song ended, another came on and had me puffing out a sharp breath. Her taste in music could be labeled as schizophrenic. Curiosity got the better of me and I walked to her iPod to find out the name of the song playing. The song was *Letters From The Sky* by Civil Twilight. I'd never heard of them and when I spotted the title of the playlist—JB3—my gut churned as I set it back down. Her footsteps began thumping down the stairs as I turned to wait for her.

She jumped when she spotted me. "Hey. You scared me."

"Sorry, I knocked a couple times. Figured you couldn't hear me."

Shrugging her shoulders and forcing a smile on her face, she walked to the kitchen and dropped off the cleaning supplies in her hands. Walking to the stereo, she turned down the music before crossing her arms over her chest. She seemed nervous and I couldn't imagine why.

"Everything ok?" Her eyes darted to mine as she nodded and I knew she was lying. "No, it's not." I sat down on the couch and motioned her to join me. Curling her feet under herself, she sat on the other end. "Spill it."

She huffed, "No. I'm good. It's personal, anyways."

Hmm. She clearly didn't want to talk about it and I didn't want to push her. "Have you eaten?" She answered that she hadn't and I got up and headed to the kitchen. "You got anything in here to make or should I order take out?"

"I'm not really hungry."

I grabbed the stack of takeout menus from the end of the counter and told her, "Your choice. Anything you want."

I looked over to her and she was examining her hands. Something caught my attention on the counter and I picked up the small folded card and opened it up. I felt all the blood leave my face as my hands began shaking. I knew exactly what I was looking at. Was Cassidy pregnant? Did Cal know? I knew immediately that he didn't because I would've heard about it.

My eyes moved to her and she was stone still, staring at me from across the room. Walking back to the couch, with the card in my hand, I sat down next to her. She wiped a lone tear from her face as I handed it to her. She looked it over momentarily and then placed it on the coffee table.

"Does he know?"

"Not yet." I could barely hear the words as she squeaked them out.

"Christ."

I didn't know what else to say. My world just came to a screeching halt. Cassidy was pregnant. I knew it was selfish, maybe it was jealousy, because I didn't want it to be true. I couldn't begin to imagine what she was going through. They were separated and now she was pregnant and we all knew who the father was. James.

~ CASSIDY ~

PAUL AND I sat there in silence for a long time. He seemed to know exactly what the card was. I don't know what kind of reaction I expected from him. I certainly hadn't planned on him finding out before I told James. Jane and Paul both knew my secret and I had to tell James before anyone else found out.

"Are you pregnant?" Jane's question from that night still lingered in my ears.

How could I have been so stupid? I had been exhausted, puking, and an emotional basket case for days, if not weeks, and that was just the tip of the iceberg.

Standing in the bathroom at my father's house, I stared at the stick I'd just peed on. Slowly, I watched as the line appeared on the stick. Pulling out the directions, for what was probably the tenth time, I examined it again. It was just the control line. Chewing my nails, I kept watch of it. I paced the small bathroom before looking at it again. A plus sign appeared in the second window. Grabbing it, I sat down on the toilet and stared at it in disbelief.

I was pregnant! I was elated. And then like a wrecking ball, my circumstances slammed into me. I was pregnant and on my way to divorce. The room began to spin and I felt the signs of my volatile stomach begin to play again. Turning on the cold water, I splashed my face and took in some deep breaths managing to hold the nausea at bay. Jane was probably getting worried. Grabbing the test, I walked back into the bedroom as Jane smiled at me.

Jane had gone to my prenatal appointment with me earlier that day. I was a coward and still trying to figure out when to tell James. I think I wanted proof, from more than a store bought test, when I told him. Now I had it. I was so petrified of what his reaction would be. Jane had assured me he'd do the right thing, but that wasn't what I was worried about. I was worried he *would* do the right thing, even if it wasn't what he wanted. And I just wanted him to want the baby *and* me.

"When are you due?"

Paul's question pulled me from my own thoughts as I said, "December 11th." He just nodded. "I'm almost through the first trimester and didn't even know it. I'm an idiot."

"Cassidy, you're not an idiot. You've had a lot on your plate."

"I know, but isn't a woman supposed to know these things? Jane's the one who figured it out, not me."

"Well, Jane's a nurse. Don't be so hard on yourself." I couldn't verbalize my response and just shook my head. "You need to tell him, Cassidy. The sooner the better."

"I know."

"Is there anything I can do to help?"

"Only if you can get him to answer my calls, because I'm guessing he won't."

"We'll figure it out."

My voice cracked as I muffled out, "It's such a mess, Paul. I didn't want this, not like this. He's made it clear to me that he doesn't want me." Paul pulled me close as I soaked his shirt with my tears.

"He's a fool. But you have to tell him. I'll be here whether he is or not."

I woke up a few hours later curled up on the couch, under a blanket. Paul was gone and he hadn't left a note. I was starving and grabbed the only thing that sounded good. Cocoa Puffs. After I had a bowl, I went upstairs and went to bed.

THAT FRIDAY I was determined to tell James about the baby, especially after some light spotting. I had called my doctor, who told me to take it easy and we scheduled a follow-up appointment for the next Monday. I didn't want to wait, but he'd assured me my hormone levels were normal and this early in the pregnancy there was nothing to do except wait. I just wanted to get through the rest of the work day. I'd finally conceded to Cecily's choice to interview Melissa. No other candidates had presented themselves. I had Linda, who I still wasn't sure I wanted to keep as our receptionist, call Melissa and set up an interview for the following week.

I had tried calling and texting James a few times and never got a response. Texting Smith, I figured he'd help me and I didn't really want to involve Paul. Paul already knew too much. Smith answered and I asked him to put James on the phone and James refused.

"God dammit." I pulled into the parking garage under the hotel as I unleashed my anger on Smith. "Tell him to stop being a little bitch." I think I heard him stifle a laugh. "Let him know I'll be at the penthouse and I'm not leaving until he talks to me. It's important."

"Cassidy, come to the office. He's here."

"No, I'll wait here."

Smith continued trying to convince me to go to their office across the street and I refused. It was a private matter and needed to stay that way. I lost signal and dropped the call as I made my way up the elevator. I was relieved to discover that all the codes were still the same and my keycard still worked.

I walked down the hall to his penthouse and used my key to get in.

Opening the door, something felt off. I couldn't explain it any other way. The faint sound of music drifted through the air. Smith had said that James was at the office. Why was there music playing? Maybe James *was* here after all.

"James?" I made my way up the stairs with my purse in my hands and the proof of my pregnancy inside.

I made my way down the hall toward the bedroom door. The music seemed to be coming from his workout room and as I approached the doorway I saw there was no one in there. Where was he? Turning back toward his room I stopped dead in my tracks. Melissa stood in front of me with a towel wrapped around her. I wasn't sure which room she walked out of and didn't care. She was running a towel through her hair and froze in her tracks when she saw me.

I was so upset that my tongue became paralyzed, thick and numb like I'd just left the dentist. I could feel myself start to shake. What a fool I was! Rushing past her, I headed toward the stairs as her arm reached out and grabbed my wrist.

"Cassidy, please stop. It's not what you think."

Whipping around to face the skank, words finally found me. "Not what I think? You don't have any idea what I think." She moved back half a step as I began screaming at her. "You two whores deserve each other."

"Please let me explain."

"Explain? Explain what? That his bed wasn't even cold and here you are warming it again." It hurt to breathe and all I wanted was to fall to the floor and scream. Instead the words continued to fly out of my mouth. "I don't know who to be more disgusted with. You're pathetic." She seemed to be speechless and I turned and headed for the stairs. "You can forget about the job, too. I won't be made a fool anymore by you or him." I had to get out of there before James showed up.

As my foot hit the first step and then the second I was jerked backwards. Turning, I saw that my purse strap caught on the railing. I wasn't aware of the tears I was shedding until they ran down my cheeks. Melissa came closer and tried helping with my caught strap as my tears began blinding me.

"Cassidy!" It was James and then I heard the front door close.

"Dammit." I couldn't clearly see the stairs due to the tears, as I attempted to get down them. My strap gave way right as I tugged on it violently.

His figure came into view just as my foot missed my intended target. One leg went out in front and the other behind me as I grabbed for the railing. I was unsuccessful at catching myself and the room tumbled around my vision as I rolled down the stairs. Pain seared me and I could hear him calling my name as my back crashed against the stairs and then everything went black.

two

Heartbeat

~ JAMES ~

REFUSING TO TAKE THE CALL, I listened as Smith laughed at something Cassidy said. He then tried coaxing her to come to the office. As I listened to the conversation I became slightly nervous. Why was she so insistent upon seeing me?

"Dammit." Smith put the phone in his pocket and glared at me. "Did you change the codes?"

"No, why?"

"She's at the hotel and headed to the penthouse."

FUCK! "God damn that stubborn woman."

He glared at me, arms crossed over his chest, "Isn't this what you wanted? Her to move on."

"Not like this." We both knew if she found Melissa there that it would crush her. I still hadn't told her that Melissa was staying with me. Cassidy would be heartbroken. Maybe it's what needed to happen to get her to let go, but why did I feel so sick about it? "I have to stop her."

"Why don't you just admit that you want her? Things would be a lot easier for everyone."

"Wanting her has never been the question. You *know* what she did, what she said. There's no going back." Smith was the only person I'd confided in about Cassidy using her safe word on me.

Smith just shook his head. "You and your stupid rules. Make some new ones. If you love her..."

I was out of the room before I could hear the rest of what he had to say. Riding down the elevator, I dropped down, my legs bent, and released a guttural groan. How was I ever going to get her out of my head, my heart, and my soul? Loving her from afar was my penance. Maybe Smith was right. What could be so important that Cassidy was willing to wait for me until I showed my face? Maybe she wanted to stop the divorce? I shook the thought from my head. Dreams weren't something that came my way.

I opened the door to the penthouse and heard her raised voice coming from upstairs. "Cassidy!"

The door slammed behind me as I made my way toward the staircase. I glanced at Melissa, in nothing but a towel, *fucking perfect,* as Cassidy stood at the top of the stairs. I saw it happen even before she was aware of it. Her foot slipped, as she lost her balance her body flung back against the railing as her body tumbled over itself and down the stairs. I was helpless to stop it from happening.

She landed at the base of the stairs and I carefully gathered her in my arms. "Cassidy, baby are you hurt?" She wasn't moving or responding to me. No, no, no.

"James, be careful. You shouldn't move her." Melissa was running down the stairs toward us.

I glared at her, "What did you do?" Looking back down to my angel I pleaded with her, "Talk to me, Blackbird."

"James, her purse was stuck, I was trying to help. I promise I didn't..." Tears were forming in Melissa's eyes as she shook her head. I knew she hadn't done anything malicious, I was just lashing out.

"She's unconscious. What do I do?"

Melissa reached into my jacket pocket, took my phone and called 911. I listened as she talked to the operator on the other end. "She's breathing. Wait, I think she's waking up."

I was stroking the hair back from her face as her eyes fluttered. Groaning, she reached for her head as she made eye contact with me. I knew in that moment that I couldn't lose her. Cassidy winced and latched on to her abdomen.

"James, the baby."

Her words were like a punch to the gut. The baby? What baby? The tears that had begun to fill my own eyes dissipated as I looked up to Melissa. She stepped away and relayed the message to the operator.

Looking back down to Cassidy, I asked, "What are you talking about?"

She started sobbing as she cried out, "I'm pregnant James, and I had to tell you. That's why I came here." She spotted Melissa then, almost like she hadn't realized she was there before. NO, NO, NO. Her eyes darted between the two of us.

"Cassidy, it's not what you think."

"I think that I'm a fool." Her eyes left mine as she winced again, trying to move. "I need to get out of here."

"You're not going anywhere, but to the hospital."

Could it be true? Was she really pregnant? My heart sped up at the thought of having a child with her. If she thought I was overbearing before, God help her.

I managed to keep her relatively still until the paramedics came. She wouldn't speak to me and Melissa had vanished upstairs, and returned, dressed, before they wheeled Cassidy out of the hotel.

I was about to climb into the ambulance with her when she refused. "No. You're not riding with me."

"Cassidy." I looked to the paramedic and proclaimed, "I'm her husband."

"We're separated!" She looked to something, more like someone, behind me and I followed her gaze. "You're a whore." Looking back to me, she choked out, "I hate you."

Melissa hadn't flinched at Cassidy's words, but I had. She then handed me Cassidy's purse, the broken strap dangling, before heading back into the hotel.

"Maybe it's best if you follow behind." I nodded at the paramedic and handed him the purse and watched as he set it on Cassidy's stretcher.

I watched as she pulled away in the ambulance. She would never hear me out, but I had to try to find a way. Jane. Jane would listen to me and Cassidy would listen to her. She had to. I ran across the street and jumped into my truck, which sat in the parking garage, and started to dial Jane, but decided to wait.

When I got to the hospital, Cassidy still wouldn't let me stay with her. She'd insisted that I call Jane, but wouldn't say another word to me. Stepping outside, I did just that. I called Jane and told her what had happened. Jane confirmed that Cassidy was pregnant, but I still couldn't process it. Why the hell did Jane know and not me? Jane found me in the lobby a short time later and asked me some questions.

Sighing, she resigned, "I'll go back and talk to her. Wait here."

Waiting wasn't something I wanted to do. She had five minutes and I was going back there, whether they liked it or not. Security would have to throw me off the premises.

Was she really pregnant? I couldn't wrap my head around the idea. How long had she known? When had it happened? I mentally chastised myself, because the last few times we'd been together, I'd left her before morning. I knew that was a hard limit for her, she'd said so herself. But I wasn't prepared to unveil all my secrets to her, while she was awake, and that's what I wanted to do. Staring upon her, asleep and sated, I would talk to her about my demons, unbeknownst to her. I was pushing my luck because I knew eventually she'd feign sleep and hear my secrets, if she hadn't already.

I looked at my watch for the third time. Time's up. Tough shit. I was done waiting. I made my way back to her curtain, which was closed and poked my head in. There was a nurse, doctor, Jane and Cassidy. Her belly was exposed and they were all staring at a small screen.

"There's your baby."

Cassidy let out a heavy breath as I asked, "It's true?" The doctor dared to question who I was and I defensively responded that I was her husband.

Nodding, he pushed a few buttons and the oddest sound filled the air. "And that is your baby's heartbeat."

The doctor said he was going to release her, but Cassidy still wouldn't talk to me. Jane and I stepped outside where Jane proceeded to cuss me out. I told her the truth, that there was nothing going on between Melissa and me. She was nothing more than a roommate. Jane seemed hesitant to believe me, but that wasn't my concern.

Before I could even fathom what was happening, Paul's voice filled the air around me. "You son of a bitch." Jane and I turned toward Paul's voice as his fists met with my chest. "She's pregnant! What did you do?"

Shoving him back, I bellowed, "I didn't do anything. Why are

YOU here?" Did he really think I was capable of hurting her?

"She called me crying."

Jane tried stepping between us, ordering, "You guys, stop."

"What's going on?"

Cassidy walked up to us with her discharge papers in hand. Paul rushed to her side and asked her something, but I didn't hear what was said. My thoughts became strewn as my temper boiled over at the sight of his hands on her. She didn't shrug him off and even leaned into him.

Doubt coursed through me and the words left my lips before I could stop them. "Is it even my baby?" Who was the fool? Me or Cassidy or Paul? Cassidy challenged me with her eyes before I lied and stated, "It's good to know I'm not the only one fucking around."

Paul was beet red. He went to step forward and Cassidy grabbed his arm to stop him. "Well, at least we understand each other."

Stubborn fucking woman. Something in her eyes hardened and I believed for a moment that she was lying. She was just being obstinate and wanted to hurt me like I'd hurt her. All thoughts of the baby were pushed aside. Well, fuck her and fuck them if they thought they could play me, whether they were lying or not. I had to leave, not just the premises, the city. Hell, maybe I needed to leave the state. I needed to decompress and sort out my thoughts before my anger took over and someone got hurt.

Storming off I went home and packed my bags. I didn't leave a note for anyone and Melissa wasn't around when I got there. I would find out later that Melissa had moved to the hotel room down the hall while I was at the hospital with Cassidy. Before I headed down to my truck, with my bags packed, I called Cassidy. It rang and rang before going to voicemail. Trying one more time, I was sent to voicemail after two rings. Point taken. Who was I kidding? No one would miss me, anyways.

~ PAUL ~

WHEN WE GOT back to her place, after the scene at the hospital, she went straight upstairs. We hadn't spoken on the way home. *His* ringtone began to play through the air and I spotted her purse on the table by the door. She came walking down the stairs in lounge pants and a sweatshirt when the phone began ringing again. Pulling it out of her purse, she hit ignore and sent him to voicemail before turning her phone off.

A couple nights later, Cassidy was quiet and distant, which didn't surprise me. I'd packed a few things and was staying in her spare room which also served as a small home gym. I didn't want her to be alone. The doctors had told her to take it easy, that there was still a chance she could lose the baby.

It hadn't even been a full forty-eight hours and no one had seen or heard from James. Smith said we shouldn't worry, that he'd be back. Cassidy was upstairs taking a nap and I was eating a sandwich on the couch. I heard the faint sound of her footsteps up above. She was in the bathroom.

I didn't think anything of it until I heard her cries fill the air. "Paul!" Dropping the sandwich to the plate sitting on the coffee table, I ran upstairs. I found her huddled on the bathroom floor. "It's gone, the baby's gone."

"What are you talking about?"

She stood up, with some help from me, "Please, take me to hospital." I just nodded my head as she slipped on some shoes.

We were headed back to her place a couple of hours later. The doctors had confirmed that she had lost the baby after all. I tucked her into bed that night and kissed her forehead. What could I possibly say or do to make it better for her? James should have been there with her, not me. Even I knew that. I also knew the pain of losing a child, but I imagined it must be different for a woman.

She grabbed my hand as I started to walk away. "Please, stay. I don't want to be alone."

Nodding, I kicked off my shoes, shirt and climbed under the covers with her, leaving my pants on. There was nothing romantic about what happened. She was in pain and if my presence next to her helped, then I was willing to do it.

"Thank you for being here."

"I'll always be here. Whatever you need, anything you want, you can count on me."

~ CASSIDY ~

That Friday, after my miscarriage, I was headed to Cal and Jane's for our usual pizza night. When I pulled up I recognized several different vehicles. Smith and Paul were both there, a patrol car and Cal's truck. I couldn't even imagine what was going on, not after the months of bullshit we'd all been through.

Walking in the door, the conversation was heated and flowing, my presence unnoticed.

"It's been a week since anyone has seen or heard from him. Something's wrong." Jane was upset. Paul and Cal seemed disinterested as Jane glared at them. "What is wrong with you two? He could be in trouble!"

Smith chimed in, "Has anyone talked to Annie?" When no one said that they had, he added, "I'm calling Annie. This isn't the first time he's disappeared."

James. They had to be talking about James. "He's missing?" All eyes were staring at me and it was the only answer I needed. "Since when?"

Jane walked over to me, "No one has heard from him since last Friday, at the hos…"

Cutting her off, "Why am I just now hearing about this?"

"Well, with everything else going on, I didn't want to worry you."

Jane was sweet, but it was just pissing me off. My husband was missing! "So, NOBODY has heard from him?"

Frank, who I hadn't noticed until then, came over. "Cassidy, have you heard from him? Anything? A text, a call?"

My breath caught and I placed my hand on my chest. "Oh, God." The emotions started seeping up to my chest as I tried to control my voice. Smith interjected then that Annie was on her way over. "He called me that night, twice. I ignored it."

Cal then asked, "Did he leave you a voicemail?"

"No."

"With everything going on between the two of you. I can't believe he just up and left. Wait, yes I can."

"Cal, please." Jane was trying to calm him down when Frank, who was clearly on duty, asked what 'everything' was.

"It's personal, Frank."

"That's why it's important you tell me. I'm trying to help, Cassidy."

"I'm pregnant, I was." The look on his face wasn't lost on me. Paul disappeared outside and Smith just looked at me dumbfounded. He hadn't known. "I lost the baby. He doesn't know."

"Doesn't know what? That you…"

"That I lost the baby." Jane sat down next to me and tried consoling me as I continued disclosing information to Frank that I didn't want to. "He found out that day, last Friday." The real fear penetrated my soul. "Dan, what about Dan? What if Dan got to him?"

"There's been no further reports of him in the area."

"Yeah, but what if..."

"If Dan was involved, we'd know. Dan would want us to know."

"This is my fault."

"This ISN'T your fault, Cass. Don't you dare blame yourself for this! This is on James." I loved my brother, even when I didn't want him to be right.

Frank nodded his head and suddenly Jane and I were the only ones left inside. I sat there thinking about all the horrible things that could've happened to James and I had been none the wiser. What if he'd called me, looking for a lifeline, or a cry for help? I'd spent my days mourning the loss of a child I'd never get to know and a marriage that seemed forever lost. No matter how hard I tried to make myself hate him, I couldn't do it. A few minutes later, the door opened and everyone came walking back in, Annie included.

"Hey, Cassidy."

"Hey."

Everyone stared at her as if they knew she'd have the information we sought. "James, is fine. He needed some time away. I assure you he's ok."

My fear turned into joy, knowing he was ok, and then it boiled into anger. I tried taking a few deep breaths to calm myself. I began shaking and stood before walking toward the door.

"Cassidy?"

"WHAT?" Annie looked a little taken aback at my tone. "What do you want me to say? All this fuss and commotion, when all the while he's fine and YOU knew he was fine. I thought he was dead when I walked in here and found out no one's heard a word from him for a week. I'm his WIFE, at least legally. What the fuck is wrong with you people?" Glaring at Smith, "You expect me to believe you didn't know where he was when she does?"

"Cassidy, I swear."

"You can all rot in hell." Cal's eyes were the last I saw as I walked out the door. There was no judgment there. He was mad, too. I could tell. For once I may have spoken before he had the chance to. As I made it to my car, I felt a hand on my arm. Whipping around, I came face to face with Paul. "Don't!"

"Cassidy, I'm really sorry. I can't begin to understand..."

"No, you can't. Please. Leave me alone. I don't want to say something I'll regret. I'm angry and I need some time."

"Ok. Just let me know when you get home safe."

I scoffed. "Please. With my twenty-four hour tail, I'll be fine." I pointed at Ryan, who was parked on the street. "This shit is getting old." I climbed in the car and drove home.

It took me hours to get to sleep that night. Horrifying scenarios ran rampant through my head of the terrible things that could've happened to James. That didn't include the things that came to mind of James and infidelity. How did I know he wasn't drowning his sorrows in some sex at the club? Maybe we were both better off. God, I just wanted all the hurt to stop.

three

Lost

~ JAMES ~

I WAS HEADED TO THE TOWNHOUSE and hoped she'd see me. We were going to have a baby together and I wanted to do anything and everything I could to get *us* back. Dr. Pratt had been more than obliging over the last week and helped me more than he knew. I had yet to turn on my cell phone or check my email, knowing I'd find a barrage of inquiries to my lack of presence over the last two weeks. Cassidy was my number one priority and I wasn't going to let anything distract me from that.

I was parked outside when her car pulled in the drive. She was home early. The license plate put a smile on my face as I watched her walk to the door. She seemed lost in thought as she closed the front door behind her. I climbed out of the truck and made my way up the steps.

Knocking on the door, I waited for her to answer. When she

opened the door, she stared at me like I was a ghost. "Can I come in?"

She just nodded as I stepped through the doorway. I couldn't help it as my eyes drifted to her still flat belly. I wondered when she'd start showing. I knew that the books I'd read said it was a little different for everyone.

The emotions were written all over her face. She avoided my eyes as I watched her own become glassy. "Cassidy?"

"No. Please." Stepping closer, my knuckles grazed her cheek as a small tremor ran through her. "I'm angry with you. No, infuriated."

"I know. I'm sorry." Before I expected it, she wrapped her arms around my torso and buried her face in my chest.

"I thought you were dead. Where have you been?"

"I was getting my head put back on straight." Rubbing my hands on her back, I buried my nose in her hair. "I wasn't prepared for the news that I was going to be a father. We have to stop hurting each other just because we can."

She pulled back and stared at me like I'd grown a second head. "James, the baby..."

"I know. We have a lot to talk about. Please hear me out."

She shook my arms off her, "No, you don't understand." I looked at her confused. "Have you talked to anyone since you left?"

"No. What's going on? I came straight here, to you."

"James, I lost the baby." The tears rolled down her cheeks and I felt the color drain from my face.

"I don't, but, what do you mean?"

She turned from me and headed toward the couch. "I miscarried a couple days after you left. There's nothing anyone could've done." I watched her curl up on the couch and place her head in her hands.

I stood there and watched her as she sat, silent, for far too long. I couldn't process any reasonable thoughts. What did I say, what did I do to make this better for her? I couldn't fathom her pain. Pain? Had it hurt? Jesus, I wanted to be sick.

"There's no baby. You're free now. It's ok."

"What? No. That's not what I want. I *want* you. I *want* the baby." I knelt down in front of her, still in denial. "I want us and our little family."

Her breath hitched as she traced my scar, "But there is no little family. It wasn't meant to be. You can go."

"This is my fault."

"We're both to blame, James. I forgive you. I just need to figure out how to forgive myself. The doctors said I should still be able to have kids, this one just wasn't meant to be."

No. I wanted *our* baby. My hands circled her hips as I laid my head in her lap. My baby, our baby, was gone. In the blink of an eye. And I'd left her, to suffer through it alone.

"I'm so sorry I wasn't here with you. I wanted to be." Her hands began stroking through my hair. God, I'd missed her touch. "I'm sorry you went through it alone. That was never my intention."

"I wasn't alone. Not really."

My head snapped up at that. What did she mean? Had Jane been with her? "Jane?" She just shook her head. "Cal?"

A tear slid down her cheek. "No, he didn't even know about the baby until it was too late." I pulled away from her. There was only one other person. We both knew that. "James. I was alone and he was the only other person who knew. He stayed with me. Night and day."

Her words were just making it worse. Innocent or not. She was just validating everything I was paranoid about. Paul was the one who was there when she needed me. ME. I was a coward and had run.

She tried reaching for me. *Breathe James, just breathe.* "No! No, it wasn't meant to be. You're right."

"James?"

"I'm sorry. This never should've happened." She took my words the wrong way and I saw the wall go up, again.

"Please go."

"Cassidy..."

"GO! Maybe Annie can help you, since she seems to be the only one you choose to confide in. You're too late. It's too late." I stood up slowly and paced the small space. "You're always too late."

The dagger was already in me, her words just twisted it. She was right. I was too late. I walked out as the rain clouds began to pour down on me. Always too late.

~ CASSIDY ~

HE WALKED BACK out the door. I didn't cry and actually thought I might have emptied my reserves, the well run dry. For the first time in years I wanted my mom, no matter what she'd done or said to me. I just wanted to confide in her, woman to woman. My grandmother would've been a great alternative, but she was gone too. My phone rang and it was Jane.

Jane convinced me I should go with her and Cal to her family's cottage, up north. I didn't want to intrude on their alone time, but Jane had insisted I wouldn't be intruding. The wedding was just over a month away and we could use some time to enjoy ourselves. Unable to deny that I could use some time away, I conceded to going. She said that they'd swing by and pick me up before dinner time.

Not sure what to pack, I threw a little bit of everything in my bag. I needed to be somewhere that didn't remind me of him and that was the main reason I had agreed to go. My heart was scattered, in a million jagged pieces, on the floor of my soul. Paul and James had each staked their claim to bits and pieces of it. The whole thing was made worse by the fact that James and Paul were friends, and Paul was still working for James.

Maybe a weekend away was exactly what I needed to figure out what, if either of them, was what I wanted. Who was I kidding? I knew who I wanted, but did he want me? I was beginning to doubt it. My head was beyond fucked up and I didn't care anymore.

Pulled from my thoughts, I heard the horn from my brother's truck, grabbed my bag and headed for the door. Opening the passenger side back door, I slid my bag on the floor and climbed up.

"Hey gorgeous."

My heart stopped and I looked over to see Paul occupying the spot behind Cal. *Fuck.* I looked to Cal who was oblivious and then to Jane who shrugged her shoulders and pointed at Cal. Being in Paul's presence all weekend wasn't going to help me with my issues.

"Hey, I didn't know you were coming."

"Cal invited me. Hope that's ok?"

"Of course." I lied through my teeth, buckled in and geared up for the three hour drive.

When I woke, I was in Paul's lap. Not sure how I ended up there, I pushed myself up and moved to my side of the seat.

"Sorry about that."

"It's all good."

We pulled up a long driveway shortly after. Eventually we came to a clearing and before us was a huge log home, not a cottage. There were lights on and I recognized one of the vehicles as Smith's. My stomach immediately sank. *What the hell?* I felt like banging my head on the wall. Odds were if Smith was there, James might show. Of course, I had no idea given he'd disappeared for two weeks. Maybe he'd disappear again. It was going to be a really fucking awkward weekend, regardless.

As we were unloading, Jane walked over. "I'm really sorry, Cassidy. I really did think it would be just the three of us."

"Story of my life. I'll survive." *Lord help me.* "He's back."

She looked to me, surprised. "James?"

"Yes. He came over before you called."

"Oh, Cassidy. Are you ok? Did you tell him?"

"I'm not sure I know what ok is anymore. He knows."

"And?"

I just shrugged my shoulders. "I'm not sure. I think he thinks I want Paul and I think he wants out."

"Cassidy, I don't know what to say? I can talk to him."

"It's ok. Let's just get through this weekend first."

Walking in the front door, after climbing up the porch, you could hear music playing. As I took in the grandeur of the place I knew it was the biggest log cabin I'd ever been in or seen.

Jane announced, "Ok. There are plenty of bedrooms, so, take your pick." Jane led Cal up the stairs and Paul and I followed suit. She went on explaining that her parent's, along with James', built the house together almost twenty years ago and had updated it a few years back. Almost every bedroom had its own bathroom and some were 'jack n jill' style.

Jane pulled Cal into a room close to the staircase and they shut the door giggling. I rolled my eyes and made my way along the open banister. Down below I saw Smith and Delaney playing pool. Delaney waved to me and I waved back. *Where was James?* Maybe he hadn't come.

I strolled past five or six more doors before picking the door at the end of the hall. I wanted nothing more than to be as far away from the couples as possible. Looking behind me, I saw Paul go into a bedroom a few doors back. Hopefully the room I picked was unoccupied and I liked that it was seemingly away from the bustle of the rest of the house.

I walked in and found a rustic looking bedroom. It was large and had a door that went into a bathroom. Placing my bag on the bed, I then walked to the bathroom. It was huge, with a giant cast iron tub in the middle of the room. There was a large shower in the corner, with no door or curtain. There were a few more doors and curiosity got the better of me. One was a linen closet, one led to a balcony overlooking the back of the house, and the other was a small sauna. *I was in heaven.* There were controls on the wall for different lights and heaters. Even the tiled floor was heated.

I was ecstatic that I had discovered that room and that it wasn't already occupied. Finder's keepers. I was fully prepared to give myself a mini spa weekend. After changing into some sweat pants, I headed back downstairs. Everyone was in a large media room. There was a dart board, pool table, a large poker table, large screen TV on the wall, couches, chairs, and a bar with six barstools. Delaney was pouring herself a margarita and I went and got myself a glass.

"How you doing?"

"I'm fine, Delaney. How are you?"

"Good. Glad to see you guys up here. We thought we'd be alone, but the more the merrier."

I wanted to ask her if James was coming, but couldn't get myself to do it. Hell, I didn't even know if anyone knew he was back and I wasn't sure if I should be the one to tell them. I took a swig of my drink and immediately sucked in my cheeks. It was strong, but delicious. Since I wasn't going anywhere, I indulged, and it wasn't long before I was refilling my glass. A few drinks later I was feeling pretty good and didn't care about the predicament I was in any longer.

"What do you say?" I looked into his blue eyes as he smiled brightly at me. "Up for some darts?"

"Why not!" I raised myself off the couch and became dizzy for a split second. Paul steadied me and once the blood got back to my head I was ok.

"How many have you had?"

"Don't start with me." I smiled, "I'm fine."

After a game of darts, I wasn't in the mood to play anymore. It was then that someone came in the front door. Nobody else seemed to hear it but me. The dread filled me. I knew who it had to be. His figure came into view and our eyes immediately locked.

"James! You're back!" Smith walked over and handed him a beer and then hugged him. "Glad to see you got my text!"

Cal was giving him the evil eye and Paul just nodded at him as Jane and Delaney chastised him for disappearing for so long.

He pulled his gaze from mine and looked to Paul, before acknowledging Smith. He took the beer and drank it down. "I see the whole gang is here."

The tone James used wasn't lost on me. He and Paul had managed to make the work relationship work, as far as I knew, which I was grateful for. Nothing had even happened between Paul and me, but Paul had made it known that he was interested and waiting for me. I didn't even know if James and I were together or not. I mean, I knew we weren't together and the divorce papers were being drawn up. We'd created a life and now that life was gone.

A solitary tear slid down my cheek and I wiped it away before anyone saw. When I looked back up I realized that James had seen. For a second I thought he was going to come over to me, but he didn't. I decided that alcohol was the only thing that would get me through the night and refilled my glass.

"Who's up for a game?" Jane was doing everything she could to lighten the mood.

Delaney chimed in, "How about 'Never Have I Ever'?"

Jane, Paul, and Smith were immediately on board. I agreed, too. With some minor persuasion from Smith and Delaney, James joined in. Cal decided to stay sober and keep score—more like he was keeping an eye on Paul and James. Smith and James flipped over the poker table to reveal a hard top. Delaney set down glasses and various liquor bottles as we began to take our seats. I sat down at the end of the table; Paul took the seat to my left with Jane next to him. Delaney took the seat to my right, with Smith next to her, putting James across from me.

He still hadn't officially said two words to me. His hair was pulled back and his expression was fierce. "Never Have I Ever kissed a girl." Everyone looked to Jane, laughing. "What?"

"Starting a little strong aren't you?" Smith was questioning her while smiling and Jane just shrugged her shoulders.

Everyone took a drink as Jane looked to Delaney and me and teased, proclaiming us "Hookers!"

"Jealous? I'll kiss you Jane, if he doesn't mind." Delaney pointed to Cal as he threw his hands up in the air.

"Don't let me stop you, Jane!" Cal was laughing and Jane was blushing.

"I kissed a girl and I liked it, the taste of her cherry chap stick." The lyrics came flowing out of my mouth before I realized I'd sung them, recalling the kisses I'd exchanged with Roxy, or was it Misty? James was glaring at me and Cal, well, I couldn't look at him. Trying to cover for myself, I rolled my eyes and blurted, "The song!" I got up and plugged in my phone, since my iPod had mysteriously disappeared, and put on *I Kissed a Girl* by Katy Perry.

"Paul, you're next." Jane ignored the building tension and elbowed Paul.

"Never Have I Ever gone to Prom."

James and I were the only ones who didn't take a drink. It surprised me that he hadn't gone to Prom. It was my turn. I didn't have any idea what to say and began to panic. Remembering something James said about Delaney, I blurted out, "Never Have I Ever role played in the bedroom."

Delaney, Smith, James, and Paul all slammed back their shots. "I beg to differ." His words caught me off guard as I looked in his green eyes. His glare was icy and locked on mine. What did he mean? Before I could think about it longer, Delaney made her statement.

"Never Have I Ever…this is hard," she looked to everyone, "had sex in an airplane." Nobody moved. Just as Delaney was about to pick up her glass, James picked up his. "Ha. I knew it!" *Who the hell did he have sex on an airplane with?* I was beginning to think the game was a bad idea.

"Ok, my turn." Smith was gazing to everyone while he rubbed his chin. "Never Have I Ever had sex in my parent's house." Laughter broke out and they all started razzing Smith that he hadn't done that. We all took our shots. My head was definitely beginning to swim. Now it was James' turn.

"Never Have I Ever let a lover tie me up." I just glared at him. I didn't know if he was trying to make a statement or if he was just being an ass. *He was never tied up? How was that possible?* Everyone picked up their glass.

"Geez, you bunch of harlots."

Laughter filled the room as Delaney said, "You're the one engaged to a cop. So I'm guessing he uses cuffs!"

Jane turned beet red before she asked, "Never Have I Ever had sex in a barn." Christ. Were the fates out to get me?

I looked to Paul and couldn't help but smile as we lifted our glasses.

I'd lost my virginity to Paul, in *my* barn almost ten years ago. Though I was pretty positive we were the only ones who knew that. Jane then asked for a bathroom break and we all agreed. I remained seated as everyone, some stumbling, moved away from the table.

"It was him, in the barn, wasn't it?" I looked up as the room shifted in my vision, making me dizzy. I was pretty sure James and I were the only two within hearing distance.

"Now you decide to talk to me?" I tried to stand up and immediately fell back down to my chair.

"How much have you had to drink?"

"Not enough! As if you give a shit." I watched the hurt pierce his eyes as he gripped his glass, turning his knuckles white. Bed, I wanted my bed, or a toilet, or both, immediately. James stood up and walked over to me. He pulled me to my feet, wrapped his arm around my waist and led me to the sliding doors. "I don't want to go outside." I tried pushing his hands off of me, but it was pointless.

Once we stepped on to the deck, the cool air felt utterly refreshing as I inhaled it deeply. Almost immediately my stomach was wrenching. I stumbled to the edge and began unleashing the contents of my stomach. He was pulling my hair out of my face and I was completely humiliated. Once my stomach calmed down, he handed me a napkin to wipe my face with. It was then I managed to shove his arms off of me.

"Why are you here?"

"I didn't know you'd be here. I'll leave in the morning. I wouldn't want to interrupt your romantic weekend with Paul."

I attempted to smack him, but he caught my wrist. Did he really think I went up there to be intimate with Paul? I wasn't ready to take that step. How could I when I didn't even know where James and I stood. I was trying to think of what to say to him, but I had nothing. It was pointless. The tears began rolling down my cheeks.

"Cassidy. Why did you use your safe word? Why did you let me think Paul was the father of the baby?"

I was leaning against the deck railing, digesting his words. "I, you, James you shut me out in every way except physically. I didn't know what else to do to get through to you." I took a deep breath, "As to the baby, you told me you were fucking around with Melissa. I was hurt and wanted to hurt you back."

He ran his hands through his hair, pulling a few strands loose, and then braced his hands on the railing. "Cassidy, there are some things that are better left unknown." He was referring to shutting me out, I thought, and didn't respond to my statement about Melissa.

"What are you talking about? What's haunting you? Please, tell me." I couldn't resist touching him and wrapped his forearm between my shaking hands. "James, please."

His other hand came down over mine as he turned to face me. "Cassidy, it's too much. Too many dark caverns that I don't want to take you down. I've proven over and over that all I do is hurt you." He interlaced his fingers with mine as my other hand covered my eyes.

I ached for him, his demons, and whatever absurd reason he had that he wouldn't let me in. "I know you have nightmares. I have them too. I wish you'd let me comfort you." Why had I told him to go earlier? If I'd asked him to stay, maybe things would be different. We could have been on our way to reconciliation.

"I wish for that too. But it's too late. You said so yourself." I looked up to him and there it was again. That distant look he got when he'd made a decision that he wasn't going back on. "We've lost too much, together and alone. I can never make it up to you. You deserve to be happy." He then pulled me in his arms, confusing me even more.

Sobbing, I cried out, "You make me happy. Please don't do this." I looked up to him, pleading, begging, and wishing I knew what to do to get him to open up and change his mind.

"You need to let me go, Cassidy." He pried my arms off of him and stepped several feet away from me.

"I will not let go. What are you so afraid of?" He rushed to me then and the look in his eyes startled me.

"You have no idea what *real* fear is. You have NO idea what I've seen, done and tolerated in this world." I'd never seen him so angry. He was gripping my upper arms so tightly that I knew I'd surely have a bruise or two. "And I won't subject you to it. Not now. Not after everything else you've been through."

"I have no idea because you won't tell me!" I tried pulling myself out of his grip and yelled, "You're hurting me." His hands dropped from my arms as the sliding door opened up.

Paul poked his head out asking, "Everything ok. We're ready to get the game back up and running when you are."

James looked to me, "She's in no condition to play. I'm done too." He then leaned in so only I could hear and whispered, "Paul loves you. Let *him* love you. He won't let you down." His words were like a dagger to the heart. I heard his footsteps as he walked away from me, but my world was spinning.

"James, what's going on?" Paul was suspicious, too, and I wasn't entirely sure if he had heard what James had said to me or not.

"Get her to bed. She's already hurled over the deck."

"Dude, where are you going? You're in no shape to drive."

"I'm not driving anywhere. Just take care of her. She needs someone she can count on."

I listened while they discussed me like I wasn't even there. He was handing me over to Paul like I was a piece of property. How had it happened? My legs gave out and I sank to the deck floor. I think, no, I knew I was in a state of shock.

"Hey, let's get you to bed." Paul helped me to my feet and walked me back in the house.

Jane came rushing over. "What's going on?"

"She just needs to rest. I'm going to take her up to bed"

"Maybe I should take her."

I was aware of my brother's voice and managed to squeak out, "It's ok. Paul can take me."

Paul walked me to the staircase and we started walking up. With every step, the stone inside my chest grew bigger and bigger. I couldn't breathe anymore with the weight of it. A sob broke free and my knees gave out. Paul swept me up in his arms and carried me to my room as I cried into his neck.

He sat me on the bed and then walked into the bathroom. I heard the water running and then he returned with a cold rag and handed it to me. I pressed it to my face, trying to get the tears to stop. When the tears finally ceased, the pounding in my head renewed. I was a complete wreck. Every part of my body ached. James was throwing us away, me away, and I didn't understand why and didn't believe I ever would. His mother said he would push me away, but I never dreamed he'd take it so far. How long was I supposed to hang on?

"I'm going to go find some ibuprofen and I'll be right back."

I sat there for a moment before getting up and I shed my sweat pants and socks. It dawned on me that I was wearing a shirt of James' and I pulled it off, throwing it across the room. I'd forgotten about Paul and that he said he'd be back. The only thing I knew was that I was angry, boiling with rage.

I was pulling a brush through my hair when my door opened again. Paul closed it and was half way in the room, holding a bottle of pills in one hand and a glass of water in the other, before he realized I was half naked. I had a fleeting thought to cover myself and decided against it. I was in my bra and panties and we both stood there, just staring at one another. Nothing mattered anymore. I didn't want to deal with emotions, I just wanted to feel. Revenge looked good right about then and so did Paul.

four

Revenge

~ PAUL ~

I WAS FROZEN, NOT BELIEVING MY EYES. I told her I'd be right back. Why was she just standing there in nothing but her underwear? Fuck. She looked amazing. Her curves were more defined than they were all those years ago. I was instantly growing hard. I'd wanted her back in my bed since that first night I saw her again all those months ago. I knew she was in love with James, hell, she was his wife, but I also knew there was still chemistry between her and I. The whole situation was fucked up. I had no idea she was with James when I got his call that he needed a new foreman and wanted me for the job. Hell I didn't even know that they knew each other. When the three of us put all the pieces together, it was beyond uncomfortable.

"Cassidy?"

"Paul, please don't leave."

She was playing dirty, whether she knew it or not. The black bra and panties she wore, against her porcelain skin, had my fingers aching to touch her again. The tattoo on her ribcage was begging to be caressed, by me. I set the water and bottle of pills down on the dresser before making my way over to her.

"Cassidy, this isn't right. You're hurt and angry." The mistake I made was placing my hands on her shoulders. She pressed herself against me before running her hands up my chest.

"Paul, stop talking. I know you want me." My eyes met hers as she got on her tip toes and pressed her lips to mine. When I didn't immediately respond she whispered against my mouth, "Kiss me, Paul."

I lost all sense and buried myself in her kiss. God, it'd been too long. Her kisses were better than I remembered them being. I bent down, running my hands down her thighs before pulling them up and around me. Walking to the bed, I sat down on the edge. I broke the kiss then and cupped her face. She was so beautiful.

She began kissing my neck and sucking on my ear. I couldn't help but press her warmth against my throbbing erection. She let a moan escape her lips as she rocked her body against mine. My hands ran over her chest and the tops of her breasts.

"Please, Paul."

"Cassidy, I've wanted you for so long." She was frenzied and not listening to me. Pulling at my shirt before she ran her hand to my groin, I had to grab her hands to get her to look at me. "I royally fucked up when I let you go all those years ago." I saw the change wash over her.

She pulled away, "Why'd you let me go, why does everyone let me go?"

I had to stop before we took it any further. "Cassidy, you're not ready for this. You're hurt and angry. I'm sorry. I shouldn't have kissed you." I lifted her off my lap and set her down on the bed next to me as her sobs picked up again. I stood up and pulled the covers down on the bed and directed her to lie down.

Once she was under the covers, I brought her the water and pills. She threw back a couple, drank a sip of water, and laid back down. She was already dozing off when I pushed the hair from her forehead. "I don't think I ever stopped loving you." I kissed her forehead and left her to sleep.

When I walked out of the room and back down the hall, I realized the house was quiet. Everyone must've gone to bed. I took it upon myself to make sure the house was locked up. When I walked past the back room, which was a full of overstuffed furniture and a fireplace, I saw that there was a fire burning. James was sitting in a corner, with a glass in his hand, just staring into the fire.

"She's in bed sleeping. I got her to take some Motrin beforehand." He didn't acknowledge my presence, just swirled the contents of his cup. "James, I know you love her, at least I think you do. And you're not the only one. I lost her once and it tore me apart. I hope you know what you're doing."

His eyes moved to mine, but there was nothing in them. Not wanting to get into it any further with him, I made my way up to my room.

~ JAMES ~

"I'M NOT DRIVING anywhere. Just take care of her. She needs someone she can count on."

I walked away and headed straight for the basement door. Once down stairs, I walked through the sliding door and onto the patio. I turned on the light, grabbed the hose, and cleaned up the mess Cassidy had made.

I was broken, worthless, and unworthy of her. She deserved someone who could show her all sides of themselves and let her in. And someone who could stand with her when she needed him most. I'd failed at all those things. I had waited too long. There were things in my past even I couldn't come to grips with. It was even worse, since everything with Derek happened.

When I confessed to killing Derek, I saw how she looked at me and she was right. I *was* a murderer, even if it wasn't Derek I was referring to. I'd killed others. Hard, cold, and unlovable is what I was, and she deserved more.

After cleaning the deck, I went to the family room and turned the fire place on. The noises from everyone else eventually faded as everyone headed to bed.

"James?" I turned to look at Smith. "You ok?"

"I'll be fine."

"I know it's none of my business, but I like to think we're friends first. She's your match. Don't let her go. You can rebuild what you had."

He left the room then and soon Paul walked in. He prattled on about loving Cassidy and how it tore him apart. For me, you couldn't tear apart what was already shredded. Letting her go would quite possibly kill me, but she was better off. It wasn't about me anymore.

I finally grabbed my bag, which was still by the front door, and climbed the stairs. Making my way to the last room, *my* room, I made my way inside. I didn't bother turning the lights on as I removed my clothes and climbed into bed. Her scent filled my nostrils and I knew immediately she was in bed next to me. Her soft breathing filled my ears and my heart began to hammer for her.

As my eyes adjusted, I took in her shape in the darkness. She had her back to me and I couldn't help but scoot closer. I briefly wondered how she ended up in my room; Jane and Smith both knew it was *my* room. Maybe they weren't paying attention or maybe it was a setup. Reaching under the covers, I trailed my trembling hand down her side and back up again.

"James…"

She mumbled my name, but she was still asleep. I was relieved that she whispered my name and not Paul's. I rested my head down next to hers and pulled her in my arms. I had to hold her one more time, even if she wasn't aware that I was there. I would always love her, but she'd do better without me. Without me in her life there would be no media hounding her, no conspiracies, no more violence, and no more miscarriages.

My hand drifted to her belly. The foreign feel of tears leaked from my eyes. She had been carrying my child and then she had lost my child. I was to blame for that, too. I had kept too many secrets from her and in the end it killed our child. She said that she had forgiven me, that there could be more babies, but I couldn't risk her health and happiness anymore. Everything she'd lost was linked to me, in one form or another.

I drifted off for a few hours. When I woke, she was in the same position and I knew I hadn't had a more restful night's sleep in weeks. I kissed her temple, "I'll always love you, Blackbird."

I crawled out of bed, grabbed my belongings and headed to another bedroom to dress. I then left her to her weekend. If she had any chance of moving on from me, I needed to be as far away from her as possible. That was easier said than done. Cal and Jane's wedding was fast approaching and I wouldn't be able to completely avoid her.

I got in my truck and put her iPod on to play. It must've been in her purse that day she fell down the stairs. I'd found it that night when I'd packed my bags and before I had left. I should've given it back to her, but hadn't. Instead I'd stepped into a little piece of her world, her treasured music. The playlist titled with my name was selected and I pushed play. *There's a Rumor* by The August Empire filled the truck. It was wrong to let her think I didn't love her. As I listened to the song, I wondered what her thoughts were. Did she really still love me? Was I a fool?

I remembered something Dr. Pratt had said. '*Your happiness is only about YOU. If Cassidy wants to bear your burden, let her, maybe that's what will make HER happy. That's what love is and also something a true submissive longs for. It's between the two of you and no one else can come between that.*'

I pulled the truck over and debated about turning around to go and get my girl. If, and that was a big if, I was going to get her back, I had to do it right. If she was meant to be mine, Paul wouldn't be a factor. Paul was my friend. But this was about more than friendship. It was about the love of a lifetime. She was still my wife, I had time. I needed to tie up the loose ends, Dan being one of them. She would be mine again, even if I had to wait twenty years for it to happen.

~ CASSIDY ~

I WAS AWARE of my pounding head as the sun poked through the curtains. For a moment, I wondered where I was and then the previous night came flooding back in to my memory. My arms outstretched in the big bed and the space next to me was warm. Did I? I was so confused. I thought I heard a door close and scrambled out of bed. I threw on a shirt and my sweats and ran down the stairs and to the front door.

His truck pulled out of the drive and I was helpless as I watched.

Now I was just mad. I shouldn't have been surprised that he was gone. I also couldn't help but wonder if I'd shared my bed with him, or maybe with Paul. Oh, God. Please tell me I hadn't. I felt someone nudge my arm and looked to find Cal beside me. He handed me a cup of coffee and stared down the driveway with me.

"You ok?"

Scoffing, I took a sip of the coffee and cringed. "What is with you and your black coffee?" He smirked at me as I chastised him, "It's gross!"

"There's three sugars in there!"

"Creamer, Calvin. It needs creamer!"

"Come on. I think there's some inside. Jane's making breakfast."

We didn't talk about anything else, just ignored the elephant in the room. Sitting at the counter, Paul walked in and I remembered kissing him the night before. *Shit!* What if he *was* the one who warmed my bed last night and not James? I pinched the bridge of my nose, willing the ache to go away. Then I started thinking about the kiss with Paul. It was nice, no, more than nice. Then I started cursing myself. I was a slut and I was going to die a filthy whore death.

"Here." I looked up as Delaney slid a glass across the counter to me. "It'll help with the headache." I looked at the green contents and back to her. "Promise. Just chug it."

I did as she suggested and gagged when I was done. "What's in that? Never mind, I don't want to know."

Breakfast continued in a normal fashion. I caught Paul staring at me a couple of times and tried to play it off. Life had to go on. There was no other choice. If James wanted me to move on, I'd move on. I was young, single, eligible. Shit. I wasn't eligible. Fucking hell.

Later that day we were all out by the pool. It was open, though the weather was still a little cool. The guys dove in as Delaney, Jane and

I watched. We were in robes, with our swim suits underneath, and decided to sit by the fire. We'd spent the day hiking and riding four-wheelers. I'd had a ton of fun. By default, I was with Paul all day since everyone else was coupled up. It was nice spending time with him. Cal had pulled me aside just to tell me to take it slow. I assured him there was nothing to worry about. And there wasn't. It was none of his damn business anyway.

"We need music and drinks, Delaney!"

"On it. You get the music and I'll get the drinks!" She and I popped up and walked inside as Jane sat by the fire playing on her phone. "Grab your phone, there's a music dock outside." I looked to Delaney as she added, "There's surround sound out there."

"Awesome."

She grabbed the margarita maker, the mix, as I helped and we setup on the outdoor bar. Once the drinks were mixed, she hooked up my phone and I skimmed through my songs. I knew exactly what I wanted to hear. *Coconut* by Harry Nilsson started filling the air. Delaney and I immediately started swaying around the fire like goofballs and pulled Jane up with us as we sipped on our margaritas.

We'd removed our robes and were swinging around in nothing but our swimsuits. We were all caught off guard when the guys snuck up behind us and grabbed us, each in their own fashion. Delaney was over Smith's shoulder, Jane swooped in Cal's arms and Paul had his arms encircled around me. We were all begging and pleading, knowing how cold that water was.

"Paul, don't you dare!"

"Sorry, gorgeous. We made a deal."

"We?" Before I could inquire further he was pulling us to the edge. "No, no, no, shit. Paul!" And we were in the water. As my head bobbed to the surface, all that could be heard was Delaney, Jane and I cursing the guys. "Holy shit, its cold!"

"Stop being a wuss. It's not that cold."

"I'll show you a wuss, Paul Vincent!"

I jumped on his back and tried taking him under. It wasn't an easy task or he just conceded as he went under and took me with him. We were face to face when we came back up. Out of the corner of my eye, I spotted Jane scrambling to get out of the pool. She was shivering as my brother helped put the robe around her. They ran off inside without another word to us. Delaney and Smith followed behind them. Smith seemed mildly perturbed, but I wasn't sure about what, and tried to put it in the back of my mind.

"Your lips are turning blue." I looked back to Paul as he said, "The hot tub. Want to get in?"

Shrugging my shoulders, I replied, "Yes, I'm freezing."

"They'll be back." He motioned toward the house. I wasn't so sure about that. He sat down across from me as we sat in an awkward silence. "Cassidy…"

"Paul…"

We both chuckled after saying the other's name at the same time. "You first."

"No, it's ok. You go first." Tilting his head at me I said, "I insist."

He examined me for a moment before taking a deep breath. "You kissed me last night."

Immediately, I felt myself blush as I looked away. "You kissed me back."

"Yes, I did." We sat quiet for another moment. "I didn't let you go, not like you think I did." It took me a moment to remember what I'd said to him the night before as I tried to explain myself, but he stopped me. "Cass, just let me talk." I nodded and waited for him to continue. "When I got back to base I wrote you a letter every day, sometimes more." His gaze penetrated me as I struggled to keep eye contact, "I know, you never got any. Just sit and listen."

I sat and listened as he told me things that I had no clue about. He had returned to base to discover the girl he'd been with, prior to meeting me, was pregnant. He did what he thought was the right thing and married her and never mailed my letters. I admired that in him—he was right about that. As he continued, the story became more and more messed up. Cal had cut off all ties with him when he married Cora and ultimately Paul and Cora were sent to a different base. The same base that James and Smith were stationed at.

He hadn't met them right away, but apparently Cora had. I stopped him from telling me anymore. I didn't want to hear or know about James' involvement with a married woman, but Paul insisted.

"Cass, he didn't know she was married. Cora really fucked him up. Smith and I became friends and he built the bridge between James and me. The three of us were sent on a tour before the baby came. When I received word that the baby had been born, I got divorce papers at the same time. Cora vanished, with my child and I was on the other side of the world, helpless to do anything about it."

"Oh, my God, Paul."

"Anyways. I was able to go home a few weeks later for some R & R to discover she'd had a paternity test done. The child wasn't mine."

"James?"

He laughed, "No. I ran into her a year later and that little girl was not fathered by either of us. Let's just leave it at that. I wouldn't have needed the paternity test to prove it wasn't mine."

I busted up laughing. "Sorry. That's funny. No wonder she left. But, she should've told you."

"Agreed. Anyways. After that, James, Smith and I were tighter than ever. We did a few tours together, until we were both injured. James and I recovered in a hospital in Germany while Smith finished his tour. James saved us both, and almost lost his life while doing it. I owe him my life."

"Paul, I had no idea. He won't talk to me about it. I know he has nightmares, but..."

"It's not an easy thing and we all deal with it differently. We saw, did and experienced some horrible shit."

I was finally beginning to understand as Paul continued telling me more about his time in the Army. I felt like a complete shithead that I'd given James such a hard time, but also didn't understand why he couldn't just explain it the way Paul had. Paul didn't seem to mind talking about it.

"He seems to carry a lot of guilt."

"He does. We lost almost our entire platoon that day. That fucks you up, especially when you're our leader." I wiped a tear away as I felt the gravity of the pressure James had been carrying on his shoulders. "Hey, sorry. I didn't mean to make you cry."

I shook my head, "No, it's ok. At least I understand a little bit more." It helped, but it didn't change anything. James and I weren't going to work, at least that's what I told myself, and I was on my way to being single again.

Paul slid in closer to me as his fingertips grazed my jaw. "Cassidy, I should've come back to find you. It's my biggest regret. Letting you go."

I looked into his blue eyes, the eyes that branded me when I'd lost my virginity, the eyes that sparked when I said those three little words for the first time. "You found me now." I tried smiling at him as his eyes traveled my face.

"Yes, I did." He leaned in as I held my breath. I wanted him to kiss me and when his eyes met mine, asking for permission, I consented. His lips tentatively brushed against mine as his hand cupped my cheek.

He took his time as his close-mouthed kisses moved and began to decorate my jawline. He was clean-shaven, not something I was used to. His hands held the side of my face as my hands held onto his inked forearms. If I touched any other part of him, I knew I would come unhinged.

five
Permission

~ PAUL ~

HER EYES MET MINE AND THE slight nod of her head was the only permission I needed. Cupping her face I let my lips touch hers. The song overhead changed and I smiled because the song reminded me of her. *Look at You* by Big & Rich serenaded us as I trailed kisses along her face in the hot tub. Her delicate hands gripped my lower arms and I felt her nails dig in slightly. Her breathing was labored as my cock pressed against my swim trunks, eager for an escape.

I had to take it slow, I should have stopped it, but I wanted her more than reason, or the devil himself could have bargained for. When my lips made their way back to her mouth, her tongue greeted mine. She tasted like tequila and sugar and I wanted more. As I pulled her closer, her arms moved to my shoulders as she floated into my lap.

Memories of that summer long ago drifted through my mind. It seemed that making out was something we were both good at then *and* that night in the hot tub. Hesitantly, my hands skimmed down her back as her tongue caressed mine. I was aching to pull her closer, but I didn't want to move too fast.

She pulled back, gasping for air. I dropped my head to her shoulder and wrapped my arms around her. "I'm sorry."

"Shh, Paul. I'm a big girl."

She lifted my chin and as my eyes met hers, she straddled my lap, but kept a safe distance away from my bulging erection. She kissed me and as her hands held the back of my head, my own ran up and down her thighs. She moaned when my hands began to travel her hips and she inched a little closer. My hands squeezed her ass as another moan escaped her lips. Sliding closer, she pressed her mound to me and we both reacted.

"Oh, I just want to feel good." Her lips seared along my neck as I rubbed against her again. "Oh, Paul, make me feel good."

"Anything you want, Cass."

What sounded like a door slamming, ripped us from our moment. She jumped in my lap and pushed herself to arm's length as she looked around. There were a couple lights on in the house, but we were still alone, as far as we knew.

"Paul, I'm sorry."

"Don't apologize. I meant to take it slower. I'm sorry."

We agreed to call it a night and I helped her put her robe on before we headed back inside. I walked her to her room and debated about kissing her goodnight, when she snuck inside. Smiling, she told me she'd see me in the morning and then closed the door.

Bracing my hands on the door frame to her room, I dropped my head and groaned. I took in a deep breath and turned to see Delaney in the hall, staring at me. She just raised her eyebrows at me before turning away and headed down the stairs. Curiosity got the better of me and I followed her down. I found her in the kitchen making a sandwich and I took her up on her offer to make me one. We sat in silence as we finished our midnight snack.

"You're playing with fire Paul Vincent."

I narrowed my eyes at her and asked, "How so?"

"You'll just get burned in the end."

Now I was getting annoyed. "At the end of what?"

"You're both consenting adults, and I don't really care who fucks who, but she'll pick James and he'll pick her." I didn't know what to say. "I thought you should know."

"We'll see. James seems to only be picking himself."

"Touché."

I liked Delaney's candor, though the topic mildly irritated me. We, James and I, both had our own history with Cassidy and I believed mine would win. If I hadn't, I never would've pursued her. I believed with every, well almost every, part of myself that she was meant for me. I was willing to walk through the depths of hell to prove it.

~ CASSIDY ~

I CLOSED THE door on Paul and sank against the door. My head was a mess and so was my heart. The chlorine that I was covered in filled my nostrils and I headed for the shower. Turning the water on, I climbed in after removing my swim suit. I shampooed my hair and as I rubbed the soapy loofah over my skin, my core tingled and my lips ached as I remembered Paul's kiss from the hot tub. My body was aching for a release and I was going to oblige.

I glanced at the removable shower head and pulled it down as the many jets of the shower soaked my body. Leaning against the wall, I rubbed my breasts and imagined Paul's mouth there as the showerhead in my other hand tickled my clit. My eyes played a trick on me as I opened them and imagined James. Blinking once, I reopened my eyes and he was gone. I closed my eyes again and imagined James in front of me. His hands traveled down my front and then he kneeled down in front of me. His mouth moved over me as I leaned my body against Paul.

Paul's hands traveled my torso while his lips sucked on my neck. James, still on his knees, lapped at my juices while two fingers entered me. I imagined reaching behind me and stroking Paul's cock as James tongued me into oblivion.

"Always, only, forever you, Blackbird."

"Anything you want, Cass."

Their words filled my ears and drove me closer to the edge. The orgasm that flooded me had me trembling against the shower wall. When my eyes opened, my fantasy faded away. A girl was allowed to dream, right? And a dream it was. I finished my shower and climbed into bed, a faint throb still lingering between my legs.

I was dreaming, or at least I thought I might be. Blindfolded and tied to the bed, hands roamed my body. I was aware that more than one pair traveled along my skin as a pair of lips lingered on my lower back. A hand moved down the curve of my hip, toward my inner thigh. My hips rose as I sought out a deeper and more meaningful caress.

"Soon, Blackbird." His voice near my ear alerted me that his was not the mouth on my back.

"James?"

"Just relax, enjoy the pleasure."

Someone knelt between my legs and lifted my hips slightly when there was a knock on the door. "Tell them to go away!"

"Anything you want…"

"Paul?"

The knock on the door came again and this time it was Jane's voice I heard. "Cassidy, you hungry? I'm coming in."

I rolled over, vaguely aware of the pillow between my legs. I had been dreaming. *Shit!* What was wrong with me? Jane poked her head in as I waved to her.

"Hey, you ready to hit the road soon?" I nodded. "Sorry, I know it's early. I have to work tonight so..."

"It's ok. Just give me a few minutes and I'll be down."

"Ok."

She seemed like she wanted to ask me something, but wasn't sure if she should. "Mind your business Jane, or tell Cal to!" She laughed at that before nodding her head and leaving the room.

On the drive home I was remembering the day Cal had come to the house. He was furious, ecstatic, overly-protective, and just plain concerned. It was the day after my miscarriage and I hadn't even told him I was pregnant yet. It was a mess.

"Cass, Jane told me. You're pregnant!" I was unable to speak as I felt myself pale. *"What's wrong? That's a dumb question, I know what's wrong. What can I do to help? Want me to rough him up again?"*

That got a small chuckle from me as I shook my head. "You should sit down."

We walked over to my couch and sat down. "I can't believe my baby sister is going to be a Momma!"

"Cal, there's no baby." He looked dumbfounded.

"What do you mean? Jane said..."

"I lost the baby on Sunday." I watched as he tried to process my words. I should've told him from the beginning.

"But, how?"

I shrugged my shoulders. "Sometimes these things happen, that's what the doctor said anyway."

"It's because of him, isn't it?"

"Cal, there really is nothing anyone could've done. I imagine Jane told you that I fell down the stairs. I'm sorry I kept it from you. I'm a klutz, we all know this."

"You wouldn't have fallen down those stairs if it wasn't for him!"

"Cal, we don't know. I had started spotting lightly earlier that day. It's just too complicated, there's really no way to know why. Please, let it go."

The tears were filling my eyes as he pulled me close and wrapped his arms around me. "Cassidy, I'm so sorry."

"I know. I am, too."

I exhaled a big breath and shook the memory away. We were close to home and Jane and Paul both appeared to be asleep. Cal caught my eye in the rearview mirror and smiled.

"Don't jump into anything new, too quick sis."

I rolled my eyes at him, responding, "Calvin David, mind your own damn business."

"Cass..."

"CAL!"

He put a hand up in defense, "Ok, ok. Geesh."

"I love you, but don't."

Jane lifted her head and scolded Cal with her eyes before looking back to me and winking. Paul still seemed to be asleep and I was grateful for that. Cal dropped me off first and Paul jumped out as I closed the truck door.

"Cassidy?"

Turning to look at him, I smiled. "Be patient with me, Paul." He nodded and dug his hands into his front pockets. I leaned up and kissed him on his cheek. "Call me."

I walked in my front door without looking back. It was around lunch time and I was looking forward to doing a whole lot of nothing for the rest of the day. I spent a good part of my day searching for my iPod with no luck. Worse case I'd just buy a new one. I could afford to, though I knew I should focus on paying off my student loans.

The next day at work, I got a call from Annie. I had debated about even answering the call, but figured it could be important. She told me that Judge Mathis had requested to see me and James regarding the divorce proceedings. My heart dropped like a brick as I took down the address and meeting time for the next day. We'd had the papers drawn up weeks ago, or so I thought, and I had no idea what to expect next. Annie warned me that we likely wouldn't be approved for an annulment. Whatever happened, I just wanted it over with.

The next day as I walked into Judge Mathis' office, my senses were on high alert. I was waiting in his office, alone. I wasn't sure if I should've expected James or not. The door opened and I turned and recognized the judge who had married James and me on that winter night a few months prior.

"Cassidy, pleasure to see you again. Though, I wish it was on better circumstances." We shook hands and he kissed my cheek before taking his seat behind his desk. "Can I get you something to drink?"

"No, thank you. I'm all set." I was gripping my hands together, trying to diffuse my nerves.

He leaned back in his chair and just stared at me. I was becoming uncomfortable when he finally spoke. "You two seemed so in love."

His statement caught me off guard. "Well, sometimes love isn't enough."

"So you still love him?"

For whatever reason, I didn't feel like hiding anything from him. What did it matter? "I'll probably always love him. I believed whole heartedly when I said my vows that he was it for me."

"So what changed?" I just stared at him. "I'll be candid. Sources tell me that you're pregnant." The expression on my face must have alarmed him. He sat up quickly, from his laid back position and clarified, "Your secret is safe, but it's a big decision bringing a baby into the world."

"There is no baby, not anymore."

"Hmm, I see."

"I lost the baby, I didn't abort it, if that's what you think."

"Sorry, I didn't mean to presume."

"I was ecstatic when I found out we were going to have a baby. Our relationship was the only problem, or lack thereof."

"Well, I can't grant you an annulment. You'll have to go through the six month separation period before it's official. At that time, if you still wish to be divorced then I'll make the process as quick and smooth for you as possible."

I'm not sure what I was expecting. Six more months of being MRSJB3 wasn't really what I had in mind, but there was no getting around it. "Thank you."

He shuffled through some papers and placed them in front of me. "I just need you to sign here and here." I signed my name, Cassidy Benedict, and scoffed when I realized I'd never even had my driver's license changed over. "Something funny, dear?"

"No. Sad really. In all the commotion of the last few months I never changed my name on my driver's license. Guess it never really mattered."

He walked around the desk and clasped my hands in his. "It matters dear. If you want my opinion, that boy is a fool. He didn't have a ring for you that day either. That was his first mistake."

My throat tightened at his kind words as I feigned a smile. "He's a good person. The circumstances were just wrong. Our timing has always been a little off."

"Well, I'll let you get back to your day. You can finalize in November, but I hope you two can work it out."

"Thank…." The door opened at that moment and James came walking in.

"James, I was just telling this lovely creature that I hope you two work it out." I was mortified and couldn't look to either of them.

I reached for my purse and made my exit. "Cassidy, wait." I continued down the hall and away from prying eyes and ears before he stopped me. "Cassidy, please talk to me."

I turned to look at him, mascara running, with no words to throw at him. "What James? You got what you wanted. In six months we'll both be free."

"That's not what I wanted."

"Ditto." We just stood there staring at one another. "I have to get back to work." He just nodded and I walked away from him, but I would never be whole again because the core of my heart was with him and always would be. I couldn't keep fighting for him when he clearly wasn't going to fight for me. Six months. A lot could change in six months.

~ JAMES ~

AFTER SPEAKING WITH Judge Mathis, my plan was falling into place. Though I wasn't sure how much of a plan it was. Annie would call Cassidy to schedule the meeting on Tuesday with the judge and we'd sign the papers. I had spent the rest of Sunday and Monday getting caught up on work and putting the other pieces of my plan into motion. I didn't like flaunting my money to get what I wanted. But for her, there was no price tag too high for me to pay to show her I loved her.

I wasn't planning to buy her love, just trying to prove my love. If a few grand gestures helped get through to her, then so be it.

I met with Paul and Smith and got down to business. I pressed Smith on the Dan front. We suspected that he'd left town, but I wanted him caught so that we could all breathe easy again. Paul and I were civil and I hated what I was doing to him. He had no reason to believe that I wanted my wife. Hell, I'd practically handed her to him on a silver platter. I shook the memory away as we discussed the house and other properties of mine.

"I want to move forward with the house."

"Ok. I'll get started on laying the foundation."

"Good. Alright, next. The Blue Horse. I want it gutted."

"I thought you were going to sell it?"

"Nope, change of plans. I have plans for some kind of memorial for my mother. I'll let you know when I finalize everything." I knew what my plans were, but I couldn't risk anything being spoiled. "It'll be quick, too. I need it finished by mid-September. Remodel and all."

"Ok. Just keep me up to date."

"Delaney will be in touch. She's helping with the final design."

"Sounds good."

That night as I headed to the penthouse, I stepped out of the elevator and ran into Melissa. Her bodyguard was with her and I pulled her aside to speak to her.

"I wanted to apologize again."

"James, it's ok." She smiled and rubbed my arm. "You've been through a lot, so has Cassidy." I nodded and she asked, "How is she, the baby?"

Shit. It dawned on me that she didn't know. Shaking my head, "She lost the baby."

"Oh, God. I didn't know."

"How would you? That reminds me, what happened with the job interview?"

Snickering, she replied, "It didn't happen. I'll find something else."

"Melissa, you're a perfect fit for that job. I think you should try to talk to her."

"No, thank you. I'm over getting my head bit off."

Smiling, "You two are more alike than you know. Her bark is worse than her bite. Ask her to hear you out. Give her the benefit of the doubt and she may do the same." She started to say something else and I stopped her. "Seriously. If you want that job, you're going to have to fight for it. Think about it." She processed my words for a moment before agreeing to think about it. "Alright. I'll let you go." She got in the elevator and I headed to my suite.

I had Cassidy and music on the brain. I'd been listening to her playlist, the one titled with my name, over and over and working on my own playlist for her. The one year anniversary of the first night I saw her was fast approaching, which meant that it had also been almost a year since Holly's death. I pulled my tie off and headed up to my room to change.

I spotted the gift box on my dresser and recalled what was inside. Grabbing the box, I put it in the closet, up high on a shelf and said a silent prayer that one day we'd get good use of the contents inside. Heading back down to my office, I pulled up iTunes and got to work.

Her playlist had exposed me to some bands I'd never heard of before and one was quickly growing on me. The Airborne Toxic Event had been completely foreign to me and now I couldn't stop listening to them. The first thing I did was download all of their work and turned it up as I grabbed a pad of paper. It took me moment, but the words started flowing as I spilled my heart out on paper to her. I wasn't brave enough to give the love notes to her, but one day I would be.

The next afternoon, I was purposely late to the meeting with Judge Mathis in order to give him some time with her. After I chased her down in the hallway, I froze and let her leave again. I had to pace myself. She wasn't ready to hear me pour my heart out and I hadn't been ready either. I headed back to his office and closed the door.

He smiled at me knowingly, "That girl is still head over heels for you."

"I don't know, she doesn't act like it."

"James, you brought her here to sign separation papers. I wouldn't expect her to be happy about it. I'm not sure what your plan is, but I'd execute it soon before you lose her for good." I knew he was right. "I've learned in my many years that most women are very forgiving. They just want to be cherished and wanted. Cassidy is no exception. That girl wants you to scream it from the rooftops."

"I have some grand gestures up my sleeve. Don't worry."

"Alright. Well, here's the paperwork. File it or win her back." I shook his hand knowing I had absolutely no intention of filing that paperwork and went to leave his office. "Hurry up before someone tries to snatch her up."

"Yeah, yeah. Thank you."

I didn't need any reminders about Paul and any other suitors who'd come calling when they found out she was single. Of course, she wasn't single, she just didn't know that. I pushed down the voice that chastised me about playing with fire. It was a daily struggle to remind myself that I wanted her, no matter what I'd done or been through, and I was going to prove I deserved her.

The next weekend I went to the club to pass time. I was a silent observer, lurking in the corners while I watched couples seduce each other on the dance floor. I recognized some as regulars, knowing they'd end up downstairs come the end of the night, and others I didn't. I threw back the rest of my drink and was headed toward the door when I saw her walk in with Paul.

I backed away so that she wouldn't see me. Her eyes scanned the room before they lingered over the door leading down stairs to where her desires awaited her. My suspicions were correct. I knew her well enough to know why she was there. It wasn't for the dancing and drinking. Paul had been down there with me, but it'd been several years. He didn't mind a little group play, some light bondage, but he was no sub and no Dom. I wondered if she'd opened up to him about her desires, but my gut told me she hadn't. She was still discovering them and coming to terms with it. If she thought he could give her what she craved, she'd be disappointed.

I stepped outside and called Annie to discover that she was downstairs as well. The next part of my plan was about to be set into motion.

six

Impressive

~ CASSIDY ~

A COUPLE DAYS AFTER SEEING JAMES and Judge Mathis, I was in my office when Linda told me my next appointment had arrived. When Linda walked Melissa back I was mildly annoyed. I'd ignored her calls, knowing it was about the job. I gave her an A for effort. She was savvy. Apparently, I couldn't avoid her any longer.

"Linda, close the door. Thank you." Linda left, closing the door behind her as I requested. "Melissa, have a seat."

"Thank you." She took a seat and I pushed my work aside and took a sip of my coffee. "Thank you for seeing me."

"Don't thank me, yet." She smiled as I commended her for her efforts. "Pretty smart scheduling an appointment for a wedding planner."

"Well, you wouldn't see me any other way."

"True. So, what do you want?"

She sat up a little straighter and cleared her throat. She was intimidated and I couldn't figure out why. "I'd like a chance at the job. I'm a great candidate and I believe I'd be a great fit."

Sighing, I knew she was right. "Your resume is impressive. I've practically memorized it." I needed her and I think she knew that. Maybe we needed each other. "Ok. You have ninety days to prove to me that I'm making the right choice."

Her eyes got big as she exclaimed, "Really?"

Shrugging my shoulders, "Cecily is confident and your resume speaks for itself. Can you start on Monday?"

"Yes, hell, I can start today if you want."

Laughing, I said, "Monday's fine. It's already Friday. Enjoy your last weekend of freedom." We both chuckled at that. "Wait. It's a holiday weekend. Make it Tuesday."

"Cassidy?"

"Yes."

"I'm really sorry about the baby." I wasn't expecting to hear that from her and was a little dumbstruck. "Nothing is or was or has gone on with James and me since he met you."

"Melissa, I really don't want to talk about it."

"I know, I just had to say it. James is yours and he wants you back, even if he's too stubborn to say it out loud."

"Ok. I can't hear any more of this."

"I understand."

"Thank you for coming in. I'll see you bright and early on Tuesday." She nodded and we shook hands before she saw her way out.

I put what she said in the back of my mind. I had plans with Delaney that night and with Paul the next and I couldn't focus any more of my attention on James, especially if the feeling wasn't mutual. Life went on, at least that's what I told myself and what I was trying to do. I had no cares in the world and wanted to live that way. It was time to live life to its fullest and just have a good fucking time.

DELANEY AND I went to dinner and then to the club for some dancing. She didn't mention James once and I was thankful. She was the most non-judgmental person I'd ever met. She and Smith still boggled my mind. I never would've put them together and it turned out that they'd known each other since they graduated high school. She told me a little bit of how they met on summer vacation. She'd spent the summer with her Aunt, in a tourist town, and Smith was working for her Aunt.

There seemed to be a lot more to their story, but she didn't dwell on it. I was looking forward to hearing more and wondered if they ever planned on marrying, knowing it wasn't for everyone. They'd been together for over two years, after rekindling their relationship from an almost decade hiatus. I wanted more details, but I'd have to wait, there was a dance floor waiting for us.

We were sitting at a table close to the bar, taking a break, when we spotted Roxy and Misty. "Your girls are here."

I nearly choked on my drink as I laughed at her statement. "Uh, they're not my girls."

"They'd like to be." She waggled her brows at me and said, "No judgment! You're free to do what and *who* you want."

I watched them out of the corner of my eye as I just said, "Mmmhmm."

She kicked my leg under the table, "You're attracted to her!"

"Ow! What? Who?"

"Please, Cassidy. She's fun, they both are." I open-mouth gawked at her. "Or so I hear." She winked and took another sip of her drink.

I was more than attracted to her, them. Fucking hell. I'd always admired the female body, but never found myself attracted to one. Not the way I was attracted to Roxy and Misty. Before I could think on it anymore, Delaney pulled me into the throngs of people as we danced and danced some more.

That night when I got home, I found myself pleasuring myself in bed, again. It was becoming a habit, but that time the bodies I imagined around me weren't male bodies. *Shit!* Roxy and Misty had tried persuading me to stay and I had found myself in a precarious situation in the restroom with them.

"Come home with us."

"Better yet, come down stairs with us."

"I, um, I really shouldn't…" *I'd spent some time on the dance floor with them and Delaney, but I wasn't making out with her. Roxy leaned in and kissed me just under my ear, sending a shiver through me.*

"Cassidy, you staying or going." *Delaney stood at the entrance of the bathroom, smirk in place, as Misty and Roxy hovered around me.*

"Not tonight girls." *I pulled myself away and walked toward Delaney."*

"We'll be here next weekend too."

I closed my eyes as the ending sensations from my orgasm flowed through me. I drifted off reminding myself that I deserved some fun and there was nothing wrong with a little experimentation. It would just have to wait. Maybe until next weekend.

~ PAUL ~

IT WAS SATURDAY, and I had a date with Cassidy. I vaguely wondered if she realized I was considering it a date. I stopped and picked her up some flowers before making my way to her place. When I pulled up, her security detail left after we spoke. James, had lightened the reins slightly. The only time she had someone watching her was when she was alone. She was slowly getting her freedom back and I knew she was happy about that.

We went to dinner and a movie before we debated our next move. I wanted to invite her back to my place, but didn't want to be presumptuous. It was a first date after all and I didn't want to move too fast. I decided then that I should be the gentleman and take her home.

Walking her to the door, she invited me in. I struggled with the decision and kissed her goodnight. Of course the kiss became heated and she pulled me inside. Fuck it. We were both consenting adults. Once the door was closed, I pushed her up against it while finding her hands and locking our hands together. Pressing my body against hers, she pushed back, eliciting a moan from both of us.

"Cassidy, we should take it slow."

"Fuck taking it slow."

Before I could agree or disagree, her mouth found mine again as we walked to the couch, our arms tangled around one another. We sat down next to each other but it wasn't long before she was on her back with me next to her. I broke the kiss as my hand skimmed over her exposed torso, her sweater lingering around her ribcage.

My eyes scanned down her body. The skirt she wore was exposing too much of her thighs for me to keep control. My hand reached down to her ankle and slowly moved up the back of her calf and up to her knee. I lowered my lips to her knee and kissed my way a little higher. I lifted my eyes to hers as she waited for my next move. My hand moved under her skirt and caressed her hip as she bit her lip.

"I don't want to move too fast, Cass."

"I know. I'm ok. Please, kiss me."

Smiling, I asked, "Where?"

Stifling a laugh she begged, "Here." She pointed at her mouth as she narrowed her eyes at me.

"Anything you want, Cass."

We continued making out and rubbing against each other for quite some time. Soon I was on my back as she dry humped my erection. Jesus. I was going to come in my pants if she didn't stop doing that. Like she read my mind, her weight shifted as her hand pressed against my groin.

"Cassidy, be careful. You don't know how bad I want you."

"This," she squeezed me gently as I sucked in a breath, "says otherwise."

"Evil. You're evil."

I sat up with her straddling my lap and crashed my mouth to hers. She smelled so good and I couldn't believe I finally had her in my arms again. The time in the hot tub had just been a tease. Her hands undid my pants and I wasn't going to stop her. Her hand slipped in between my briefs and jeans as she grabbed on to me. My hands gripped her hips and pulled her closer. She shifted slightly so that she was humping my thigh as her lips worked down my neck and she continued stroking me.

Before I could slow it down, her hand jerked me off as my orgasm flooded over me. Shit. She encouraged me on and didn't seem disappointed, but I was. That was NOT how I wanted that to go. She went to get up but I stopped her.

"No way. I'm not done with you." The mess in my pants forgotten, I laid her back on the couch as I kissed her lips.

My free hand found its way up her leg and skimmed over her wet panties. Her moan was a welcome sound as her arousal drifted through me. She spread her legs wider as the fabric stretched and exposed more of her to my hands. I continued rubbing her through the material, her clit swollen and waiting for more.

"Touch me, Paul."

Her words had me hard all over again. I pulled the fabric down her hips with her assistance before resuming my task. She was eager to move against my fingers and I loved her enthusiasm. Her kiss became scattered as her body started showing the signs that she was close. I wanted to kiss every part of her, but knew I couldn't, not at that moment.

She started crying out as I made sure to keep my movement steady, to draw out her climax. She latched her arms around me as I whispered in her ear how beautiful she was and how much I'd missed her. There was an innocence to her, even though she wasn't innocent anymore. I didn't know how to explain it.

A little while later, she was walking me to the front door. We'd both agreed that doing anything else, wouldn't be the best idea, not for that night. I climbed in my truck and pulled away once Ryan pulled back in. I climbed in the shower once I got home and released another load as I yearned for the time when I would become one with her again. It almost seemed too good to be true.

That Monday was Memorial Day and we were getting together at Cal's for a BBQ. Cassidy and I had a hard time keeping our hands to ourselves and Cal was really cool about it. Jane was in a tough place too, being that James was her cousin. But I appreciated that she never treated me any differently. We found ourselves alone for a moment.

"I just want you to know that her happiness is my top concern." Jane squeezed my upper arm and hugged me.

"Mine too, Jane. I promise. I know this puts you in an odd spot."

"Hmph. I know how frustrating he can be. I just hope he doesn't regret his choice."

I just nodded at that. What was I supposed to say? I knew what it was like to regret choices made where Cassidy was involved.

Cassidy and I weren't able to see much of each other the rest of that week. We were both slammed with work which was understandable. We were able to meet for a couple of quick lunches, but Lena and Anthony were there both times. Cassidy and I made plans for that weekend to go out dancing and I was looking forward to letting loose and having some fun.

We walked into the club that night. Drinking and fun the only thing on tap. "I want to get drunk. Get me drunk, Paul!"

"I'm not sure that's such a good idea."

"Spoil sport. You'll keep me safe. Won't you?"

"Of course." She smiled that killer smile of hers and leaned up to kiss me. I still couldn't believe that we were back to that place. Her in my arms and kissing me. I was the happiest man on earth.

We danced for hours, at least it felt that way. I took a break and when I came back from the restroom she was dancing with two girls that she'd introduced to me earlier, though I couldn't recall their names. I sat at the bar, watching and downed my shot. As I observed more closely I became jealous and intrigued. With two shots in hand, I made my way to her and she eagerly downed the shot I handed her before pulling me closer.

A waitress walked by and we discarded our empty vials and when I turned back to her I was met with a deep and passionate kiss. As we licked the traces of liquor from each other's lips our hands took liberties. Her hands pushed under my shirt and around my back as she rubbed her belly against my aching cock. I wanted her so badly that I was ready to pull her into a dark corner. She broke the kiss and turned around, her ass pressed tight against me.

The blonde began dancing with her as the other sandwiched in behind me. Before I could comprehend what was happening, Cassidy and the blonde were kissing. What the fuck was happening? I was turned on and jealous and pulled Cassidy toward me. She was drunk, or close to it and I was feeling the effects of the alcohol, too.

~ CASSIDY ~

ONE MINUTE I was kissing Paul and the next, Roxy and then Paul was pulling me back toward him. I was on my way to drunk and so turned on I was ready to hump a barstool. He wasn't the dancer that James was. *NO!* I chastised myself for thinking about him. That night was about me, my wants, needs, forbidden desires, and there would be no regrets! I went there that night with the hopes of running into Roxy and Misty and I knew it wasn't fair to Paul, but I didn't care.

I took Paul's hand and Roxy's in the other. If Misty followed, then the more the merrier. I headed toward the small bathroom in back, all my scruples pushed aside. I walked through the door and found it empty. Paul didn't hesitate when I pulled him in as I man-handled him the best I could. Leaning up against the wall, I tugged him to me and kissed him.

"Cassidy?"

"Shut up, Paul."

Groaning, he succumbed to my kiss and leaned into me. I pulled my mouth from his and began kissing down his neck. I spotted Misty and Roxy as they locked the door and watched. It just fueled my fire as I plunged my tongue back into his mouth. If he knew we had an audience, he didn't seem to care.

Undoing his belt and pants, "Do you have protection?" He simply nodded as his hands roamed from my ass to my breasts and back again.

His hand moved down to my knee and up my inner thigh. My tight skirt was pushed up higher as his hand found me. I was wet and aching and he didn't waste any time pulling my panties aside to rub his fingers over me. My eyes drifted to Roxy as her seductive stare devoured me.

Fueling my fire, I pulled Paul's boxers down and clasped his hard-on. "Paul, get the condom on!"

"This is crazy."

"That's what makes it fun. I want you. Take me!"

Bending over, he pulled a condom out of his pocket and quickly sheathed himself. I hiked my skirt up as he moved closer. He spotted Roxy and Misty and before he could object, I molded our mouths together and draped a leg around him. Moaning, he wrapped his arms around my legs and held me against the wall as his tip pushed against me.

"I've wanted you, this, us, for so long."

"I know, baby. Don't make me beg." I reached between us and guided him in as he hiked my legs up a little further. My thighs clenched around his hips as he slowly sank into me.

"Cassidy. Christ, you're so tight."

"Fuck me." It wasn't a plea.

He was talking too much. I just wanted to feel him pounding away inside of me. I don't know how else to explain what the feeling of having a hard cock inside of me did to me. Like I was complete, full, and whole with another human being. A hot, tatted, muscled, sexy man who wanted nothing in that moment but me and my wet pussy. His entire being focused on me was a complete turn-on.

Paul began fucking me, the way I liked as I dropped my head against the wall and reveled in the feel of it. My eyes opened to find Roxy standing next to us, Misty forgotten. Paul hesitated for a moment, almost as if gauging what she'd do next.

"Don't stop, she's enjoying it, Paul." Roxy encouraged him on, her eyes never leaving mine. "But I think she needs a little more."

Her hands moved over my shirt to caress my breasts. Paul gripped me tighter, the only part of my body left against the wall was my shoulder blades. Roxy leaned in and kissed me as Paul fucked me. Paul released some curse as his dick plunged in and out of me. Roxy moaned and pulled away. When my eyes refocused, I saw Misty sucking on her neck as her hands rubbed against Roxy's crotch.

My hand traveled to my clit and Roxy placed her hand on top of mine. Dropping my head to the wall, I pulled my hand away and let her work my clit while I fondled my breasts. She pulled her hand away and brought it to my lips. I sucked on her fingers briefly before she returned them to my clit.

"Fuck, I can't hang on much longer, Cassidy."

"Control it Paul. Let's make her come first. Don't worry, she's close."

He slowed his pumping, but angled himself to hit me a little deeper. "Oh, God. Right there." I don't know who I was encouraging, Paul or Roxy. Roxy released a moan of her own as Misty's hand massaged her like she was massaging me. "Oh…don't…shit."

"That's it pretty girl. Harder Paul, give her all of it."

Paul moved faster and I couldn't stop it. My vision left me as bursts of ecstasy coursed through my body, from my fingers and down through my toes. As the sensations began to cease, Paul was convulsing as well, his head dropped against me. Roxy's hand left me as I pulled Paul's mouth to mine. We broke our kiss when there was a bang on the door.

"Wrap it up. Some of us have to take a piss."

I couldn't suppress the giggle as Misty told them to hang on. Paul pulled out of me, tied off the condom and flushed it down a toilet while I situated myself. Once he was dressed, we all walked out of the bathroom like nothing happened, ignoring the stares from those in the hall. I'm not sure what caught them more off guard, that there were three or four of us who emerged from the bathroom.

I don't remember how it happened, but we ended up downstairs at the bar as Misty allocated a room for us. Paul didn't need too much persuasion as I asked him to do this with me.

"Paul, I want this experience and I want it with you. It's just one night."

I finished the drink in my hand before setting the glass down on a table. When Misty returned with the room key we followed her down the hall.

The techno music could be heard in our room and I pulled Paul closer. I kissed him and he broke the kiss just long enough to tug my shirt over my head. His eyes drifted over me as he gently ran his fingers over the tops of my breasts. For a split second I regretted that we had re-consummated our relationship in the fashion we had. It should've happened alone, in the privacy of his place or mine.

I had no further time to think about it as he walked me back toward the bed and fell down on top of me. The bed dipped on either side of us as Roxy and Misty flanked us. Misty reached in and pulled Paul's shirt off. His entire torso was covered in ink. 'Love' and 'Rage' stood out prominently as I traced them with my fingers. He leaned down, kissing my shoulders as he pulled my bra strap down. He quickly discovered my phoenix tattoo and grazed it with his lips before unclasping my bra.

Kneeling in front of me, he stared down at me in admiration. I went to touch him but my hands were restrained by Misty and Roxy. I consented as they tied my hands to the headboard above me and began moving their mouths over my body and Paul's. Soon, they moved him to a chair, ordering him to watch.

seven
Ashamed

~ CASSIDY ~

WHEN I WOKE UP, NOT SURE if it was minutes, hours or days later, I was face down in the bed. Paul was next to me, Roxy on my other side, but I didn't see Misty anywhere. *FUCK!* What had I done? My head began pounding as I took in the nakedness of all of us. I was suddenly ashamed and embarrassed as I recalled the torrid things we'd done to one another.

My primary focus became fleeing. I had to get out of there. Music still played overhead which made me believe it was just very late in the night, or early in the morning. I managed to crawl out of the bed, Roxy and Paul undisturbed. As I finished dressing, Misty walked back in the room and regarded me casually.

"I, I should go."

"No worries, sweets." She just smiled and I became freakishly nervous. "Calm down. What happened here stays here. Roxy and I may be known for our transgressions, but we don't kiss and tell."

I just nodded my head as I mumbled, "Ok."

"You just going to leave him here?" We both glanced at Paul and I was unsure of what to do. I'd rode with him, how was I going to get home? "You shouldn't feel embarrassed, or whatever. We're all consenting adults."

"It's a little more complicated than that."

"James?"

My stomach flipped, "Yes, no, I mean Paul and I. Dammit." My emotions were going to betray me and I felt my throat tighten. "I have to go." I grabbed my purse and fled.

I was halfway down the hall when I bumped into someone. I mumbled sorry as I tried to get past her. "Cassidy?" *Shit!* Slowly, I turned around and was face to face with Annie. "You ok?"

Those two words broke me. Of course I wasn't ok. She took my hand and pulled me in a room and closed the door. We sat down on a couch as she waited for me to speak.

"I messed up, but it felt amazing. Why do I feel so guilty?" She smiled at me before we talked for a while.

~ JAMES ~

I HAD BEEN TALKING with Annie, down a hallway and away from prying eyes and ears. I was mid-sentence when her red hair caught my attention. Annie's eyes followed mine as we observed. She was holding Paul's hand, pulling him behind her, with Misty and Roxy in tow.

"God dammit!"

I went to move and Annie put her hand on my chest to stop me. "James. Don't. Let her do this."

I glared at her, but didn't need to say anything. She knew how I felt. We watched as the four of them walked into one of the dozen bedrooms. I was going to be sick. My heart ached, stomach churned and my body was raging. Misty moved the indicator on the outside of the room so that people knew it was occupied. I felt Annie's eyes on me before she grabbed my hand and pulled me down the hall. She walked us into her room and closed the door.

"How do I sit here knowing what's going on?"

"You have to let her do this."

"The fuck I do!" I grabbed the small table in front of us and threw it against the wall and watched as it shattered to the floor. "She's my wife!"

"And *YOU* set this plan in motion. She thinks you don't want her. She's doing what any hot-blooded woman would do. You know if it was me, I'd be fucking anyone who came into my path."

"Dammit!"

"Set her free. If she comes back, you know she's yours. Isn't that what you want? Her to come back to you."

I dropped to my knees as the emotions flooded me. "She has to come back. She's a part of me. Annie, I can't breathe without her."

She pulled my head into her lap as I cried. "You stupid, stupid man." I left a short time later, our plan falling into place, or so I prayed.

I got in my truck and drove around aimlessly. It was all my fault. I'd deliberately pushed her to the edge. I knew what desire I'd awakened in her and I was wrong to think she'd only want that high with me. She was searching for a fix, like a junkie, and I prayed that she'd realize I was the only dealer for her.

I scrolled through my playlist and put on *End of Me* by A Day to Remember. What if I lost her to Paul? Was group play what she really wanted? Was that something I could give her? Sharing never bothered me before she came along, but she was different. I wanted to be the only one to give her pleasure and I wanted to be the only one she wanted to receive her pleasure from.

I KEPT BUSY with the house and the renovation of the bar over the next week. The anniversary of Holly's death was fast approaching and I wondered how Cassidy was dealing with it. Could I reach out to her as a friend and show support? I wanted her to know that I remembered. Annie had stayed in touch and just told me that Cassidy had listened to her, but made no decision.

That Saturday afternoon I couldn't get Holly and Cassidy out of my mind. I spent a few hours at the bar checking the progress. Paul seemed on edge, but I didn't inquire. I wasn't sure I wanted to know what was bothering him. Walking out the back door, the scene from the previous year played out in front of me.

Holly was cradled in Cassidy's arms, both of them covered in blood. Holly was gone, but I couldn't relay that to Cassidy. Sam was conscious and had been holding Holly's hand when the paramedics pried him away. I still believed that he died of a broken heart and who could blame him. He watched the woman he loved get gunned down right in front of him. He'd been wounded himself, but didn't die until a few hours later, at the hospital, after insisting on an update about Holly. I never confessed that information to Cassidy. What good would it have done?

"You ok, man?" Turning to Paul, the memories faded away. "You look like you've seen a ghost."

"Eh, something like that. We all set?"

"Yup."

We each walked to our vehicles and I wondered if we'd ever get back to a place where we could talk like comrades again. We were too old to let a girl come between us. Of course, that was how we'd met in the first place. Maybe it was kismet. I left a few minutes after he did and drove by Cassidy's place. Her car was out front and as I was working up the courage to go talk to her when she walked out the door and got in her car. She hadn't seen me and as Ryan pulled out behind her, he waved to me. I nodded and pulled away, following them, though I knew where she was headed. Calling Ryan, I asked him to stay outside the cemetery to wait for her.

She surprised me when she walked to my mother's grave first. God, I loved that woman—my mother, too. She laid a flower down and then walked the hundred yards or so to Holly's grave. I gave her a few minutes alone before I started to approach her. I didn't have any idea what I'd say to her, but just wanted to be there for her. All our differences put aside. She was sniffling when she stood back up, wiping a tear away, she turned and spotted me.

She looked around briefly, almost seeming confused by my presence. "Wh, what are you doing here?"

"What do you think I'm doing here?"

"You remembered?" She was surprised that I had remembered what she'd lost and it baffled me.

"How could I forget?" She looked so frail and broken. She tried to speak and then tried containing her sobs. I took a step toward her and she took a step back. "Cassidy, let me hold you."

She searched my eyes, probably gauging if I was up to something else. "I miss her so much. This last year…"

"I know." I took another step toward her as she buried her face in her hands. "Shh." I wrapped my arms around her and gently pulled her to me. She didn't resist and I buried my nose in her hair as her citrus scented shampoo assaulted me. "It's going to be ok."

~ CASSIDY ~

ANNIE AND I were walking out of the club in silence, her words running through my brain. I'd confessed what I'd done and she was really cool about it. She told me that if I was looking for a no emotions and no commitment relationship, she knew a Dom who would love to work with me. It felt strangely like a proposition. I told her I'd think about it. I mean, really, I didn't know what to think. No emotions and no commitment sounded really appealing, but was it possible?

"Cassidy!" *Shit!* Looking to Annie, she stepped a few feet away as Paul caught up to me. "You just left?"

"I'm sorry. I freaked out."

He moved a little closer and lowered his voice. "Cassidy, if I did something wrong, please tell me. I'm really sorry. I shouldn't..."

"Stop. You didn't do anything wrong. I just want to go home and go to bed."

"Cassidy, we need to talk about this." He put his hands on my shoulders and leaned down to meet my eyes. "Let me make this right. I'll take you home. Please."

Nodding my head, I agreed. Looking to Annie, I apologized and assured her that Paul would get me home. The sun was slowly rising and Annie encouraged me to call her. I climbed into Paul's SUV and he headed toward my place. We drove in silence and he reached over and placed his hand on top of mine. I'd really screwed everything up.

He pulled in my driveway and I jumped out before he had a chance to get out. "Hey." He ran up the steps fast on my tail. "Cassidy, stop running."

"Paul. I'm so embarrassed. Can't you just let me wallow?"

Snickering, he whispered, "No. Why don't we sit and talk and you can tell me why you're so embarrassed."

I could feel my cheeks burning up as I turned the key and let us in. "Please give me a few hours." I stopped short of letting him in all the way and turned to face him. "I can come over for dinner and we can talk. But, I have to sleep."

He let out a huff of breath and rubbed his hands over his face. "Ok. But if you're not at my place by six, I'll be here by six-fifteen."

"Ok. Deal." He kissed my cheek before walking back out.

I fed Chessa and climbed into the shower after stripping my clothes. My brain was a complete fog as I let the water seep into my bones. Flashes of myself tied to the bed while Roxy and Misty worked me over drifted in and out of my thoughts as Paul sat and watched. Then they had worked Paul up into a frenzy as I watched, unable to move since I was still tied to the bed. When we were both ready to explode, they'd untied me and I'd straddled Paul, pulled the condom down his length and joined our bodies again.

How could something that felt so good also feel so wrong? How was I going to explain that to Paul? Ugh. I rinsed the soap off my body and got out of the shower. Wrapping the robe around me and towel around my head, I stared at myself in the mirror. I had bags under my eyes and remnants of mascara on my bags. I was a hot mess. Pulling the towel from my head and the robe from my body, I climbed into bed.

My dreams were filled with beautiful men and women, some naked, some not. I felt like I was on a carousel as different scenes played out before me. I began to recognize the faces of the people around me. Roxy and Misty, Annie, Delaney and Smith while Paul and James stood next to each other. Both of them had a hand stretched out toward me as the carousel began to spin faster and faster. How did one choose when the love I had for each of them was so different? Paul had been the first to make my heart truly pitter-patter, I'd given him my virginity and then he broke my heart. James, he owned my heart and locked it up tight, but not before he broke it, too.

When I woke, it was just after four p.m. I'd slept long enough that I should've felt rested, but I didn't. I wanted to pull the covers over my head and sleep for days. My mind was filled with way too many emotions. The anniversary of that horrible night was fast approaching. I sucked the sentiments down, that tried to take over, and forced my thoughts to dwell elsewhere.

I wandered downstairs and made myself some coffee. While it brewed, I searched around for my iPod and still couldn't find it. I sorted my mail and discarded the junk mail before opening my student loan statement. Sighing, I put the statement back in the envelope. I needed to start paying more on them. I didn't feel like I was making any headway on it and felt like the debt was going to swallow me whole. Grabbing my coffee, I headed upstairs to get dressed.

I pulled into Paul's driveway and took a deep breath. The flashes from the night before were dancing circles in my head as I tried to push them aside. A shudder ran through me, a good one. I was a dirty whore. I climbed out of my car and headed to his front door. Knocking, he opened it a few seconds later and held the door wide for me. His place was laid out similar to mine. He had music playing and candles lit. He had that huge grin plastered on his face, but he was nervous. I was nervous, too.

I set my purse down on the couch, unsure of what to say or what to do. He moseyed to the kitchen and pulled something out of the oven. It smelled delicious. Paul could cook! That pleasantly surprised me.

"I hope you're hungry." He smiled at me and I slowly headed his way.

"Starving."

"Good. Hope you like pasta."

I looked over to the pans littering the stove to find bread, salad and a pan full of pasta that was smothered in cheese. "Love it. You didn't have to go to all this trouble."

Smirking, "Yes, yes I did." I smiled back and took the plates from him and set them up on my side of the counter. "Sorry I don't have a table yet."

"No worries." His place was lacking some furnishings, but it wasn't barren by any means.

He offered me some wine, which I refused, and took water instead. Drinking probably wasn't a good idea, for many reasons. We sat in silence as we started to eat. I couldn't take it anymore.

"Paul, I'm really sorry about last night. I don't know what came over me."

Setting his fork down, he placed his hand on mine. "You're shaking. Cassidy, I'm the one who should apologize. Shit." He seemed lost for words and who could blame him.

Struggling to look at him, "I can't imagine what you think of me. I've never done anything like that in my life." His eyes skimmed over my face as one side of his mouth turned up. "What? Stop that."

"Stop what?"

"Undressing me with your eyes." I abruptly stood up and began pacing. "I acted like a wanton hussy."

"Woah, woah, woah. Hang on." He leapt off his own barstool and stood in front of me. "You are not a hussy. What happened was unexpected and *hot*." He winked at me and I covered my face with my hands. "And it never has to happen again."

What? Did I want it to happen again? Hell if I knew. "It wasn't how I expected things to be with us." I sighed, "Shit, I never expected *us* to *be* again."

"Cassidy, Misty assured me that they wouldn't tell anyone what happened. Well, maybe it was Roxy. I don't know. But whatever. I don't want last night to ruin things for us." His hands were on my shoulders and I felt so lost.

"I'm so confused, Paul." I recognized the song that came on and was immediately taken back to that summer.

~ PAUL ~

CAL HAD GONE to a buddy's party and I had contrived that I wasn't feeling good. Cal and Cassidy's dad, Dave, had gone to dinner with his girlfriend. Cassidy and I had a few hours to ourselves. She'd told them she had plans with a friend, but was hiding out in the barn until they both left.

I was sitting in the living room, ready to go find her when she burst back through the back door. Standing, I strolled to the back of the house and she met me half way. She jumped in my arms as I twirled her around. A few hours alone, we were so excited and had been looking forward to it all day.

She turned the stereo on and put a mixed CD in to play and turned it up. She'd made the compilation a couple days earlier and we listened to it when we could. Wherever You Will Go by The Calling started playing. She pulled a frozen pizza out of the freezer and turned the oven on. I pulled her away from her task as we danced around the kitchen.

"I've been waiting for this all day!"

She looked up to me and smiled that brilliant smile. "Let's run away together." She was teasing, but part of me wanted to.

"Anything you want."

Laughing, she retorted, "Don't tease me, Paul. You can't just leave the service." She kissed me before saying, "I'm not going anywhere."

I squeezed her tightly and wished that I could just leave the service. I *loved what I did, but she was beginning to mean more to me than any other thing in the world could ever mean. I'd heard guys talk about this. I was falling for her. No question about it.*

"It's our song." She closed her eyes and dropped her head to my chest. I pulled her close as she wrapped her arms loosely around my waist. We held on to each other as I gently moved us to the song. How I wished I could turn back time. All I wanted was to make her mine, just like the song stated.

That song ended and another began as she looked to me, "Is this the CD I made…"

"Yes."

Her mouth hung open for a moment before she stated, with a hint of shock in her voice, "I can't believe you kept it."

"Of course I kept it." She smiled at me before laying her head on my chest again. "Cassidy…" I didn't know what to say. The words stuck in my throat. I knew what I *wanted* to say, but she was fighting a battle with herself that I had to let her fight.

"Yes?"

"Nothing. Just know that I am truly sorry about how things went down last night, but I want to move forward. I don't want one night to wreck things for us."

Her eyes left mine as she gazed at my shirt. "I know. Let's finish dinner and just see where we end up."

We were on the couch some time later, watching a movie. There was a pretty intense love scene playing out on my TV as we sat and watched, her curled into my side. I didn't make a move on her, though I wanted to. When the movie was over, she sat up and I could tell she was still uncomfortable.

"Paul, I think I should go."

Sighing, "Is there anything I can do or say to change your mind?"

I rubbed my hands over my face before leaning on my knees while I waited for her answer. She searched my face and then hung her head while she stared at her own hands.

Barely above a whisper, she confessed, "I care about you so much. You were the last thing I expected to walk back into my life."

I waited for her to go on and when she didn't I grumbled, "But?" She lifted her tear filled eyes back to mine, "What do you want, Cassidy?" I didn't dare ask 'who' because I was terrified that it wouldn't be me.

"I think I need time and space. We jumped in head first way too fast. My divorce won't even be final until November." She stood up abruptly and I joined her. "I'm so sorry."

I was paralyzed and didn't know what to do or say. I was losing her all over again, but this time by her choice and not mine. "Cassidy." She turned to me and I closed the distance between us and wrapped her in my arms. She didn't fight the hug, in fact she may have squeezed me as hard as I did her.

"I really am sorry, Paul. I understand if you hate me."

"I don't hate you. I could never hate you. I don't think I ever stopped loving you."

She jerked her head up at my words, her baby blues branding my soul. Her hands held my face as she pulled my lips to hers. My heart was on the line and didn't know whether to jump the line or run from it. She'd just told me she needed space, hadn't she? I didn't care. I was going to take the kiss as far as she'd let me.

Our tongues became tangled, competing for power. I couldn't pull her close enough and I vaguely recall that her shirt hit the floor before her fingers dug into my scalp. "I'm not going to stop unless you tell me to." We were both panting as I trailed my teeth along her neck. If it was a goodbye fuck she wanted, I was going to do it right. When she walked away from me—if she walked away—it would be with trembling legs in a passion induced coma.

Her hands pushed at me as she backed away from me. "Wait." She was shaking her head, "I can't, we can't do this." She bent over, picking up her shirt and put it back on. "This isn't right."

I slumped against the wall, my raging hard-on quickly shrinking. Staring at the floor, I watched as her feet moved toward me. Her hands reached for me and I pushed them away as my eyes found hers. "Please don't."

She took a step back and nodded her head as if understanding. "I'm sorry, Paul."

"I am, too." She turned toward the door and as her hand turned the knob I reminded her, "Anything you want. Is he willing to do that?"

She froze for a moment before opening the door and then walked out, leaving it open. Pushing myself off the wall, I walked to the door and slammed it shut, but not before confirming her security detail was still there. He was.

Feeling sorry for myself, I grabbed a beer and plopped on the couch as I scanned the channels. I wanted her more than she wanted me. I knew that I had waited too long and pondered what I would've done differently. I woke up on the couch a few hours later and hauled my sorry ass up to bed.

The next week came and went without a word from her. I knew she was dealing with a lot and I debated about reaching out to her. Deciding against it was one of the hardest things I'd ever done. She knew I wanted her and there wasn't much else I could do to prove it. She asked for space and I had to give it to her. I focused on work because that was all I had.

eight

Broken

~ CASSIDY ~

I PULLED OUT OF HIS DRIVEWAY and headed home. Once I pulled into the driveway I broke down. It would've been so easy to stay with him and let our bodies take over. I was attracted to him, there was no question there, but he wanted more than I could offer him. I was married to the only man I wanted, but my husband didn't want to be married to me. I started sobbing as another memory bombarded me.

I found myself in the barn, up in the hayloft. Collapsing on a pile of hay, I grabbed the blanket that Paul and I had left there and pulled it to me. His scent, though faded, still lingered there. The hayloft became an easy hiding spot for us on the cooler nights. I wasn't ready for him to leave. I knew he had to go, but I thought I had more time with him.

"Cassidy?"

"Paul!"

"No, Cal. Are you ok?"

I pulled myself up and wiped my tears away, unable to make eye contact. Cal sat down next to me and wrapped his arm around my back, cupping my shoulder. Shaking me gently when I resisted him, he pulled me to him. Burying my face in my hands, I was aware of my brother rubbing my back.

"I know it's hard here without me. I'll miss you, too, but everything will be fine. I'll be home again before you know it."

"I know, I just…"

"What's going on with you? You've never taken it this hard." I felt my eyes bug out and the flush spread across my face. Cal always knew when I was hiding something. "Why did you think I was Paul? I swear to God if he's put a hand on you."

"NO! No, everything is fine. There's nothing going on with Paul."

Cal was raging inside—and out—with the thought that Paul had taken advantage of me, when in reality Paul had been a perfect gentleman. I had been the one throwing myself at him.

"Cassidy Arianna Charles, you tell me the truth right now!"

"I swear, there's nothing going on between Paul and me. It's just a stupid crush, nothing more. I promise." I lied to Cal through my teeth, probably for the first time, and prayed that he'd believe me.

He bought the lie and convinced me to come finish breakfast. When I returned to the kitchen Paul's plate was empty and he was nowhere in sight.

Paul made himself scarce the rest of that day. I felt like an idiot. Had the last few weeks been a waste? I became angry. That night, when I was sure everyone else was asleep, I snuck into the guest room that Paul was occupying. The lights were off and his bed was empty. Where was he?

I crept down the stairs to the front door and stepped outside, after slipping on my shoes. Walking to the back of the house, I peered out into the night desperate to find him. I started walking to the back lot where our tree was. He'd carved our initials into that tree a couple nights prior. It *was very childish, yet romantic. When I was far enough from the house, I began calling his name. Nothing. Maybe he was in the barn. When I made it to the barn, the full moon in the sky illuminated his figure standing in the hay loft opening. I was so relieved to have found him.*

There was a tap on my window. Ryan. I turned off my car and stepped out as he asked, "Is everything ok Mrs. Benedict?"

"Please don't call me that. You can call me Cassidy." He nodded. "I'm ok."

"If you need anything, please let me know."

"Thank you." I walked up my steps and straight up to my room.

The next morning when I was going through my mail I found a letter with a return address that made my heart sink. It was from the gallery Holly had worked at. I opened it and found that they were selling all of her artwork in a few weeks. I was livid. Sara had assured me that they didn't have any of her art and Cal and I had thought that odd. Holly loved to paint and draw. I had a few small pieces of hers, but couldn't believe there wasn't more. Sara had blatantly lied to me and now they were going to benefit from it. And there was nothing I could do about it.

The next couple of days came and went. Cecily was present less and less as Melissa and I took over. Melissa and I were eating lunch in my office together that Wednesday. I could tell she wanted to say something; I just wasn't sure what it was.

"Cassidy, can we talk woman to woman?"

I gazed up at her and realized her eyes weren't blue, they were brown. Colored contacts? I wasn't sure I wanted to hear what she had to say. But if we were going to be business partners, we needed to be able to get along. I nodded my consent. She got up from her spot and closed my door before sitting back down.

"I wanted you to know the truth. I have a lot of demons and I always looked to James as the person who could vanquish them. After my attack, I realized that only I can do that." She stopped, as if waiting to make sure I was still with her before she continued. "James and I haven't slept together in nearly two years. I know you may not believe me, but it's true. Not that I didn't try."

I wanted to believe her, but still wasn't sure if I should. "That doesn't explain why you're living with him."

"He was trying to protect me. He keeps those he cherishes close to him." I must've paled because she immediately tried retracting her statement. "That's not what I meant."

"It's ok. He's made it clear that he doesn't cherish me. He couldn't get far enough away from me." I pushed my lunch away, unable to eat anymore.

"Cassidy, he cherishes *you* above anyone else and that scares him to death. I've known him almost my entire life. That's why I acted the way I did at the auction. You changed the ballgame and I knew he'd never be mine again, not with you in the picture." I sat staring at nothing as I listened to her words. "I was jealous, envious, whatever you want to call it. You sunk my battleship."

I chuckled at that. "I don't know about that."

"I originally plotted with Dan to get you away from James. I had no idea he would take things so far."

I wasn't really surprised by that admission. We had all figured that was the case. We sat in silence for a little while before she apologized about the day I had found her in the penthouse in nothing but a towel.

"You should know that I moved out that day." That made me happy to hear. "I'm sorry about the baby. I…"

I cut her off, "It's not your fault. I should've told him sooner. Maybe things would be different."

"He was devastated, Cassidy. He wanted that baby."

"I did too." I was about to say more when there was a knock on my office door. Sighing, "Thank you, Melissa. I appreciate it."

"It's not a problem. I'm really happy to be here and excited for the future for the first time in a very long time." I wished I could say the same. "I hope you can make it work with James. I don't know your history with Paul, but even I can see the pull between you and James." Another knock on the door came.

"There needs to be more than a pull." She smirked at that before we both stood and walked toward the door. I opened it up to find Annie. I'd forgotten our appointment. "Annie, sorry. I totally forgot."

"It's ok. I was nearby and just figured I'd swing by." She looked to Melissa, "How are you doing, Melissa?"

"I'm good. I should get back to it. QuickBooks beckons me!" We chuckled at that before she looked to me and said, "Anytime you want to talk, I'm willing to listen."

She made her exit as Annie took a seat at the table. I closed the door behind Melissa and sat down next to Annie. "She means well."

Looking to Annie, I acknowledged her. "I know."

"So, this art gallery. Tell me more." I divulged all the details to her as quickly as I could. "I really don't know if there's anything we can do. With Holly not having any family, well, it's complicated."

"Well, it was worth a try. If I had the money I'd just buy it all myself. I should've been more persistent last summer. I *knew* there had to be more."

"I'm really sorry, Cassidy." She smiled at me and inquired, "So, what happened with Paul?"

"Ugh. It's complicated. But, needless to say, we're not speaking. I told him I needed space and time." She nodded. "It was foolish of me to, well, whatever."

"And James?"

Shaking my head, "What about him? I haven't talked to him in what seems like weeks. The wedding will be interesting."

"How's that going?"

"Good. Jane is probably the calmest bride I've ever worked with. Beverly on the other hand…" We both laughed at that.

"Have you thought any more about what we discussed?" I just stared at her, unsure what to say. "Well, here's his email address. He's very discreet and prefers to start up a rapport with his subs through email."

She slid a business card across the table and I picked it up and scanned it. There was no name on the little black card. Just an email address that gave nothing away about his identity. "I'll think about it. Hell, it'd be nice to just have someone to talk to."

"I'm sure he'd enjoy that. I should run. Call me if you need anything."

"Will do. Thanks, Annie."

That night when I got home, with Holly on my mind, I called the tattoo shop and booked an appointment with Styx. I'd had the phoenix for almost a year and it was way past time to get the color filled in. He couldn't get me in right away, but it was fine. I put the appointment in my calendar and came across the card that Annie had given me. I stared at it for several moments before placing it back in my wallet.

That Saturday marked the one year anniversary of Holly and Sam's deaths. Friday night, Cal and Jane had come over for pizza, just the three of us. Jane and I worked on her seating chart as best we could since there were still a few RSVPs we were waiting on. She had her final fitting the next week, as did I.

"Cassidy, you doing ok."

Without looking up at her I replied, "Yup. I'm good." I felt her hand on mine and looked to her. She clearly doubted my quick response.

"Cass, you've been through a lot the last few months." Cal had joined in on the interrogation as I rolled my eyes.

"You guys I'm fine."

"Cassidy…"

"STOP. There's no point in talking about it." Taking in a shaky breath I whispered, "You don't understand. No one understands. I lost my baby and my husband in the span of days and now Paul."

"What do you mean 'and now Paul'?"

"Ugh." I ran my hands through my hair before confiding in them. "I called it off with Paul. I wasn't ready, probably never will be." I couldn't bear to look at either of them. "I don't want to cry anymore. Can we please stop talking about it?"

"I told Paul to back off."

"Cal, this isn't his fault."

"I'm very well aware of whose fault it is." I laughed at him. "Why are you laughing?"

"Cal, I love you, but I'm a big girl. I can take care of myself."

Huffing, he walked to the kitchen as he mumbled, "I doubt that."

"Really?"

"Alright you two." Jane tried diffusing the squabble between Cal and I, but it was too late.

"I never once questioned you and all those hussies you brought 'round. Not once. Who I fuck is none of your concern, even if one is your best friend and the other your fiancé's cousin."

Cal stared at me, glancing to Jane, whom I had clearly offended. "Ok. I think that's our cue to go."

"Jane, I'm sorry."

"Nope, it's ok. I'll see you next week at the fitting." Jane grabbed her things and walked out the door.

"Nice, Cass." Cal walked to me, anger radiating off of him. "If she calls off the wedding it's on you."

"Oh give me a break. She's not going to call off the wedding. I didn't mean to offend her, but I'm not sixteen anymore, Cal. You have to stop treating me as such."

Sighing, he resigned. "I know. I'm sorry. I came over here because of Holly. It's a year today. We didn't want you to be alone. I don't want to fight with you."

I rubbed his arm, "I know and I appreciate it. You should go after her before she leaves without you." Nodding, he kissed my cheek and left.

The next morning I woke up feeling like crap, but attributed it to what day it was. I went to the flower shop and picked up some flowers, leaving them on the front seat and ran back inside to grab my phone. I drove to the cemetery, almost on autopilot. I was barely aware that Ryan was behind me and had remained at the entrance, giving me some privacy.

I parked between Eva's grave and Holly and Sam's. I headed to Eva's first and placed a single rose on her grave as my thoughts drifted to her. I imagined how things would've been different had she not passed away. It was futile. Rising, I walked toward Holly and Sam. A chill ran over me.

I placed the bouquet on Holly's grave as a tear rolled down my face. How I wished I had her to confide in. She wouldn't have judged me or my indiscretions. I laughed at the thought of her meeting Paul and wished she would've gotten to know James. Ugh! What was wrong with me?

"Holly, show me a sign. Please." I whispered the words not quite sure what I was asking for.

Another chill ran over me as I stood. When I turned, his muscled figure greeted me. His hair was down and he wore jeans and a well-fitted polo. *Was he my sign?* I shook the thought away.

"Wh, what are you doing here?" My voice was shaky as his presence rattled me.

"What do you think I'm doing here?" He tilted his head and smiled that smile at me that made my toes curl.

"You remembered?" I couldn't believe he remembered. I mean, I could, but I was shocked to see him there.

"How could I forget?" He was silently beckoning to me, I could feel it. What the hell was he playing at? I tried to speak, but the emotions were too potent to contain. He made a move toward me and I immediately stepped back. "Cassidy, let me hold you."

Hold me? He wanted to hold me? Why now? I scanned his eyes trying to figure him out. But that proved an impossible task. *'He must be close to seven feet tall!'* I remembered Holly's description of James when she first saw him. "I miss her so much. This last year…"

"I know." He made a move toward me again and I didn't have the strength to walk away from him and I didn't want to. I covered my face with my hands and he pulled me close. "Shh." I let my body mold into his and when he inhaled my hair, it wasn't lost on me. His own scent, mixed with cologne, drifted through me and immediately relaxed me. "It's going to be ok."

Was it? How could he say that? I wanted to believe him. Was it possible to just forget everything and move on? Together? He guided me to a nearby bench and handed me a handkerchief which I used to wipe at my eyes. I sat down and he followed suit. His arm was draped around the back of the bench, rubbing my shoulder. Another chill ran through me and I was beginning to think I was getting sick.

"Are you cold?"

I shook my head, "No, I don't know."

His hand moved to my forehead, "Cassidy, you're burning up."

"What are you talking about?" I'd been feeling a little run down that whole day, but just figured I was tired.

"You're running a fever."

"I'm fine, I assure you."

"You need to see a doctor."

"Stop!" He looked startled at my outburst. "Stop pretending you care. I know you don't."

He attempted to place my hands in his, but I evaded him. "I care, Cassidy. More than you know."

I stood up. I couldn't listen to anymore of his lies. "I can't listen to this." My head began to spin and the aches in my body became more prevalent. "You keep saying you care, but, but." The cemetery began to spin around me. "Shit."

"Cassidy?" I dropped back down to the bench. "You're not fine."

"I'm fine." My protest was a weak one. "I just want to go home. Take me home." I dropped my head to his shoulder and listened as he made a phone call. It sounded like he was sending Ryan to come and get me—or my car—I wasn't sure which.

"Cassidy, give me your keys." Reaching in my pocket, I handed them over. "Alright. Up you go." He helped pull me to my feet and we started walking.

"Oh, no."

"What is it?" Before I could answer, I stumbled to a bush and discarded the contents of my stomach. He handed me his handkerchief again and I wiped my mouth. Standing back up, I tried walking to my car. "Not so fast. You're riding with me."

I didn't have the strength to fight him. I just wanted to go home and go to bed. He helped me up into his truck and buckled me in. As we drove, I became aware that he wasn't taking me home. Where was he taking me?

"James, I want to go home."

"I know, but not before you see a doctor."

"I told you I'm fine."

"You're so pale you're almost green. You're not fine." I just closed my eyes, knowing arguing with him was pointless.

He took me to the ER and checked me in. We waited in the lobby for a few minutes before being called back. I didn't bother telling him he could wait in the lobby. The nurse asked the usual questions and ordered some labs. James was playing on his phone and I tried to get some rest. The doctor came in to let me know my pregnancy test was negative. *Thanks ass-wipe.* Way to make an uncomfortable situation even more so. They hooked up a bag of fluids, since I was dehydrated and told me to rest as they waited for the other labs to come back.

James was resting his head on the wall behind him when I glanced over at him. His eyes were closed and I couldn't help but scan my eyes over him. His arms were crossed over his chest and his legs stretched out in front of him. His polo was unbuttoned just enough to glance at the muscles of his neck and the sleeves barely contained his biceps. My eyes traveled to the buckle of his jeans and then lingered on his package. The jeans were fitted on his muscled thighs as I pictured tugging them off of him.

I sensed the movement in his upper body and my eyes landed on his staring back at me. *Busted!* I looked away and dropped my head back to my pillow. No one would argue that he was a fine fucking specimen.

"Nice to see some color back in your cheeks." I could tell by his tone that he had that fucking sexy as hell smirk on his face. There was no need to look at him and confirm it.

"Shut your face."

"Yup, definitely feeling better." I just shook my head as the corners of my mouth turned up.

I must've dozed off because he woke me to let me know they were releasing me. He confirmed with the doctor that he'd keep an eye on me and get me to rest. The doctor wanted me to take a day or two off work, yada, yada, yada. They could try, but I had shit to do.

We pulled into a pharmacy parking lot on the way home. He ran in and said he'd be right back. A few minutes later he came back with a bag full of goodies. He handed it to me and it was full of every possible flu medication you could think of.

"You're lucky they didn't arrest you with all the meds in here."

"They tried!" We chuckled at that.

I walked in the front door, not expecting him to stay. "James, I'm fine. You can go home."

"Nope, not a chance."

Sighing, "What are you trying to prove?"

He mimicked my sigh and said, "That I care, Cassidy."

He grabbed the bag of meds from me and encouraged me to go to bed. I walked up the stairs and asked him to feed Chessa and he assured me he would. My body ached so badly that I couldn't remove my clothes without cringing. I plopped down on the side of my bed and just sat there. Apparently I sat there for longer than I thought because his voice was the next thing I remembered.

"Why aren't you in bed?"

"Everything hurts and I'm stuck." I turned to show him that I had one arm in and one out of my shirt and I hadn't even attempted to remove my jeans. I looked to him and he was trying to contain his laughter. "Don't you laugh at me! You'll be lucky if you don't get sick, too."

"Is this what you want to wear?" He held up a shirt, not sure if he knew it was his, and a pair of pajama pants. I just nodded. "Alright. Let's get you changed."

"I, no, I can't."

"Cassidy, I've seen it all before."

"It's not that."

"Then what is it?" I sat there, staring at him as another wave of nausea hit me and I closed my eyes. "Come on."

His hands were tender as he removed all my clothes, everything but my underwear. I was shaking as he pulled the shirt over my head and down my body. Stepping into my pajama pants, his hands lingered on my waist a little longer than necessary, or I imagined it. Pulling back the covers, he had me lay down.

"I'm going to go get you some broth and medicine. I'll be right back."

I watched as he left the room. My body began shaking terribly. I was so cold. How I wished at that moment that I had an electric blanket. I must've dozed off because I woke to him saying my name.

"Here, take this." I swallowed the vile liquid and dropped my head back to the pillow. "I have some warm broth here if you want it." I took a few sips before setting it back down. "Do you need anything else?"

I was still freezing and broke down and asked, "I'm sorry, I know it's awkward and I wouldn't normally ask..."

"What is it Cassidy?"

"I'm freezing. Can you find some blankets or..."

"Or what?"

"Hold me, just until I warm up?"

He didn't say anything, just nodded, turned off the light and started undressing. The room was cast in darkness as I listened to him disrobe. I heard his shoes hit the floor, followed by the buckle of his belt. I felt his weight on what had been his side of the bed as he climbed under the covers and moved closer.

"Front or back?"

I knew exactly what he was asking. My front to his front or my back to his front. He asked it most nights when we were in bed, when we were still together. "Back." I rolled to my side as he moved in closer. I could already feel the heat of him surround me. He was a damn furnace.

"You're still shaking." He wrapped his arms around me and tucked me back against him. The only things separating us were the damn separation papers and my pajamas. "Dammit." His hand grazed my hip as he adjusted himself.

"Can't you keep him under control?" I snickered, but couldn't keep my eyes open. I was back in my James cocoon and felt myself drifting off as the chills finally started to calm.

"Not around you. You should know that by now." His words were quiet as he wrapped his arm around me again.

nine

Illuminated

~ JAMES ~

S HE WAS SHAKING FROM HEAD to toe as I pulled her close. My cock immediately reacted to her closeness. She was lucky she was dressed, though helping her change her clothes just about did me in. I had to pry my hands off of her hips before I took advantage of her. When she asked me to hold her, I knew what she needed before she had asked. I just wanted to hear her say the words.

I hated seeing her like that. She was sick and hurting and if I could help in any way I was going to. Her shaking slowly subsided as her breathing slowed and evened out. She was asleep and I soon followed.

When I woke, we were still on our sides, but she was facing me. Her face was so close to mine that it was torture. The moonlight was shining into the room, illuminating her face. She was so beautiful and I was a fucking idiot. I leaned in and ran my nose up hers and kissed her forehead. She started to stir and I panicked. Closing my eyes, I feigned sleep, just as her eyes were beginning to open.

She inhaled sharply and I felt her pull away slightly as her body stiffened under my arm, still wrapped around her. A moment later she relaxed and moved her hand to my chest. Soon I felt her fingertips barely touch my face as they trailed down the scar of my left eye and then over my cheek.

"I'm so sorry I hurt you. I never meant to hurt you." I debated about waking and begging for forgiveness, knowing I had hurt her too. "Now, now even if you wanted to, you probably wouldn't take me back. I missed you, miss you still, so much."

Why did she think I wouldn't take her back? Before I could ponder it further she continued talking. I should have stopped her, but didn't. I wanted to know her secrets more than I wanted anything in the world, except maybe her.

"I've hurt you, Paul, myself, and for what?" She sighed. "My baby," she stroked my chest, "our baby." I heard her sniffle and wondered if she was crying as my own heart constricted. "God is punishing me." I couldn't take it anymore.

"Cassidy, nobody is punishing you." She jumped out of my arms as her eyes scanned my face.

"How much did you hear?"

I tried to pull her closer, "Enough. The miscarriage isn't your fault." I pulled her back into my arms as she cried.

"I wanted our baby, so much."

Her words opened my own floodgates as I felt the tears fall from my eyes. "I wanted our baby, too. If anyone is to blame, it's me. I should've stayed and fought for you, for our baby. I'll never forgive myself for that. Instead, I ran."

Her sobs continued as she croaked out, "It's not your fault. The doctor said there was nothing that could've been done."

"See. You're not to blame either." I tilted her chin so that I could see her face. I wanted to kiss her desperately, but stopped myself. It wasn't what either of us needed. She tucked herself in closer, her head under my chin, and I rubbed my hands over her back and through her hair. "There are so many things I wish I could change for you, for us."

"Me too."

Several minutes later I stroked her face. "Cassidy?"

"Hmm." She was dozing off again.

"Nothing. Get some rest."

Groggily she inquired, "Where did you go?" I knew she was referring to the day I left her and Paul at the hospital. She had the right to know and I was planning on telling her. She started shaking again.

Placing my hand on her head, her fever was back. "You're burning up again. Hang on." I got up and got her some more meds and took them to her. "Here." She downed the meds and laid back down. "We have a lot to talk about. Right now you need rest."

She was already breathing softly when I crawled back into bed. I grabbed my shirt and threw it on real quick before settling in next to her. As she slept in my arms I recalled the conversation I'd had with Jane the previous evening.

She had come over after Cal was called in to work and laid in to me about everything. She told me that they'd recently had dinner with Cassidy and that she was a wreck. She wouldn't divulge any details about Paul, maybe because she didn't have any. The words from Jane that hurt me the most were when she confided in me about her own miscarriage. I had no idea she'd been pregnant and what Derek had done to her.

"*I sat and talked to her for hours when she found out, James. She was scared and elated at the same time. She wanted that baby.*" *I just sat and listened as Jane disclosed more to me.* "*She's put up a huge wall since the miscarriage. You need to break it down.*"

"I want to, Jane, but I don't know if I can."

"Man up! She's your wife and I know you love her. Prove it."

"How?"

"I don't know. Just because you and I don't like grand gestures, maybe Cassidy does!" I had plans for the Blue Horse but kept that to myself. "Go big or go home cousin! The only question is do you want to make it work with her?"

"I do."

"Forever?"

Smiling, "Of course. She's it for me."

"Does she know that?"

"Ok, ok. I get it. Christ."

She walked over and hugged me. "I should go. Call me if you need any ideas or help!"

"Will do."

"I love you, James."

"I love you too, meddling woman. You're as bad as your mother." She smacked my arm as we both laughed.

"Just remember. Men like to feel wanted, women need to feel wanted."

"Get out!" I lovingly shoved her out the door as she smirked and walked down the hall.

~ PAUL ~

I KNEW SHE'D asked for space, but I had to talk to her. I drove by her place and saw his vehicle parked in the drive. First I felt sadness, then anger and it was the anger that took over. The only thing stopping me from smashing his windshield in was the security detail parked out front. Had she been playing us both? No, that wasn't like her. Was it? I knew she'd never intentionally hurt anyone.

Of course, I knew better than most what a devious woman was capable of. I just didn't want to believe that Cassidy was one of them. I drove around aimlessly before I ended up at the club. Sex, drugs and alcohol sounded good and were just the fix I needed. If a woman—or two—ended up under me, even better.

~ CASSIDY ~

WHEN I WOKE up, I felt significantly better. Though my throat ached and I wasn't sure if it was from the crying or the sickness. He wasn't next to me and when I looked to the clock, I saw that half the morning was gone. He'd probably left hours ago, declarations that we needed to talk long forgotten. Pulling myself from the bed, I headed to the bathroom and turned the shower on. I needed the heat and steam to cure my aching bones.

I stood in the shower and went over the previous night's events in my head. He'd taken care of me, confessed his emotions about the baby, but not about me. I didn't know what to think or what to do. After several minutes with the hot water branding my body, I washed, shampooed and rinsed before getting out. Wrapping myself up in my robe, I walked into my bedroom to find a steaming cup of coffee on the dresser with a note.

> I'm downstairs and ready
> to talk when you are.
> ~James

I was speechless and grew nervous. Trying not to think about it, I got dressed in sweats, dried my hair some and headed down with my coffee. He was sitting on the couch reading the paper. When he spotted me he folded it and set it down.

"You look better, hopefully you feel better."

Shrugging my shoulders, I replied, "Yes. A little better."

"You should sit down. Are you hungry?"

Hesitantly, I walked to the couch and sat down. "Not really. I'll stick with coffee for now. Thank you."

"It's no problem."

We sat there, in uncomfortable silence as I sipped my coffee. I broke the silence. "You said you wanted to talk." He changed position and sat facing me, his back against the arm rest at the opposite end. Placing his hand on the back of the couch toward me, he smiled.

"Yes. I think we need to." I just smiled and nodded. "Guess I'll just dive in. When I left that day, I went up to the cabin after calling Annie. She knew I wasn't in a good place and called my therapist, Dr. Pratt."

"Ok."

"I drank away my sorrows for a couple days before Dr. Pratt showed up. He sobered me up and waited for me to open up." He looked to me and I nodded for him to continue. "Dr. Pratt is who helped me when I finished my time in the service. I had, err have, wounds, mentally and physically that he helped me work through. I had PTSD pretty bad and he, Annie, and Smith were the only ones who could get through to me.

"Alcohol became a vice for me then and it's still an issue if I let it be. Anyways, I was terrified to tell you all of that. You deserve someone better…"

I cut him off, "James, I didn't want someone better. I only wanted you. All of you."

He sighed, "I know that now. I'm sorry I didn't have more faith in you." His eyes dropped to his lap. "I was so blinded and angry that day at the hospital. When I doubted you and thought that Paul might be the father, I lost all sense and let you believe that I was screwing around."

My eyes dropped to stare into my coffee. I couldn't look at him. Knowing he hadn't cheated on me, at least not with Melissa. But, I had ultimately cheated on him. Even if we were separated.

"I wasn't, Cassidy. You're the only person I've been with since I first saw you over a year ago." He moved closer and put his hand on my knee. "Please look at me." He took the coffee from my hands and set it on the coffee table before taking my hands in his. "Cassidy, you can talk to me."

I had to tell him, there was no point keeping it a secret. "I slept with Paul." His hands still clung to mine as I choked out, "and Roxy and Misty. I'm so ashamed." Pulling a hand free, I swiped it at my face.

"When?"

"I, um, I kissed Paul for the first time at the cabin. After you threw me away. We didn't sleep together till last weekend. I was drunk and Misty and Roxy were there too." I wanted to look at him, but didn't want to see the disgust that would surely be plastered on his face. "Please say something. Anything."

"I know."

I tried prying my other hand free, "What, what do you mean you know?"

"I know about Misty, Roxy and Paul. At the club, right?" My insides convulsed as realization hit me. Had he been there that night? "Annie had to stop me from interfering." He released my hand as I buried my face. "Cassidy, I don't care. I drove you away. Just tell me it's over."

Over? That *what* was over? "I, you, you knew? Tell you what's over? I'm so confused."

"Do you love him?"

"What!" He didn't seem angry or sad; in fact, there was no emotion on his face. "Paul?" He nodded. "James, it's complicated."

He dropped his head. "When did you stop loving me?"

Was he a fool? My heart broke at his question. "I never said I stopped loving you. Paul holds a piece of my heart and probably always will. But, you." My voice barely above a whisper, "You own my heart. All of it." He lifted his eyes to mine as a smile full of hope slowly spread across his lips. "How could you, why did you just throw me away? I don't know if I can get past that."

"Please, let me try to fix it."

"James, we've both caused so much damage." He moved in closer and placed his hands on my cheeks and looked into my eyes. Whispering, I admitted, "I want you in my life, need you. But I don't know if I trust you to not hurt me again." A tear rolled down as his thumb wiped it away.

"I want you in mine, need you, too. Please. I'll do anything to prove that I won't hurt you again." He dropped his forehead to mine and kissed the tip of my nose.

My head became fuzzy. Having him so close to me was bound to make me so. "James..." I couldn't stop it. My mouth was drawn to his like a magnet.

He groaned as my lips pressed against his and his fingers moved into my hair. I gripped his biceps as our bodies immediately fell into sync. He hovered over me as I moved lower so that he could nestle his body on top of mine. The weight of his body on mine was euphoric, the one thing I'd missed more than anything.

My hands reached around him as I pulled him closer. My fingernails found the skin of his lower back and dug in. Moving my knee up, he cradled his crotch against mine, causing me to gasp and press up into him. His hand moved under my shirt and found my naked breast. He then moved it to my sternum as he pulled his lips away from me. I opened my eyes and found him scanning my face.

When his eyes found mine again, he smiled, "I can't lose you, Blackbird." He shifted his hips against mine as I closed my eyes at the sensation that ran through me. His hand moved higher and gently gripped my neck as he kissed me again. My lips were swollen and tender as his goatee tickled me.

"James, wait. Please, stop."

Leaning up he questioned me, "What is it?"

"It's too fast. Please."

"Please what?" His hand moved back to my breast, he thought I was joking.

"No! We have to stop." My tone alerted him that I was serious. He got on his knees as I pulled myself up. "This has never been the issue with us. We can't just hop back into bed together."

Running his hands through his hair, I could tell he was digesting my words. Nodding, "You're right. I'm sorry." He sat down and took a deep breath. "I said I'd do anything and I will. What do you want me to do?"

"I, I don't know." I had an idea and started chewing on my nails because I didn't think he'd like my idea.

"You're thinking. What is it?"

"Umm, maybe Dr. Pratt could help?" He stared at me a moment before looking off into space. He stood and walked to the kitchen counter and picked up his phone. "Who are you calling?" He put his index finger in the air and I immediately quieted. Was he really calling Dr. Pratt?

"Hi Dr. Pratt. Yes, I'm good. I, no, we, Cassidy and I were wondering if you'd be willing to see us. Yes, together. Ok. I understand." He looked to me, "Um, can we come in tomorrow night?" I just nodded. "Yes, we can do that. Ok. We'll see you then." He put his phone back on the counter and leaned against it. "Tomorrow night."

"Ok. I, ok, wow."

"What is it?"

"I just, I'm surprised. I didn't think you'd be ok with my suggestion."

Smiling, he replied, "I agree that our chemistry isn't the problem. We need to work on all the other things first." I yawned. "You should take a nap and some more meds. You need to be better if we're going to go see Dr. Pratt tomorrow."

"What about you?"

"I have some things to work on." I nodded. "Cassidy, I have to ask. Do you want me to stay here or at the hotel?"

My heart skipped a beat. Of course I wanted him with me, but that wasn't going to help us keep our pants on. "I, well, maybe we should see what Dr. Pratt suggests."

"Ok. I'll be back in a few hours with dinner." He walked over and pulled me to my feet and hugged me. "Thank you."

"For what?"

"For everything. I know we have a lot to figure out." He kissed my forehead and then ushered me toward the stairs. "Nap. I'll be back."

I started to head up the stairs and heard him open the door. I grew panicked and my thoughts became erratic as I wondered if it was real. Was he really there, wanting to make it work? "James!" I ran down the stairs and leapt in his arms, my own clinging to his neck.

Clasping me tightly, he consoled me and kicked the door shut, "Hey, I missed you too."

Talking into his neck I asked, "You're coming back? We're really going to work on this, together?"

His hand smoothed down my hair as he replied, "Yes. I'm coming back. I promise." Pulling my face back, I tried to smile at him as the tears threatened. "I can't do this without you. I love you, Cassidy."

I wasn't able to respond, my throat was so constricted with emotion.

I simply nodded as I buried my face against him again. We stood like that for a moment. I just wanted to remain in the comfort and safety of his arms. Eventually, we pried our bodies apart and I carried myself up the stairs. He promised he'd be back in a few hours with dinner.

After I heard the door close, I turned on my laptop. I needed music and since my iPod was gone, my laptop would have to do. I knew I should have just splurged and bought a new one. I placed it on my nightstand and scanned through my songs and playlists. I wanted this to all be real, but I was scared to death, waiting for the other shoe to drop. I put on my favorite Thirty Seconds to Mars song, on repeat of course, and climbed under the covers.

ten

Stay

~ JAMES ~

WAS IT REALLY HAPPENING? I WAS throwing my plan away, unable to stay away from her any longer. I sat in my truck outside her place as her iPod sang songs through the cab. A piano infused melody caught my attention and I started it over. Her playlist titled with my moniker was the only thing I listened to in those weeks. *Stay* by Thirty Seconds to Mars echoed through as I fought with my body's desire to claim her or to let her rest.

No sex. That's what we agreed upon. At least not till we talked to Dr. Pratt. Fuck me. She was my home. I could live buried inside her for eternity. I told her I loved her and she had just nodded. *Please tell me I haven't lost her.* She confided in me when I didn't think she would. I knew I had to give her time. She was receptive and seemed willing to work on us and that's the most I could hope for and more than I deserved.

I spent the next few hours at the office. I'd seen the flyer on her counter and started making phone calls. I tried calling Paul about the house and got no answer. Deciding I had time, I drove out to the property. The terrain had been cleared and the foundation would be poured soon. I really needed to sit down with Cassidy. I wanted it to be *our* house, not mine. She had a right to help with the design, but I didn't want to put too much on her plate either. I knew she was swamped with wedding preparations for Jane and Cal.

I stopped by the local deli and picked up some different types of soups. Granted, it was June, but figured chicken soup is what she'd want. When I walked in I could hear music blaring and when I walked upstairs the shower was running. I made my way back down to the kitchen before I was tempted any further. I took it as a good sign that the loud music and shower running meant she was feeling better. Placing the soup on the stove, I pulled out some bowls and spoons and waited.

I placed the blueprints for the house on the table and waited for her to make her appearance. Chessa joined me on the couch and curled up in my lap. I was scratching her head when I heard her steps coming down the stairs.

"Looks like I'm not the only one who missed you."

Smiling back at her, I picked Chessa up in my arms and walked over to Cassidy. She quickly turned her face so that I kissed her cheek and she was right to do so. *Slow, James. Slow.* "I picked up some soup. Hope that's ok." She nodded. "Are you feeling better?"

"Yes. Still a little achy, but I'm hungry." I set Chessa down as Cassidy walked past the dining table. She spotted the blueprints and pointed her finger, "What are these?"

"The drawings for the house." She just stared in my eyes, back to the prints and back to me again. "Ok."

Smirking, "I'd like your input."

"Uh, I, ok. Why?"

"Why do you think?" She shrugged her shoulders. "My hope is to live there with you. It's your house, too."

"No pressure, right!" She shook her head at me and turned toward the kitchen.

"Cass…"

"It's ok. I'll look at them with you, but I'm not sure that me getting invested in a house is such a good idea." I followed her to the kitchen and watched as she opened the various soups. "It's a lot to process."

"I know." It was too much. A day earlier she thought I still wanted a divorce and there I was talking about building a house. "Sorry. I'll back off."

"James, its ok. Really. Why don't you show me what you got?"

She poured herself some soup and I did the same before we sat at the table. I pointed out the general layout and floor plan to her. She didn't say much, just smiled and nodded. "We can change anything if you don't like it, but if we want any hope of moving in before the end of the year, we need to get moving." She started coughing on her soup, probably inhaling some. "Too fast?"

She smiled as she got her coughing under control. "That fast, huh?" I confirmed. "It looks really big."

"Only about four thousand square feet."

"*Only*, he says. James, that's huge."

"It's not *that* big, but thanks for noticing." I winked at her as she rolled her eyes at me.

"You're not cleaning it."

"You don't have to clean it either."

"Now you're playing dirty." She scanned her eyes over the drawings again.

"Want bigger?"

She smacked my arm, "Knock it off. We can always add on, right?"

"That's the spirit." She laughed and it was then that I realized how much I missed her smile and laughter. It filled me up with hope.

"What are you staring at?" She started checking her face as I shook my head at her.

"You. You're beautiful."

"Please. My hair's up and I'm in yoga pants and a sweatshirt."

"Exactly. Even like this, you're simply stunning."

"Whatever. Back to the house." She never could take a compliment.

"So, what are some things you'd want in your dream house?"

"Hmm. A huge kitchen would be nice."

"For all that cooking you do?" We both knew it wasn't her specialty.

"No. For the chef you'll hire to cook for me." She stuck her tongue out and carried on. "A library, an amazing bathroom, guest bedrooms because it seems silly to have all that space and not enough bedrooms to hold friends and family."

"How many bedrooms?"

She scrunched her lips together as she mulled it over. "I don't know. Five or six in addition to ours would be nice."

"Five or six! It needs to be bigger if you want all that. At least five thousand square feet then."

"Oh, Jesus. Knock it off." We were both laughing. "With the right design, is there a basement?" I nodded and she continued, "If the rooms are big enough you could have multiple sets of bunk beds, like at the cabin in some guest rooms or the basement. Murphy beds are making a comeback too."

"Definitely five thousand…OW!" She punched me in the arm, "Ok, six thousand." She crossed her arms over her chest as we laughed at one another.

"What about you? What are some things you want in a house?"

"Game room, media room, a sweet ass bar…"

"You're such a guy. Ok, I want a craft room and an office."

Smiling, "I need an office too. Maybe we could share."

"It would need to be a big office. My craft room and office could be one. With the event planning it should be together anyways." She was still thinking, "Oh, and a big closet with lots of storage for shoes."

"Shoes? I didn't take you for a shoe girl."

"Eh, I could learn. I prefer boots anyways, not heels."

"What about a playroom?"

She seemed to grow nervous. "Um…isn't that what our bedroom is for?"

"Will our bedroom be off limits to guests, because if it is then that should work?"

"I've always fancied hidden passageways. Bookcases that open to secret rooms. Think you can do that?"

Noting her sarcastic tone, I played along. "Anything is possible. I can check with Paul." She grew uncomfortable when I said his name and I couldn't blame her. "Sorry."

"It's ok. He works for you. It's just weird. Are you sure he's going to be ok with all of this?"

"If he's not, I'll find someone else to do it." She started chewing on her nails and I took her hand. "Hey, it's going to be ok. We'll find a way around it all. Can I ask where things stand with you two?"

She sighed, "I told him I needed space. Time."

"I see." I tried to keep my anger in check. I was the one who pushed her into his arms. The question would be where she stayed and would he respect her choice if it was me. Because I knew I'd have a hell of a time respecting it if she chose him.

"I'll talk to him." She placed her hand over mine. "I want *this*."

"I can come with you."

Shaking her head, "No. We all have our own history. This needs to be between Paul and me." Taking a deep breath she said, "He told me what happened with Cora."

"Yeah, I guess we're even now. But in my defense, I didn't know she was married."

"This isn't a pissing contest."

"I know. Sorry."

"This is all my fault. I've probably ruined your friendship."

"Don't worry about it. You're my number one concern, not Paul."

"Me too." Finally, some validation!

We watched a couple movies and half way into the second one, she fell asleep curled up next to me. I struggled behaving myself before she relaxed against me and got comfortable. Her head was in my lap as I ran my fingers through her red locks. I pulled a blanket over her and dropped my head to the back of the couch. There was no way I was going to disturb her.

I woke to her trying to tip-toe out of the room as she made her way for the stairs. Her blanket was now covering me as my eyes adjusted to the dark.

"Cassidy?"

She stopped and turned slowly, "James?"

Standing, I walked over to her. "I should probably head out." She nodded slowly as I asked her, "You still up to meeting with Dr. Pratt?"

"Yes, of course."

I pulled her into a hug, whispering, "Are you going to work? I can pick you up, but if you're already downtown…"

"I'll stay in touch. I'll probably try to go to work."

She was a very hard worker and I couldn't recall a single day that'd she'd taken off work just for the sake of taking off work. "Ok. Get some rest." She lifted her face to mine and stared into my eyes. "Cassidy, you should go to bed."

She blinked her eyes a few times, acknowledging, "Right. Sorry. Habit I guess."

Fuck it. It was just a kiss. I yanked her closer and dropped my hungry mouth to hers. The moan that escaped her lips sent a thrill through me. Her body immediately relaxed into mine as she let me lead the kiss. I loved her so much. She was the breath that filled my lungs. I wanted, no needed, to possess her and she'd let me if I pushed her. Showing no fear or hesitation, she'd always given her body over to me willingly. I had to treasure that. I cupped her face and slowed the kiss as her hands clung to my side.

It took all my strength to separate our mouths as I dropped a kiss to her forehead. "I should go."

Her eyes were still closed as she dropped her head to my chest. Mumbling, "I hate you," I grinned from ear to ear knowing her words weren't true.

"Got to leave the lady wanting more."

"Who said anything about me being a lady?"

I chuckled as she smiled up at me. "Maybe the lady can take care of herself, but I want details, or pictures."

"A lady wouldn't send you pictures or give you details." She winked as I turned toward the door.

"You won't be the only one taking care of things alone." She pursed her lips and if she thought I missed her eyes dropping to my groin, she was wrong. "Harlot!"

Her eyes sparkled as she gave me her 'come hither' look. "No sex. That was the agreement. And I'm the furthest thing from a harlot! Maybe." She walked around me and opened her front door. "You've overstayed your welcome Mr. Benedict."

She could barely contain her grin as I stepped out to her porch. Making sure one of Smith's guys was parked out front, I looked back to her. "Goodnight, Cassidy. I'll talk to you tomorrow."

"Looking forward to it." She didn't close the door until I was in my truck. I saw the light come on in her bedroom as I pulled away.

~ PAUL ~

How could she change her tune so quickly? I pulled in the drive several minutes after his truck left and banged on the front door. Her light was still on upstairs so I knew she was awake. When the door finally opened, the smile on her face quickly changed to one of surprise.

"Expecting someone else?"

"Paul, I, no. What are you doing here? It's late."

"What was *he* doing here? I thought you said you needed time and space."

"Paul, I told you it's complicated. He's my husband."

"And he threw you away like yesterday's news. I sat by and watched the way he treated you. How can you go back to that?"

"Paul, I know he's your friend and I know you care about me. I do." She tried putting her hand on my arm and I shook her off. "I don't need to justify or explain my relationship with James to you."

I stumbled as I tried to stand a little taller. "What relationship?" Her face contorted as my breath hit her in the face.

"You're drunk!"

I took a bow and smiled at her. "Yes, I am. Congratulations! I'm not the only man you've driven to drink." She went to say something, but stopped short. "Cat got your tongue? Or maybe Misty or Roxy? Hell, I can't keep them straight."

I wasn't expecting the smack that came, but I should've. The girl had a temper and only put up with so much. As my eyes focused on her face, I could see the tears welling in her eyes. "How dare you! I feel horrible about that night, but at least I know Misty and Roxy won't hold it against me."

"And what about James?"

"What about him? He knows, if that's what you're asking."

"You told him!"

"I didn't have to."

She didn't have to? I stood there for a minute as my thoughts tried to make sense of her words. Fuck! My head was spinning. All I wanted was her and I was too late. "Cassidy, I'm sorry."

"Paul, I'm sorry too. You need to go." She averted her attention to someone behind me. "Can you call him a cab or something?"

"I don't need your pity."

"It's not pity. You're drunk."

"Screw you. Oh, wait. I already did that." I had to get out of there. I got in my SUV and dropped the keys on the floor too many times to remember. My forehead found its way to rest on my steering wheel and I closed my eyes. A knock came on the window and I recognized Frank. *Shit!* How much time had passed?

I opened the door and stepped out. His partner was standing by a patrol car and Cassidy was nowhere to be seen. *FUCK! What had I said to her?* I was a mean mother fucker when I drank.

"Cassidy said you could use a ride home."

"Shit. Yeah. Probably not a bad idea."

"I could arrest you Vincent. You owe me. Where are the keys?"

I pointed to the floor and stumbled around to the passenger side. Frank drove me home as his partner followed. It was a quick drive and I was grateful, knowing I shouldn't have been behind the wheel.

I needed to apologize to Cassidy, but I didn't even know what to apologize for. I just needed sleep.

~ CASSIDY ~

SLEEP WAS HARD to come by that night. Paul had every right to be angry with me, I just hadn't expected him to lash out at me the way he did. I had been trying to put my feelings of embarrassment aside and he had made it ten times worse. Quickly, I sank into a horrible depression. I was a hussy, a harlot, a slut, and certainly no lady. Who sleeps with their ex—and two chicks—at the same time just days after making a legal separation from her husband? I turned my alarm off, my phone to mute and crawled under the covers. Happiness didn't owe me any favors and I deserved all the misery I brought upon myself.

I slept the day away, only getting out of bed to pee. I hadn't even bothered checking my phone. For all I knew the battery was dead. Music was the only thing of joy I allowed myself and even they weren't chipper songs. Hell, they were bordering on suicidal and I was happy to wallow in their dark melodies. I was listening to *Break* by Rebecca Roubion and had put it on repeat. The haunting piano driven song was feeding my depressed soul. I had it up louder than necessary, in my usual fashion.

"Are you still sick?" His deep voice startled me as I bolted up in bed. "Cassidy, are you ok? I've been worried sick about you." I couldn't manage to make eye contact with him and watched as he pulled my phone off the dresser and confirmed that it was dead. "I've been trying to call you all day." He sat down next to me and turned my face toward his, "Baby, what's wrong."

"Don't call me that. I'm not your baby. I'm no one's baby." He sat quiet and I could feel his eyes on my face. "You should hate me."

"Cassidy, what happened? Everything was fine when I left last night; at least I thought it was. What changed between then and now?"

The lyrics of the song playing were fresh in my mind and I used them as I saw fit. "You need to be free of me. I'm a landslide and I'll just bury you in my path of destruction." He caressed my cheek and I tried to pull away, but I couldn't. "Please, let me be. I'm a horrible person; you should hate me for what I've done."

He sighed, "He came here last night didn't he?" I just shrugged my shoulders. "He left me a pretty nasty voicemail that I didn't listen to until this morning. I should've suspected that he paid you a visit."

"He was drunk."

"He's lucky he has a fucking job. What did he say to you?"

"It doesn't matter. He wasn't wrong in what he said."

James didn't say anything, just crawled in next to me and pulled me to him as I cried. "You're not defined by your mistakes and neither am I. Lord knows we've both made them. If people want to judge us by our mistakes, let them. But I know YOU, the *real* you. You're amazing, loving, giving, creative, loyal, and fucking stubborn."

"You don't want me. I'm broken."

"Are you listening to the lyrics at all? You're the one who taught me to listen to them. You're a diamond in the rough and you won't break for nothing. Wake up. If you want me to be free and you want to run, then I'll run with you because I'm only free when I'm with you."

His tone was louder than it needed to be, but I didn't flinch. I focused on the lyrics and on his heart hammering away under my ear. "I'm sorry."

"Don't be sorry, Blackbird. That's what I'm here for. To smack some sense into you when necessary. I hope you'll do the same." I just nodded against his chest. "I'll reschedule Dr. Pratt."

I jumped up, "No! What time is it? Are we too late?"

He chuckled, "No, it's not too late. I just figured you wouldn't be up to it. We can still go."

"Ok. I want to go."

"Well, you need to get up and get ready. I'll wait for you downstairs." He climbed out of the bed and leaned over to kiss me. "Don't forget about the amazing person you are. You're amazing. I'll tell you every day if I need to."

I fought back more ridiculous tears as I wiped at my nose, "Stop making me cry. You're pretty amazing yourself."

He simply smiled before disappearing downstairs. I looked at the clock to discover it was after four in the afternoon. There were no words to describe him and my gratefulness for him. I was an idiot to have so quickly turned my back on him. *Deep breaths, girl.* I turned on the shower and hopped in. When I got out, I wasn't sure what to wear. What did one wear to meet a therapist? It was June, but the summer weather had yet to make a full appearance. I opted for a maxi skirt, peasant top and sandals. I grabbed my cardigan before heading downstairs.

He was finishing up a phone call and standing by the fireplace when he spotted me. My hair was still damp and I'd put on very little makeup, also a norm for me. He grinned and ended the phone call.

"You look great."

"Thanks. I wasn't really sure what to wear."

"I was thinking we could grab dinner after, if you're up to it."

"Yes, I think that would be lovely."

eleven
Therapy

~ CASSIDY ~

W E WERE DRIVING BACK TOWARD the city and it felt like old times. I was riding shot gun in his truck admiring the view— him. He looked *way* too good behind the wheel of that big black truck. I immediately remembered his bike. I wondered if he'd pulled it out of storage and was eager to go for a ride.

"What is it?"

"Hmm. Nothing."

"You're a terrible liar."

I smiled at him as I made it obvious that I was checking him out. "I want to go for a ride on your bike."

"Eager to feel the roar of the engine between your legs." He started laughing as my eyes got big and I blushed.

"Why do you have to make it sound so dirty?"

"You like it dirty."

"Touché. Ok. Enough of the innuendos. Focus Mr. Benedict."

"We can go for ride tonight if you like." He gazed at me and added, "On the bike, of course."

"Right, the bike. Of course." I looked out my window as I felt his hand on the back of my neck. "I would like that. A ride, on your bike."

He was grinning like a fool when I looked over at him. He just nodded and soon pulled into a small parking lot a few blocks off of Main Street. "We're here."

He took my hand and we started walking toward an old Victorian home that had been converted into an office space. We walked in to a cozy living room with oversized furniture. I was about to sit down when a door from above opened and footsteps followed. I grew nervous as I waited. A pair of tanned legs made their way down the stairs and I became possessive as James smiled at her.

"Angeline, nice to see you." They shook hands and I chastised myself for assuming Dr. Pratt was a man. "This is Cassidy. Cassidy, Angeline. She's Dr. Pratt's secretary."

Thank God! "Hi, nice to meet you." We exchanged a handshake as James wrapped an arm around my waist.

"Dr. Pratt is ready for you. He's looking forward to meeting you." Her eyes were directed toward me. She was stunning, but seemed unaffected by James. He motioned to the stairs and we made our ascent.

"Don't worry. That's Dr. Pratt's wife."

He smiled as my eyes made the connection. "Oh. Ok."

We walked through some double doors at the end of a long hallway. He was standing at a bookshelf and turned to greet us. He had on a three piece suit, though the jacket wasn't on, narrow black glasses and thinning hair that was highlighted with gray. He was almost as tall as James but slimmer.

"You must be the infamous Cassidy? His description didn't do you justice." I smiled as he added to James, "She's beautiful."

He winked at me as he responded, "Yes, she is." Turning back to the doctor, "Dr. Pratt, thank you again for meeting with us."

"Of course. Let's get started." We took our seats on a couch as Dr. Pratt sat in a chair across from us. "So, tell me what brings you here. You've been through quite a lot the past several months."

"Well, Cassidy brought it up," he took my hand in his, "and I think it's a good idea. We're not the best at communicating with one another and we want to be. At least I think that's why we're here."

Dr. Pratt looked to me and I nodded. "You seem nervous, Cassidy." I nodded again. "James, can I have a few minutes alone with Cassidy?"

"Is that ok with you?"

"Yes. That's fine." He kissed me before walking out the door and closed it behind him.

"So, it's just the two of us. Coming here was a big step, for both of you. I'm here to help any way I can. Why did you feel coming here was a good idea?"

I took a deep breath as I tried to organize my thoughts. "He's been through so much and kept his whole time in the Army a secret from me for a long time."

"Yes, he has some pretty deep scars from his time in the service."

"When his mom died, it got worse. I pushed him, probably too much, to open up to me." I could feel my chest tightening as I repositioned myself on the couch. "I care about him so much." My voice cracked, "I'm sorry, I don't know why I'm getting emotional."

"You care for him deeply and he does for you, too." He passed me a box of tissues, "Do you want this marriage to work?"

His question tore at me, in a good way. "More than anything. But we've both made so many mistakes."

"We all make mistakes. You've both proven by coming here that you want to try to make things right." He waited for a moment as I twisted a tissue around in my hand. "He's given me permission to answer any questions you may have. I assume you're aware of the PTSD."

Tilting my head, "I assumed. I don't really need the details, I don't think. I just want to be able to comfort him. He has nightmares and doesn't sleep much."

"That's pretty common."

"And the more frequent the nightmares get, the more he drinks."

"Yes, that is a problem of his."

"Is he an alcoholic?" I struggled getting the words out, but had to ask.

"Do *you* think he's an alcoholic?"

"I don't know. My mother was one, I think. He seems to be able to decide when he drinks, whereas some alcoholics can't be around it at all."

"You're correct. He has great restraint when he wants. Does it concern you?"

"Sometimes. When he decides to drink, sometimes it's a lot. That scares me." He looked to me and I felt I had to add, "Not that he'll hurt me or anything. Just that he'll hurt himself. He busted his head open a few months ago because he was drunk."

"He told me."

"How, er, has he been coming here long?"

Shaking his head, "He started again a couple weeks ago, after I went to the cabin. He's made a lot of progress and is willing to do whatever it takes to make things work with you." I just smiled at that, not sure what to say. "How's your physical relationship?" I balked at him, "I'm a sex therapist as well."

"Ok. Well, there are no complaints, except." How did I say it without sounding like a prude? "We may rely on sex too much? I don't know how to explain it. We're very attracted to one another and there are no problems there."

"So the intimacy isn't an issue?"

"No, yes, just that it's hard to keep our clothes on and our hands off each other. I refused to have sex with him last night because I didn't want to just hop back into bed."

Chuckling, "Well, that's a good thing. How long did you two wait before consummating your relationship?"

I knew I was blushing when I told him. I explained the timeline and how we'd pretty much slept together within twenty-four hours of reconnecting. "I don't regret it, I just, well, we didn't really have a 'courtship' per se. Even saying courtship sounds ridiculous."

Smiling, "It's not ridiculous. Ok. Are you willing to try an experiment? I think you're worried he's going to hurt you again and we need to rebuild your trust." I nodded. "Before I bring James back in, I want you to know that you can call me too, anytime. If you'd like to make an appointment to see me, I'm here to help." He handed me his card and said, "I'll be right back." He walked out of the office and returned a moment later with James.

James sat down next to me and kissed my cheek, "You ok?"

"Yes." I interlaced our hands as Dr. Pratt sat down.

"Ok. James, would you agree that your physical relationship with Cassidy isn't a problem?"

He coughed, not expecting the question. "Umm, I have no complaints there." He looked to me as I hesitantly made eye contact with him. "You're embarrassing the lady." He winked and said, "She's an amazing lover and I couldn't ask for more." He thought I was an amazing lover and it sent a tingle through me.

"Cassidy, what about you?" Hadn't I already told Dr. Pratt I was good there? "This is all part of better communication." I knew he was trying to reassure me.

"Ok. I have no complaints; he's the most attentive lover I've ever had."

James went to say something and Dr. Pratt cut him off. "Great! So, it's safe to assume you *both* want this relationship to work?" We nodded. "Now, I have something I want you to try. Hear me out before you say anything." We both agreed. "No sex." I felt his body stiffen next to mine as Dr. Pratt tried to negate any rebuttal, "James, hear me out. No sex for four weeks, twenty-eight days. No 'I love you's', it can lead to too much pressure. Just dating. I know you're married, but you two missed the whole dating phase that most relationships start with. Separate living quarters, the works. You're dating. Holding hands, cuddling, kisses are fine, but no sex, of ANY kind." He eyed us as his words sank in. "Thoughts?"

My brain was running a million miles a minute. Twenty-eight days? Ugh. How the hell was I supposed to be around him and *not* have sex with him for a month! Shit, that put us past Cal and Jane's wedding. There was no way he'd agree to it. Maybe we could try it for two weeks.

"I'll do it. I don't like it, but if that's what you think we should do, I agree." What! I looked to him and he started chuckling. "I think the lady may have a problem with that. I've clearly spoiled her." I smacked his arm. "Hey now! I don't think resorting to violence is what the good doctor had in mind."

"Cassidy. Do you agree?"

"I, yes, it's just, that's a long time." James was beaming ear to ear as I shook my head at him. "I'm afraid he's getting a big head." He started belly laughing at my unintended pun. "For the love...that's not what

I meant." I looked to Dr. Pratt who was watching us with a smile on his face.

"I'd say you two have the humor and light-heartedness down. Work on rebuilding your trust and the foundation of *why* you want to be together. We can meet back here next week at the same time if you like." We both agreed as James put the appointment in his phone.

Standing to leave, we all shook hands before James led me out of the house. "That wasn't so bad, was it?" He turned me to him and pushed some hair out of my face as he leaned in closer.

"Twenty-eight days! Are you high?"

"Come on, it's not that long."

"I'm shocked that you're agreeing to this." I pulled my face back and glared at him.

"Hey! I've gone longer without sex, maybe longer than you have." He pressed his forehead to mine, "He said we could kiss, hold hands. Kiss me, Cassidy."

"We're both going to be so sexually frustrated."

"He didn't say we couldn't sext or take care of ourselves."

Smiling, "Always looking for the loop hole. Perv!" He smiled as I got on my tiptoes and kissed him. I pulled away quicker than we both wanted. "Feed me." His eyes got big. "Dinner, you ass! I want food that doesn't involve your cock." I thought he was going to come in his pants. He adjusted himself as we started walking down the street toward the restaurants.

"Two can play that game, Blackbird." His hand moved to cup my ass as I swatted his hand away. Leaning into my ear he whispered, "I can't wait to devour your sweet ass—with my cock—and my mouth."

My wet panties clung to my aroused mound as I said the only thing I could, "I hate you."

"I hate you, too."

~ JAMES ~

Twenty-eight days. I knew it would be hard, but I knew it would be harder for her. I wasn't trying to be cocky about it and I knew what kind of pull we had to one another, but I knew I could handle it. The question was if Cassidy could and would handle it and if she begged me, I knew I'd concede.

We enjoyed a laid back dinner at a small Mexican place. We sat out back enjoying the weather and food. It was something I'd been looking forward to for a long time. Her and I in the summer and enjoying life. Summer days, summer nights, I didn't care what it was, I just wanted her and summer.

When I dropped her back off at her place, she'd invited me in and I declined. She was pouting her lips at me as I backed her up against her front door. "Stop tempting me. You can do this, we can do this."

She huffed and narrowed her eyes at me, frowning. "I call shenanigans."

Smiling, I tilted my head at her. "Excuse me!"

"You and Dr. Pratt; this is a setup, a bet, right?"

My laughter bellowed around us. "Cassidy, I promise you, there's no bet or setup." Her arms were crossed over her chest as she scowled at me. I dropped my voice and leaned in, "Don't think I don't want you, I do, always will."

"You sure about that?"

I fell into her trap without even knowing. I lowered my arm and began pulling her skirt up until my hand found the naked flesh of her lower thigh, "I'll hike this skirt of yours up and take you against the door." Her eyes closed as I leaned in closer, her citrus scent filling my nostrils. "I'll bury myself so deep, you'll think we're fused together."

The soft moan that escaped her lips wasn't lost on me. Her hands latched onto my forearms as I said, "I can't wait to be with you again… in twenty-eight days."

Her eyes flew open, her pupils enlarged as she took a deep breath. "You suck." Grumbling, she turned and put her key in the lock. I dropped her skirt as she opened the door. She stepped through the entryway and asked, "When can I see you again?"

She faced me and I molded my mouth to hers, stealing her breath and making it my own. Her tongue glided over mine as her hands worked through my hair. My hands were wrapped tight around her, my rock hard cock pressed against her soft belly. She sucked my lower lip between her teeth as I smiled against her lips.

"How about tomorrow night?" She just hummed and refused to stop kissing me. "Weather should be perfect. We can go for a ride." My tongue joined hers again before she pulled away, both of us trying to catch our breath. "I'll take that as a 'yes'. I'll pick you up at six."

Gently, I pulled her hands from my scalp and kissed the top of each hand before pushing her away. "Don't go."

I smiled, "You're the devil." She just smirked at me. "I give you permission to think of me tonight while you pleasure yourself. I'll be thinking of you."

"I didn't know I needed permission."

"Goodnight, Cassidy."

Sighing, "Goodnight, James."

She closed the door and set the alarm before I walked down the steps. I checked in with Ryan, who was parked in front of the house. There'd been no sign of Dan, or his existence, since the incident with Melissa, but that didn't mean anything. I wanted him found and the sooner the better. Jane's wedding was only a few weeks away and we'd all rest easier knowing he was locked up. Or dead. Dead was better.

I was almost to the hotel when my phone chimed. Pulling up my text messages, I had one from Cassidy.

Thinking of you.

There was a picture of her from the waist down, hand in her undies and it looked like she was lying in bed. A car horn blared from behind me and I dropped the phone. The light was green and I was holding up traffic. Christ. At least she had enough common sense to not include her face in the picture. I pulled into the parking garage, parked and headed to my suite.

I was already disrobed by the time I reached my bedroom. And Rock. Hard. I fisted myself and snapped a pic and hit send. My phone began ringing, almost immediately.

"James." Fuck, she sounded sexy on the phone.

"Cassidy."

"I miss you."

"I miss you, too, baby." A soft moan came through as I stroked myself. Walking back to the bed, I threw the covers back, yanked my socks off, keeping one handy for cleanup, and crawled into bed. "Are you touching yourself? I'm touching myself."

"Yes." Another moan had my cock pulsing. "I miss your dick."

I was so turned on and surprised, which made it even hotter. She'd never really shown interest in phone sex and I was going to eat it up, though I'd prefer to be eating her. "Are you wet? Let me hear how wet you are."

"Ok." I heard some ruffling and the faintest sound of her fingers sliding over her slickness came over the line. More ruffling and then her breathing came back through the line. "I miss your hands on me."

I kept stroking myself at her words, picturing myself holding her wrists above her head as I slid into her deep and hard. "Put it on speaker. Touch your breasts with your free hand." I waited a moment. "Are you close? I'm so hard, baby."

"Yes. James…"

"Harder, do it harder."

Her whimpers of need had me closer than I wanted to be. "Oh, right there. Don't stop."

"I won't stop. Fuck. I'm close, Cassidy."

"Oh, God."

"Come for me. Fuck."

"I want you inside me, oh."

"Cass…shit…" I spilled my load into my sock as I imagined her body surrounding mine. "Cassidy, let go, come for me." Her moans became more fervent and she started crying out. "That's it. I'm right there with you, my beautiful Blackbird."

A few moments later, when we'd caught our breath, she was able to talk again. "I hate you."

With a smile a mile wide on my face, "I hate you, too. Get some rest."

"You, too."

THE NEXT DAY was business as usual. Lunch was approaching when a knock came on my office door.

"Come in." The door opened and Paul stood there, a silent challenge on his face. I knew that I owed him an apology, an explanation. I'd told him I hadn't wanted her, just to change my mind. "We doing this now?"

He nodded, "Looks like it," and walked in and closed the door. He stood on the other side of my desk and I took a seat hoping he'd follow suit. He did.

"I owe you an apology, Paul. But you also owe her an apology."

He leaned back, scrubbing his hands down his face. "Fuck. She told you."

"Told me? No. She was a wreck and I put the pieces together. What did you say to her?"

"I, I don't know. I was drunk." He looked to me and then looked around the room. "This was a mistake."

I sat and tried to ponder his meaning. Talking to me, talking to her, the job; I wasn't sure what he was referring to as the mistake. "I'm the one who made the mistake."

"You can say that again."

"Paul. We've done enough fighting. You're one of my best friends. I fucked up. I know that, Cassidy knows that, hell, everyone knows that. I can't lose her. I won't."

"And what makes you think I can? I've lost her twice now. I almost didn't survive the first time. I knew there was a chance I'd run into her moving back up here, but shit. I didn't expect to find her with you."

"I need to know that you're going to back off. We're trying to make this work."

"How's that? You seem to change your mind week to week."

"God dammit, Paul. I know you love her and whether you believe it or not, I do too. I'll spend the rest of my life proving it. She's my wife and I'll fight for her till the end." His gaze was icy as he stared at me. "Don't make me fight you for her."

His eyes moved to the window that stared out over the city. "You fuck this up again…," He didn't finish his statement. He was about to speak again when my office door opened.

We both directed our eyes to Cassidy. She stood there, a deer in headlights with what appeared like carryout in her hand. Paul turned his eyes from her as I made my way over to her.

"Sorry, I can come back." She was white as a ghost. "I should've called."

I kissed her temple and took the bag from her. "It's ok. Paul and I were just finishing up. Can I have a couple minutes?"

Nodding, she agreed. "I'll be back in a few minutes."

I turned as Paul got out of the chair he occupied. "You need to find someone else Benedict. I can't do this."

He was quitting on me. I understood, but I didn't want to lose him. "How long do I have?"

"I can stay through till the wedding. That's almost four weeks. Then I'm going back to Atlanta."

"Ok."

"If the prints are finalized this week we can start pouring the foundation. Might be able to have it framed before someone else takes over."

He brushed past me, "Paul?" He turned to look at me, hand on the door. "You'll always have a job waiting if you change your mind. But I understand why you're leaving."

"Don't make me regret walking away."

I didn't respond and watched as he walked out the door. A few seconds later, Cassidy walked through the door. She must not have seen him in the hall because she was looking for him.

"He left."

"Oh, ok. I'm sorry."

"Stop. It's ok. I'm famished. What'd you bring me?" I didn't have the heart to tell her that Paul had quit. That was his story to tell. And I hoped that if he was gone all of her attention would be on us. She pulled some Thai food out of the bag and I grabbed some bottles of water from my mini fridge.

"Is everything else ok?"

"Yes. Everything's good. I need to finalize the prints so they can pour the foundation."

"Cool." She was holding back.

"Do you want to see them again?" I placed my hand on hers, "Cassidy, as far as I'm concerned this is your house."

"No, it's *our* house." She smiled brightly, "I'd like to look at them again."

Over an hour later her phone started ringing. She pulled it out of her purse and began cursing. "Everything ok?"

"Yes, no. I'm supposed to be at the dress shop for Jane's final fitting and mine. I have to go."

"Ok. We still on for tonight?"

She kissed me quickly and said, "We better be." She stood and headed for the door and I followed.

"Hey, Ryan with you?"

"One of the guys is in the lobby, impatiently waiting I'm sure."

"Ok."

We walked to the lobby and I put her and security in the elevator. I didn't catch his name, but knew Smith had it covered. We'd finalized the foundation, a little bigger than she originally wanted, but I knew we wouldn't regret having the extra space. Plus, we could always add on if we wanted. I sent the drawings down to Paul's office and got back to work.

twelve

Foundations

~ CASSIDY ~

"THERE YOU ARE! YOU LOOK AMAZING. What's going on with you?" Jane was full of energy as I laughed at her. "You have a secret! Tell me."

I dropped my bag and my body to the couch and she joined me. "I have too many secrets."

"Oh?"

"James and I. We're trying to work it out."

She flung her arms around my neck and squealed in my ear. "Thank God."

"Cal's going to have a coronary."

"Bah. Don't worry about him. I'll handle him." She grabbed my hands, "Details. Well, not too many."

I snickered, "Um, we're taking it slow and going to therapy. Together." She just nodded and then asked about Paul. "Jane, I care about him, I do. But, James is my husband and at the end of the day, he's who I want." We sat quiet for a moment. "I feel horrible. I've really hurt him."

"James?"

"No, well probably him too, but I was referring to Paul."

"Hey. He'll get over it. He knew you were married. I don't know what he expected. He's a big boy. He can handle it." I smirked and she added, "I'm pretty sure I know at least one girl who's interested in him."

"Oh?"

"Lena." I laughed and agreed. It was pretty obvious that Lena had a crush on him.

I smiled at her and then it was time to try on the dresses, again. She'd scheduled another fitting, having changed a couple things on the dress, but hadn't told her mom. She wanted to surprise her and I was a little envious of their relationship. I'd never get that experience with my mother and while I was at peace with it, it deeply saddened me.

When I pulled in the drive after the fitting and work, James was waiting for me, his bike parked in front. He was sitting on the front steps dressed in boots, dark jeans and his leather jacket. *Fuck!* He was sexy as sin. Even his hair was down and I momentarily thought that he was tormenting me.

"Hurry up woman! We have things to do."

I chuckled as I made my way past him on the steps, trying to ignore his presence. His arms circled around my knees and pulled my back into his lap. With a big grin on his face, he lowered his mouth to mine. Just before I got lost in the kiss, he put me back on my feet and told me to hurry up.

I put on some jeans, boots, a t-shirt and found my purple jacket that he'd given me for my birthday. He was standing in the foyer waiting for me. I was walking down the stairs and pulling my hair back as he opened the door for me. He handed me my helmet and then got on the bike. I climbed on behind him and grabbed on tight as he peeled out.

We rode for a while and I soon realized he was headed up to the lot. A lot of the land had been excavated and dug up, but our tree was still there. He parked and we started walking around after removing our helmets.

"They'll pour the foundation later this week or next week." He started talking about things and pointing out where the front of the house would be. I was in awe of him. "I saved the tree. Come on."

He pulled me toward the tree and when we got there, he yanked a pocket knife out of his jacket and started carving our initials. It took him a while, but soon there was a large heart with 'JB3 & CC' carved in the side of it.

"There. James Benedict the third & Cassidy Charles." He was smiling like a big dork and I didn't have the gumption to remind him that my name was no longer Charles, but Benedict, legally speaking.

"So, remind me. How much land do you have here?"

"Enough."

"Well, if you weren't on my brother's shit list, I'd say we should convince them to build here too. Benedict Commune."

He laughed and added, "Maybe Smith and Delaney on the other side."

"We'd always have family and friends nearby."

"Yes, we would."

The rest of the week flew by. That weekend was the auction at the art gallery. I tried to not think about it, knowing I couldn't afford to do anything. Even Annie had said there was nothing I could do. Things at work were going great. Jane's wedding was keeping me busy as Lena handled the other events going on. Melissa and I were getting along fine and she was actually growing on me. I wasn't ready to spill my secrets to her, but she seemed to be a great fit in her new role. The only issue was Linda. I couldn't help but feel the woman was off somehow. Who knew, maybe she just didn't like me? Oh, well.

James walked in my door that night and ordered me to get dressed up. "Nothing too fancy, but put on a skirt or a dress."

"Ok."

Forty-five minutes later I walked downstairs in the dress I'd planned to wear to the rehearsal dinner with my hair and makeup done. "Where we going?"

"You'll see."

We pulled into the parking lot across from the art gallery and I paled. "James, I can't. How'd you find out?" He just smiled. Annie. Had to be. "I, James, I don't think I can."

He grabbed my hand. "Yes you can. I'll be with you the whole time."

There were some news reporters, who of course flocked to us, to him. I smiled and tried to ignore them as we made our way inside. A server walked by with a tray of champagne and I snagged one and downed it.

"Slow down." I turned and he was smiling at me, trying to lighten the mood. He winked as he took my hand and led me through the gallery.

There were several different artists work up for sale, but Holly's was the main feature. I didn't even know how much work of hers they had that I didn't know about. My stomach felt like a lead ball as we approached the room where her work was featured. I was still livid with Sara and the owner of the gallery.

As we made it to the door, I stopped in my tracks and James looked to me. "What is it?"

"I, I just need a minute."

He came in closer and cupped my cheek. "It's ok. I'm here with you."

"I know. I just wish she was here to see this. Her work deserved to be featured, but not like this."

"I know, baby. I got you."

I took a deep breath and we headed into the center room. Some of the pieces I recognized and others I didn't. She had a LOT of work. It immediately caught my eye as I walked over to a huge painting which was the focal point of the room. It was the profile of a woman with ivory skin, blue eyes and long flowing red hair. She was looking down to her hands, where she held something that was hidden to onlookers. I was drawn back to her hair. Hair so red and it flew out behind her, like the wind was blowing. As my eyes took in the whole painting, not just the details, my heart broke as I realized the red hair blended into the wings of a phoenix.

"Holly!" Her name was barely a whisper as I realized that the painting was of me.

His hand held the small of my back as he confirmed, "She captured your likeness very well." I turned to smile at him as he wiped my tears away. "Do you know what she has in your hand?" I just shook my head.

"I have to have it. I'll pay you back."

"You don't have to pay me back. And, I want it. You can't have it." I smiled at him. "I'll be right back."

I stared at the painting for a moment longer before circling the room to look at her other pieces. She'd even painted one of an anchor and wings with the quote that was the inspiration for our tattoos. I wanted them all and I knew I couldn't have them. There were several candid paintings. She loved to capture people on film and then paint them. I recognized a couple of Sam, as well. There were a few landscapes and some of people I didn't recognize. She had been so talented.

"Hey. I talked to the curator. It's already sold." My heart sank. "But the one with the anchor is available. I told her we'd take it."

"Ok."

"I tried, I really did."

I squeezed his hand. "Thank you. It's better than nothing. I'll take what I can get." I turned back to my painting, burning it into my memory, before I asked if we could leave.

We drove to the little spot he used to take me on his bike and he parked the truck. "Come on. Time to cheer you up." I looked to him as he ordered, "Get out of the truck. I'll be there in a sec."

I stepped out as he rolled down all the windows and cranked the sound system. *Summer* by Calvin Harris began to play as he walked to my side. He started swinging me around and I couldn't help the laughter that filled me. He was the best medicine, my antidote for any ailment. When the song was over, another started and I wondered about his song choice. *Take Me Home* by Cash Cash played next and I knew this wasn't his kind of music.

"Your choice of music is a little surprising Mr. Benedict."

"Haven't you learned by now that I'm full of surprises?"

"Hmm. Yeah, yeah."

"So. I invited Delaney and Smith over to play cards. I hope that's ok."

I pursed my lips at him, "Worried you can't be alone with me?"

He laughed, "Maybe. Twenty-four days."

"But who's counting?"

"Exactly."

We picked up a pizza on the way back to my place and found Smith and Delaney waiting for us on the porch.

"'Bout time love birds." Smith was ribbing us as we made our way inside. He and James lingered back by the door as Delaney and I headed toward the kitchen.

"So. What's going on, girl?"

I laughed. "Not much. Why?" She knew I was being sarcastic as I filled her in. "We're working on it."

"Well, I'm glad. You two really are a great match. I've known him a long time, but I like you more." She winked at me as we giggled. "I got your back anytime you need it."

"Thanks."

"So," dropping her voice, "what about Paul, the club?"

I blew some air out and whispered, "He knows." We both knew that the *he* I was referring to was James. "We're working past it."

"He has a knack for that." I titled my head at her as she added, "knowing everything. He *knows* everything. It's frustrating."

"Well, that might have been something to know before I, err, did whom I did." She shrugged her shoulders as we laughed. "Live and learn I guess."

"Right-O."

We were playing Texas hold-em and Delaney was out of cash. She upped the ante and started propositioning Smith. "I don't know why you bother. You can have me any way you want me. You know that Laney!" It was the first time I remember him referring to her as Laney and not Delaney.

Smith folded and so did James; I had been out long before that. Delaney pulled what was left of the pot to her side of the table, the smile of victory all over her face, as James dealt another hand.

I had two queens in my hand, with another queen and a pair of sevens in the flop. Full house, queens high! James and I were the only ones left and we both raised until I was out of chips.

"You raising or calling?" His green gaze gave nothing away.

My cards covered my mouth as I attempted to return his icy stare. "We could always make it a little more interesting." His eyes got big for a split second as Delaney suppressed a chuckle. Smith pushed himself back in his chair and got comfortable, awaiting the show.

"How so?" He was challenging me and I debated about how far I was willing to take it.

I focused on the friends on each side of me, my man across from me deciding distraction was my best tactic. I grabbed my phone, leisurely scrolled through it and put on *Eyes On Fire* by Blue Foundation.

"You're stalling. Not confident?"

"Oh, baby, I'm confident." I wanted to see if he really did learn to listen to the lyrics. He'd left me wanting more all week, it was my turn.

Smith was grinning from ear to ear, "This just got very interesting. Fair warning, Cass. He's a sore loser."

"Hmm…sore is just what I had in mind." I looked him dead in the eyes as he fought the smile trying to break across his supple lips.

"I'm waiting. Bet away, Blackbird. You can't scare me."

Even then, I couldn't believe I was about to do it. He'd let a secret escape without meaning to and it was one of few things I remembered from that night. "If I win," I looked to Smith, Delaney and back to him, "I get to be the first…"

"Honey, I don't have any 'firsts' left." He let his man-bun down and ran his fingers through his hair. It was his turn to distract me.

"I wasn't finished." He leaned back in his chair and waved his hand at me. "I get to be the first to tie you up."

The room went silent, only the song filling the air. My cheeks were burning and I could see Smith and Delaney staring us both down, waiting to see what his response would be. He'd said that night at the cabin he'd never been tied up. I played my 'ace' so to say and waited for his move. He looked at his cards again, examining them, the river and me keenly.

"I'm waiting, JB3. Or should I call you Beast?"

Delaney was ready to fall over with laughter as Smith concluded, "She's beat you at your own game, Benedict. You either lied that night and confess to that now, or raise the stakes."

"I don't need your help, Smith." He looked to Delaney as she gave him the bird when he told her to zip it. "I accept your bet, on one condition."

"What's that, because I fully intend to see this through, tonight."

He leaned over the table and brought his mouth to my ear so only I could hear. Breathing heavily against my neck, a chill ran down my back. He whispered, "You can't have sex with me. Doctor's orders." He sat back down and smiled at me.

"Oh, I didn't have any intention of doing that." He licked his lips as I smirked at him. "So, you're accepting defeat? There's nothing you want from me if you win?"

Delaney and Smith looked like bobble heads as they watched us play out our game. "If I win, we shred the divorce papers and have a proper wedding." My heart stopped as I felt like I was about to suffocate. "One you deserve."

"Oh, snap." I darted my eyes to Delaney who mumbled, "Sorry. I'll hush."

My brain started firing off and I couldn't stop it. Did he know he had a winning hand or a losing hand? Was he fucking with me? What the FUCK? I pictured myself walking down the aisle in a white ball gown. *Knock it off, Cassidy.* Was he just offering something he knew he couldn't give me?

"Breathe, Cassidy."

I took in a breath as Delaney handed me my water. I took a swig and pushed my crazy thoughts aside. "Accepted. Show 'em."

"Ladies first."

Damn him! "You're a jerk." I laid my cards down and wondered who I wanted to win more. Who did he want to win?

"Boom! Full house, Benedict."

James looked at the cards I laid down and dropped his, face down, to the table. "Congrats. You win."

"Ahhhhaaaahhhaaaa!" I stood up and did a little dance. "I win!" Smith was laughing at me as Delaney swiped James' cards and looked at them. She gave him an odd look as I asked, "What is it?"

She threw the cards in the pile and said, "Nothing. You won. Nicely played." She turned her eyes back to him, "Time to pay up, James." I continued dancing around the table like a jerk, boasting in my glory.

"Well, I'd say it's time for us to leave." I frowned at Smith as he and Delaney gathered their belongings. He looked to James and said, "Have fun, brother." James just nodded at him as we walked them out.

"Call me!"

"Will do, Laney." She winked and then slid on to the back of Smith's bike, latching her arms around him.

Walking back inside, James headed straight to the table and put the deck of cards away. I watched him clean as I debated my next move. Could I really tie him up and *not* have sex with him? Probably not. Maybe he really was leery of the whole thing. I was an ass.

"Hey, I'm sorry. If it's a hard limit for you, I'll take it back."

He stood to his full height and turned to gaze at me. Slowly, he closed the distance between the two of us as I became increasingly more nervous. What had I done? His hands each circled a wrist and pulled my arms behind my back as he leaned into me. Hovering over me, I closed my eyes as his facial hair tickled the delicate skin of my neck. His lips circled my ear and pulled gently as I dropped my head against his chest, trying to stop myself from falling over.

"It is a hard limit for me." It took longer than it should have for his words to register with me. "I want you so fucking bad."

"James, I don't have to tie you up." Panting, "Oh, God, you have to stop that." He was biting and sucking on my neck and released my wrists only to hold them with one hand while his other grabbed my ass and pushed down between the back of my legs.

We both moaned as he rubbed my wet panties with his broad fingers. As I cried out, his mouth seized mine and he released my hands to turn me around. He maneuvered us to the wall and pressed me up alongside it. My breasts heaved against the wall as his hands rubbed over my torso.

"James, please. Make me come."

"No sex, Blackbird."

I almost started sobbing in my body's desperate need of him. My voice cracked, "I, no, I can't do it. It's torture." He stopped what he was doing and turned me to face him.

"Can't do what?"

"I can't wait. I, I..." I suddenly became unsure if I should tell him what it was I wanted. "I'm not as strong as you."

"You're strong."

I shook my head in protest. "I'm not."

"Tell me." I closed my eyes as he gripped my chin and ordered, "Look at me," and when I did he demanded, "Tell me!"

I continued shaking my head as I whimpered, "I need you inside me. I'm starting to forget what it felt like. I don't want to forget. Please, don't let me forget."

The green pools of his eyes mesmerized me as he stared at me. I'm sure he was fighting with his own emotions, wants and needs, let alone doctor's orders. He released my chin and stepped away from me as I sagged against the wall. My clit thrummed away, pleading to be touched as I watched him pace the room.

"I'm sorry."

Turning to me, "Don't be sorry. Never be sorry for telling me what it is you want, what you need."

Before I knew what was happening, he had grabbed my hand and was pulling me up the stairs. I didn't know what to think or what to expect as he pulled me to the center of the bedroom and kissed me, almost violently. My lips began to swell as our mouths fought for control, teeth bumping while our lips tangled. I tried to remove his clothes, but he denied me while he removed mine.

He pushed me to arm's length and took in my body. I stood, legs trembling, in my bra and panties as he tried to push down his erection through his pants.

"Fuck." I jumped at his outburst and watched him remove his socks, leaving him in only his shirt and pants. He climbed the bed and I watched him as he sat up against the headboard, legs spread wide. "Come here."

I climbed the bed as gracefully as I could, not sure where he wanted me. He directed me to sit down in front of him and I did as I was instructed. I felt him tug his shirt over his head, dropping it to the floor. Pulling me back, the warmth of his chest soothed an ache in me I hadn't known was there. I completely relaxed against him as his hands began to travel down my abdomen. Turning my face back toward his, I found his waiting mouth.

His hands singed every part of my torso, avoiding the parts most desperate for his touch. I even tried to move up against him and stopped when he pulled down the cup of my bra down and molded my breast to his hand, while he released the other. He lifted me slightly so that my bum was resting against his cock, enveloped in his lap. His legs moved under and in between mine as he spread my legs. He caressed my inner thighs until I was trembling again.

"Touch yourself." My body stiffened at his words. "No sex with each other, of any kind. Touch yourself."

He kissed me again as my hand slowly moved to my panties. I didn't have the energy to fight him, I just wanted my release and if touching myself was the only way to get it, then so be it. At least he was there with me, helping to guide me over the edge.

As my fingers found my soaking lips, a rush of desire charged through me. He groaned and pressed his groin against me. His hands pushed my hair to the side as he tortured my neck with his mouth. My fingers did what they knew how to do best. In and out, round and round, up and down as he kept pressing himself against me. My breathing was picking up as my hand increased its pace.

"Slow down. Enjoy it. Make it last." His own words were raspy and strained as he held on to me.

His arms encircled me, one at my neck and the other around my waist. "James..." I slowed my movements, circling in the opposite direction before pulling my fingers away. Lifting my hand, he sucked on my fingers when they reached his mouth. When he released them, I resumed my own demise as he encouraged me on. We were panting and moaning our own song of longing and desire.

"Kiss me." Turning my face to his, he breathed in my mouth as my climax came closer. "Come in my mouth. I want to breathe in your release."

My body tensed as his tongue explored every part of my mouth. His arms held me tighter as my release overpowered me. He didn't stop kissing me until my trembling ceased, his fingertips drawing lazy circles over my skin.

My eyes opened a few minutes later and we were face to face under the covers. He was asleep and I didn't have the heart to wake him. I crawled out of bed, threw on his discarded shirt and climbed back in next to him. Habit and instinct both took over as he tucked me against his body. I was safe, back in his cocoon embrace.

thirteen

Unbreakable

~ JAMES ~

I WOKE UP WITH A RAGING BONER, her hip pressed up against it. *Fuck!* I wanted to take her, fuck doctor's orders, but I wanted to make sure when we did finally fuck again, that it was it for us. *She* was it for me, but I knew she still wasn't convinced of that. Of course, the act we'd performed that night probably broke doctor's orders, but I wasn't about to tell him. I had to get out of that bed before I buried myself inside her.

I debated whether I should leave, shower, sleep on the couch, run on the treadmill; the choices were boundless. My hard-on was relentless so I decided on a shower. I made my way to the guest bath in the hall, not wanting to wake her. Turning the water on, I removed my pants and briefs before stepping in.

The room was already filling with steam when I soaped up my hand and started stroking myself. I replayed the scene we'd acted out, but it wasn't my hand that brought her pleasure in my thoughts. My desire was quickly building, my balls rising and falling with the pulsing of my cock. Through the sheer curtain, I envisioned the door slowly swing open. Her figure came into view, red hair falling down her shoulders. She was wearing my shirt and slowly came closer. Her eyes were locked on mine as she slowly pulled the curtain open.

"Don't come any closer, woman." I was naked and not prepared for her to see the tattoo that graced my back. She couldn't see it. Not yet.

She smiled at me and in her sirens voice said, "I'm not going to get you off, but I thought I could help you like you helped me." She climbed in as my eyes dropped to her nipples that were poking through the shirt.

I closed my eyes and when I opened them again, she was gone. I was losing my shit. Blue balls were making me loopy. I stroked harder and faster until my release came. I washed up before I got out and got dressed—thankful I still had some clothes there—making sure to cover my tattoo.

Knowing we were breaking every recommendation Dr. Pratt had given us, I crawled back into bed with her and pulled her close. It had been so hard not telling her how much I loved her, telling her I had won the poker hand—four of a kind—I wanted to marry her, properly. Delaney held my secret in her hands and I wasn't sure why she kept it, but she had. Maybe she knew as well as I did that Cassidy needed more time. When my brain stopped battling itself, I slept for a few more hours.

I WAS PUTTING my socks and shoes on when she woke in the morning. She stretched and smiled coyly at me. "Hey."

"Hey, back at ya." She sat up as I said, "I have some work I need to do. Will you be around later?"

Nodding, "Yeah, I'll be around. I'm supposed to get the color filled in on my phoenix today."

"Oh, yeah. Do you want me to come with you?"

"You don't have to. I'm sure Ryan, or whomever, will follow me if you're not there."

I walked to her side of the bed and kissed her forehead. "Ok. I'll keep in touch then. I'll talk to you soon."

"Oh, ok."

I stroked her cheek. "Don't do that. Everything's fine. But we need to pull back the reins."

"I know. I'm sorry."

"You really need to take this time to figure out what you want, what you need. I know I haven't made it easy on you and I can never apologize enough for that." Her eyes were transfixed on my neck as I tilted her chin up. When her eyes met mine I reiterated, "I'm not going anywhere. You're what I want. End of." She went to speak and I put my finger to her lips. "This is serious. Three more weeks. We can do this."

I kissed her again and left her sitting on the bed as I walked out the door. Knowing she was going to see Styx, I called him and asked him not to mention the anchor tattoo I'd gotten. He said it was no problem. Later that day I made it to the shop about half way through her session.

THE NEXT WEEK flew by. The foundation for the house had been poured and the Blue Horse was coming along nicely. Of course I needed to rename it, considering what I had in store for it. It had been gutted and was awaiting Delaney's magic touch. All of Holly's artwork had also been delivered. I had stored it in the spare bedroom at the penthouse, the room Melissa no longer occupied, and locked the door. I couldn't risk Cassidy or anyone else finding it. I had taken Cassidy to the gallery that night having already purchased every single piece of Holly's art. When Annie called to tell me, I was furious and did what I did best. I made it happen.

I was still replaying our second session with Dr. Pratt in my head. We'd met with him early on in the week and dove into some deep territory. I'd had my own session with him and after our joint session, Cassidy made her own appointment with him.

"You guys need to slow it down. Enjoy just being a couple. I know, but you know what I mean." He made eye contact with both of us after we disclosed our struggles with not being intimate. *"I'm not trying to be cruel, but right now we need to focus on your mental and emotional connection. We know that the physical one is there."* Cassidy was sniffling when he added, *"I'm not saying the emotional and mental connection isn't there, it is. We just want it unbreakable."* She nodded and then he brought up the miscarriage. *"You two lost a child, no matter how early in the pregnancy, it's a significant loss."*

With a shaky breath she murmured, "I don't want to talk about it. We, James and I, have already talked about it. I don't want to keep trudging it up."

I interrupted her, "I can't imagine her grief, because I know how torn up I was." I took her hand as my other ran through her hair, "I did everything wrong when I found out and you'll never know how sorry I am for that." She didn't look at me, just rested her head against my chest as she wiped her tears away. "We didn't even really have a chance to process and enjoy the fact that we were expecting a child before it was taken away from us."

"Had you two discussed the topic of kids before that happened?" We both shook our heads. "Do you want kids?"

We both visibly stiffened. It wasn't something we'd really discussed and we needed to. She sat up and looked to Dr. Pratt, "I, well, I never thought I did. Never thought of myself as the mothering type. But when I found out I was pregnant, I was overjoyed." Her eyes turned to me, "The thought of your baby growing inside me, I'd never felt joy like that before." The tear fell from my eye before I was able to hide it from her. I swiped it away as she smiled at me.

"James?" Dr. Pratt was awaiting my answer.

"I never wanted kids; at least I didn't think I did. But when it all happened, I'd never wanted anything more." She tangled her hand with mine and leaned into me.

"So it's safe to say you both want kids. When? I'd suggest giving yourself time as a couple before you become parents, but I know every couple has to decide on their own." He looked to us and added, "Think about it. We'll discuss that next week. Our time's almost up."

As we stood to leave, he suggested Cassidy make an appointment to see him, alone. She was open to it and once they found a time that fit both their schedules, we headed out.

THAT WEEKEND WAS Jane's bachelorette party and Cal's bachelor party. They were originally planning a joint event, but Cassidy and I had convinced them—well Jane since I wasn't quite speaking with Cal yet—to at least go to dinner separately. Even though Cassidy was standing up for Cal and I for Jane, she went out with the girls and I with the guys. I tried to get out of it, knowing that Paul would be there and I didn't want to bring any unnecessary tension to the party.

"You can't not go, James. They'll know you're avoiding them."

Sighing, I knew Jane was right. "Take Smith and I'll take Delaney."

"I can't just invite someone."

Jane said, "Yes, you can. Cassidy, invite Delaney. Melissa is coming, too. More the merrier." Cassidy had agreed and promised she'd stay in touch via text when the time came.

Hearing that Melissa was going and Cassidy hadn't objected surprised me. Though, she'd mentioned that their work relationship was going really well. Cassidy got off the phone with Delaney and spouted, "It's done!"

The girls were going to The Benedict lounge for dinner and then planned to hit the town. I waited with Cassidy and Jane at the townhouse until Smith and Delaney pulled up. The girls hopped in Cassidy's mustang as I gave her a warning stare.

She just laughed as she burned rubber while pulling out of the driveway. Jane and Delaney's squeals sailing out the open windows. Smith clapped my shoulder before we climbed into his vehicle. When we got to Cal's, Paul's SUV was parked out front. Work had been a breeze since he was on site all week at the house or the Blue Horse. Last we'd spoken was when he'd put in his notice. I really should have started looking for his replacement, but hadn't.

We walked in the open door and I recognized Paul, Frank and some other guys from the force. Dave was there, too. He walked over to me and shook my hand. We exchanged hellos, but he didn't interrogate me like I had expected. I had every intention of doing right by his daughter, though I'd told him that before and broken my word.

Gripping my shoulder and with a lowered voice he said, "Relax James. I've talked with Cassidy. I just want you two to work it out and I hope you do." I looked to my father-in-law as he smiled at me, shocked at his words. "I like having you around. Mostly cuz it makes Cassidy happy, but because it irks Cal. I enjoy it." He winked and we shared a laugh.

"I never intended to 'irk' him. But if it makes you happy, I'll see what I can do."

He let out a boisterous laugh that gained the attention of everyone there. Cal was clearly irked. "See, working already."

Frank took the lead, "Alright boys. Let's head out. We're headed to Duke's for dinner. Where the rest of the night leads, we'll find out. Load 'em up!"

I had no idea how it happened, but I think Dave had something to do with it. Cal and Paul ended up with Smith and I in Smith's vehicle. To say it was uncomfortable was an understatement. Thank God the restaurant wasn't a long drive. Cal and Paul talked about Cal's job while I played on my phone. Smith turned the radio on. I was oblivious to the song until the lyrics started to sink in. *Sleeping with a Friend* by Neon Trees was playing and silence filled the vehicle. Glancing in the rearview mirror, Cal was glaring at me and then at Paul.

"Simmer down everyone. That shit's funny." Everyone looked to Smith as he turned and grinned at all of us. "You fuckers need to lighten up. First rounds on me!"

"You're a dick."

I recognized Paul's laughter as he chastised Smith. "Not a dick, a Frank-n-wiener, right Frankie? You got us. Douchebag."

"Don't call me Frankie!"

"That's right. I apologize. It's Francis, right?" Cal looked confused as Paul and I started cracking up. Smith tried reaching through to the back seat to slug Paul as I yelled at him to watch the road.

Looking at Cal I revealed Smith's secret. "His name is Francis, Smith is his last name. Guys in the Army liked to call him Frankie just to piss him off."

Cal chuckled and looked to Smith. "Frankie huh? I'll remember that. Frank is fortunate that his parents named him Franklin, not Francis!"

Dinner was uneventful as we had a few rounds and filled our guts with too much food. When we left the restaurant, Dave walked to his car, encouraging us 'boys' to have fun, but to behave. I watched Dave drive off as Cal walked over toward me.

"Hey."

"Hey." His hands were in his pockets as he lifted his chin, standing as tall as he could, but not taller than me. "You in this, like really in this?"

"Why do I have a feeling you're not referring to this night out?"

"You know I'm not referring to this night. I'm referring to my sister."

I glanced at Smith and Paul a few feet away as they discreetly observed Cal and me talking privately. "I owe all of you an apology. But I'm not going to make excuses or explain my reasoning for the things I did, to you." The cop in him had him scrutinizing me as I continued. "I love her, Cal. I thought she was better off. Maybe she was, but I wasn't. I don't work right when she's not around." I refused to disclose anything more unless he asked specifically.

Nodding, "I get it. I know you've done a lot for her. Just don't make me bash in your face again."

"Well, if I deserve it, I expect it to be you."

He chuckled as we shook hands. "Paul's really messed up about this." His eyes darted to where Paul stood. I sighed as he informed me that Paul had told him about Cora. "I love Paul like a brother, but my sister's happiness is most important. I hope you all figure it out and friendships aren't lost."

"I hear you. It won't be easy."

"It's funny, now that I have all the pieces, I know that it was Cassidy who changed him all those years ago. The guy I met after basic training wouldn't have stepped up with Cora, but he did and I know it's because of my sister." I watched as he seemed to be reflecting on what might have been. "Don't take her for granted. He's proof that things can change in the blink of an eye."

"All right shitheads," Smith strolled over, "enough of the bullshit. We've got some things in store for this man. The titties await."

"No man. I don't need or want strippers."

"No way man. It's not a bachelor party till you get at least one lap dance." I laughed as Frank and the guys from the force taunted Cal until he gave in.

"Alright. ONE lap dance. That's it."

We didn't stay long at the strip club and Paul, Smith and I barely took notice of the chicks trolling around us. I was too busy texting back and forth with Cassidy. They had just left the restaurant, heading out to go dancing. She'd let it slip where they were going, the same bar we went to on her birthday the previous fall. I knew Cal wanted to go out dancing with Jane and decided to use the information to my advantage.

We were in the parking lot outside the strip club when I said, "I know a place. Nice bar, good music, laid back."

Cal chimed in, "I'm in. Lead the way Benedict!"

We drove back to the respectable part of town, parked the cars and walked the few blocks to the bar. We all cozied up to the bar, ordering our drinks. It was the first time I saw Cal drink more than a few drinks. Who was I to judge? He deserved to have a good time. I kept my eyes out for the girls and spotted them in the back corner on the dance floor. No one else seemed to notice as we headed toward some barren space on the other side of the bar.

From what I could see across the dark expanse of the crowded bar, all the girls were there. Lena, Cassidy, Melissa, Delaney, Jessica, Jane, and a few more girls I didn't recognize. Ha! Anthony was there, too. They were dancing to some song I didn't recognize that kept repeating *Boom, Clap* over and over. It was annoying, but they seemed to know all the words. I enjoyed watching her. She was carefree, happy and seemed to be in her element. She had a drink in her hand as they all swayed to their liking, though my eyes were fixated on her.

As if she could sense my eyes on her, she turned with her eyes searching the crowd. Leaning against the wall, I waited for her eyes to lock with mine as I took a swig of my beer. She paused momentarily, before her smile beamed at me. She didn't say anything to the other girls, just kept dancing knowing that I was watching her. The song ended and another began as she pretended to ignore me. I wasn't sure if she knew we were *all* there or not.

Dammit! Smith, that pussy-whipped fucker, was already dancing with Delaney. Why the fuck weren't they married? They might as well have been. They were like love sick puppies and had been for years. It was inspiring and depressing all at once. Cal strolled over to me as he spotted Jane.

"Well played man."

I looked at him as I took another swallow of my beer. "I don't know what you're talking about."

"Yeah. Whatever." He took a drink of his ale and said, "Thanks. I'm going to go request a song. I'll be back."

I nodded as my eyes went back to Cassidy. I was surprised to see her and Melissa laughing and talking with one another. Looking to my left, I spotted Paul sulking. We needed to find him a woman, STAT. Just then, Lena came over. She looked nervous as she approached Paul. Did Lena have a thing for Paul? Huh. More power to her.

A new song started as the dance floor emptied. A country song began to play as the girls headed back to their table. As Jane turned, Cal was standing there, hand outstretched. She beamed at him before she jumped in his arms. Not one to be showed up, I put down my empty bottle and made my way over to Cassidy.

When I reached her, I offered her my hand and she chirped, "I thought you hated Country?"

"I do. But I hate you more." I winked as she laughed and took my hand. I pulled her close as we rocked to the rhythm.

"This may be the *Best Night Ever*. JB3 dancing to country music and all." She giggled and whispered in my ear that it was the name of the song.

As I swung her around to the beat, I spotted Lena walking away from Paul as he moped some more. Ryan, who I hadn't realized was there—he must've been Cassidy's tail that night—swooped in and asked Lena to dance. She smiled as they joined us on the floor. I maneuvered Cassidy around so that we weren't right in Paul's line of sight. I held her close, enjoying the feel of her soft curves against my body. When the song ended, she started to pull away, but I kept her close.

She nuzzled back into me asking, "You ok?"

Stroking her hair I nuzzled her temple, "Perfect. Just enjoying the moment."

As the night started to come to a close, those of us that were still there walked back to our separate cars. Melissa had already left and so had Frank, Paul, and the guys from the force. Paul had been in no shape to drive and I hoped he'd found a ride or called a cab. The four of us, Jane, Cal, Cassidy, and I up riding home in Cassidy's mustang.

Snuggling up to her before we got in the car, I offered up my suggestion. "Why don't you drop me off at your place first so I can get my truck and go home?"

Scrunching her brows, she protested. "Why?"

"Cassidy, you know why. Let's not push the boundaries." She took a deep breath as I continued, "You know I want nothing more than to spend more time with you. But it's late."

"I know. How many days left?" She smirked at me and my cock twitched.

Leaning into her ear, I said, "Careful. I'm starting to worry you just want to make it through these twenty-eight days so you can fuck me again." She pulled back and narrowed her eyes at me. "I want you back in my bed, but only if it's forever, Blackbird."

I kissed her cheek as Cal proclaimed, "Get a room!" Cassidy rolled her eyes as Cal added, "Or at least take Jane and I home first."

"Shut up and get in the car!" We all laughed at Jane's order as the two of them crawled in the back seat.

"There's not enough room. Here baby doll, sit on my lap." The door shut and their voices were drowned out.

"You're really going to make me ride home with the two of them making out in the back seat?"

"Yup. You can do it."

"Have I told you lately that I hate you?" I just shook my head at her, smiling. "Well, I do." She pushed me away as I smacked her ass and watched her get in the car.

Cal and Jane seemed a little confused when Cassidy dropped me off first. I was tempted to stay and surprise her, but we didn't need any more temptation. I hopped in my truck and headed to the hotel. It was well after two a.m. and we could all use some sleep.

~ CASSIDY ~

I crawled into bed that night exhausted and craving him. What else was new? Cal had inquired about why I'd dropped James off first, but Jane quickly distracted him. I just told him to mind his own business. Their wedding was two weeks away and I still had so much to do. I knew that it would get done, but the next two weeks would be a whirlwind of final prep. Programs, seating charts, song lists, and the list went on and on.

That Tuesday I had my second private appointment with Dr. Pratt, followed by a joint session with James. I left work early to make it on time and recalled our session from the week prior. He'd asked me about my childhood and we'd spent most of the time discussing my relationship with my mother, or lack thereof. I was sure that we'd pick up where we left off when I got there that afternoon.

I waited in the library for a short time before Dr. Pratt was ready for me. I sat down on my usual spot on the couch and we exchanged some pleasantries before he picked back up with my mother.

"So, last week we left off just after your mother's death." I nodded. "You mentioned that you took her death pretty hard. Can you tell me about that?"

I sighed. "A few months later I ended up in the hospital, having my stomach pumped." He gazed at me cautiously as I picked at my fingers. "My dad hadn't emptied out the medicine cabinet and I found a bottle of my mom's sleeping pills. I'd started taking one here and there. School was hard for me. I didn't have a lot of friends and after mom's death, nobody looked at me the same way. I heard the whispers, 'There's Cassidy. Did you hear about her mom?' It was horrible and I couldn't take it anymore."

"What happened after that?"

"My Dad found me and I spent a few days in the hospital and went to therapy twice a week, sometimes more. The joke was on me, too." He looked at me, wanting to know what I had meant by that statement. "The whispers just got worse, but instead it was about how I was crazy, just like *her*. It was horrible. The only thing that helped was Cal. He was popular and he put a stop to most of it, him and his girlfriend. He was Mister Popular and protected me at all costs."

"So there was never a relapse or recurrence?"

"No. I went to therapy for several years on and off. Life goes on and I knew that once I got away from those people things would get better. I started counting down the days to high school graduation and my start at a new life. I could be anyone I wanted to be, though I didn't know who that would be."

"Do you know who that person is now?"

I blew out a breath. "Do any of us really know who we are?" He smiled. "I'm stubborn, a hard worker, I have a temper, I'm too sensitive, too analytical—clearly because I can't just answer the question."

"Well, we're all a continuous work in progress. If we weren't trying to better ourselves and learn from our mistakes, what would be the point?"

"Agreed."

"So, tell me about the first time you met James."

I couldn't stop the smile that spread across my face. "I'll never forget the first time I saw him."

fourteen

Fireworks

~ CASSIDY ~

Soon our session was over and I headed to the bathroom before James joined us. I spotted him when I walked out of the bathroom. I'd never get over looking at him. He was totally casual in jeans and a t-shirt. His hair was up in a man bun and he was staring out the window. His dark jeans clung to him perfectly as the sleeves of his shirt were pulled taut around his biceps. As the door closed, he turned and smiled at me. He'd shaved his beard, but the goatee remained. Damn, he was fine.

"Hey, you." He walked over and wrapped me in his arms.

And for how hot he was, he smelled a million times better. I took a deep whiff as he squeezed me tight. "Hey yourself."

"You up for dinner afterward?"

"Yes. Food sounds excellent. I'm starving."

"You two ready?" We turned at Dr. Pratt's voice and took our seats on his couch. "So, how'd it go this week?"

"Much better." Our words were identical and spoken in unison.

"No sex, of any kind."

I shook my head as James answered, "Only alone." I smacked his arm as we laughed.

"Well, you're over half way there. I know next week will be very busy for you, Cassidy. Can we schedule now to meet in two weeks? At that time we'll discuss where we're at and you can both make a decision about your marriage. Does that Monday, after the fourth work, say six p.m.?"

We both checked our phone calendars and agreed as we programmed the appointment in. Two weeks and we could finally move on. I already knew what my answer would be and believed I knew what his choice would be too. We'd been through too much together to walk away.

We walked to a nearby restaurant and had dinner after our session. After, he walked me to my car and I found his truck near mine. I was a little surprised he hadn't taken his bike. He told me to hang on and ran to his truck and opened up the back door. He pulled out a square flat board, closed the door and made his way back over to me.

"What's this?"

"Your painting. The one with the quote."

Gasping, "Right! I almost forgot." I popped my trunk and he laid it in. "Now I need to find somewhere to hang it." Just then, like on cue, Ryan pulled up. That meant one thing. James wasn't coming over. I looked to James and pouted.

"Work calls. We're almost there, baby."

"I know." I knew it wasn't the time or place, but I had to ask. "Nothing on Dan?" He shook his head. "I don't understand. Where could he be?"

"I don't either. He's probably left town, but I'm not risking your safety."

"I know." I dropped my head to his chest as he held me. Mumbling, "I just want this all over so we can all have some peace."

"Me, too, Blackbird."

THE WEDDING DAY was finally upon us. I couldn't believe how fast that week and a half went, but I didn't have time to think about it either. The ceremony was going to be at four, with pictures following and then dinner. Fireworks would begin just after ten and James and I had made sure to secure the staff, DJ included, to remain late into the night. They'd be well compensated and we planned on partying all night long. We all deserved a party of epic proportions and that's what we'd planned.

I was headed to Jane's room at The Benedict, awaiting the elevator to open in the lobby. The doors opened and I was greeted by James. He smiled brightly and whisked me into the elevator. He didn't even say hello before his lips were cemented to mine. The past week had been the easiest to restrain ourselves, simply because I'd been so busy.

As I savored his mouth on mine, I realized it was no ordinary kiss. It was fevered, but not rushed; desperate, but not sloppy; and I became lost in him. With his hands in my hair and mine gripping his waist, he pressed me up against the elevator wall and I could feel every pulsing inch of him against me. I pushed back, and he let me, and then his back was up against the elevator wall. Smirking that 'I dare you' smile at me, he awaited my next move.

I ran my hands down his arms, starting at his biceps and down until our fingers entwined. Raising his arms up, I let go and told him not to move. I was sure he was holding back a laugh as I took the lead.

Burying my face in his neck, I bit and sucked at the exposed flesh. His hair was neatly pulled back, still damp from his morning shower. His cologne saturated my senses and the result was my muddled head and wet panties. Sighing and sagging against him, my hands tugged his shirt out of his pants, desperate to feel his skin against mine. He was always so warm. My hands ran over the ripples of his abdomen before moving to the muscles of his back.

"Come back to the penthouse with me." His deep baritone sent a thrill through me.

I wanted nothing more. Our twenty-eight days were almost up and he'd been more than strong during that time, me the weak one. Now it was my turn to be strong.

"I can't."

Groaning, "You can." His arms dropped and pulled me closer as he sucked on my ear. "I can't manage another three days without you. It's been too long." My eyes closed, I listened to his words as my body felt weightless against his. "Blackbird…"

Stammering, "James, we, we can't, it's only three more days." He worked his mouth harder against my skin, "Oh, you have to stop that. You know how hard it is for me to say no to you."

The elevator chimed and we were on the floor for the penthouse. How had he managed that? Before I could object, he was pulling me after him, toward his door. He swiped the key card and opened the door, slamming me up against it once it was closed and we were inside.

"James, Jane is waiting for me."

"She can wait." He growled as he lifted my legs to circle his waist.

It was only three days. He removed his suit jacket as I pulled his tie loose. Buttons hit the floor as I yanked open his shirt. He snarled at me, and without removing his shirt he crushed his lips to mine as my nails raked down his chest leaving red lines in their wake.

"You owe me." Pulling back, he looked at me, lost at my meaning. "Poker. When do I get to tie you up?"

He smiled and simply said, "Soon."

Loosening his hold on me, my feet hit the floor as he pulled my t-shirt over my head. Slowly, his fingertips trailed over the mounds of my breasts where the lace of my bra met my skin. My chest was contracting as my eyes found his. I nodded my head once, knowing the question his eyes were asking.

"Cassidy, if you cross this line with me it's done. There's no going back. I won't go back."

I nodded my consent and he tugged my yoga pants down and cupped my bare cheeks with his hands. His thumb slid into the back of the thong before he ripped them from my body.

"Stop destroying my underwear collection, you brute."

"You know I'll just buy you more." His nose was buried against my short strip of curls, "I've missed your scent. You smell so good. Only one thing is better." Pulling my leg aside, his tongue licked at my seam, "You taste like heaven."

I couldn't suppress the moan that fell from my lips and then my phone started ringing. *Shit!* "James, I have to go."

Kissing up my belly he begged, "Make them wait. Please." He was back at his full height, hovering above me as his fingers released the front clasp of my bra. His eyes were engrossed on my breasts as he massaged one and lowered his head to consume the other. His free hand massaged my hip, working to the back of my thigh.

"Hurry up." He groaned against my breast before releasing it and standing. I watched as he pulled a condom out of his wallet and dropped his pants. Commando! My eyes looked to his cock and back to his eyes as I said, "Shocking. Hoping to get lucky, Mr. Benedict?"

"A guy can hope." My hand found his length as his eyes closed and he hissed a breath. "Cassidy…"

He grew even harder in my hand as I kissed his chest. I heard the foil packet rip open as he gently pushed my hands aside. Once he was sheathed his fingers grazed across my lips. It was embarrassing how wet I was for him; you could hear his fingers slide in and out of me.

"James...make me remember."

Without another word, wrapping my legs around him, he pushed me back up against the door. He waited for me to look at him before he began the slow torture of sliding into me. My legs were already trembling when he pulled out and finally pushed in to his full length. My womb clenched as a rush of love flooded me. My eyes began to water as I tried to pull him closer to me.

"Baby, did I hurt you?"

"No. I forgot how good you feel. It feels so good, please don't stop."

He smiled before he kissed me. My fingers tangled in his hair as I worked some strands loose. My hips rocked in rhythm to his, grinding against him to gain the most contact. His shirt clung to his shoulders as my hands cleaved to them. He pulled me away from the door and walked us to a dining chair.

Slowly, he sat down as his tongue explored my mouth. His hands held my shoulders as he pushed me back. The angle had me gasping as he slid out and back in again. My head dropped back as I let him manipulate my body. One hand gripped my hair is it hung down my back, longer than normal from months of neglect. His other hand moved to my hip as he demanded I touch myself, coming before him.

"Do it, Cassidy."

My fingers began to circle my clit as I sought out my orgasm. The flutters started as he continued his assault on me. I leaned back a little further as he tightened his hold on my hair, loving how he felt so deep inside me.

"James!"

"I got you. I'm never letting go."

I gazed to him and I used his words for the first time, crying out, "Always, only, and *forever* you."

The smile overtook his face as he pulled me to him and whispered against my lips, "You and me. No one else."

I felt the tear roll down my cheek and I knew he saw it, too. "You're mine and I'm yours."

Then it was his turn to use my words, "Only you."

He leaned me back again as we rode each other into a frenzy. I could feel his pace quickening as my fingers worked my clit feverishly. Wanting to see his face, I picked my head up and he easily released my hair and brought my mouth down to his. Both his hands held me tight as I started moaning louder.

"I'm going to come, James. Don't stop."

My body tensed and went limp all at once against him. I couldn't stop squirming and he bellowed out his own release as I ground my hips onto his. His fingers moved to the back of my thighs, each touch causing me to quiver even more. We were both suffering from new born giraffe syndrome—what we'd jokingly named it months prior—and needed time to recover our legs.

We were rudely interrupted as my cell started ringing again. "Shit!" He was panting into my neck as I snuggled up closer to him. "I have to go."

"I know."

I was pulling my clothes back on as he watched me. "Sorry about the shirt."

Shrugging his shoulders he replied, "I have more." The tension was in the air, but in a good way. "You're nervous. Why?"

"It's, I just..."

He sauntered over to me and pushed my hair behind my ears. "I want you. I'll move my stuff back in today. It's up to you."

I wanted nothing more, but I was worried about Dr. Pratt. "Maybe we should wait till Monday. I just want to get this wedding over with and then you'll have my full attention."

Smiling, "Understood. You should get going before they call a search party." I nodded and picked up my purse and headed toward the door. "I hate you, Blackbird."

Blushing, I smiled brightly and turned to him. "I hate you too, JB3." He winked at me as I walked out the door.

I headed back to the elevator, checking my phone. I had missed calls from Lena, Jane, and Mrs. Whitford. I made it to Jane's room just as my phone began ringing again. The door was slightly ajar as I made my way inside.

"There you are! We were beginning to worry."

"Sorry, I was caught up, err, traffic was a wreck."

Jane looked at me and knew I was lying. She walked over, hugged me and whispered, "He's written all over you."

I asked, "What do you mean?"

"He's all over you. I can see it, like in your aura, your vibe, and I can smell his cologne. It's about time you two got your shit in order. Please tell me this nonsense with you two is over?"

Smiling, with emotion in my voice, I mumbled, "I think so. I love him so much."

"I know you do. The feeling's mutual."

The morning and afternoon flew by as we got ready. Lisa, Bev, Jane and I had our hair and makeup done in the bridal suite as the photographer and videographer fluttered around us. When it was close to time, I made my exit. I had to make sure Lena had everything handled and I needed to check on Cal. Jane looked amazing in her dress and I'd meet her in the bridal room before the ceremony, before I took my place with Cal at the altar.

I found all the guys downstairs wandering the terrace overlooking the garden where the ceremony would take place. I walked through the reception hall and spotted Lena. Everything seemed to be in place. The room was a sea of green, light yellow and white. It was beautiful.

"Cassidy, you look amazing! The cake was just delivered and everything else is all set."

I let out a big breath, "Excellent. You've really pulled this off. I couldn't have done it without you."

"It's no biggie. I was glad to help and I love my job."

"Ok. I'm going to go check on the guys. The guests are starting to arrive. I'll see you soon."

I made my way back out to the terrace as guests were being asked to take their seats. I spotted my Dad, my uncles, and some cousins and made my way over. I was bombarded with questions of where my own husband was and did my best to explain that he was with the bride. If I started trying to explain it all I'd just end up with diarrhea of the mouth.

I managed to snag Cal and pull him to a private corner. He tugged on his collar as I noticed the sweat beading on his forehead. Was he hot, anxious, or both? I smiled at him and asked if he was ok.

"Me? I'm great. Just ready for it to be over. You know me. I'm not a suit and tie guy."

"I know, but you look great. Remember to breathe. You may faint when you see Jane." I looked around and Lena nodded that it was time. "Ok. I'm going to go make sure Jane's all ready and I'll be back."

"Ok."

I knocked on the bridal dressing room door and James opened it and smiled at me. He stepped out and closed the door as he kissed my cheek.

"I can smell you on me and vice versa."

Giggling, I smacked his arm. "Knock it off. You cannot."

"I can."

Rolling my eyes I inquired, "Is she ready?"

"Yup. You can go in. I just wanted to give her and her parents a minute."

I tapped the door gently as I opened it. Bev was holding back tears and Jane's father looked like the proudest man alive.

"Sorry to interrupt." Jane beamed at me as I continued, "They're ready when you are."

Nodding she responded, "I'm ready."

I hugged her and took another look at her. The lace dress hugged her perfectly. She wore a long veil that would trail behind her. The dress was almost entirely backless and would probably cause Cal to have a coronary, in a good way. Her hair was pulled in a low side bun, accentuating her delicate frame and features. We were forehead to forehead and the photographer caught the moment.

"I always wanted a sister."

She smiled, "Me too!"

Her eyes began filling with tears, "Oh no you don't. Cock! Balls! Schlong! No tears, Jane!"

Everyone started laughing and I nodded at her and made my way out of the room. James clutched my wrist and pulled me back to him.

"Say cock again. It makes me hot." I shook my head as we laughed and I made my way back down the hall.

~ JAMES ~

I WATCHED HER walk down the hall, to where Cal was most likely waiting. She looked stunning in that green dress. It made her look like a fairy with all its flowing layers and I wanted to get her out of it. Slowly. I'd been determined to wait the twenty-eight days, but when I saw her that morning in the elevator, I couldn't wait any longer. All my resolve pushed away. I had also told myself I wouldn't be with her again until I knew she was wholly committed to us. Please, God, let her be wholly committed.

We waited a few minutes before it was time to walk Aunt Bev to her seat. I walked back up the aisle and Cal and Cassidy then took their turn down the aisle and took their places. A chill ran up my spine and as I scoured the crowd an eerie feeling settled over me. My eyes found Smith and he sensed it in me too. He discreetly walked out and made his way to the back of the garden. He radioed a few guys as my eyes continued looking over the crowd. There were close to two hundred people in attendance. I swore to myself he'd pay if Dan ruined this day for Jane.

The curtains closed and the music changed. I looked behind me to see Jane and my uncle walking my way. It was time. She was so happy and my fears about Dan were pushed aside. I kissed her cheek as Lena told me to take my place. It was all a little untraditional, me standing beside Jane and Cassidy beside Cal. But, it made sense. Once I took my place across from Cassidy and Cal, the music stopped and the minister asked everyone to stand.

The curtains opened again and everyone spotted Jane. There were a lot of 'ohs' and 'ahs' as she made her way to the altar. Cassidy deserved a day like Jane was having. One way or another I would make it happen, I just didn't know when. Though, I had some ideas. It was nice standing across from Cal, watching him pledge his life to my cousin. I knew he wouldn't hesitate to take another dozen bullets for her. Staring at Cassidy, she dabbed at the tears in her eyes as they threatened to fall.

"You may kiss your bride."

The cheers filled the garden as Cal and Jane gave their audience even more to applaud about. They were introduced as Mr. and Mrs. Charles and walked down the aisle. I smiled at Cassidy and kissed her cheek when we met in the middle. She looped her arm through mine as we followed behind the bride and groom.

fifteen
Miracle

~ JAMES ~

Too soon we were all thrown into a flurry of greetings and tasks to achieve. Dinner was going to be a drag as Cassidy sat next to her brother and I sat next to Jane. I wanted her close to me, needed her close. My thoughts were interrupted when both fathers took their turn at thanking everyone for attending. *Screw this.* I moved my chair and sat at the end of the table so I could be close to her. Smiling, she shook her head at me as I joined our hands under the table.

Then the microphone was handed to Cassidy and she stood. I let go of her hand as she took a deep breath and unfolded a piece of paper that had been clutched in her other hand.

"I'll try to make this quick. As you all know, Cal is my big brother and he's done his brotherly duty well. Maybe a little too well." The crowd laughed. "You're my best friend and all I've ever wanted for you was to find someone as loving, kind, generous, funny, and as spectacular as you are. I hate to break it to you, but you didn't find that. You found something more. Jane, where do I begin? You're the sister I never had and I'm so happy you're a part of my family. I wish you nothing but the best. May you be the anchor to keep his feet on the ground and may he be the wings to keep your heart in the clouds. I love you both." Everyone clapped as she added, "Cheers to Jane and Cal."

The DJ took the microphone back as Cassidy hugged Jane and Cal in turn. She sat back down and I squeezed her hand as I leaned into her. "You're amazing."

She chuckled, "It sucked. Took me forever to write and it was lame."

"It's not lame. It was short and sweet. Everyone loved it." I kissed her softly as she leaned into me. "I know now's not the time, but we need to talk." She looked deep in my eyes and nodded her agreement. "You should eat first and then I want to dance with you!"

After dinner and before the usual festivities I found Smith and chatted with him. "So nothing suspicious?"

"No. All my guys are here, but nobody's seen anything."

"I don't like it. I have a bad feeling."

"I know, me too."

Sighing, "All right. Try to enjoy yourself. I don't want Cassidy or Jane worried."

"Will do."

During the cake cutting, Jane got Cal good with a fist full of cake to his face. He dabbed some icing on her nose and left it at that. They danced their first dance to two different songs. One that Cal picked and one that Jane picked, both god awful country, before Jane danced with her dad. I spotted Paul by the bar with Melissa and wondered if they'd come together. Ryan and Lena were nearby as the four of them began chatting. Looking for Cassidy, I spotted her with her father and Lisa.

I requested some songs and headed over to meet some of Cassidy's family. I was given a quick round of introductions. Some chastised us for eloping and others encouraged our choice. Cassidy was uncomfortable with the whole topic, but just played along with it. Soon the DJ made an announcement as one song ended and another began.

"This song goes out to Cassidy. You'll know who it's from."

She looked to me, confusion in her eyes as *Miracle* by Foo Fighters began to play. It was the song I'd played for her on the ride back to her place after the masquerade last year. I hoped she would remember the importance of the song. I put my open hand out between us as she excused herself and let me lead her to the floor.

She let me pull her in tight and started to question me. "James?"

"Shh, just let me dance with you, my miracle. You're mine, Cassidy; I need you to know that."

She looked into my eyes as I stroked her face, leaning into her as she closed her eyes. I kissed her soft and sweet before she laid her head on my shoulder. Her breath was sweet as I dropped my lips to her temple. She held on tight as I sang some of the lyrics in her ear.

I couldn't hold it in anymore. I knew we were supposed to wait till Monday, but she had to know how I felt. "I love you, Cassidy. I know, I'm breaking more rules, but you need to know. I don't expect you to say anything in return. You're the only thing I want and I'm so sorry for all the mistakes I've made. I hope you can see it in your heart to forgive me one day."

The song was ending and she lifted her tear filled eyes to mine. "I forgive you. I forgave you long ago. I'm so sorry for the mistakes I made."

I placed my finger over her lips, "I forgive you. I want us to have a fresh start, a clean slate." She sniffed as I asked, "Can you do that? Just nod your head if you agree." She nodded without hesitation. I motioned to the DJ and he played the next song.

"I don't deserve you."

"I've said it before and I'll say it again. You deserve more. Now kiss me." *I Won't Give Up* by Jason Mraz began playing. "I'm sorry I gave up on us so easily. It won't happen again."

"Me too." She clung to me until the song ended and a more upbeat tune filled the air. "I'm going to go freshen up."

"Ok. I'll be waiting."

As she walked away I saw Paul follow her. I took a deep breath and didn't intervene. As far as I knew he still hadn't told her that he was leaving town. I didn't want him to go, not really, but I understood why he felt he had to go. When I turned toward the bar, Melissa was making her way toward me.

"Hey stranger." She smiled as she asked, "How you doing?"

"Good, things are good."

"You and Cassidy looked cozy. I hope that's a good sign."

"Me too. I think everything's finally going to work out."

"I'm happy for you. You were right, too."

"Oh, about?"

"Cassidy. I like her." I snorted. "Yeah, don't get used to hearing that. I'll never tell you that again."

Laughing, I asked, "That you like her or that I was right?"

"I plead the fifth."

~ PAUL ~

THE MONTH BEFORE the wedding had been exhausting. The only things that kept me sane were work and the club. I worked from sunup to sundown and then overindulged in alcohol, women, and I was ashamed to say, drugs as well. I knew I needed to reel it in and had cut myself off—from the drugs—cold turkey. Women, well, meaningless sex, was an older habit that I struggled to get out of. I knew Lena had expressed some interest, and I'd told myself to stay away, though I hadn't listened.

I made it through the wedding and fought to keep my eyes off of Cassidy. Of course, she couldn't keep her eyes off of him. I had been such a fool to think I'd come here to find her single and available. She hadn't been either, but then I'd gotten my hopes up when it looked like things wouldn't work out. I fucked it up with fucking, like I usually did. The one time I wanted more from a girl after fucking her—ok, second time, but same girl—and she broke my heart. I guess it was my penance considering what I'd done to her years ago.

I knew I had to tell her I was leaving. She deserved that. I knew she'd done nothing wrong, but I knew she felt otherwise. She walked into the hall while James stayed in the ballroom. I seized the moment and called after her.

"Cassidy. Wait up."

She turned and smiled when she saw it was me. Putting her hands on her hips, I knew she was trying to play it cool. "What's going on?" I walked closer, but not too close. "Everything ok?"

I shook my head and stuffed my hands into my pockets. "Yeah, everything's good. Well, considering."

She started chewing on her lip as her hands began to fidget. She was so damn easy to read. I was going to miss that. She looked down to the carpet and softly said, "I'm really sorry, Paul. I know I hurt you. It wasn't my intention."

I took a step closer and fought the urge to touch her. "Hey. I should've known better. You're married, he's an old friend. I just couldn't get you out of my head and believed that *we* belonged together. It was too much pressure, for us both."

I could see her emotions start to get the better of her as she struggled to apologize again. "I really fucked things up for all of us. I'm sorry I got you caught in the middle."

"I let myself get caught in the middle."

"I hope you know that you'll always own a piece of my heart, but he occupies my soul and I can't let him go."

"I know. I won't be around to interfere anymore."

Her head jerked up as she exclaimed, "Why does this sound like a goodbye?"

"Because it is. You shine brighter when he's around. I knew it the minute I saw you two together. I fought for what wasn't mine and he won." She started crying and I couldn't watch her do that and not console her. I pulled her into my arms and reveled in the feel of her one last time. I had to let her go, had to let go of us and the dream of her being mine. "You're going to be ok."

"I'm not worried about me."

She pulled away as I looked down to her face. "I'm going to be fine."

"Where are you going? Am I allowed to know?"

"My family's in Atlanta. My brother's running the business, but I know he could use my help."

"Does Cal know?" I just shook my head. "He's going to be bummed."

"I know. I'm bummed too."

"You don't have to go."

"Yes, I do."

She closed her eyes and took a deep breath. "When do you leave?"

"Sunday."

"You're not going to tell him are you?"

"I, I don't know. It's not like I won't stay in touch."

"Paul…"

"Everything ok?" James walked up and took in the situation. He took a possessive stance close to Cassidy and I took a step back.

"Did you know he's leaving town?" He didn't say anything as she put the pieces together. "James Benedict. If you had anything to do with this…"

"Cassidy, it was my decision." She looked between us both, trying to decide what to believe. "I should go find Cal and Jane." I turned and walked away.

"Paul," I turned back to face him, "I meant what I said. You'll always have a job here if you want it."

I nodded, "Thanks, man. I appreciate it." I walked away from them knowing full well I had no intention of ever returning. The only way to move on was by staying away.

~ CASSIDY ~

PAUL WALKED AWAY and James smiled at me, concern across his face. "You ok?"

I nodded and took a deep breath. "Yeah. I really hurt a lot of people. Why don't you hate me? I hate me."

He was a little rougher than he intended as he gripped my shoulders and began rubbing them when I winced. "Don't say that! I don't hate you. I could never hate you. Cassidy, you're my world. Please tell me you believe me."

I was shutting down, drained, so tired and I just wanted to go home. There were still a few hours left in the night and I prayed I could hold on. He leaned down to meet my eyes and I just smiled and nodded. "I believe you."

I could tell by the look on his face that he didn't believe me and I didn't care. He walked me back through the ballroom and out to the terrace. Everyone was gathered down in the garden or on the terrace. Judging by the crowd it was clearly time for the fireworks to begin. James stood behind me, his arms circled around my waist. I placed my head back against his chest and he easily supported me. I knew without a doubt he loved me and I loved him. Why did life have to be so fucking complicated? When the first firework boomed overhead, I jumped. He squeezed me tighter and kissed my temple before we enjoyed the rest of the display.

Cal and Jane were next to us and when the fireworks were over she pulled me into a hug. "Thank you so much. This night has been wonderful."

"You're welcome. It was my pleasure."

"Really, Cass. You did wonders tonight. Thanks, sis."

"Imagine what I could've done had I been given more than three months to plan!" We all laughed.

James chimed in, "Hey, I wanted to give you guys something without all the theatrics." He pulled an envelope from his pocket and handed it to Jane. "I hope it's not taken the wrong way. I just want my family close to me."

Jane looked at the envelope and back to James before Cal said, "Well, open it."

Even I was clueless as to what James had gifted them. Jane unfolded a piece of paper and scanned her eyes over it. Looking up to us, disbelief in her eyes, "James? Are you serious?"

"What is it?" Cal and I asked in unison.

"It's land." Jane's voice was barely audible.

"Land. For what?" Even I understood, Cal was clueless.

I squeezed James hand and smiled up at him. He was amazing. "I have all that land out by the cider mill. I thought it'd be nice if you guys built a house, too. We'd be neighbors."

I knew from the look on Cal's face he was worried about the cost. Living on his salary had never been easy. "Wow. That's, well, wow. Thanks, Benedict." My brother and James shook hands and then Jane gave James a big hug and thanked him again. Cal made eye contact with me just as I noticed Paul hovering nearby. I motioned toward him and Cal turned to see him.

"Paul! Where've you been buddy?" I looked to Paul who asked to talk to Cal and Jane. "Sure, everything ok?" The three of them walked off and I hoped everyone would give them some privacy for a few minutes.

"Why didn't you tell me what you had planned for their gift?" He just shrugged his shoulders. "It's amazing."

"Really, I didn't want to make a big deal out of it. It was your idea, anyway. I have more land than I could ever need. I know how close you are to both of them. It was the right thing to do."

Smirking, I said, "It'll be like our own little commune." He laughed as I tried to suppress a yawn.

"Cassidy, let me take you upstairs. You're exhausted."

"I can't just leave. All my family is here." He frowned at me, but I managed to hold on for another couple hours.

Cal and Jane left and decided to drive up to the cabin that night. She had to work on Monday so they only had a couple days alone. She gave me the key to her room and I assured her I'd get all her belongings home to her.

James and I were headed up the elevator and I pushed the button for the floor Jane's room was on. He looked at me and I told him I wanted to get my purse from Jane's room. I'd gone without my phone all day, and while it was liberating, I needed it back. We made the quick detour and walked into the bridal suite.

"You know, since Cal and Jane aren't using the room, we could."

I looked at him and laughed. The room was very decadent, with a Jacuzzi tub, and a huge king sized bed.

"Mr. Benedict. I'm exhausted. Keep dreaming." I threw myself back on the bed, still in my dress and my exhaustion hit me like a two by four. "Shit. I'm not getting up."

He smirked and crawled on the bed next to me. He pulled me into his embrace and soon we were both asleep, he in his tux and me in my dress.

WHEN WE WOKE it was early morning. I turned to look at him and he was wide awake, staring at me. I smiled, blushing while I stretched my body out.

"Stop looking at me." He laughed and asked why. "Um, I probably have raccoon eyes and look horrible."

"You're beautiful." He climbed out of the bed and offered me his hand. "You hungry?"

"Yes."

"Get dressed and meet me in my room in thirty minutes. I'll order breakfast for us."

"Mmm, sounds perfect. I'm going to take a quick shower and I'll be up."

He kissed my cheek and said, "Hurry."

He winked at me before he walked out the door. I gathered up my bags and pulled out my clothes from the day before. I hadn't packed extras because I hadn't anticipated being gone all night. The hotel toiletries would have to do. I checked and there was even a toothbrush and toothpaste. I was about to remove my dress when there was a knock on the door. He was relentless. What could he possibly want? One thing was my best guess.

I flung the door open and exaggerated my tone, "Yes, Mr. Benedict."

Fear ripped me in half as I tried to shut the door, but it was too late. I started screaming and ran for the hotel phone. He pushed me back, the receiver in my hand, and he ripped the phone from the wall. I had to get away from him. I knew what he'd done to Melissa and knew in my gut he wouldn't hesitate to do the same to me. He pulled a gun and put it to his lips and I hushed.

"One more scream and he's dead, after I make him watch me kill you."

"Dan, please don't do this. He's expecting me back in his room. He'll know something's wrong."

He looked around and knew he had some time. "Guessing since the shower is running, clothes are laid out, and you're dry, I have plenty of time." He stared at me and I started to get sick to my stomach as his eyes scanned my body. "Get up!" Slowly, I stood up from the bed where he'd pushed me, and he motioned me closer. "Get a pad of paper and write him a note. Tell him you aren't feeling well or something. I have plans for you before I involve him."

My emotions were getting to me as my throat clenched and my voice cracked. "Dan, you won't get away with this. Let me go and we'll show mercy. My brother's a cop, he can get you a lighter sentence."

He smacked me as he spit out, "Do you think I'm some kind of fucking idiot? Now do what I said. NOW!"

I tasted the blood on my tongue as I grabbed the pen and notepad off the side table. As I wrote the note, I remembered the safety word that Smith had put in place. All the security guards and James knew what it was. I just prayed it worked.

Dan grabbed the note and scanned it. "What the fuck is this?"

"I, he, we were supposed to go grocery shopping. If I give him a list it'll keep him busy, give him something to do."

He looked at me and at the note with the small grocery list and shrugged his shoulders. "He's in for one hell of a surprise. Grab your shit. Let's go."

I grabbed my small clutch, knowing my phone was in there, but not knowing if it had a charge left. Smith had also installed a tracking app on my phone. *Please God, someone help me.* We walked out of the hotel room and he motioned me toward the stairs. It was very early and the halls were quiet, maid service not at work yet.

"You do ANYTHING to make anyone suspicious and they're dead." He put the gun in the front pocket of the hoodie he wore and walked behind me. We made our way down the dozen flights of stairs, I was guessing to the parking garage, when he sneered, "You'll get in your car and drive."

I pulled my keys out of my purse as we made our way down the last flight of stairs and walked into the hall that lead to the garage.

"Cassidy! You're up early." NO! "You headed out?"

Dan lingered back in the stairwell as I held the door open. "Hey, Melissa. I was just heading home." I had no idea what Dan had in store for me, but I didn't want Melissa hurt anymore.

sixteen

Hostage

~ CASSIDY ~

"**H**EY, WHAT'S WRONG?" IT WAS THEN that I felt the tear slide down my cheek.

"Are my eyes watering? Stupid allergies. I forgot my allergy pills at home and…"

I heard her gasp as Dan yanked me back against him. "Run and you're dead, Melissa."

"Go ahead you piece of shit. After what you've done to me, I'd rather be dead." She was challenging him and I didn't know whether to sing her praises or scold her.

"You're a stupid bitch. You'll make a good hostage. Let's go."

She willingly walked with us as we walked down the corridor and continued to bait him. "You'll never get out of here with both of us, Dan."

"Shut your whore mouth."

We entered the garage and headed toward my mustang. He put the gun on Melissa and told her to sit in the passenger seat as he climbed in the back. I got behind the wheel and slowly pulled out of the garage after buckling up. I used my clicker to open the gate and pulled out onto the road. He told me where to go and I followed his instructions. Soon we were in a bad part of town and we pulled up behind an older model car.

"Get out."

He started walking toward the car and Melissa refused to go with him. He pointed the gun in her face and began cursing at her.

"Please stop. Let her go, Dan. I'll do whatever it is you want. Just let her go."

Melissa seemed surprised by my words and then repeated the same thing, adding, "Dan, she can't give you what you want. I can. Anything you crave, need, desire, you know I can give it to you."

I felt like I stepped into a movie. She had some kind of connection with him that I didn't understand and didn't want to. I saw a change wash over him as he digested her words.

Suddenly he shouted, "No!" He turned to me and pointed at my car, "Pop the trunk." I vehemently shook my head as he stuck the gun to her forehead, "POP THE TRUNK or I'll kill her."

"Cassidy, it's ok. Pop the trunk."

The tears were flooding down my face as my shaking hands released the trunk on my key fob. She willingly climbed in and just before he closed it, he smashed the butt of the gun against her temple as she fell to the floor of the trunk. I screamed before he turned the gun on me.

"Shut the fuck up and get in the other car."

He grabbed my purse and threw it in the backseat of the other car and told me to drive to my place. I was on autopilot, my adrenaline pumping. I prayed to God that James would realize something was wrong and save me. They'd probably find Melissa first.

Dan had me give him the code for the garage and the security system and had me park inside my garage. Chessa greeted me and scurried off back inside when he kicked at her.

"Upstairs." He had my purse in his hands. I had to find a way to distract him and get my phone so I could call for help. "Don't get any ideas." My eyes darted to his as he caught me glancing at my purse. I walked into my bedroom and he ordered me to sit down in the chair.

He pulled my phone out and noted that it was low on battery. I motioned to the cord on my bedside table and he plugged it in. Whatever he had in mind, he was going to torture both James and I. He set the gun down on the dresser and unzipped his hoodie before removing it. Dropping it to the floor he walked over to me, a disgusting smirk on his face. I refused to make eye contact with him as my stomach roiled. He gripped my chin and grabbed my breast roughly with his other hand.

"I hear you're a pain slut." I looked at him, not sure what he meant. "I know what he's into, thanks to Melissa. He's stayed with you long enough that you must be into it too. This is going to be fun. All those weeks of screwing you, I had no idea pain was what you really wanted. I would've accommodated you."

"Screw you." I fully expected the smack that came.

"See, we'll get along just fine." He pressed his lips to mine and I bit him. "Someone likes to bite." He sneered at me, "So do I. Get on the bed."

I refused and he manhandled me until I was on my back on the bed. I didn't recall him being so strong. He was on top of me when our attention was diverted to my phone and the ringtone that filled the room. I'd changed it a couple weeks prior to *Come Get it Bea* by Pharrell Williams because it reminded me of James and all the rides we took on his motorcycle. It stopped ringing and started right back up again.

"Why is he calling?"

"He's persistent. You should know that." It rang a third time, he wasn't leaving voicemail and then my text messaging started going off. "He won't stop until I respond."

It started ringing again and Dan was becoming increasingly agitated. I managed to kick him in the groin and dove for my ringing phone on the night stand. Pushing the answer button frantically, I began screaming, "JAMES! I'm at home. Dan's here…"

"Agh! You bitch!"

Dan jumped on top of me as his fist met the side of my face and we fell to the floor. My phone was dropped to the floor in the struggle and I don't know where it ended up. I was searching for it frantically and heard the drowned out sound of James screaming my name on the other end.

"James! He has a gun." Everything went black.

I don't know how long I was out. A minute, an hour, a day, I had no idea. I opened my eyes to see Dan pacing my bedroom floor. It must not have been long. My phone screen was smashed and lying on the floor next to me. Discreetly, I grabbed it and hoped to God it was still somewhat functional. I shoved in down the front of my dress, into my bra before Dan saw. I closed my eyes and waited to see what his next move would be, trying to figure out what mine would be as well.

"Get up." He kicked me in the gut as I gasped for breath.

Pulling me to my feet, he dragged me down the stairs and back to the car. My head was still reeling and I tried moving as slowly as I could, trying to delay, in hopes that James or someone would show up. As he opened the car door and pushed me into the passenger seat, I noticed the door to the house was open. Chessa was standing on the stairs and ran out the door. She'd never been outside before and I worried for her. I tried getting out and running after her, but I came face to face with the barrel of his gun.

"Get back in the car."

As he pulled out of the driveway, tires squealing, I heard another set of tires squeal and looked to see Paul's SUV heading toward us. They wouldn't know it was us and I frantically grabbed at the wheel to get their attention. Dan pushed me off him, but not before my eyes met James in the passenger seat of Paul's SUV. Paul slammed on the brakes and turned to follow us. Another car flew by us and I guessed it was Smith or Ryan, if not both.

Dan had a good head start, but he wouldn't so easily lose Paul. Paul had a need for speed and used to race stock cars in his spare time. Dan ran a red light and traffic jammed up in the intersection, putting some more distance between us and Paul and James.

"Before you die there are some things you should know."

"Fuck you. There's nothing you can tell me I don't already know."

"Is that so?"

"You killed my mother and probably your uncle, too." I was screaming and crying as I asked him why.

"Your mother was a whore, just like you."

"She wasn't a whore! She was pregnant and you killed her!"

Sneering, "Yeah, with MY kid." I couldn't believe what I was hearing. "Your bitch mother was banging me too, not just my uncle. He didn't have any kids and that's why his first marriage fell apart. He was sterile. Your mother convinced my uncle that the child was his. Everything that was supposed to be mine would go to your mother and her bastard kid."

I couldn't believe his words. Even if it was true, he was willing to kill his own child just to get to the money. I was doomed. He'd never show mercy on me. I sat motionless as he pushed a few buttons on the stereo.

"I know how much you like music and how *meaningful* it can be to you." He was being sarcastic as he pushed play. "Listen to this and take it for what you will."

Water's Edge by Seven Mary Three began playing. He was fucking twisted. I looked behind me and I couldn't see Paul and James. As we drove further—I was shocked we didn't have cops on our tail—it dawned on me where he was headed. I wasn't quite sure what he had planned, but he was going to kill me in the same place my mother had met her fate. I remember thinking if he was going to kill me that I hoped he would just shoot me. Drowning was my biggest fear, knowing it's what took my mother. Was I destined to repeat my mother's mistakes, suffer her same fate?

I pulled my phone out of my dress and Dan didn't try to stop me. I powered it on, but with the screen cracked, I couldn't make much of anything out. I pushed the buttons where my phone icon should have been and called him, at least I hoped it was him. I couldn't hear anything and just started rambling.

"James, I'm so sorry. I love you, please know that. I choose you. It's always been you."

The phone was taken from me as he tossed it out the window. I didn't fight him, convinced that there was nothing left to do or say. I was a dead woman. My only solace was in the fact that James and Cal would never rest until Dan was in jail or dead himself.

The sound of sirens in the distance floated to my ears and I began looking around. We were close to that old bridge my mother had driven her car off of. I started believing that it hadn't been an accident and I felt guilty for all the hatred I'd harbored over the years. She may have cheated on my father and been carrying another man's child—it didn't matter who the father was—but she hadn't killed herself like I thought. I refused to believe that any longer. Somehow Dan was behind that murder too. Looking behind me I was almost positive I saw Paul's SUV turn the corner.

"They won't stop me. It's over and you're coming with me."

I was thrown back in my seat as he floored it. The bridge was still old and rickety; after all those years no one had properly reinforced it like they should have. I tugged on my seat belt to make sure I was strapped in and took a deep breath. I couldn't go down without a fight. I undid his seat belt and when he reached for the gun I grabbed the wheel. The curses flew out of his mouth as the gun fell at my feet. I reached down for it as his fist slammed down on my back.

Pulling up, I pointed the gun at him and demanded he pull the car over. He refused and before I could beg him again the car smashed through the flimsy guardrail. I braced myself, gun still in my hand, refusing to let it go. He lunged for me and I pulled the trigger, knowing the gun wouldn't work once it got wet. I don't know where I hit him, but he grabbed his side. Next thing I knew, we hit the water and I was thankful it wasn't night time and not that far of a drop. Dan must have hit his head because blood was pouring down his forehead when I looked to him, thanks to my unbuckling him.

Water.

It was flooding in his partially opened window and I undid my seatbelt as I became soaked. I tried the button for my window and nothing happened. I don't know what I was thinking. Water was coming in too quick as I banged on it. The gun. I could use it to try to break the window. Dan's screams filled the remaining air as he tried getting his window down too. The water came in too fast and I couldn't get out. I took a deep breath, face pressed to the ceiling of the car as my hair and neck became drenched. The car was fully submerged and I had no escape. My eyes became clouded by the water as I tried to search, for what I don't know, anything to give me hope. My life was flashing before my eyes.

The green dress floated around me, like an abyss. My lungs were so tight that they felt like they were on fire. I was lost, trapped, and couldn't hold my breath much longer. He would never know my true feelings, but at least I knew his. He loved *me*, wanted *me*, no matter what. Thinking about how my loss would destroy him, I banged on the glass one more time with everything I had. The glass broke, but not before my lungs betrayed me and I inhaled a mouth full of water. Hands grabbed at me, pulling me under—or above—I wasn't sure. He was the only thought in my drowning mind.

I woke to a stranger's mouth on mine as I gagged and choked on the water pouring out of my lungs. I recognized Paul standing over me, but if he was there with me then where was James? I scrambled to my feet, pushing the EMS worker aside and spotted Ryan in the water. He was frantically diving under and coming back up. More Police and EMS started trickling down the embankment as I scurried to the water's edge.

"Paul! Where is he?" He was panting and I knew it must've been him who pulled me from the car or at least he who dragged me to shore. He looked miserable as my heart refused to believe it. "Paul!"

"Cassidy, I don't know what happened. I had to get you out."

He walked over to me as I pounded my fists on his chest. "No, no, no. Please, Paul." I was sobbing as he let me hit him without flinching. "Go in after him."

"I had to get you out. He made me promise."

I looked back to the water. Smith was pulling a body behind him and that body appeared lifeless. I saw the hair and knew it was him. "James!"

Paul ran back in and along with Ryan helped Smith carry his body to the shore. His lips were blue, I'd never seen anything like it, and the EMS workers started working on him immediately. Questions were flying about how long he'd been under and if there was anyone else in the water. I couldn't take my eyes off of him as I silently offered my soul to the devil, anything just to save him.

~ JAMES ~

I WAS EAGERLY awaiting her arrival for breakfast. I wanted to give her back the necklace. I'd found it all those weeks ago, after her attack. But, I knew I should wait. I placed it back in the velvet box in the drawer in my closet. Monday, that's when I'd give it back to her. I checked my watch again before putting it on. She was taking her time and I was being impatient. Thirty minutes hadn't yet passed. I pulled the towel from my waist and dried myself off and got dressed.

I threw on a t-shirt, cargo shorts, socks and shoes, after pulling some boxers on. Leaving my hair down, I headed down the stairs. I wanted her to relax today. Whatever she wanted to do was what I had in mind. If she wanted to sleep, I'd let her sleep. I could probably squeeze her into the spa if she wanted a massage. Grabbing my phone, I called the spa. They had a few openings and I told them I'd get back to them. Breakfast was delivered a while later. I was scrolling my phone when Smith called.

"Hey man. What's up?"

"Are you with Cassidy?"

Fear ripped at me, "No, she's in the bridal suite."

"Her car just left the garage, her phone is there, too. Ryan isn't with her."

"God dammit." I grabbed my keys and bolted out the door. "Meet me at the bridal suite."

"I'm on my way up."

Not wanting to wait for the elevator, I took the few flights down and ran down the hall. Her door was closed as I began pounding on it, praying it was some kind of mistake. Just as I was about to try to kick it in, Smith stepped in front of me and swiped his card, opening the door. We walked in cautiously. The shower was still running, the phone was ripped from the wall and disposed of on the floor. I was about to head out the door when Smith handed me a notepad. I didn't need to read it given the look on his face, but I did anyways.

James,
I'm not feeling well and just need some time
to myself. If you could bring the groceries
I need tomorrow morning, I'd appreciate it.

OJ
Eggs
Bacon
Fruit

XO,
Cassidy

"Jesus Christ." I threw the notepad down as Smith and I ran out the door. She'd managed to write a note and remembered the trigger word Smith had put in place. Bacon. She was in danger and I knew who it was. "I let my guard down. This is my fault."

Smith looked back to me as we ran down the stairwell to the garage. "We all let our guard down."

We barreled through to the garage as Paul pulled by. He stopped, his window already down. "What's going on?"

"Dan has Cassidy."

"WHAT!"

Without thought, I jumped into Paul's SUV and Smith jumped in my truck. Ryan came running through another set of doors and jumped in with Smith. Smith and I were on the phone as he told me where Cassidy's car was. Thank God I was so overbearing and had a tracking system installed. I just hoped it wasn't a diversion.

"Smith, did you call the cops?"

"Ryan's talking with them now. Her car and phone are still together. They're near all the abandoned warehouses on Canal Street. The cops may beat us there."

When we pulled down the street, there was a squad car pulled up behind Cassidy's mustang. We all jumped out and Smith told me that her cell tracker was on the move. *Shit!* Her car was empty. The cop didn't want us touching anything because it was a suspected crime scene. That was when we heard banging coming from inside the trunk.

Frantically, I pulled out my keys, her spare fob on my key ring and popped the trunk. Melissa was there, holding her head. Smith helped her out of the car as we all started questioning her.

She looked to me and tried to keep her composure. "I'm sorry. I tried to negotiate with him. He wouldn't listen."

"Where did he take her?"

"I, I don't know. It was an older car, silver I think, maybe a Buick."

"James, her cell is heading north. He might be taking her back to the townhouse. He's a good five to ten minutes ahead of us, easy." We left the cop with Melissa as the four of us hopped back into our two vehicles and sped off. The cop yelling at us the whole time that we should let the authorities handle it. Fuck them.

Paul used his phone to put Smith on speaker in his SUV as I tried calling Cass on my cell. I tried over and over again, sent some text messages and got nothing. Finally, she answered and all I heard was her screaming.

"Cassidy!"

"JAMES! I'm at home. Dan's here..."

"Cassidy? Cassidy answer me." I listened as I heard a scuffle before the phone went dead. "FUCK! Dan has her, they're at the townhouse." I knew Smith heard me as Paul floored it. We were doing ninety on the freeway, headed toward her townhouse, Smith right behind us.

"How did this happen?"

"Paul. Don't start with me."

"Sorry, I just."

"I let my guard down. I fucked up. Don't you think I know that?" Smith confirmed over the speakers of the SUV and I directed my next words to all three of them, but specifically Paul. "Whatever happens, you get her out and to safety." Paul looked to me and understood the gravity of it all. "No matter what."

"I got it."

"I'm talking to all of you."

"We got it."

Too many minutes passed before we were burning rubber down her street. I spotted a car swerve and saw her red hair in the passenger seat as her desperate eyes met mine. Paul spotted them too and turned the wheel as he slammed on the brakes. We were turning to follow them as Smith pulled down the street and followed suit.

"Ryan, he's got her in the passenger seat. Call everyone you know."

"He's already on it." Smith responded as we drove with more caution than Dan was exhibiting. We'd be lucky if he didn't get in a car accident; of course maybe that was his plan all along.

We were driving for far too long. He was taking her to the country and dread settled over me. "He's taking her to the old Reynolds Bridge." Smith and Paul both questioned me. "It's the bridge her mother died at all those years ago."

"Jesus Christ."

"You don't think…"

"I, no, I can't, Ryan tell the cops." I put my head in my hands as I thought about what that sick motherfucker had in mind for her.

"We'll get her."

My phone rang and it was her. "Cassidy!"

"James, I'm so sorry. I love you, please know that. I choose you. It's always been you."

I tried talking to her, but it was clear she couldn't hear me. Her voice was garbled and then the connection was gone. It took everything I had not to break down. I just looked to Paul, dread filling me. It was a goodbye call because she was convinced she was going to die.

"Do you have your tools?" He pointed to the back seat as I grabbed anything I thought might be useful. We had to stop him before Dan did something crazy.

We lost sight of his car for a few moments and found it as we approached the bridge. Paul floored it again once we hit a straightaway and gained on them.

"You don't think."

"No, I know." We watched in terror, nothing we could do as we witnessed the car fly through the side of the bridge and into the water. "Paul, drive to the embankment. Remember what I said. You get her out."

"What happened?" Smith came through the speakers and Paul answered him.

"The cars in the water..." Their voices faded away as I waited for Paul to get close enough.

Once Paul pulled a ways down the embankment, I jumped out of the SUV. I grabbed a crow bar and ran toward the water. Paul was right behind me with a piece of pipe in his hands. I prayed that the cops and Smith were close behind. The car was at least fifty yards away as it disappeared under the water. Before diving in, I turned and saw Smith. He knew to stay put, the cops would need to know where the car went under.

Paul and I began swimming out. Once we were above where the car had sunk, we took deep breaths and went under. My eyes burned against the filmy water, but I could make out the car. The water wasn't extremely deep and it was the only thing I was thankful for. We swam to the passenger side and all we could see was her green dress. It had swallowed her whole, but she was banging on the glass. We began smashing on her window and it finally broke. I grappled for any part of her I could reach and pulled her out. Dan's body came into view and I was determined to finish it.

Paul grabbed onto her other arm and started pulling her to the surface as my body was tugged back violently. I was becoming fatigued, trying not to inhale water. I found him tugging on my leg and I smashed his face with my fist before wrapping my hands around his throat. There was no way he was making it out of that lake alive.

His eyes were bulging as something heavy smashed against my head. I couldn't hold on much longer. I needed air. I started to become disoriented and as his body went limp, eyes wide, I pushed up with my feet and hit my head again and my thoughts went blank as my lungs caved and sought breath, finding murky water instead.

WHEN MY EYES opened I was aware that I was in a hospital room. A gorgeous redhead in scrubs was leaning over me, calling my name. I looked around as a few people began standing around my bed. Smith and my father were there and another nurse walked in. What the hell was going on? I tried to sit up, but my head began pounding when I tried that.

"James. Thank God, you're awake." The redheaded nurse was being a little inappropriate as I pulled my hand from her.

"What's going on? What happened?"

A doctor in a white coat came over as the redhead moved aside. Smith stood close to her and I wondered who she was. "James, you've been in an accident. Do you know where you are?"

"Clearly. I'm in the hospital."

"Yes, that's correct. Do you know the people here?"

I looked to the faces I recognized, "Smith, Dad," my eyes went back to her as I drew a blank.

She stepped forward and whispered my name, "James? It's Cassidy."

"James, do you know who she is?"

I laughed, uncomfortable and confused. "I, sorry, I don't." She stared at me as Smith and my father flanked her.

"She's your wife, son."

Scrunching my eyes, I looked to the doctor, Smith, and then my father before my eyes went back to her. My wife? I took in her appearance again. No, I never planned on getting married. This had to be a joke.

"Haha, guys. Seriously. Who's the redhead? Where are the cameras? We all know I'm not the marrying type."

seventeen

Amnesia

~ JAMES ~

THE REDHEAD GASPED AND TURNED into my father's arms as they stepped further away.

"James, do you know what day it is, what year?"

My attention back on the doctor, I thought about his question. "Umm, yeah." I racked my brain. "August 2011." The doctor took a breath and asked to talk to my father and the redhead in the hallway.

Smith stayed with me. "Smith, what the fuck is going on?"

"Maybe we should wait for the doctors."

"Tell me what's going on. Who's the redhead?"

He moved closer, running his hands over his face. It was then I noticed he was wearing scrubs, too. What twilight zone had I stepped into? "She's your wife, Cassidy."

"No, I...what?" I shook my head. "What happened, what day is it?"

Smith told me and I was shocked. It wasn't August and it wasn't 2011. It was July 5, 2014. What the fuck happened to me? The doctor came back in and confirmed what Smith had told me before I could ask more questions about the redhead, my wife.

"You need to rest. You've been through a trauma. Can you do that?"

"Can I get something to eat? I'm starving."

"Sure. I'll have your nurse bring you something."

Everyone walked out of the room, leaving me to my thoughts. I closed my eyes, not sure what to think, say or do. Several minutes later, the redhead walked in with a tray of food. She set it on the table by my bed and avoided eye contact with me. She was extremely nervous and I couldn't blame her. I was still trying to wrap my brain around everyone telling me that I was apparently married to her.

"I went to the cafeteria and got a few things I thought you'd like."

"Thank you. You didn't have to do that." She looked to me briefly and smiled. She had beautiful blue eyes and it was evident she'd been crying. It was then I noticed her bruised face. Had she been in the accident with me? I heard her own stomach growl and smirked. "Are you hungry? I'm sorry, what was your name?"

The emotion flitted across her face as she tried to keep her composure. "Cassidy, my name's Cassidy. It's ok. I can eat later." I placed my hand on hers and insisted she eat, too. "Ok. Do you want the pizza or the lasagna?"

"No matter to me." She took the pizza and sat on the edge of the bed by my feet.

I pulled the bedside table over and started eating. She seemed quiet and reserved and definitely submissive. That explained a little bit. But married? I still couldn't wrap my brain around it. I caught her staring at me as the door opened again. A nurse came in and asked to take my vitals. She then asked Cassidy if she was staying overnight.

"Um. I, that's up to him."

"I imagine you probably want to sleep in your bed and not here." The nurse looked at Cassidy sympathetically before leaving the room. "I'm sorry. I'm not quite sure what to do here."

She attempted to smile, assuring me it was ok. "You're right. I'd prefer my own bed. You've been through a lot and need your rest." She looked around the room and then gazed at me stating, "I'll be back tomorrow," before walking out the door.

~ PAUL ~

I GOT DRESSED and headed out without waking her. She'd tried so hard at the bachelor party to be a friend and I'd pushed her away. I reached out to her later on and told her I couldn't be more than friends. Well, that quickly turned into friends with benefits and she knew she wasn't the only one warming my bed. If that's all we were, why did I feel bad about sneaking out? Probably because I knew she deserved more.

When I walked down to the garage and hopped in my SUV, I had no idea that I'd run into James and Smith in the garage. Thank God I had. After all the chaos that came, I was second guessing my decision to leave town. I needed to decide if I was going to hop on that plane home or if I was going to stay.

The next morning I rolled over and saw her naked body, a curvier and more voluptuous one than from the previous morning. Her hair was a bit longer, darker and was fanned out behind her. It all made no difference to me, I wasn't picky. She was asleep. She and I had started making a habit of warming each other's bed, long before I cared to admit, and she understood it was casual. Hell, it'd been her idea. We'd left the hospital together after awaiting news on James, though no one else knew and we both wanted to keep it that way.

I had to visit the hospital to see how everyone was holding up before I made my decision. At least we were all alive, barely. Well, not *everyone* was alive, but I didn't give a shit about his, hopefully, dead ass. I contacted Smith on my way home and he had confirmed that the body had been pulled out of the water overnight. Dan was dead.

At Cassidy's insistence, we hadn't contacted Cal and Jane. She wanted them to enjoy their honeymoon since it was only a weekend retreat up at the cabin. They'd left before everything went to shit and they'd be home on Monday, which was the next day. I had a decision to make. Stay or go. I sat in the hospital lobby later that morning, waiting for Smith while I reflected on the previous evening.

We were in the lobby waiting for word. Smith, J.J., and Cassidy walked in and we all grew silent. Melissa, Lena, Anthony, Frank, Annie, Ryan, Delaney, Jane's parents, and I all stood or sat in our various places in the room as J.J. filled us in.

"He's awake. His memory is a little off right now, but the doctor's think he'll make a full recovery."

J.J. continued answering questions and I got the sense he was being vague. Smith had his arm around Cassidy and she wouldn't make eye contact with anyone. I had a feeling something more severe was going on, but they didn't want to disclose it just yet.

Melissa came forward, "Cassidy, you look exhausted."

"She's right. You've had one hell of a day." Delaney seconded Melissa's words.

"I, yes, but...Lena, did you get a hold of my dad?" Cassidy looked to Lena who nodded. "Is he coming down?"

"He should be here at any moment."

Just as Lena finished her statement, Mr. Charles walked into the lobby. Cassidy ran to him and he checked her over as he held her. She was crying into his chest as he pulled her to a corner of the room, Lisa walked in a few moments later.

J.J. got our attention and thanked everyone for coming. "Please give James some time and privacy. Please check with Smith, myself, or Cassidy before you pay him a visit." We all agreed and began heading our separate ways.

I walked to my SUV and she was standing there waiting for me. We didn't have to exchange words. I just nodded and she followed me in her car as we headed back to my place. It was one weekend I knew I wanted to forget and I'm sure she did, too.

Smith gripped my shoulder and pulled me from my thoughts. Shaking hands, he reiterated that Dan's body had been pulled from the lake and his body was at the coroner's office. I'd never been so relieved to hear that someone was dead.

"Don't you have a plane to catch?"

I looked to Smith, "That's what I'm trying to decide. Did he find a replacement for me?"

"Nope. He was planning to take it on himself. Before, all this."

Sighing, I had my answer. "Alright. I'll cancel my flight. I'm not sure how long I'll stay, but I'll keep things running so the projects are on schedule until he's back to work."

"It's worse than that." I narrowed my eyes at Smith, as he confided in me. "You can't say anything. He has amnesia. He's thinks it's fucking 2011."

"Jesus."

We talked a while longer and I knew I had to stay. We shook hands again before I left. I pulled out my phone and dialed.

"Hey Mom. Yeah, I'm not coming home just yet."

~ CASSIDY ~

I WAS IN THE hallway with J.J and the doctor. I couldn't comprehend anything he was telling me. The only thing I knew was that James didn't know who I was. Devastated was an understatement to how I felt. Dan was finally gone—I hoped—and everything had been falling into place.

"Mrs. Benedict?" I jerked my head to the doctor as he said my name again. "Give him time. Sometimes these things take time. Don't put too much on him too soon."

Nodding, I complied as J.J. rubbed my back. "Don't worry dear. He'll remember."

"I hope so." The doctor headed back in to see James as I murmured to J.J., "You heard him. He never planned on getting married."

"He's a silly boy. Don't listen to him."

Smith came out of the room followed by the doctor. "He's hungry." Looking to me he suggested, "Why don't you go to the cafeteria and get him some of his favorite foods? It might help." We all agreed and the doctor walked away.

"I don't want anyone to know just yet. He's fine and that's all they need to know for now." Smith and J.J. agreed.

"I'll wait here while you and Smith go get him some food. We can talk to everyone together."

"Ok."

When I was in line getting food for James, Smith got a phone call. He looked to me as he gave generic answers that didn't tip me off to anything. He paid for the food and took the tray from me as we headed back to the elevator.

"I don't know how to do this."

"How to do what?"

I looked to him, "Pretend I don't know him." I sniffed, "It's not fair. After everything…"

He nodded and sighed, "They just pulled his body from the lake. He's dead."

A weight was lifted from me and immediately replaced with another. "And James has no idea." Then it hit me. "Oh God."

"What is it?"

"Smith, he has to remember. How far back does he remember?"

"I, he thinks it's 2011."

My gut wrenched as I started crying. "His mom! He thinks she's still alive." The doors opened and we stepped outside and into another hallway. He set the tray down and pulled me to him. "I can't do this, Smith."

"Shh, yes you can. Just one day at a time. All you have to do is go eat with him, not fill him in on the last three years of his life."

I knew he was right, but every memory that was ingrained in my soul, James no longer had. It hurt to breathe thinking about him suffering through all of that again. If he asked about his mom how was I going to explain it?

"One day at a time, Cassidy."

I wiped my tears and took a deep breath. "Ok."

I walked into his room, set the tray down, and we exchanged a few words. I was fidgeting and it took everything I had not to throw myself in his arms when his hand touched mine. I was so happy that he was alive and just wanted to imbed myself in his arms. He had to ask me my name and it cut me deep. When the nurse came in and asked if I was staying, I knew I had to get out of there. I left more abruptly than I had intended to. Smith and J.J. walked with me to the lobby where our friends and family awaited news.

I vaguely recall J.J. filling everyone in, without telling them that James had amnesia. When my Dad walked in I rushed over to him. He was the only other man who could make me feel better. I filled him in quietly as he shed some tears of his own. Next thing I knew, everyone seemed to be gone except for the three of us, and J.J., Smith, and Delaney.

"Has anyone called Cal and Jane?" Lisa asked and we all shook our heads.

"Please don't. James is alive. Let them enjoy their honeymoon." Reluctantly they all agreed and J.J. confirmed that Bev hadn't called Jane either.

"Cassidy, can Lisa and I take you home."

"Yes, but I don't have my car or keys to get in."

"Here." Smith pulled out some keys and handed me one. "It's for your place." I nodded, knowing he wouldn't need it anymore, I grabbed on to it. "I'll try to get your car back to you tonight or in the morning. I need to find out if the cops impounded it or not."

"Thank you, Smith."

"Mr. and Mrs. Charles, I can put you up at the hotel if you like."

"I don't want her to be alone. We'll make due. Thank you." My dad turned down the offer and we headed out.

I fell asleep in my dad's truck on the way home. It'd been one hell of a long day. The sun was already starting it's decent in the summer sky when we walked in my front door. I missed the sound of Chessa's bell greeting me and started crying.

I filled Lisa and my dad in on what had happened as they consoled me. They walked me up the stairs and into my room. Most everything was in order, but a chill ran over me. Just that morning I'd been Dan's captive in that room. My only comfort was knowing he was dead. Now I just had to deal with the memories.

"Why don't you take a bath, dear? I'll make you some tea."

I agreed as Lisa and my Dad started picking up the broken pieces of my table lamp and the turned over chair. I pulled some clothes out of a drawer and walked into my bathroom, closing the door. I stood there for several minutes. I didn't have the energy to take a bath, though I knew I needed one. Changing my clothes, I discarded the scrubs and re-entered my bedroom. The mess was gone. I crawled into bed and I think I was asleep before my head hit the pillow.

I WOKE TO the smell of bacon and pancakes. Bacon. Smith had told me that they found the note, but not before he figured out my car had left the hotel. I needed to get to the hospital. I looked for my phone on my night stand and remembered Dan had thrown it out the window. Now I needed a new phone.

"Ugh!"

Hitting the side of my bed with my fists, I then climbed out of bed and into the shower. Once I was dressed, I headed downstairs where Dad and Lisa awaited. I ate way too much, but I was famished! When I was close to finishing, there was a knock on the door. My Dad answered it and Smith walked in.

"Hey, I have your car." I walked over to him and took the keys. "These are James' keys. We'll have to order another spare set, so don't lose them."

Smiling, I thanked him. "You're a lifesaver, literally."

He just shrugged his shoulders. "I took it upon myself and got you this too." He handed me a new cell phone. It was charged and seemed to have all my info in it. "Good thing he's overbearing and backed up all your stuff."

"Right! Thank you. I was dreading having to go replace it." He said hello to my father and Lisa and they asked if he'd heard anything new.

"No. I haven't heard anything. I was planning to head up there now. You want a ride?"

I looked to my dad and he said, "We'll probably head home soon. Its ok, you go ahead. We'll lock up here."

"Ok. I'll follow you so you don't have to cart me around." I headed to the door and realized, "Shit, I don't have my license or anything. Guess I know what I'm doing tomorrow."

"I can still drive you. I'll check and see if your purse was in the car wreckage."

"No, wait, hang on. I think it's here." I ran back upstairs and found my purse on my dresser, license inside. "Got it!"

I hugged my dad and Lisa and told them I'd stay in touch with any update. Dad didn't want to overwhelm James and I understood. Smith followed behind me as I pulled out the drive. I started to wonder how he got my car here and his car, but knew he had plenty of resources at his disposal. When we reached the intersection, the same one that Dan had flown through the night before, I panicked.

I was stopped at the red light, oblivious of when it turned green. Everything grew quiet as the previous day's events flashed through my mind. A tap came on my window and I was sinking again, banging on the glass. Someone was saying my name, but I couldn't figure out from where. I looked to my left and saw Smith, looking nervous. Shaking my head I saw the honking cars driving around us and giving us dirty looks.

I rolled down my window as he asked, his voice full of concern, "Are you ok?"

"Yeah, sorry. I don't know what happened."

"I can drive you. Pull over to the side and you can ride with me."

"No, it's ok. Sorry."

"You sure?" I nodded. "Alright. Just call me if you panic again."

"Ok." The light was red again and I watched as he climbed back into his car.

We made it to the hospital without further incident. Smith and I headed up to his floor and I knocked on the door before entering. He was still roommate free, which never happened and I couldn't help but wonder if it's because of *who* he was. It didn't matter.

"You first." I motioned Smith ahead of me and he didn't hesitate.

"Hey, man. You getting me out of here?" I walked in hesitantly and watched their exchange. He was oblivious to my presence.

"That's up to the doctor's, not me."

They had some special handshake and were laughing when he spotted me. I should've done more to get ready. I had on no makeup and my hair was pulled back. *Way to impress, Cassidy!* I hung back and waved, unsure what to say. The man I loved, more than life itself, didn't know me anymore. I became uncomfortable as I felt his eyes scan my body, like he was seeing me for the first time.

"I can leave if you don't want me here."

He smiled and eyed Smith before returning that seductive glare my way. "No, you should stay. We should probably talk."

"I'll give you two some privacy." Smith pulled another cell phone out of his pocket and handed it to James. "Here you go. New phone." James looked the phone over and commented on how thin it was. "Yeah, technology's come a long way in the past few years."

"Right. It's 2014." He shook his head as Smith smiled at me and headed out. "So, where should we start?"

I was fidgeting as he watched me like he had all the time in the world. "Um, I don't know. What do you want to know?"

He chuckled, "Everything, of course."

"Right." I took a deep breath and went to sit down on the window seat, the furthest spot from him, when he interrupted me.

"You can come closer. I won't bite, unless you're into that sort of thing." I felt the blush spread as I opened my mouth to speak and shut it just as quick. "You *are* into that sort of thing. Ok. Noted."

I closed my eyes and sighed. "I don't think I can do this." I started pacing and he grabbed my wrist and pulled me closer. He was wearing a t-shirt and sweats. Someone must have brought him some clothes. Why hadn't I thought about that?

"Relax Cassidy. We're married and while I don't remember, I know that I wouldn't marry someone who didn't have similar likes and desires." I just stared at his chin before he tilted my chin up, my eyes meeting his. I took a shaky breath remembering all the times he'd done that when he knew who I was. "There's no need to be embarrassed. Smith sat with me last night and answered some of my questions. But now I want to hear from you."

He pulled the bedside chair closer and directed me to sit. What had Smith told him? Not sure why, I apologized. "Sorry. Did you get any rest last night?"

"Eh, as much as to be expected in this place. The docs want to keep me another day, but I'm doing everything I can to get out of here today." I pulled a leg up underneath my body and tried to get comfortable in the chair. "Are you ok? Smith told me that we both almost drowned, but they didn't admit you, only me."

"I'm ok." His hand reached out as he ran his fingers over the bruises on my face. "I didn't, I mean, shit. How did that happen? The accident?"

"Yes, it was the accident. It wasn't you."

"Smith said the same thing, but I had to make sure. I've never hit a woman..."

"I know that. You've never hurt me, well, not like that, I mean... ugh." His expression was priceless as we started laughing.

"Another mental note taken." I just shook my head. His charm was still there and I wasn't immune to it. "So, how did we meet?"

The doctor came in at that time and gave me a reprieve to get my story together. He was ordering some tests and as long as they were fine, he'd release James in the morning. He stressed the importance of taking every precaution due to his previous brain injury.

"Understood. I don't like it, but I get it." James conceded and I was grateful.

The doctor walked out and I looked to James, "I'll be right back." I left before he responded and stopped the doctor in the hall. "He's asking questions and I just want to make sure it's ok to tell him things."

"It's hard to know what helps in these situations. There's a good chance he'll remember everything in an instant. Others, it takes longer and only small pieces come back. But you need to prepare yourself that he may never remember." He placed his hand on my arm as I rubbed my fingers across the pounding that was beginning to form in my head. "Try to keep any traumatic events at bay. I understand that his mother has recently passed. Don't lie to him, but I wouldn't jump right into it either. Just follow your heart and be patient with him."

"Ok. Thank you." I headed back into the room and James wasn't in his bed. The door to the bathroom popped open and he barreled into me. "Sorry."

His hands were on me, just like that night at the Blue Horse. I gently pushed myself out of his arms as he apologized. I walked back to the chair as he took his seat on the side of the bed and faced me.

"Where were we?"

"I think you asked how we met."

"Yes, so, tell me everything."

"Ok. We met at your bar, the Blue Horse."

"Wait, my bar?"

"Yes, on 4th Street."

"Shit. I've really missed a lot. Ok." I went to speak as he stopped me again. "Wait. We didn't meet," he stopped and looked to me.

"At *the club?* No, it was the bar."

"Huh. Ok. Go on."

"We met there. I was there with friends and we flirted off and on for several weeks." I thought about my tattoo and showed him my wrist. "We first started talking about my tattoo after several bouts of eye ogling."

He took my wrist and looked at my tattoo. "Eye ogling, huh."

I wasn't about to tell him I called it eye-fucking and there he was, eye-fucking me in his hospital bed. "That, right there. Stop it!"

He smirked as his gaze returned to my wrist. "Cool. It's a raven, right?"

My heart plummeted to the floor of my stomach. "Yup. So anyways." I pulled my wrist back and continued my story. I told him how it was a few months before we saw each other again. Leaving out the nasty details about Holly and Sam's murders and Dan's involvement. "We saw each other again at your Aunt Bev's masquerade and, well, the rest is history."

"So, this all happened last summer?" I nodded. "And we're already married? Are you pregnant or something?" His eyes traveled to my abdomen as I tried not to react. He didn't know, didn't remember. *Breathe Cassidy.* "Why'd we get married so quickly?"

"No, I wasn't pregnant. It was a spur of the moment kind of thing."

"Wow. Ok."

A technician came in then and took him out for some scans. He told me he'd be back and I told him I'd be there. There was a knock on the door and Smith came in holding two coffees, one frozen, one not.

"I got you a vanilla frapp thingy. Delaney said that's what you like."

"Thank you." I was grateful for the distraction and filled him in on James potential release.

"Ok. Well, I just talked to Paul downstairs. He's going to stay for a while to help out at work. James was planning to take over, but given everything that's happened."

"No, that's great. I'm happy he's staying." I sighed and pulled out my phone, checking my notifications to kill some time. "So, what all did you tell him last night?"

He shook his head and smiled at me. "Just what he needs to know." I narrowed my eyes at him as he chuckled. "That you're the love of his life. That's the only thing that matters."

"You told him that?"

"Of course I did. I'm his best friend. He's told me on more than one occasion and I let him know that."

"Thank you."

"I know what it's like to lose someone and have no control over the situation. If I know you like I think I do, you'll do anything and everything to prove your love."

I wasn't sure what he meant about losing someone as it related to him and didn't feel it was the time to inquire. "You're too kind. I really fucked up while trying to prove I didn't love him."

"He made his share of mistakes, too. Don't stress too much over it. Everything will work out."

"I'm not sure what to do with him when he's released." Smith tilted his head and after a moment seemed to understand my quandary. "He offered to move back in and I told him to wait. Most of his things are at the penthouse. How do I explain that?"

He thought for a minute and then said, "You don't. I'll move his stuff to the townhouse today."

"Wait, are you sure?"

"If you said he offered to move back in, then that's where he wanted to be. Being with you is most likely the thing that'll help him remember. He doesn't even know about the hotel. That was a pipe dream in 2011." I nodded, still unsure it would work. "It'll work."

"If you say so." Then all the things about him moving back in with me ran through my head. We were married, that meant sharing a bed, and all the other stuff. "Christ."

"What is it?"

Sighing, "It's just so complicated. I probably shouldn't be discussing this stuff with you."

"What stuff?"

"He doesn't remember me, but I remember him and, well, I find him irresistible. How do I not have sex with him?"

He snorted, "Well, why do you have to not have sex with him?"

"Never mind. You're a guy; of course you'd say that."

He was laughing and trying to apologize at the same time. "Hey, I'm sorry. In all seriousness, just take it slow. I know how intense his connection was, is with you. Maybe sex is what will trigger his memory."

"Perfect. I can see the headline now. 'JB3 amnesia cured by wife's mad vagina skills.'" I was cracking up as he pretended to be offended.

"Not quite sure any headline would include the word 'vagina' in it. And I don't want to hear you talk about your vagina again."

It was my turn to start snorting. Delaney had walked in and we weren't aware until she spoke. "You better not be talking about her vagina!" Smith and I were laughing hysterically as Delaney established, "Clearly I missed the joke."

eighteen
Unhinged

~ JAMES ~

IT SEEMED LIKE I SPENT HOURS inside machines as they scanned my brain. I'd been through it before and knew the routine. I was eager to get upstairs to her, my wife. The word was so foreign to me. I'd gotten married. It just seemed crazy. Smith and my Dad all confirmed so it had to be true. Dad and Mom. It wasn't like my Dad to stay away, or my Mom. I wondered if she was out of the country getting more treatments. I was sure I'd see or hear from my dad later in the day.

I was still having trouble wrapping my brain around the fact that I'd lost almost three years. What the hell had happened in the 'accident' and what the hell *was* the accident? Smith had just said it was bad and involved a car, a bridge and us almost drowning. How the hell had we driven our car off a bridge in July and who was driving? Cassidy or myself? I had to find out.

I would be lying if I said I wasn't attracted to her. I was. Almost instantly, too.   Redheads weren't usually my MO, but there was something about her. My dick was twitching just at the thought of it. Where were we living? What did she do for a living?

"Alright James, you're all set. The orderly will be here in a moment to take you back to your room."

As the machine turned off and I was able to stand, I stretched my legs and waited. When I made it back to my room Smith was there playing on his phone and Cassidy was asleep on the window seat. As I got back in my bed, she began to rouse. She smiled sweetly and grabbed what appeared to be an almost gone frozen coffee and took a drink.

I got as comfortable as I could on the hospital bed as Smith and Cassidy tried to make small talk. I couldn't suppress the yawns that continued to escape me.

"You should rest, James. I can come back later." Smith nodded, agreeing with Cassidy's words.

"Talk to you soon, brother." He shook my hand and walked into the hallway.

Cassidy made her way to follow him and as she paused by my bed, her body language revealing all, she waved and said she'd be back around dinner time. I reached out and snagged her hand. I wasn't sure why, but I had plenty of time to think about what she must be going through. With us being married and as close as Smith assured me that we were, I couldn't imagine the grief she was feeling. A tremor ran through my fingers as her eyes examined our joined hands. I pulled her a little closer and she tried resisting.

I was now standing at the edge of my bed and she was in front of me, avoiding my eyes. "James." It was barely a whisper and her voice was broken. Her free hand traveled to her face and swiped at her eyes.

I bent my knees so that we were face to face. "Cassidy. I'm not sure what I should say or do, but I can only imagine what you're going through. I'm sorry. I want to remember." In less than twenty-four hours she had captivated me. Why the fuck couldn't I remember? I wanted to remember. My body reacted to her immediately, every time she was near, and I could sense that it was the same for her. Looking up to the ceiling, "Please, God, let me remember."

A small sob broke from deep inside her and instinct had me pull her close. Slowly, she relaxed against me as I released her hand and wrapped my arms around her back. She squeezed her arms around my waist as her scent assaulted my senses. Oranges. She smelled like oranges, or tangerines, maybe it was both.

Between heaving and broken breaths she whimpered, "I thought you were dead. After everything we'd been through, everything was finally falling into place. Then, then Dan almost killed us both, and…" She stopped talking, almost like she knew she'd said too much and just held on to me.

What was 'everything'? Dan, Dan who? I knew a few, one was from high school. What the hell had happened to her, to me, to us? Dan who and why had he tried to kill us? I was about to ask her when my nurse came into the room.

"Fucking hell." Cassidy bolted her head up and looked at me, eyes narrowed. "What?"

"Well, that's something I always say. I've never heard you say it." She pressed her lips together and tried smiling. "Sorry, it just caught me off guard."

"I hate to break this up, but I need to check his bandage and he really should get some rest."

"It's fine." She looked back to me as she gingerly pulled herself out of my embrace. "I'll be back later. Is there anything you want or need?"

I grabbed her hand and looked at the raven tattoo on her wrist.

Something told me there was more to the story, but I didn't have any idea what it was. I just nodded as she slowly let her hand fall out of mine.

"Is that a yes you need something?"

"What? Oh, umm, no. I think I'm good. I'll see you soon."

"Ok. Get some rest."

I watched her leave before I climbed back in the bed. The nurse made a positive comment and asked if I'd remembered anything. I told her I hadn't and she told me to give it some time. I couldn't help but feel like time was the enemy.

It didn't take me long to sleep, but it didn't last. My thoughts were running amuck, willing myself to remember something, anything. I was missing her and had an almost uncontrollable urge to strip her naked and bend her over the bed, or my lap, every time she walked in the door. *Shit!* What the hell was wrong with me? It was like my body remembered her, but my mind didn't.

"Fuck!"

I heard the door open and spotted my father in the doorway. "Everything ok, son?"

I exhaled and pounded my fist on the bed. "Define 'ok'. Why can't I remember her?"

He walked over as he digested my words. "Her who?"

"Cassidy, of course. Who else would I be talking about?" He sat down in the chair next to me and folded his hands in his lap. "In my mind I'm single, well, seeing Melissa, but that's just casual. When in reality I'm married to, to her. Cassidy. And she's stunning, funny, kind, at least from what I can gather."

"She is and more. You found a gem and we love her dearly."

"She's not my usual type at all." I knew that wasn't entirely true. "I don't understand."

"What's to understand? You changed when you met her. Your mother and I both saw it. That's how it happens for most of us. We find the one girl who unhinges us and it changes everything. To say that Cassidy unhinged you is an understatement." His gaze scrutinized me as I tried not to take offense at his words. He smiled and added, "In a good way, James. She reached a part of you that had been closed off to all of us for a long time."

I sighed. He was probably right. I didn't do love and romance, even I knew that. I also knew that I wanted to romance her, this woman I didn't know, and it sounded ridiculous to me.

"How is mom?" He stared at me and I was becoming uncomfortable as he shifted in his chair. "What is it?" Realization hit me that mom had been battling cancer for two years already back in 2011. Now it was 2014. "Dad?"

The door opened and in walked my redhead. She was the stranger my body already ached for, my wife and my memory had no recollection of her. She smiled at me before she spotted my father. She noted his somber expression and returned her blue gaze to mine.

Stopping in her tracks she asked, "I'm sorry, am I interrupting?"

"Cassidy, please join us." My father motioned her into the room and hesitantly, she did just that. She set her bags down and stood nervously at the end of my bed. "I was just about to talk to James about his mother."

The unease that washed over her face told me everything I didn't want to know. My dad started to talk and I put my hand up to stop him. My lips barely moved as I made the statement. "She's gone, isn't she?" My eyes shut as I took a deep breath, dropping my head into my hands. I winced when my hand tugged on the hair by my wound a little too hard.

"Yes." He was straight to the point, something I admired in him, but at that moment I wondered if he could've been gentler when he broke it to me. When I asked when he told me that it had only been a few months prior.

"Jesus. Was it the cancer?"

"Yes. She stopped treatment in November." He continued speaking as my ears turned themselves off.

I didn't want to believe his words. That meant that she'd battled it for over five years. I couldn't listen to any more. "Please, stop." The suffering my mother had gone through was too much to think about. It was making me ill.

"James, do you feel alright?" I was aware of her voice as her hand touched my forearm. I didn't mean to flinch at her touch, but the harm was already done. She took a step back saying, "I'll get you some water and a cool rag." The emotion was gone from her voice as she turned and left the room.

"I'm sorry, James. I didn't want to break it to you this way, but you needed to know."

"I know, Dad. I just. My last memory of her isn't really my last one." I looked to see that Cassidy was still gone. "Did she meet her?"

"Your mother loved her. I think before she even met her. They spent a lot of time together." I nodded. "She was disappointed you two eloped so quickly, but only because she missed out on celebrating with you."

I felt like a jerk for taking that away from my mother. As her only child, I knew how important my wedding day would've been to her. "Is there anything else I need to know, that I've missed in this three year time-warp."

"No. The only thing you need to know is that your mother loved you, loved Cassidy and she wanted you two to be happy." He gripped my shoulder as he stood. "Take comfort in her. She loves you." The door opened and Cassidy walked in with a pitcher of water and some cups. "I was just leaving dear." She placed the cups and pitcher down and I watched as my father embraced her. "Take it easy on him. Call me if you need anything."

"Ok."

When he was gone, she poured two glasses of water and handed me one. I took a sip and then a few more before I set the cup down. She was drinking her own water while trying not to make it obvious that she was gauging my reaction to the news that my mother was gone. Our eyes met as she stared over the rim of her cup before she moved to sit down in the chair my father had been occupying.

"I'm ok."

My words seemed to surprise her. She muttered, "Ok."

She was holding back. I could sense it in her. "What is it? You can tell me."

"Well, it's just…"

"Out with it!" I huffed, "Christ, are you always like this? You're like a simpering child." I regretted my words immediately as I watched the flush of anger spread over her cheeks.

"NO. I'm not always like this. I was told to tread lightly, by your doctor, so that we didn't re-traumatize you."

"I didn't know…"

"No, you don't know. Do you have any idea what I've been through, what I'm going through?" She was angry and started pacing the small path by my bed. "There are so many things I want to tell you, but I'm so afraid I'll do something to make it worse. So, instead I sit here biting my tongue, desperate for you to remember anything about me, about us." She swiped at a tear and then angrily pointed at the tears falling down her cheeks. "And this! I FUCKING hate this. When I'm angry I cry and I know what I must look like. But I also throw shit and say things I don't mean." Turning on me she hissed, "Remember anything yet?"

Hot damn! She was a firecracker with a submissive side. *I think I'm in love! Fuck. Focus.* "Cassidy, I'm sorry."

She inhaled and exhaled a big breath before she grabbed her purse. "I should go."

I jumped off the bed and blocked her path. "No. Please don't go." I tried to touch her, but she backed away and I took a step closer. She had nowhere to go. "Please stay." I wiped the last remaining tear off her cheek with the pad of my thumb and licked it away.

"Don't do that."

"Do what?" I pulled my thumb from my lips as I savored her salty tear.

"That! Wipe my tears with your thumb and then lick it." I was a little confused when it dawned on me that it must have been something she was used to me doing. "It gives me a glimmer of hope that you remember when you don't."

Damn. Everything was so messed up. "Cassidy, will you sit with me on the bed? I don't want you to go."

She looked to the small bed and then back to me. "There's hardly room."

"We'll make room." I took her purse and set it back down before taking her hand in mine. I sat down on the bed and moved as close to the other side as I could. Patting the space next to me, she sat down awkwardly. Laughing, "You can come closer. I won't bite…"

"Unless I ask. I know." Her tone had me smiling as she settled in next to me. "I miss your mom. More than you know."

I put my arm around her and we sat hip to hip and side to side. "Strangely, that makes me very happy."

"I don't know that it's strange."

"Yeah, well. I just know that if you two were close then I made the right choice." She turned and smiled at me. Before things had a chance to get uncomfortable, she dropped her eyes and put her head on my shoulder.

Softly, she said, "I've missed you, too."

It was the oddest feeling because I felt the same way. How could I miss someone I didn't know? "Did I handle her death badly?"

"Um…badly is an understatement."

"Oh, boy. I don't think I can handle that discussion. Tell me about her service."

"Are you sure?"

Nodding, I replied, "Yes. We'll save my deplorable behavior for another time."

Snickering, she said, "Ok."

I reclined the bed a little as she lay in the crook of my body. She began describing in great detail the beautiful ceremony. Apparently my mother had planned out the entire thing out in advance. That was so like her, planning every single detail, no matter how minute. Cassidy had dozed off and I was staring at her left hand as it dangled over her side. There was no wedding band on her ring finger. I looked to my own and saw the same thing. Maybe we'd both lost them in the accident. I couldn't imagine not giving my bride a ring. My stomach grumbled and she started to wake.

"You hungry?" She looked up to me sleepily, "Did you eat dinner?" I shook my head. "James, you need to eat. Did they bring your dinner?"

"I forgot to order."

Sighing, "What am I going to do with you?"

"Feed me hopefully!"

Giggling she said, "I have some snacks or I can run down to the cafeteria and get you something warm to eat."

"It's going to be late soon. Do you have to work tomorrow?"

"Nah. I'm good. Melissa has it covered. We need to get you home and settled."

"Melissa?" What were the odds that we were even thinking about the same Melissa? I couldn't imagine that she was working with the girl I was—used to be—screwing. This time lapse was bound to get me in trouble.

She sat up, "Yeah. Something else you don't know. Melissa and I work together." She started laughing. I'm sure it was in response to the look on my face. "Relax, I know about your history and she was on my shit list for a while. That's all I'm saying about that for now."

THE NEXT MORNING I was released from the hospital. Cassidy was there to take me home. Funny how I didn't even know where 'home' was. We walked out of the hospital and her mustang was pulled up in the valet lane. It was a sweet ride and I was eager to drive it, though I wasn't about to over step my bounds. We both buckled up before she pulled out of the hospital.

"Nice ride."

She smirked, "Thanks. It was a gift," she paused and looked to me before adding, "from you."

"Really? I have good taste!"

"Ha. I picked it out. You were driving foreign when we met and now you have a Ford pickup."

"What? Why?"

She giggled and shrugged her shoulders. "My Ford love rubbed off on you is my guess." Before I could respond, she pulled onto the freeway and opened her up. "Hang on!"

She gripped the stick like a pro as she flew down the freeway. It was a miracle that she wasn't pulled over. Soon, she was exiting and headed toward a part of town I was fond of. I figured out almost immediately where she was headed. The townhouse. The last I recalled I was in the process of gutting the place. It was my baby, my side project and what I worked on in my down time.

When she pulled in the drive, the outside changes were well evident. It looked great. "So, we live here?" She just nodded and got out of the car. When I walked around the back of the car, I spotted the license plate. "MRSJB3? Really?"

"Really!" She walked up the few steps to the front door and sniggered over her shoulder. "That was all you, too!"

"I hate that nickname."

"I know, but I like it!" She winked and walked in the front door.

"Wow. I really did it." She smiled at me before walking into the kitchen. "So, how did we both end up here? Did you move in after we got married? It wasn't my plan to keep the place."

"That's another funny story that I still don't have all the details to. I rented the place from your Aunt Bev, thinking she was my landlord. Your cousin, Jane, later told me that you were the landlord." Her revelation baffled me. "I'm still not really sure what your intentions were, but it doesn't matter now."

"Wow. I surprise myself."

"Hopefully that's a good thing." I smiled and nodded.

There was a knock on the door and when I saw Jane on the other side I was surprised and happy to see her. Apparently she was happier. She threw her arms around me with some guy covered in tattoos hovering behind her.

"Jane! What are you doing here?"

She leaned back and was examining me. Looking to Cassidy she scolded, "Why didn't you call us? Are you ok?"

Cassidy shrugged her shoulders and said, "It was your honeymoon and we're both alive. I didn't want to worry you."

Honeymoon? To *this* guy? "Fuck. I've missed a lot."

Jane and—whomever he was—walked in as I sat down on the couch and Jane joined me. "It's true? You don't remember?" I just shook my head. "Oh, God."

Jane was married and I wanted details. "So, fill me in. Who's this guy?" Her guy smirked at me and his eyes seemed familiar.

"Well, this is Cal, my husband and your brother-in-law." That's right. Cassidy had mentioned that her brother married my cousin. Was that weird? I didn't have time to think about it.

I looked to him and he smiled. They had the same eyes, that's why they seemed familiar. I stood and held my hand out. He shook it as I said, "Cal, right? Nice to meet you. Well, you know what I mean."

"I do. I'll give you two a few minutes while I chat with my sister." Jane and I nodded as Cal followed Cassidy upstairs.

~ CASSIDY ~

I WALKED INTO the bedroom and looked around. Smith and I had moved the majority of James clothes back in the day before. He'd never know he hadn't been staying there. I felt guilty, like I was pulling one over on him. I walked to the bed and sat down as Cal followed. He sat in the chair across from me and leaned forward, elbows on his knees.

"So he really doesn't remember anything?" I just shook my head. "How far back?"

"He thinks it's 2011. He's lost everything and anything that had to do with us. How do I get him back, Cal?"

"You have him back. You guys mended things, right? Before

everything?" I nodded. "Fuck! If that asshole wasn't dead. I should've been there."

"It's not your fault, Cal."

"I spoke to Frank. You're sure you're ok? I can't believe what he did."

"I'm ok. I really don't want to talk about it. It's too disturbing and fucked up." I saw his face change and remembered what Jane's ex had done to her and Cal must've assumed. "No! He didn't get a chance."

He dropped his head to his hands as he grumbled, "Thank, God." He muttered something else, but I didn't catch it. Then he asked, "So, how's this supposed to work?" He motioned around the room and I knew what he meant.

I tried to clear my throat, but it didn't help. "I don't know. I remember everything about him; he just knows I'm his wife." I was picking at my fingers, while saying, "I don't know what he'll expect from me. I don't know if I can give myself over to him again and risk losing him, Cal."

He looked at me for a moment before his eyes drifted over the room. "So, set some boundaries. I know it's easier for us men to separate emotions from sex. I can't imagine how hard this is for you. I know how important he is to you."

"Am I being punished?" I started crying and he got up to sit next to me. "I hurt him and I don't know what's worse, that he knew and did nothing or that he doesn't remember anything now."

"Hey. Shh. You're not being punished."

"Do I tell him? I mean. What the fuck? 'Hey, thought you should know that I cheated on you—but you knew—and you let me believe you were cheating, too, when you weren't.'" I stood up and peeked into the hall and quietly, closed my door, and turned back to Cal. "Who would believe that? It's a little far-fetched."

"I hadn't thought about it that way." He took a big breath and admitted, "I don't know what to tell you, Cass. I want to believe that everything will come out in the wash, if he remembers."

I know that I paled as I said more to myself than to Cal, "I can't live with that secret for the rest of my life."

"It was a complicated and messed up situation. We can ALL testify to that. You slept with Paul, an old boyfriend, when James *abandoned* you." He scrunched his eyebrows together at the look of remorse on my face. "It was *just* Paul, right? Cassidy!"

"It's complicated."

"Jesus Christ. Who?" My eyes bulged as I knew he really didn't want to know. "No, never mind. I don't want to know. I might go to jail when I break his jaw." He walked back to the chair and sat down.

Little did he know it wasn't a man, but two women I slept with, while with Paul. I shook the memory away as someone knocked on the door. I opened it and saw Jane standing there.

"Am I interrupting?"

"No."

"Good! Cal, go chat with James. Cassidy and I have some catching up to do."

My brother smirked at her and stood from his chair. "Yes ma'am." He closed the door behind him and left Jane and I to our girl talk. We sat on the bed facing each other. She could tell by the look on my face that I was barely holding on.

Putting a hand on my knee, she said softly, "I'm so sorry, Cassidy. Is there anything I can do?"

I shook my head as I sniffed, "No. If I think of anything, I'll let you know."

"He feels terrible. His top concern is you." That surprised me as she smiled, "I think that's a good sign. Somewhere deep down, he remembers how important you are to him."

Sighing, "I know I'm over complicating things, but I don't know how to be around him."

"What do you mean?"

"Well, he's your cousin. I'm not sure you want to hear about it."

Rolling her eyes she insisted, "Just spill it. What is it that has you worried?"

"Do I sleep with him? I mean, I want to, but we haven't even kissed. And I don't just mean sex. Do we sleep in the same bed? I'm a stranger to him, but he's also a guy."

Like she read my mind, "And if you're sleeping in the same bed together, he'll want more."

"Exactly. It's not that I don't want that, but, ugh."

"I think I get it. You should just be candid with him. He appreciates that. Set up some guidelines."

"Cal suggested that too, boundaries."

"I knew there was a good reason I married him." She winked as we both laughed. "Try to focus on other things. You like to read right?" I nodded. "When you're not at work, spend some time reading. You should check out the Cursed Series by T.H. Snyder. If you think you have issues, her characters will make your problems seem like nothing. And they make for some hot book boyfriends! I just finished the first one and I'm getting ready to start the second one."

Laughing, "Well, I love a good book boyfriend. I'll check it out."

nineteen

Alone

~ CASSIDY ~

Later that night, after Smith dropped off his truck, James was deciding what he wanted for dinner. I had insisted he pick since he'd been the one stuck in the hospital. He'd chosen the Thai place and I offered to go pick it up since I needed to grab a couple things from the grocery store anyways.

When I walked back in the door, there was music playing and he was sitting down scrolling through an iPod. Was that mine? When he spotted me, he took the groceries out of my hands as I ran back to the car for our food. As I walked by the table, I noticed it was indeed my missing iPod. I'd lost it around the time I miscarried. Had he found it or had he had it all along. He noticed me looking at it and asked if he should change the song.

"No. I'm just, well. That's mine. Where'd you find it?" I smiled, "It's been missing, for months, that's why I ask."

"Oh. Well, it was in a bag on the front seat of the truck. I assumed it was mine, but maybe it's yours. But I don't recognize a lot of the songs."

"It's ok. I'm glad you found it. I'm beginning to think you've had it all along."

"Maybe so. So, you called me JB3?"

Smirking, "On occasion."

"Hmm. I'm not sure I like that."

"I know. You got over it." My cell phone rang and when I looked at the caller ID, I recognized Dr. Pratt's number. "Shit." Answering the call, "Hello. Yes, sorry." James watched me and his eyes narrowed when I said, "Hello, Dr. Pratt. Yes, he's home now. I'm sorry, I should've called to reschedule. Um, now? Hang on." I put my hand over the phone and asked James, "Dr. Pratt would like to stop by. Is that ok?"

"Dr. Pratt? Um, sure. Am I seeing him again?"

I had yet to fill him in on that detail. "Yes, we both were."

"What?"

I put my finger up, making him wait, and put the phone back up to my ear. "Yes, we're eating dinner. We'll be here. Ok. See you soon." I put the phone on the counter and sat down at the table where our carryout awaited us.

"What's going on, Cassidy? Why are we seeing Dr. Pratt?"

"We were working through some things, together and separately. He was helping us. We had a scheduled appointment for tonight, but with everything that's happened, I forgot to cancel it."

"So, why is he coming here? Can't it wait?"

Shrugging my shoulders I concluded, "I assume he's worried about you, maybe both of us. If you're not comfortable with it I can call him back."

"No. It's fine. I just wasn't expecting it."

He started eating and didn't speak again until Dr. Pratt showed up. I ate as well and hoped that having Dr. Pratt over wouldn't be a mistake. When he got there, we'd just finished eating.

I opened the door and he said, "You've got a stray cat under your porch."

"What!" I ran past him and started looking at the porch, trying to get a glimpse under it. A moment later a black cat darted out, hissing at me, and ran away.

"Are you missing a cat?"

I looked to Dr. Pratt and responded, "My cat, Chessa. She ran away on Saturday."

"I'm sorry to hear that." I just nodded.

We walked in and I sat down on the couch. James was putting dinner away and had missed the exchange about Chessa. He came over and sat at the other end of the couch as Dr. Pratt sat in a chair across from us.

"So, fill me in. How bad is the memory loss?"

Dr. Pratt looked to James, who took a breath and filled him in. Occasionally Dr. Pratt's eyes would travel to mine and I'd smile or nod in accordance with what James revealed to him.

"Cassidy, how are you handling this?"

Shrugging my shoulders, "As best I can. I'm not sure how I'm supposed to act."

"What do you mean?" James question caught me off guard because I expected Dr. Pratt to ask it, not James. Looking to him I voiced my concerns. The same ones I'd discussed with Jane, Cal, and Smith. James didn't seem upset or offended and said that my concerns were valid.

"Ok. Cassidy, I have some questions for you and I want you to be honest." I agreed. "When was the last time you two had intercourse."

I looked at him and he just shook his head saying, "Just the truth."

Like he knew we broke the rules, I told the truth, "Friday morning, before the wedding at the hotel." I couldn't bear to look at James and then Dr. Pratt asked when the last time was that James told me he loved me. "I, um…"

"Doc, this is awfully personal." I glanced at James, uncertain of what to say and how to answer.

"I know it is, but there's no reason for either of you to hide it. You two had been coming to me for almost a month. Sex was a vice for you both and I asked for you two to commit to twenty-eight days of celibacy and no 'I love yous' so that you could work on your communication."

"Twenty-eight days! What the fuck!" His reaction was priceless. I started laughing as he glared at me. "What are you laughing at?"

Trying to contain myself I said, "Because that was MY reaction. You were more than willing to do the time. I was the one throwing a fit."

His brows scrunched together as he simply said, "Oh."

"Ok, so back to my question. Cassidy, when was the last time he told you he loved you?"

"At the wedding while we were dancing."

"And what about you?"

"I, well, I didn't say it back." I looked to James who seemed a little surprised and I added, "I called him before the accident, but I don't know if he heard. I told him then."

"Wait, we weren't together during the accident? What the fuck happened?" He was growing agitated and I didn't know what to do.

"James, calm down. If you want Cassidy to explain everything you need to sit down, shut up, and listen." I liked Dr. Pratt more and more every time I saw him. "That is, if you're committed to this marriage."

His eyes darted to mine and then back to Dr. Pratt's. "Well, yes. I don't remember, but I know that I wouldn't have married her if I didn't love her. I'm committed."

I explained in great detail what had happened with Dan, the bridge, and the accident. I added in the nefarious things too, how I had been dating Dan when James and I met for the first time. James seemed to handle everything ok, but he was visibly upset and looked exhausted. I felt bad, but was glad that at least the Dan portion of our life was out in the open.

"And he's dead?" I nodded. "Did he drown?"

"I got a hold of his gun and shot him in the car before we went under, but you and Paul pulled me out of the car. Paul got me to shore, but you stayed under. I don't know what happened, if there was a struggle with you and Dan. I don't know."

"Paul? Vincent!"

"Yes. He's back in town and working for you." I left it at that. He'd heard enough for one night.

"Ok. Cassidy. I understand your concerns. Honestly. I don't know how to suggest you two handle this. I think it's pretty evident that you two had a break through and were effectively communicating, and clearly you love one another." Looking at James, "I know you don't remember, but I can tell you from the private sessions you and I had; you were willing to die for her and you almost did. I think you should take it slow, but don't deny what's there, either. Tread lightly, be cautious, and enjoy one another. After I leave, why don't you two discuss it a little further? It doesn't have to be tonight, you can discuss it tomorrow, but please talk candidly with one another."

I was heading up the stairs as James closed the front door behind Dr. Pratt. I heard his footsteps follow me up the stairs and a thrill of nerves and excitement trailed up my spine. It wasn't that late in the evening, but I needed to try to go back to work the next day and we needed our rest. I pulled some pajamas out, since sleeping nude probably wasn't the best idea, and walked into the bathroom to change.

When I walked back out he wasn't in the room. I found him in my spare bedroom, where his treadmill sat and my bike sat. He was sitting on the edge of my old twin bed and looked to be lost. I walked over to him and knelt down in front of him, unaware that the stance I was taking would be appealing to him.

Placing my hands on his knees and looking to his face, his eyes scanned over my own. "Are you ok?" He had circles under his eyes and he pulled back slightly before I trailed a finger over that scar of his. "Sorry." I pulled my hand back to his knee and asked again, "Is there anything I can do? You're exhausted. Go to bed."

He placed his hands around my wrists in a vice-like grip as his eyes crawled over my body. Pulling us to our feet, we stood as he held my arms between us. "Do you mind if I take a shower? I can sleep in here."

I shook my head and protested, "James, you can sleep in our bed. All of your things are in there." I pointed to our bedroom as he released my hands and walked away from me. I found him searching the closet and he emerged with some clothes in hand. "James?"

He walked into the master bath and turned to me. "I, it's just that I don't share my bed. Hell, my bed has always just been a place for me to sleep. Alone." I started to object but he cut me off, "I know we may have, but I need time. I'll be just down the hall."

I smiled, though it nearly killed me, and told him I understood. "I get it. It's fine." Pointing to the bathroom, "All of your toiletries should be there."

"Thank you."

He closed the door and I may have jumped at the sound. I crawled into bed feeling defeated and like we were back to square one. A sudden change seemed to have swept over him and I didn't understand. When

I woke in the morning, I was still alone. I wasn't sure what I expected. I walked down the hall and found his door closed. My hand reached for the knob and then pulled back. He needed time.

SEVERAL WEEKS LATER I was on my way home from work. I was looking forward to the weekend, but it had also become the hardest part of my week. James and I were still living like roommates and it was killing me. We talked about everything, when he was around, and wasn't gone. We'd both thrown ourselves into work and it was our only solace. Paul had moved back to Atlanta a couple weeks earlier, once they were all convinced James could handle the workload.

James still hadn't remembered anything and we were all losing hope that he'd ever remember. When he wasn't working, he was working out and constantly walking around the house shirtless. I was beginning to wonder if he was trying to torture me or if he had no idea what he was doing to me. I wondered how he'd react if I started walking around without a shirt on. Hmm, maybe that was a good idea.

I'll never forget the first time I saw it. He was running on the treadmill that first week he was home and I was on my way to work. I realized when I got downstairs that I'd left my phone on my night stand. I ran back up the stairs and he had his bare back to me as he wiped his face with a towel. He had earbuds in and didn't hear my gasp.

Shoulder blade to shoulder blade and down the center of his back was a huge anchor tattoo. I tripped on the last step up and landed on my knee. It was a blessing because I was able to disguise my tears when he ran over to see if I was ok. I told him I was a klutz and that he should get used to it. The last thing he needed was more pressure from me to remember.

I stared at that tattoo whenever I could, but knew it was pointless to bring it up. I knew him—well the old him—well enough to know that it was *my* tattoo. Then it started eating at me. When had he gotten it? Scenario after scenario ran through my head. I had a pretty good idea about the timeframe and hated myself.

That fateful day I had used my safe word, changing the path we were on, he wanted to show me something. That tattoo had to be it. Had I just kept my mouth shut, he'd have shown me that tattoo and I probably would've forgiven him, let him back in. I had to try to let it go, but it was eating me alive. I'd never lose my faith in him again; no matter how long it took I was going to get him back. I just had to be patient.

Part of being patient apparently included masturbating to his image almost every night. It got me off, but it wasn't enough. I wanted him and knew he wanted me, too. At least I hoped he did. I just couldn't figure out what he was waiting for. I was becoming desperate, thinking about making the first move, but scared to death and worried he'd reject me.

~ JAMES ~

THE WEEKS FLEW by and summer was going to end before I knew it. Delaney, Smith and Paul had done a great job of getting me up to speed on all the projects I had on my plate. The Benedict was a dream and I was still in awe of it. It had been a pipedream, last I remembered, and I'd made it happen. I'd come to terms with losing mom, but it would always hurt.

Cassidy had been wonderful, but it was like having a really hot roommate that I couldn't touch. Of course, I knew that was all in my head. She was my wife; of course I could touch her. That was the hardest part for me. I had rules when it came to intimacy, or at least I had at one point. Only at the club, or a hotel, my terms, no kissing, and those were just the beginning of my long list of regulations. What had happened or changed that I'd let her in? I couldn't believe that we didn't have sex at home, in our bed, but we also hadn't discussed things like we had agreed to and Dr. Pratt had suggested. I didn't want to believe that she was a cold fish, but she'd also made no attempt to become intimate either.

I spent many nights watching her as she slept and wondered if she ever did the same. I should have just kissed her and gotten it over with. I knew the attraction was there, but. Nothing. I was being an idiot. Enough was enough. I'd take the bike out for a ride like I planned and then I'd come home and make my move. I just hoped I wouldn't disappoint her.

I was putting my helmet on when I heard the purring and looked down to see a cat weaving in and out of my legs. I tried shooing the thing away, but instead, it walked up the steps and made itself at home. I fucking hated stray cats.

Then I heard a different purr, the one of her mustang as it pulled in the drive. She was home early. I watched her long legs slide out of the car and watched the skirt fall from mid-thigh back to her knees. Her hair was down and my fingers curled up with a need to touch the red strands.

"Hey. I was just heading out." I watched as her eyes scanned my body and the bike. Had I missed the signs? She was looking at me like I was a piece of meat. "I'll be back in a bit. Will you be here?" I saw her posture change slightly. Did she want to go for a ride?

"Ok. Be safe." She turned and headed toward the front door.

"Cassidy!" She turned and I said, "Careful, you've got a stray cat on the porch. Have you been feeding it or something?"

Her eyes darted to the porch as she cried out, "Chessa!"

The cat made no qualms about letting Cassidy pick it up. "Friend of yours?"

She turned to me with the most beautiful smile on her face. "I can't believe you found her!" As I walked toward her, she filled me in on the fact that the cat was hers. "She ran away the day of the accident. I can't believe she's back." She walked in the front door and set the cat down, who then ran off somewhere toward the kitchen. She looked to me and said, "I have to feed her and make sure she remembers where her litter box is."

I nodded and waited for her to return from the laundry room. "So, do you want to join me?"

"For a ride? Are you sure?" I nodded. "Yes! Give me five minutes."

She ran in the door and I went to the garage and pulled down the other helmet. I was an idiot. Why had it not occurred to me that I had two helmets for a reason? Of course the second one must have been hers. I wasn't waiting long and I wasn't disappointed when she walked out the door. Her tight jeans hugged every curve just right. She wore a grey shirt and had her hair pulled back in a low pony.

She walked over, the excitement radiating off of her. Handing her the helmet, I watched as she slid it over her head. I straddled the bike and turned the engine over. Revving it for optimum effect, I motioned her to climb on. *Preferably my lap.* I shook the thought away as she braced herself on my shoulder and swung her leg behind me. She latched her arms around my torso without reserve and I peeled out of the drive.

We rode out of town and came across a small festival and I decided to check it out. They had a beer tent with live music and you could smell the funnel cakes in the air. Not really sure if she was hungry, but assuming she was, I found somewhere to park.

"Want to check it out?"

"Sure. I could go for an elephant ear or two, too."

We walked toward the music, stopping to check out a few vendors who were set up in tents, before they closed up for the day. I told Cassidy that we should make plans to come back the next day to check out the other tents that had already closed for the day. She happily agreed. We stopped and each ordered some food. She opted for a corn dog, an elephant ear—as she called it—and a lemonade. We ate as we walked and made our way toward the bright lights of the Ferris wheel and arcade games.

"Want to go for a ride?"

She cringed and said, "I don't know. Last time I rode one, well, let's just say I left my lunch on the pavement."

I laughed, "Seriously. It's a Ferris wheel." She just shrugged her shoulders as I continued to rib her. "Alright, Benedict. I'll ride the Ferris wheel with you on one condition," she looked around and pointed at one of the arcade booths, "I want one of those! The big one."

I followed her finger to see stuffed animals of all sizes. I couldn't even tell from our distance what kind of animals they were. "Deal. This will be easy enough." I pulled out my wallet and she gawked at the wad of twenties I pulled out.

"No! That's cheating. You have to win it; you can't buy it, big shot." Huffing, I shoved the money back in my wallet, grumbling the whole way over. "And I'm pretty sure you have to win like three times before you can trade in the smaller ones for the big one."

"Why did I agree to this?"

She just laughed and as we got closer I realized it wasn't even a game of skill. It was the stupid water gun on the bulls-eye game. This would be easy enough. I paid my money and she sat down next to me. She was going to compete against me. She was rotten and I was going to thoroughly enjoy wiping that smile of hers off her face when I won.

She won the first game, I won the second, then some tween in baggy pants won the third game. His girlfriend squealed like a banshee and I had a hard time hiding my disgust. Looking to Cassidy, she was smiling from ear to ear. She had a great smile.

"Ready. Just you and me. Hurry up and pay the man." Her spunky side was contagious.

"Yeah, yeah. Prepare for my wrath woman."

She turned her blue gaze to me and winked, "Don't make promises you don't intend to keep, James."

Was she flirting with me? The buzzer sounded and I missed the start. "Dammit. You're cheating!" She just laughed as she squeezed the trigger. The bell chimed and she threw her hands up in the air, boasting her victory. I just shook my head as she pointed to me and made an 'L' with her finger and mouthed the word loser. "You're vile!"

"Ha! You love it!" The attendant handed her another animal and she thanked him. "You ready to go again or you had enough?"

Shrugging a shoulder I quipped, "I think I'm done."

"Well, I'm glad that you're comfortable enough in your manhood to accept defeat by a girl." She was teasing me and I could dish it out, too.

"Alright big talker." I handed the attendant enough money for two games. Looking to Cassidy I said, "Double or nothing."

She seemed confused. "I already have two and you have one."

"Yup. And I just gave him enough money for two games, but we're only playing one. Double or nothing. If I win the prizes are all mine AND you ride the Ferris wheel. If you win you get your big stupid stuffed animal and you don't have to ride the Ferris wheel." She looked at me and agreed before I added, "Though, I'm not sure you'll have a ride home if you win."

She just shook her head as we waited for the bell to sound. I won and wondered for a moment if she'd let me win, but it didn't matter. I turned in my three small animals and picked the exact one she'd wanted. I made sure she knew that it was mine as I started walking toward the Ferris wheel.

"Who's boasting now?"

twenty
Tension

~ JAMES ~

As we walked, me with my huge prize and her with her two smaller ones, we came across two parents and a small child. The little girl was running in a small circle near us and when she ran into my leg, she let go of her balloon. I tried to snag it, but it was gone before I could stop it. She started crying and I felt horrible. Her parents tried consoling her as I apologized.

"It's not your fault." The mother looked at her daughter and said, "We have more balloons at home. But you need to watch where you're going next time, ok?"

"Yes, Mommy."

As Cassidy and I started to walk away, I knew what I had to do. "Hang on." Cassidy stood back and watched as I approached the family. "Hey," the little girl and her parents turned to me, "I have this big stuffed animal and he needs a good home. Maybe if it's ok with your mom and dad he can go home with you."

The little girl gasped and looked to her parents, "Please, please, Mommy and Daddy." They both laughed and said that it was fine with them.

"Remember to take good care of him."

"Oh, I will, I will. I promise." I handed over the stuffed animal that was almost as big as the little girl was.

I turned and headed back toward Cassidy. She was smiling from ear to ear when I rejoined her. "Now you're just showing off."

I feigned being offended as I asked, "Who, me? Never."

"Mister." The little girl was tugging on my pant leg and I turned and bent down to her level, caught off guard when she threw her tiny arms around my neck. "Thank you, mister." I looked to her parents who were both smiling. She kissed my cheek and then skipped back toward her parents.

"Looks like I have a little competition." I stood back up and scoffed at Cassidy's remark. "She's cute and she has game. I'll give her that much."

Without thinking about it, I grabbed Cassidy's hand as we walked toward the Ferris wheel. I made a detour and headed toward the tent with the music. She looked at me and I just said, "I have no desire to deal with you puking. No offense."

"None taken. Here." She handed me her second prize and said, "All's fair in love and war."

I smiled at her and enjoyed the feel of my hand holding on to hers. I entwined our fingers and tried ignoring the surge of energy that ran through my fingertips. Leading her through the tent, I quickly took in our surroundings. The band was taking a break and a slow song was playing. Couples littered the dance floor and I caught her gaze as she watched them. I remembered her saying that we used to dance and wondered if I should ask her.

The song ended and another slow one started. I recognized *Pink* singing and didn't bother asking; instead I weaved us through the throngs of couples and then faced her. She only hesitated for a moment as I pulled her close. Her body stiffened slightly, but I was almost positive that it was from nerves, not discomfort.

"Relax."

"You're not making it very easy."

I looked to her, "What do you mean?"

She shook her head and smiled, "Never mind."

Before I could ask anything more, she turned her face into the crook of my neck and I felt her inhale and exhale as her body relaxed. The hand that held her lower back pulled her a little closer as feelings I didn't recognize stirred inside me. I suddenly felt very protective and possessive of her. I let go of her hand as my arms came together to encircle her. It was like I couldn't get her close enough. That hand of hers I had released ran down my back and I felt her nails gently dig in as she held on tight.

I tried to focus on the lyrics of the song, ignoring the throbbing my body began doing. I had to try to take things to the next level with Cassidy. Not since Cora—my biggest mistake—had I felt emotions remotely close to what I was feeling. But unlike Cora, Cassidy was mine, my wife. If I wanted her I could have her. What the hell was I waiting for? The song was right. We could learn to love again, or maybe it was only me who needed to learn again.

Lifting my head I whispered her name, "Cassidy?"

She raised her own and met my eyes. My hand pushed some of her hair behind her ear as I took in the features of her face. She looked so vulnerable and I couldn't wait any longer. I leaned in and watched as she closed her eyes, awaiting my kiss. I could smell the mint from her gum and realized she was holding her breath, though her lips were slightly parted.

"Cassidy! Cassidy Charles!"

Her eyes bolted open as my lips pulled back and my ears were assaulted by whoever was calling her name. A brunette I didn't recognize came running up to us and I could feel the tension begin to pour off of Cassidy. Whoever the chick was, Cassidy was not happy to see her.

"I knew it! I told Carl here that it was you. We were all the way over there." She pointed to the other side of the tent as the guy she was with took a swig of his beer, though he clearly didn't need anymore. "Aren't you going to introduce me?"

"Right, sorry. Umm, James this is Kim. We went to school together."

She thrust her hand into mine, she knew exactly who I was and her next statement proved it. "The famous JB3! Cassidy, how'd you manage to snag this one?" Cassidy smiled nervously as Kim continued jabbering on. "Cassidy and I were practically best friends growing up, she's just being modest."

"Um..."

"Really! Wow. Is that so?" Kim was visibly excited that I believed her bullshit and Cassidy had already picked up on the fact that I was playing along. "Best friends, huh? You must know *everything* about her."

"Yup, yes sir. Everything!"

"What's her middle name?" Kim smiled and laughed nervously as I added, "What about her favorite color, favorite food, or favorite boy band?" I was aware of Cassidy standing next to me, staring on in disbelief. Kim tried to make excuse after excuse and I cut her off. "See, I'm going to take a gander that *your* favorite color is green." Her eyes bulged and her mouth dropped open. "Arianna, purple, pizza and Backstreet Boys. And Arianna was her grandmother's name." I took Cassidy's hand and we left Kim and the festival.

We were practically jogging back to my bike when I realized she was calling my name. We were secluded, away from prying eyes as I stopped and looked around us.

"James, that was. Wow. Thank you. I couldn't stand that girl. We were friends in elementary school, but it didn't last." She kept talking on and on. Did she ever stop talking? I mean, I enjoyed talking with her—it's the only reason I knew those things about her—but that wasn't what I wanted her mouth doing at that moment.

I turned to face her and when her eyes met mine she went quiet. I took a step toward her and she took one back. I took another two and she took a second. I was enjoying our new game. Moving forward again, she backed up and met the wall behind her. Smiling, I reached out my hand and when she looked at it I took her by surprise.

With my hands in her hair, my teeth mashed against hers, harder than I intended, and I crashed my lips to hers. She moaned in surprise, but quickly succumbed to my brutal kiss. My hands worked through her hair, over the back of her neck and back again till I was stroking her jaw with the pads of my thumbs. I licked at her lips as she moaned again and sagged against the wall. My dick was rock hard and I couldn't remember wanting someone more. I didn't give a shit that we were on a public street and anyone could see us. Her tongue found mine as she had me release a growl of my own. Fuck, she tasted good. Her hands were frantically pulling on me as I leaned into her and pressed my hard-on against her.

Gasping, "James." I silenced her with another kiss as I ground my pelvis against hers.

I had to stop this. What the hell was wrong with me? She was making me lose my mind and I didn't care. I wanted to sink my dick into her so bad that I was willing to do anything, almost anything.

"James, take me home."

Pulling back, I looked to her. Fuck my rules. I grabbed her hand as we walked back to my bike. I handed her the helmet as I put on my own and started the bike. "Get on!" It wasn't a request and she climbed on and gripped my hips as I drove us home.

We walked in the front door and I pulled her up the steps behind me, eager to spread her out on that big bed. I yanked her close once we were in the room and was torn between taking my time and devouring her that very instant. I slowed down the kiss and worked my mouth back to her ear as my hands ran under the hem of her shirt. Her skin was soft as she trembled against my fingers and I wanted to touch every part of her. She was very responsive and I knew immediately it must have been one of the things that drew me to her.

She was timid, but in a good way and not abrasive like many women I'd been with. While I already knew she was unlikely to ever make the first move, she wouldn't back down once things began. Her fingers were tangled in my hair as she pulled on its length. It wasn't something I was used to. Usually my women were restrained or discouraged from touching me. This was a whole new ballgame to me, well, not new, but one I hadn't played in a very long time. Even Melissa and I had guidelines we followed, until she tried changing them.

"James, are you ok?"

I was totally distracted and she knew it. Focus James! "Sorry, I, am I moving too fast?" She just shook her head and tried pulling me closer.

"No, I've been dying of anticipation for this moment. Please, tell me you'll move back in here with me. I want this to be our bedroom again." I pulled away and she tried to close the distance between us. "James. Don't go." She already knew.

"I, we, I should've taken you to the club. I can't do this."

"Yes, you can." She pulled her shirt over her head and I sucked in my breath at her beauty. My eyes immediately falling to the tattoo on her ribcage, but the lighting was all wrong for me to make it out. "Please James, I'll do whatever you want. Please don't go. Stay with me."

It was too much pressure. The intimacy she was used to I couldn't give her and didn't know if I'd ever be able to. Backing away from her, I confessed, "I'm not ready for this. We need a contract." It was the only thing I knew that could protect us both.

"What!" She grabbed her shirt off the floor and put it back on. "I'm not one of your subs! I'm your wife. Take me to the club if you want, but don't insult me with a contract."

"I didn't mean to insult you." Before I could say anything more, she threw her purse at me, just missing my head. The contents fell to floor and scattered after it hit the door jamb. "I just, I'm so fucked in the head I don't know how to do this." I pointed around the room and she knew what I was referring to.

It was barely a whisper as she pleaded, "Try. For me, please try."

I walked toward the door, stepping over the contents, and said, "I just, I can't. I need more time." I don't know if she knew I heard her next words, but I did and they hurt.

"You always leave me alone in the dark." She got on her knees and started shoveling the discarded items back into her purse. I handed some things back to her and she snatched them from me aggressively.

Once she had everything, she stood and the door closed immediately in my face and soon music was playing loudly. I paced the hall for a moment and spotted a business card on the floor. Picking it up and examining it, I became confused. Why did Cassidy have one of my DOM business cards?

I walked to what had become my room and kicked the door closed. I fell asleep to the drone of her music. Her image haunted me in my dreams; at least I was pretty sure it was her image. I woke in a cold sweat and the clock told me that only a few hours had passed.

Getting up, I used the bathroom and music was still coming from her room, but it was quieter than before. I opened the door and saw her image lying in the bed. Chessa came running in and jumped on the bed and curled up next to her. Someone was glad to be home.

I walked to her side of the bed and touched the strand of hair that was lying across her cheek. She whispered something and I thought that it might have been my name, but figured that was silly to assume.

"I'm so lost, Cassidy."

I jumped when she whispered, "You're my anchor. We'll find our way back." My eyes scoured her face. Her eyes were still closed. Was she talking in her sleep? "The baby!" What the hell was going on? She must've been dreaming. "I wanted the baby, but I wanted you more."

I didn't know what the hell she was rambling on about and I needed to leave the room before she really woke up. I tried to go back to sleep, but I couldn't. I called the one person who I knew would be up if she was working.

"Jane. Yeah, everything's fine. You're working right. Ok. I was worried I'd wake you. I just, well, I have an odd question and I don't even know if you'll know the answer."

"Ok, what is it?"

"Cassidy was talking in her sleep and she mentioned a baby. Is she just dreaming? I'm so confused."

I heard her sigh. "James, you should talk to Cassidy about this."

My gut wrenched. "Is she pregnant? You know something."

"Not that I know of, but..."

"But what?"

"She was." I dropped down to the bed and pressed my hand across my forehead. "Are you there?"

"Yes. I'm here."

"James, she lost the baby. It was yours. You should talk to her about this, not me. I'm not surprised she hasn't said anything to you though. She took it really hard, but there was nothing anyone could have done. These things happen."

"Is it why we got married?"

"No. It happened after your mother passed away."

"Ok. I'll let you go. Thank you."

I hung up the phone before Jane had a chance to say goodbye. I lay in the tiny bed mentally crushed. Why hadn't Cassidy told me? Should I bring it up? I didn't think it would be a good idea because Lord knew I didn't want her to suffer any more.

I managed to fall asleep and my dreams—or nightmares—had me tossing. In one I remember having a woman bent over a bench at the club and I was fucking her in front of everyone. The room spun and I was in another corridor, alone, and a door closed, but I didn't have any clue who went into the room. Then I was talking with Annie and smashing furniture.

When I woke, the morning was half gone. I carried myself down the stairs and didn't see Cassidy. Her car was still out front and I went back upstairs. Knocking on her door, I opened it slowly and she wasn't there. I started to get worried when I heard the front door open. She saw me at the top of the stairs, closed the door, and walked into the living room without as much as a hello. I'd really fucked things up, again.

~ CASSIDY ~

I was finally back in his arms, his hungry mouth on mine never tasted so good. Then he pulled away after I opened my big mouth asking him to move back into our bedroom. I thought we'd made so much progress. Could I blame Kim? Because I wanted to. Her interruption hadn't stopped the kiss that came later, but, FUCK! Now everything was screwed up again. After putting everything back in my purse, I slammed the door behind him and turned on some music. Loud! If he didn't like it, he could leave. *God, I hope he doesn't leave.*

Pulling off my clothes, I put on a cami and scrolled through my playlist. Walking around in my cami, panties and socks, I put away a basket of clean clothes while the music blared. I was angry and trying to focus on that emotion. *Over You* by Ingrid Michaelson came on and I couldn't stop the tears. I was a sucker for a piano ballad and the song opens with her singing about him wearing his three piece suit. The song was on my playlist for a reason. It reminded me of James.

Wouldn't everything be easier if I could just get over him? I knew that would never happen. I couldn't give up; I swore to myself that I wouldn't. Weeks had passed and he was still there. Something was keeping him there. And if it was pride, then I'd take advantage of it. If the club was the only way I could have him, then the club it would be. I knew immediately that I'd sacrifice having him in my bed at home if it meant I had him in my bed at the club. It was a start. A glimmer of hope buried itself deep inside me. Maybe the club would be the thing to help him remember.

The next morning I woke and swore that my dreams were filled with him. I didn't have time to think about it. I showered, got dressed, and Delaney picked me up for coffee. Before I left, I opened his door to find him sleeping. Hopefully he'd still be home when I returned.

Deciding to confide in Delaney about his reservations, she responded, "Damn! You two still haven't?" I shook my head. "Wow. I'm surprised he's exhibited so much restraint, though not really. You're there for the taking. What's wrong with him?"

I laughed at her remark, "I don't know."

"Maybe you should make a move on him. He won't turn you down."

Staring at my coffee cup, I muttered, "I doubt that. He turned me away last night."

"Well, try harder." She sighed as she saw me fighting internally. "I'm sorry. What are you going to do?"

Shrugging my shoulders, "I'm going to agree." I looked to her, knowing I was blushing. I lowered my voice, "I want him Delaney, and if this is the only way I can get him…"

"Well, I'm going to warn you now. The James you knew and the James you're with are two different beasts. Pun intended."

"What do you mean?"

Sighing, "He had rules, has rules. Most of the girls couldn't handle how well he could compartmentalize everything. Sex and emotions don't mix for him. That's why we were all so happy and surprised when he started pursuing you. He changed."

"Yeah, everyone keeps saying that. I hope I'm doing the right thing."

"I think you are. There's no other choice and time's running out."

"I can't let the divorce happen, but I don't know what else to do. This wall between us needs to come down. If I tell him about it now I'm worried he'll just walk away. Why would he stay if he finds out we were separated?"

"But you said…"

"Yes, we reconciled, but he doesn't remember."

"Cassidy…" She looked to the ceiling and took a deep breath. "I shouldn't be telling you this, but I'm going to. It was more than just a reconciliation for him."

I shook my head, not understanding her meaning. "What do you mean?"

"The poker game." I nodded. "You didn't win, he did. He wants to marry you, the right way."

"But, you said I won."

"He was worried it was too much too fast and didn't want to push you too hard. Don't you see?"

"I see and know it's just something else he doesn't remember."

"He was willing to do anything for you."

"I know and now it's my turn."

I walked in the front door after Delaney dropped me off and he was standing at the top of the stairs. I knew what I was going to do, but I was still hurt. Attempting to ignore him, I shut the door and walked into the living room. I heard his steps pound down the stairs and watched him circle into the living room. He was wearing jersey shorts and nothing else. I groaned and tried to look away.

"You ok?"

"No, I'm not. Unless you want me to start walking around half naked, I'd appreciate the same consideration." He seemed surprised at my words and I added, "You're dangling the carrot when we both know you won't hand it over."

He looked to his crotch before he realized I was being facetious. "Right. Sorry." He walked to the laundry room and walked back out with a shirt on. "Can we talk?"

"Yup." He sat down in the chair facing me as I played with my phone.

"Do you think you can put that down?" I looked up to him, rolled my eyes and set the phone down. I was being a bitch on purpose and I think he knew it. "Listen, about the club."

I put my hand up, "I agree."

His head jerked back a little as his eyes blinked a few times. "Wait, agree to what?"

Huffing, "The club. If Beast wants to come out and play, I agree." I just stared at him, deadpan as he processed my words.

"Cassidy, I have rules. You can't just agree."

"I have rules too and I *can* just agree." We stared at each other, each waiting for the other to speak. "So, what are these rules?"

He leaned back in the chair and quietly observed me. I kept eye contact and smiled, assuring him that he wasn't going to scare me off. "Why don't we start with your hard limits? If you know what those are."

"No blood play, electricity, ball gags, I don't like sleeping alone, umm…" He was surprised at how quickly I continued to rattle things off. "Surprised?"

"A little. I wasn't sure how much I educated you before."

"Anal is ok, but it needs to be worked up to. I enjoy being restrained, spanked, man handled…"

"I'd like to figure out on my own what you enjoy." His tone was serious and I nodded. "What's your safe word?" He didn't think I saw it, but he adjusted himself as my eyes traveled back up to his. "Focus, Cassidy."

"Oh, I'm focusing." I wasn't sure if I should use the same safe word when, "Unicorn," fell from my lips. It was time for a new word.

"Unicorn? Ok." His gaze lingered over me and I wasn't sure what he was thinking about, but I was dying to know. "Are you always so challenging?"

I narrowed my eyes at him, "What do you mean?" He didn't say anything. "If you mean the banter, we've done that since day one. I'm not sure it's something I can turn off with you."

"Ok. We'll manage. I don't mind it." He shifted positions and said, "Now for my rules." I was dying of anticipation, yet dreading what his requirements would be. "I know that they call me Beast, but you'll refer to me as Master or Sir, preferably Master. No kissing, unless I say so. It muddles emotions."

God, Delaney was right. How could I go with no kissing? Why hadn't I listed that as a hard limit? "No kissing!"

"I'm not finished." His demeanor was so different, intimidating and sexy. My clit was already tingling. "You will always wear a blindfold unless I tell you differently. Satin panties, no bra, stockings are optional. I want you to make a playlist of songs that turn you on, that you enjoy, and email it to me. I'll make sure it's playing. And try to steer clear of super sappy songs. They annoy me." I nodded and was looking forward to that. I already had a good start on a list of songs I could send him. "I always wear a condom, but you must use a method, too."

"I, um, I have an IUD." He nodded. I wasn't going to bother telling him I had it put in after the miscarriage because that would just start a whole new conversation I didn't want to have.

"We won't always have intercourse, but pleasure is always my top priority. We, I, need to build up our trust. Can you be ready tonight?"

Tonight! Fuck, yes! "Yes. Tonight should be fine."

"When we're here, there will be no sexual intimacy. You will not instigate and we will continue on as we have been. If and when the time comes for that to change, we'll sit down and discuss it." My heart sank. Baby steps and I kept repeating it to myself. "Do you still agree?"

I returned my gaze to his and thought about everything he'd said. "Yes. I agree."

He headed toward the stairs, "Oh and no masturbating. Your orgasms are mine to claim from now on. Send me the list and be ready to leave at seven."

"Ok."

I sat on the couch in disbelief for a few minutes. Soon, I heard the treadmill and I grabbed my laptop. I started on my playlist and tried to keep sappy songs out of the mix. Of course, I added in some of *our* songs. He'd never know and maybe they'd trigger a memory. Over an hour later he walked down the stairs dressed in jeans and a button-up shirt.

"I emailed you."

"Already?"

"Yup."

He smiled. "Ok. I have to run to the office. I'll be back in time to pick you up." He didn't say anything more and he was gone.

I'd titled the playlist 'The Club' and emailed it to him, including the link to my streaming playlist, as well. I had no idea how he planned on utilizing it. If he hadn't figured out my eclectic music taste, he'd get a taste of it with that playlist. He'd be back in a few hours. I got a few chores done and then headed upstairs to shower again and primp. New razor, salt scrub, lotion, and all the essentials for extra smooth skin were awaiting my use.

I did my hair, leaving it down and lightly curled. It was longer than it'd been in years, of course so was his hair. I applied my makeup the way I remembered him liking. Heavy eyes with a nude lip accentuated my eyes and features. I had music playing and heard a door close. Turning it down, I listened to him walk to his room and then into the hallway bathroom. Looking at the clock, I knew I needed to get dressed. I stared at the two outfits in front of me and debated making a decision.

There was a knock on the door. I was standing in the middle of my room in nothing but my satin panties and bra. I smiled at the torture I was about to unleash. I strolled over to the door and opened it before walking back to the outfits lying on my bed.

"Hey, I, uh…" He stopped talking and when I turned my head, his eyes were planted on my ass. Slowly, I turned around, hands on my hips. His eyes traveled up my body, leisurely, before meeting my gaze. "Sorry, I was just checking to see how long you needed."

Turning back around, because I couldn't keep the smirk off my face, I responded, "Just trying to decide what to wear. Did you want to pick?" I heard his steps approach behind me. "I'd need help with that one."

"Help with what?"

"It's a corset. I can't lace it up alone." I could if I really wanted to, but he didn't know that.

"You can't leave the house looking like that."

"I can't. Why not?"

A low growl vibrated in his throat as he looked at me, "Stop that."

I chuckled, "Stop what?"

"Wear whatever you want as long as you're covered up when we leave." He stormed out of the room and bellowed, "You have five minutes."

Quite pleased with myself, I put on my usual hot pants, my black bra—not caring that you could see the straps—the purple corset that I could easily lace up myself, and my black boots. I pulled a small black jacket out of my closet and put it on. It only covered my shoulders and I hoped he would find it satisfactory to being 'covered up' as he put it.

twenty-one

Consummate

~ JAMES ~

I DROVE IN SILENCE TO MY OFFICE, her words playing over and over in my mind. She couldn't be accused of not being assertive. If she wasn't familiar with the things the club brought to my life, she was a great pretender. And she had one of my business cards and it was eating away at me. I made a mental note to see if I had any emails in that specific account from her. I doubted that she'd be able to handle the no emotions part of it all. Hell, I doubted if I would be able to handle it. But fuck if I wasn't going to enjoy trying.

The Blue Horse renovation was almost complete. The dedication ceremony and grand opening was in a few weeks. We'd managed to keep the surprise from Cassidy and Cal, Jane and Smith had filled me in on the details of that fateful night. Cassidy hadn't discussed much about Holly to me and I understood why. My own actions had me confused. I was planning this great surprise for her, I was attracted to her and I knew I cared about her. But why wouldn't I consummate our relationship like a normal human being?

Sitting at my desk, I scrolled through my DOM email and found nothing. Maybe it was a fluke that she had one of my cards, maybe not.

Pondering my next move, I called Dr. Pratt. He was surprised to hear that we had yet to consummate things. I told him what I was struggling with and he advised against my plan.

"If she's agreed, I can't stop you, but I think—if you want this to begin to function properly—you need to live as normal a life as you can."

"But doc, the club is my normal."

He sighed, "Touché. Please don't shut her out at home. The only thing you'll do is build animosity between the two of you. And if you still have that ridiculous no kissing rule, get rid of it. You can't do that to her. She's your wife."

"Gee, doc, just speak your mind."

"You asked for my opinion as a friend. I'll gladly bill you and give you my professional opinion if you like. Though you'll only hear the same thing." I laughed at that and we said our goodbyes.

Pulling up her email, I opened up the playlist. Scrolling through it I recognized some songs and some I didn't. She had songs ranging from Rob Zombie to Ginuwine and everything in the middle. I compiled the list onto my iPod and began listening. She had a thing for guitar riffs and pianos, which was evident, but not necessarily together in the same song. I laughed wondering if I should have her checked for schizophrenia.

Looking at the clock I realized the day had flown by. After locking up, I headed back home. She wasn't downstairs and I concluded she was in her room when I heard the faint sound of music drifting through the air. She was always listening to music and a lot of it I'd never heard before. She loved her top forty, heavy metal, but she also liked her obscure indie rock. If anything, she was quickly catching me up on the music scene and introducing me to bands I didn't even know.

I knocked on her bedroom door and waited for a moment. To say I was flabbergasted when she opened the door didn't even begin to describe me. She was in her bra and panties and I nearly became irrational. She totally played it off like it was no big deal. I don't even remember what we talked about when I left the room and told her she had five minutes. What the hell was wrong with me?

She walked downstairs and my eyes traveled up her bare legs to the shorts she wore—if they could be considered shorts. Gauging by the look on her face, there was no point in asking her to change. She wouldn't be seen by many anyways. There was no way I'd be able to walk around with her for long without her being propositioned. That's when it dawned on me that she had no collar. People would think she was free game. I'd have to remedy that, but there was no time.

We were halfway to the club when I asked, "You sure you can do this?" She looked to me and nodded. "No emotions, Cassidy. Just pleasure." She was looking out the window and I wasn't sure if I was asking her or myself. Christ. I needed a drink.

We walked in and headed straight downstairs. Checking in at the desk, I was told that my room was ready and waiting. With my hand on the small of her back, I guided her through the corridors. I had no intention of stopping to make small talk with anyone. I opened the door and she walked in with no hesitation and looked around.

"Is the room ok."

She shook her head, "It's our room. It's fine."

It had momentarily slipped my mind that we'd been here before. It was *my* room, so of course she was familiar with it. "Do you want a drink?"

"I wouldn't turn it down."

"Anything in particular?"

She shrugged a shoulder, "Something fruity. Fuzzy navel is fine."

"Ok. I'll be right back."

I walked down the hall to the secured bar that was for those with private rooms. I ordered her drink and got myself a shot of whiskey. I downed mine and headed back to the room with hers. She was sitting on the end of the bed and stood back up when I entered the room. I handed her the drink and she began sucking on the straw.

"I'll be back in a few minutes." I walked over to the stereo system and docked my iPod and hit play on the list she'd provided. "Your list is quite...eclectic."

"I warned you it would be."

"Remove your boots and the jacket. You can leave the top on, for now. There's a blindfold in the dresser. I want you kneeling right here, hands on your knees, with the blindfold on. Understood?"

"Yes."

I walked to her and let my height intimidate her. "Yes..."

Her eyes slightly rolled as she said, "Yes, Master."

"Good girl. I'll be back."

I left the room and took a deep breath. I had to get myself under control. I was known for my ability to be brusque, but control was a big part of it. Women stood in line to be my next playmate, but soon regretted it. I told them over and over I wasn't some challenge. I didn't do love and many of them found that out the hard way. Fucking emotions. They always ruined a good sub.

I grew distracted and spent too much time watching the couples milling about. An old sub of mine caught my eye and I smiled at her. She was collared and she knew the rules. I had to get back to Cassidy anyway. I entered the dimly lit room and found her in complete obedience.

"It's me. Just nod your head unless I ask you a question that requires more than a yes or no. Ok?" She nodded.

I watched as her breathing slowly metered back, having quickened when I entered the room. Removing my shoes, socks, and shirt, I discarded them to the couch. I had no idea what I was going to do with her. Usually I was better prepared. I unbuttoned my jeans after removing my belt and held it in my hands. Walking to her I asked her to stand.

"Give me your wrists." She stuck her hands out in front of her and I wrapped the belt around her wrists. "Is it too tight?" She shook her head. I wanted to do everything with her and knew there wouldn't be enough time. "Come." I pulled her bound wrists behind me and sat on the edge of the bed.

She easily cooperated as I laid her across my lap. Her hair fell down, surrounding her face. My hand touched the back of her knee and I was aware of her body stiffening at my touch. As I moved my fingers up the back of her thigh, she relaxed. The muscles of her neck and shoulders were exposed and I enjoyed watching them flex as I continued my exploration of her legs. She wore the corset she claimed to need help with lacing.

"You lied to me. You didn't need help lacing this."

I tugged on the ribbon and took my time as I pulled it completely apart. The ribbon dropped to the floor as the corset fell to the side. She sighed as my warm hand moved along the now exposed skin of her back. I noticed her bra had no clasp in back as my eyes moved down to the curve of her ass. My hand landed on one cheek and then the other. Tugging her shorts down, I ran my hands over the satin of her panties. I should've instructed her to remove the shorts, but I hadn't.

"Stand up." I helped her to her feet as the corset fell to the floor. "You're trembling. Are you cold?"

"Just a little." I stood and walked to the thermostat and increased the temperature a few degrees. As I walked back to the bed, the heater kicked on. "You didn't have to…"

"Shh. I want you comfortable. Come here." I took her tied hands and pulled her between my legs as I sat back down on the bed as a new song started. The song playing overhead intrigued me and I didn't recognize it. "What song is this?"

"It's *Desire* by Meg Myers."

"I like it." I listened to the words as I trailed a finger over her collar bone and then down between her breasts. "Do you want to please me?"

"Yes…Master."

Goosebumps trailed up her arms and across her abdomen. "Do you want to taste me?" She nodded as she licked her lips. "If you're good, I'll let you taste me, but first I'm dying to taste you."

I stood up and moved around her as she fought to remain still. I imagined her eyes were fluttering, trying to find me through the blindfold. Bending my head into the crook of her neck, I buried my nose in her hair just above her ear. I breathed deep, letting her scent penetrate my soul, before I pulled her earlobe between my teeth. Her breathing increased as she moaned softly. Releasing her ear, I trailed my lips down her neck and bit down on the flesh by her bra strap. My cock was straining against my pants and I undid the zipper, making sure she heard the metal slide apart.

Leaving my briefs on, I pressed my cock against her. I didn't realize how long I'd been craving her until that moment. Turning her, I ran my fingers to the center clasp on her bra. I'd have to undo her hands to remove it without ripping it. Her breasts sprung free as the cups were pushed aside. I pushed her tied hands over her head and began kissing, licking and sucking across her chest. Playing with a nipple in one hand, I sucked on the other as it beaded into a perfect bud in my mouth. I felt her hands gently fall to my hair as her fingers clawed at the band holding my hair in place.

Growling, "Hands up!" She whimpered but did as I ordered.

I fell to my knees and licked my way to her belly button as I pulled her shorts down, making sure to leave the panties in place. Having to get closer, I buried my face between her legs while my hands gripped her hips and ass. Her scent was intoxicating. Looking up to her face, her lips were slightly parted. My hand trailed over her mound and I watched her face as I cupped her and pressed my fingers against her. Her head dropped as she cooed in response to my touch. I fingered the fabric on the inside of her thigh as her hips bucked with excitement.

"You're so wet. I can't wait to fuck you."

"Yes, Master."

Smiling, "It wasn't a question." She didn't respond, only moaned as I continued to rub her through the fabric. I pulled her panties down her legs and removed them and the shorts from around her ankles. "Sit down."

She lowered herself to the bed as I pushed her to her back. I lifted her arms above her head and watched as her torso stretched out in front of me. My eyes fell to the tattoo on her rib cage. It was a phoenix, but the colors were blue and green like a beautiful peacock. Interesting. Grabbing her hips, I pulled her to the edge of the bed and spread her legs. She was already shaking and I didn't know how much more she could handle, but I was going to find out.

Starting at her knee, I kissed my way up her legs until I reached the junction where her thigh ended and her pussy began. I lapped my tongue against her silky soft skin as her hips tried to arch closer. Just as her hips relaxed, I tongued her slit, licking every part of her. Fuck. She tasted better than any dessert and I needed more.

"Don't come. You will wait till I give you permission."

Her cry of objection was quickly overcome with cries of desire as I let my tongue travel into her as deep as it could. I placed my left hand on her pelvis as my right trailed from her leg and up to her opening. Inserting two fingers, she clenched down on them as her back arched. Slowly, I began rubbing them in a come-hither motion as she tried rocking against my hand. If she wanted harder, she'd have to wait.

"Hold still and relax." Her head was lightly thrashing against the satin bedding and I wondered what she'd say if I asked her what she wanted. "Tell me." My fingers continued their motion as she panted. "Cassidy, tell me what you want."

"I, I want you."

"Want me to what?"

Crying out, "Ohh…I want you to tie me up and fuck me till I come. Please."

I couldn't contain my smile as my hands left her body. "Please, what?"

"Ugh! Please, Master!"

"Scoot up higher, to the center of the bed and roll over."

I walked to the boudoir and pulled out various lengths of binds and cuffs. Attaching cuffs to her ankles, I hooked them to the bed and moved to her arms. Having her face down would restrict her more and it would be easier to resist the temptation to kiss her. I removed the belt from around her wrists and replaced it with the fur lined leather cuffs after discarding her bra. I left enough slack in both her arms and legs so that she could get up on all fours.

"Get on all fours." As she did, that I removed my briefs and climbed over her binds and knelt in front of her face. My erection was inches from her mouth as I said, "Open up. It's your chance to taste me."

She parted her lips and I smirked, knowing she wasn't sure how close or far my cock was from her mouth. I pulled her blindfold off as her eyes focused on my naked length. She inched closer and moved her eyes to mine, pausing, and waiting for my consent. I nodded and hissed in a breath as her tongue glided over my tip. She sucked my tip all the way in while her tongue coursed round and round my head. I pushed in farther and she let me. Before I knew it, I was holding her shoulders as I fucked her luscious mouth.

Holy shit! I was going to come if I didn't stop. I pulled out abruptly as she looked at me startled.

"Did I do something wrong?"

Taking a deep breath, I cupped her face. "No, you surprised me." She smiled, like she knew a secret. I tilted my head, "Tell me."

"You said once that I was one of the only ones to ever get you off that way." She licked her lips as she stared into my eyes. "Let me please you."

"Not so fast." I removed myself from in front of her and knelt beside her, running my hands over her back, down her ass, and to her clit. "So wet." She closed her eyes as I slipped my finger around her clit. She was more than ready and I couldn't wait any longer. Grabbing a condom off the table, she watched as I sheathed my length. "Stop looking at me that way. You're asking for trouble."

"I like trouble, Master."

"That's what worries me." Kneeling between her legs I gripped her hair and pulled on it viciously. "Is this what you want?"

Panting, "Yes," her eyes closed as her mouth curved into a smile, "Master."

Now I understood my appeal to her. She came off all shy, demure, innocent, but she was a harlot when pushed the right way. She was the perfect mix I'd sought for so long. She aimed to please, but sought her own pleasure as well. In another life she could've been a switch. Hell, maybe she still could be. I knew she'd give as good as she got, if not better. *Stop with the nonsense and fuck her!* I fisted my cock and rubbed it over her clit. Her warmth easily penetrated my layer of protection and I suddenly wanted the condom gone, but I left it on and slipped my tip into her.

I felt her hips move and demanded, "Don't move, Cassidy!" I smacked one ass cheek and then the other. "Good girl." I slid in a little further and smacked each cheek in turn; repeating the action until I was fully seated inside her. She felt incredible as her walls pulsed around me.

My hands surrounded her waist and moved up to her shoulders as I dropped kisses against her neck. I pulled her up as far as the restraints allowed as my hand wrapped around and held her neck. She dropped her head to my shoulder as my other hand fisted in her hair. Pulling back, I slid out and then back in. The hand the held her neck moved down her abdomen to finger her clit. Her back bucked against me as she cried out.

"Hold on and no, you don't have permission." She whimpered. "Soon, little bird." I wasn't sure why I called her that, but didn't have time to think about it.

I let her drop back down on all fours as I gripped her hips. I pulled almost all the way out and slammed back in to her. I stilled to ensure I hadn't hurt her and had my answer when she pushed back against me. My finger teased and taunted her clit as I fucked her mercilessly. Sweat was dripping down my back and her back was glistening with it as well. Her hips were moving uncontrollably as she whimpered. She was ready and dying for her release.

"Do you want to come, little bird?"

"Yes, James, please."

"It's Master."

"Yes, please, Master. Make me come."

I let the action of my fingers become more deliberate as my hips became more direct in their motion. "Come for me, Cassidy. I want to feel you lose control."

Her hips pushed back repetitively as she milked my cock. Christ, she was tight. "Don't...right...oh. Fuck."

She stopped talking and I noticed she was holding her breath. "Breathe and let the fuck go." Her back relaxed and a calm came over her before her whole body tensed. "That's it. Fucking scream, baby." She let loose a groan that increased with intensity as she came on my cock. I couldn't hold on and pulled my hand from her clit and pounded into her. My balls were already sucked up so high I thought I might die. "Cassidy! Hold. Still." She ceased moving, but her walls continued to clench and release me over and over until I burst into the condom. "Fuck, woman."

I dropped my head to her back as her body sank to the bed under my weight. We were both trembling as I moved out of her. She was sensitive, but not in a way that couldn't take more. She didn't try to fight me when I released her ankles and wrists and pulled her on top of me. I needed to taste more of her. Immediately.

"Straddle my face." She moaned in protest and I just said, "Do it." With shaky legs, her knees sat on each side of my face. "Hold the bed for support." She grabbed onto the headboard as my tongue slowly circled over her.

"Oh!"

Her eyes met mine as she began to slowly rock against my mouth. Her pupils were dilated as I slowly devoured her pussy. It didn't take long before her juices were dripping down my chin. I let her take the lead as she rocked her pussy over my tongue and goatee. Making sure not to move my face, I moved my hands up to her breasts as she rode out the climax that shortly followed. It didn't take much strength to roll her to her back, legs still around my neck as I lapped up her juices, shuddering like a leaf in the wind.

I fingered her the way I had before as she begged for me to stop. "Where there's one, there are usually two and when there are two, there are most definitely three."

I left her clit alone and worked her g-spot until she moaned like a woman possessed. Her legs were spread wide, no energy to hold them up as her hips occasionally flinched against me. When her grip tightened on my fingers, I gently sucked her sensitive clit. Her orgasm left her nearly comatose. Pulling the covers out from under her, I covered her up as she drifted off to sleep. I cleaned myself up and wanted her again, but knew she'd be incredibly tender. Maybe in a few hours she'd be ready for me.

~ CASSIDY ~

WHEN I WOKE I was aware of the dull ache between my legs and that I was alone. We were still at the club so I knew he had to be close by. I used the bathroom and got dressed to go search for him. I found him in a small gathering room and he was talking with Misty and Roxy. SHIT! I tried to slink out of the room before any of them spotted me.

"Cassidy!" Fuck. Roxy had seen me and my chance to hide was gone.

I turned around and put a smile on my face as I walked over. James took a sip of his drink and winked at me. I wasn't sure how to act. I just knew he said no emotions and I was trying to do that. Roxy and Misty continued their usual flirting with me and while I enjoyed it, it no longer interested me like it had before. Trying to hide my yawn, James took notice and put his arm around me.

"Someone needs her sleep. I'll be in touch ladies."

He escorted me back to our room as I told myself that there was no way in hell he'd be in touch with them. This was going to get messy and I was done with messy. I sighed and dropped to the bed.

"We didn't discuss group play." He looked to me as I felt myself pale. "I'm not interested in sharing you with another man, but Misty and Roxy are definitely into you."

"No!"

He looked a little surprised. "That's it. Just no. You don't get to decide. As my slave…"

I dropped my head to my hands and cut him off. "Yes, just no."

"Ok. It wouldn't be considered cheating…"

"NO! Please drop it."

"Why are you being so wary?" He stood and glared at me as I felt the walls closing in on me. "What don't I know?"

Fuck! Why was he so fucking observant? "James."

"Master!"

"Fuck you!" I stood and walked closer to him. "You wanted no emotions while we were here. If you want to ask me at home, where it's ok to talk about personal things, that's fine. But while we're here, we're just fucking. Right? Wasn't that the agreement?"

He glared at me and if he thought I'd just lie down and take his shit he had another thing coming. Turning me around, his arms encased me and I couldn't move as he breathed in my ear. "That was the agreement. Do you want me to fuck you, again?" His hand moved to my crotch and I whimpered at his gentle prodding. "Because you will *not* control this. I control *this*." He released me and took a step back. "Get your things. We're leaving."

THE NEXT WEEKEND we were headed to the club again as I reflected on what'd happened after our mild confrontation. We'd talked earlier in the week and I just decided to let everything out. I told him that we'd separated after the death of his mother and during that time he led me to believe he was fucking Melissa which ultimately led to me fucking Paul. I told him that on one occasion Misty and Roxy were part of it. He was furious and I wasn't sure if that was good or bad. He could only be furious if he cared, right?

After a couple days of silence he had said he wanted to move past it and agreed to no group play. I was shocked, but relieved. He also said he wanted to stop the divorce proceedings and while I wanted to jump for joy into his arms, he was still keeping me at arm's length. I told him we'd need to call the judge and Annie, but that it was up to him to do so.

It almost seemed too easy, like I was waiting for the rug to be pulled out from under me. But life was short and I didn't want to fight about it. We'd fought enough. I just prayed he wasn't playing me.

twenty-two
Desperate

~ CASSIDY ~

It was September. I had grown accustomed to our arrangement and easily made it through the days, knowing that come the nights and weekends I'd have my Beast and Master back. Though, I missed kissing him more than I could admit.

"Any requests for tonight?" I looked over to him and wondered how far I could push him.

"I'd love to dance with you, first." He observed me quietly and said he'd think about it.

We arrived at the club a few minutes later and he escorted me to the dance club instead of directly downstairs. I couldn't wipe the smile off my face as he ordered me a drink and smiled back at me. He was being affectionate and I had a hard time remembering that it only happened in the club. His hand was caressing my back and he held my hand when he led me to the dance floor. It would've been all too easy for me to lose myself in him. And I did, knowing the club was the only place I could do so.

Dancing was clearly something he was able to do before the amnesia. He grinded up against me like a pro and I grinded back, losing myself in the music and not him—or so I told myself. A few songs later we headed downstairs, clearly both primed and ready for action. He had demanded silence that night and I was playing along, eager to let my other senses guide me. I'd also gotten good at compartmentalizing, too. While at the club I only referred to him as Master and not James. It helped.

I was blindfolded, hands tied behind my back, the way he liked it. Master leaned in and I could feel his breath on my forehead. His hand turned my chin up, slowly. I inhaled his sweet breath and something inside me shifted, yearned to touch him, ached to kiss him, and look upon him more than the other nights. My tongue licked my lips, without permission to do so. I knew the rules. No kissing, no talking, always blindfolded and no emotions. Just pleasure. We had an agreement. Fuck, if he wasn't evoking emotions from me, this man whom didn't know me like he once had. It wasn't supposed to happen.

"Little bird..." My footing was compromised when his body pressed up against mine, his lips hovered above mine and he abruptly stepped away. His arms braced my shoulders as I felt his breath against my lips once more.

He backed me up against the wall as a shudder ran through me. He was going to kiss me and if he kissed me I wouldn't be able to go back. "Please don't."

"I said no talking." His hands held my hips as he pressed his groin into me and his mouth traveled my neck. I was vaguely aware of my fingernails digging into the palms of my hands when he asked, "Don't what?" His voice was deep and soft and turned my insides to mush. His lips kissed my cheek, across to my ear and back again.

"James, please. You may not remember what your kisses did to me, but I remember. Please don't kiss me if it's only something you want for tonight. I can't..."

"Can't what?"

"You're right. Kisses evoke emotion. I can't kiss you and not fall in love with you all over again."

I didn't expect what happened next. I knew he'd walk away from me, get himself under control and we'd go back to our no kissing arrangement. Instead his lips crucified my own. My arms strained behind my back, desperate to touch him. My chest hurt as my heart constricted. I was dreaming. There was no way he was really kissing me. When he pulled away he took my blindfold with him. My eyes remained closed, I couldn't look at him.

He stroked my face, down my neck and across the top of my chest. His hands cupped my face as his thumbs moved across my cheekbones and then over my lips. He brought his mouth down to mine again and when his tongue licked at the seam of my lips I whimpered. Pulling back, he wiped the tears falling from my closed eyes.

"Cassidy, look at me." I hesitated before opening my eyes. "Why are you crying?" He quickly unbound my hands and looked in my eyes awaiting my answer.

"Because this isn't real."

He held my wrists between his hands and then kissed each hand. "What if it was real?" His green eyes penetrated my soul. He was killing me.

My chest heaved as my words came out in broken breaths. "If it was real I'd tell you that I was falling in love with you, again. I loved you then and I love you now." He just stared at me and I wasn't sure if he was in shock, angry, confused. I couldn't tell. "And if it was real you'd tell me emotions just get in the way. So, let's go back to our agreement. You never kissed me, it didn't happen."

A wicked grin spread across his lips and my breath caught, scared to death at what he might say. "If it was real I'd tell you that I was falling in love with you, too. My memory of you, of us is almost non-existent, warped, scattered, but I'm falling for you, Cassidy."

I shook my head, "But it isn't real…"

His lips closed over mine as he whispered, "It is real." I stared into his eyes, looking back and forth between each green globe. "I love you, Cassidy." He smiled.

I let out a short laugh as the tears fell, but they were happy tears and I threw my arms around his neck. "I love you, James. Promise me it's real."

"Promise. Now kiss me."

I leaned in slowly and kissed his full lips. He lifted me up and held me above him, his arms around my ass. Pulling the tie from his hair, I did what I'd wanted to do for weeks on end. I tangled my fingers in his dark chocolate locks and tugged as I heard the growl I loved so much. He sat down on the couch as I straddled his lap.

Breaking the kiss he asked, "Do you want to go home?"

I smiled, "I love it here, being here with you, but yes. Take me home." He set my feet on the floor and I put my hand on his chest, "Only if you're moving back into our bedroom."

Shrugging his shoulder he sighed deeply. *Shit!* "If I have to." He winked and I smacked his chest. "Get dressed. I'm taking you home and we'll continue this there." He smacked my ass as I turned to get dressed.

He'd been kinder and gentler with me when we were at home, but my punishment—which we both knew wasn't really punishment—at the club had grown more severe. He'd been pushing my limits with different kinds of bondage and I was growing fond of rope and the many knots he was able to tie around my body. Had his walls been breaking down this whole time, me oblivious to it?

He took a detour as we headed home and pulled into the alcove he always used to go to, when he remembered me. When he got out of the truck, I waited for him to open my door. He offered me his hand and I hopped out of the truck. It was a warm September night and it smelled like it might rain. He dropped the tailgate and pulled me back against him as we stared at the stars in the sky.

"I've never brought anyone here before, but something's been nagging at me to bring you here." His chin was resting on the top of my head as he pulled me a little closer.

"I hate to break it to you, but you used to bring me here." He turned me to face him. "Sorry."

He shook his head, "Don't be sorry. That makes me happy. Did I ever tell you why I loved this spot?" I shook my head. If the place had importance to him I was clueless about it. "Jason and I used to come here in high school." He was staring into the field below us as he pointed. "We learned how to play football in that field as kids and partied here when we were teens."

Turning, I dropped my head to his chest and held him. He'd never confided that in me. And while this new-old James didn't remember me, he opened up to me easier than my original James had. We'd discussed his time in the Army a lot since the accident and he did it freely. We got to know each other on a level that had never happened and probably wouldn't have had the accident not happened.

"You should pick a song to play. I want to dance with you."

I smiled and ran to the cab of the truck and scrolled through the playlist. The song I chose was fitting—as usual—if you listened to the words. The twilight was finally lifting and I could see the sun rising. He was the only star in my night sky *and* my day, another would never compare. *Cosmic Love* by Florence and The Machine began to play as he held me close and we danced. I listened to his heart beat and a peace settled over me. I knew he may never remember our life together, but we were building a new one. I had him back. I squeezed him a little tighter as I counted my blessings.

His hand found my chin and lifted it to his lips. The kiss was sensual and full of promise. "I'm sorry I left you in the dark."

"You didn't mean to."

"I want you to know this. No matter if I ever remember or I never do; I'll never leave you alone in the dark again, Cassidy. You stuck by me when I think any other person would've walked away."

"I love you."

He smiled, "I know. I love you, too."

Our kiss was slow and passionate as our hands took their time roaming over the body of the other. He picked me up and set me on the tailgate as his hands moved under my shirt and my own did the same. I hadn't been able to touch him like that since before our arrangement and I reveled in the feel of my fingers roaming over his chest and through the hair that graced it. The heavens opened up and we were soaked by the time our lips pulled apart.

I was laughing and looked up to the sky as the warm rain fell down on us. He seemed to appreciate it as well as he grabbed my face and kissed me again. Our tongues glided and teased one another and before I knew it, we were both shirtless.

"I should take you home."

I shook my head, "Make a new memory with me. A new first for us both, together." He tilted his head. "Make love to me, James, in the rain."

He didn't speak, simply acted. Pulling a jacket out of the back seat of his truck, he laid it on the ground. Our clothes were piled on the tailgate and I laid myself down on his jacket, supporting myself on my elbows. His figure towered over me in the moonlight. The rain dripped over him and I wanted to lick every inch of his body. He knelt down between my legs and held my leg in his hand, kissing my knee before he laid me down.

"I, I don't know if I can be gentle."

"I didn't ask you to be gentle." His eyes narrowed as I added, "I said to make love to me. I didn't say you had to be gentle."

Before he could say anything, I grabbed his face and brought his lips to mine. When he slid into me we both groaned, our eyes locked on one another. It was the first time we'd done missionary since rediscovering each other and it was the only way I would've wanted it. He pulled my leg up and the angle had me crying out in pleasure. His wet hair dangled over us and threw droplets of rain on me as he pounded away.

"Cassidy."

"It's ok. I want you to come."

"No! Not yet."

We grappled with one another searching for the perfect position to drive us both mad. Somehow he managed to get us to a seated position, still on his jacket, as I wrapped my legs around his waist. Leaning back, I cried out as I found the friction I needed. My clit rubbed back and forth against his rain soaked skin as I rode him. His hands squeezed my breasts as my hair slapped against my back with each thrust. It wasn't long and I was crying out.

"Come for me little bird. Just like that."

My body became frenzied as I recognized the signs that he was close, too. I continued to ride him until his release claimed him. He bit and sucked on my neck as he shot into me while I tugged on his hair. We were both catching our breath when a gust of wind came through. A shiver ran through me and he insisted we get dressed and go home. I couldn't wipe the smile off my face the whole drive.

We ran up the stairs and I started the shower. We both had chattering teeth like it was the middle of winter. He climbed in with his clothes on, saying it'd be easier to take them off once he could feel his fingers and toes. I climbed in after him in nothing but my shirt, having already removed my shorts. The warm water almost felt painful against my cold skin.

I started to pull the shirt up and over my hips as he pleaded, "Please leave it on. I don't think I can handle the sight of you naked and wet."

I noticed the tent that had already formed in his shorts and smiled at his amazing libido. Dropping the shirt I cooed, "Turn around, then you won't have to look at me."

His eyes struggled to remove themselves from my figure and then moved back to my eyes as he refused. "No."

The water sprayed down my body as we stared each other down. "I, but why?"

"Cassidy." What was he thinking about? Plotting, I had no doubt. "Take off the shirt." I was more than willing to oblige. I removed the shirt and threw it over the shower door. "If you want to help me, you have to do as I say."

"Am I speaking with James or with Master?"

Smirking, he replied, "Who do you think?" I just stared at him. "Turn around." He grew quiet as I turned away, but I let my eyes linger on him. He lowered his head into the stream of water, his hair dropped past his shoulders. His eyes moved to mine as he ordered, "Put your hands up."

I raised my arms above my head as he watched the curves of my body change with my movement. He was fisting his cock under his shorts and his free hand ran up my spine. He pulled the shorts down, still stroking his dick. Tangling his fingers in my hair, he pulled my head back as he peered over my body. He was exquisite as the water trickled over his body and onto mine and down my breasts.

My breathing increased as my body responded to his. His head dropped to my shoulder, nipping and sucking as I moaned.

"Kiss me little bird." I turned my face up and awaited his lips. My hand fell back into his hair as I ran my hands through it. "Fuck."

He was stroking himself more vigorously and I was so turned on watching him do it. Our lips were barely touching when I panted, "Do it, James. Come for me."

He increased the pressure and speed of his hand as my other hand gripped his hip, pulling him closer. He aimed just in time, his seed shooting onto my back. His free hand clutched my breast as the waves rolled over him. When he'd regained himself, I turned around as he backed away. He walked into the stream of hot water and pulled me to him. My hands ran over his lower back as his own washed the remnants of his orgasm from mine.

WE WERE LYING in bed, wrapped in his arms, I knew without a doubt that with him was where I belonged. His strong hands ran up and down my back and to my hip as I fingered the hair on his chest, staring up into his eyes. We were both glowing. We spent a while talking when I remembered something he said at the club.

"What did you mean when you said your memory of us is almost non-existent and scattered?" I watched his face as his eyes looked to the ceiling and then down to me and back again.

His hand was in my hair as he confessed, "I've been having dreams for a while now. I didn't really think about them, but as things started coming together, I realized that the dreams are memories. They have to be."

Emotion tugged at my heart as I smiled at him, "You're dreaming of me?"

His hooded eyes looked to mine as he rolled us to our sides, facing one another. "I think I've always dreamed of you, before we even met." I closed my eyes as he stroked my face and kissed my eyelids. I knew if I tried to speak I'd just start crying. "I've tried so hard the past few weeks to be only your Dom, your Master, but I can't do it. I want to be your friend, your confidant...your lover." He pulled me closer to him, my face tucked into his chest. "And most important I want to be your husband. I tried waiting for the memories to return, feeling like my body was betraying me. But, my body knew it before I did. You're my wife. We belong to each other; every part of me is yours." I lifted my chin and tried to speak and he shushed me. "We're both exhausted. You need to sleep. Remember, sleeping with someone is still new to me. I'll stay with you as long as I'm sleeping."

I snuggled back into him and said, "I'll take it."

When I woke, the early signs of morning were penetrating the curtains. He was still wrapped around me, quietly snoring in my ear. I glanced at the clock. At least six hours had passed and he was still in bed, sleeping. Finally.

~ JAMES ~

SHE'D JUST CONFESSED that we had been married, though apparently separated, and she slept with Paul. What the FUCK? Then she told me her actual history with Paul. I was livid, furious, and didn't want to believe the other things she'd said. I didn't give a shit about the Misty and Roxy part of it all. It was Paul. He'd worked alongside me the whole time screwing my wife. I screamed and yelled at her and then left before things got out of control.

I was pacing my office, trying to process it all. "FUCK!" I swiped everything off my desk and watched it crash to the floor.

My door flew open and Smith barged in. He took in the scene and closed the door behind him. "Do you want to talk about it or keep destroying shit?"

"Don't you fucking antagonize me." He crossed his arms and leaned against the wall and waited. "Did everyone on the planet know, but me, that my wife was fucking one of my best friends?"

"Whoa. Sit down." I glared at him. "James, sit the fuck down and shut up." It was rare that Smith got mad, but when he did, you listened. I threw myself down on the couch and he handed me a bottle of water. "Do you remember anything?"

Pulling the bottle from my lips I replied, "No. She confessed."

"Well, did she tell you that you made her life a living hell? You let her believe that you were fucking around with Melissa."

"That's no excuse!"

"Dude! Melissa tried breaking you guys up for months and then you let Cassidy believe Melissa was sharing your bed. As far as I know, Cassidy didn't sleep with Paul until AFTER you two signed divorce papers."

"Separation papers."

"What the fuck ever. I'm not going to argue the specifics with you. She's been loyal to you when I've debated walking away. You put her through hell."

"What the hell?"

"What the hell, nothing. If I did to Delaney the things you did to Cassidy my balls would be dangling around her neck. And you never even slept with Melissa as far as I know." He glared at me as I thought everything over. "I don't know what's worse. That you didn't sleep with Melissa or that you let Cassidy believe you did."

"Alright. Enough. I get it."

He sat down across from me. "Why do you care so much? I mean, I know you care, but I thought you were keeping emotions out of it."

How the hell did he know that? "God dammit, Delaney!"

"Don't blame her."

"Cassidy's opening her big mouth and now I know to whom."

"They're friends. In case you forgot, Cassidy doesn't have many of those."

"Well Delaney didn't need to tell you what Cassidy told her in confidence."

"Give me a break. It's me. I know about the fucking mole on your left nut."

I glared at him. "I don't have a fucking mole on my left nut!"

"Dude. I was just making a point. Chill the fuck out." I finished the bottle of water and crushed it between my fingers. "You need to decide if you're in this or not. She's one tough broad, but she's been through enough. Do you remember anything?"

Running my hands through my hair, I rubbed my hands over my face and then propped my elbows on my knees. "I keep having dreams about a woman."

"Cassidy?"

Shrugging my shoulders, "I don't know. There's never a face and everything is in black and white. What do you know about the pregnancy?" I looked to him and saw a sliver of grief in his own eyes.

"It was your kid and you were both devastated by it. We all were." He stared off into space for a minute and I wondered what he was reflecting on. He and Delaney didn't have kids and didn't have any desire to have any as far as I knew.

"I can't stop thinking about her."

His hand clapped down on my shoulder. "Dude, stop torturing

yourself. You're falling for her." I looked at him out of the corner of my eye. "Your secret is safe, for now." He winked and then walked out of my office.

I just wanted one thing. To remember everything as it happened. The fucking glimpses from my dreams and stories from my friends weren't enough. My life had become a fucking jigsaw puzzle and I'd had enough of it. It'd been almost two months since the accident and nothing. I wanted to make it work with Cassidy; I just wasn't sure what all that entailed.

THAT EVENING I brought dinner home and told her I didn't want to move forward with the divorce. I knew that much was true. She smiled brightly and I wanted nothing more than to kiss her, but I just couldn't. My head and heart still hurt from the knowledge she'd been unfaithful. Though, was it really considered cheating given all the circumstances surrounding it?

"I forgive you." Her mouth dropped open as she stared at me.

"James."

"No, it doesn't change anything. Not yet. But, I get it and I meant what I said about the separation, divorce, whatever it is. I don't want to give up on it…this."

She stared at her plate and nodded. "Ok, but you have to do it. You need to call Judge Mathis." I nodded and retreated upstairs for the rest of the evening.

A couple nights later, we got home from the club late. We both had work to do the next day and agreed to sleep in our own beds. I carried her up the stairs. She was exhausted and I'd been exceptionally rough on her. She refused me at first when we pulled back in the drive, but when she stepped out of the truck she almost fell over.

"Stop being stubborn." I swooped her up in my arms and into the house.

I laid her down on the bed and undressed her. Leaving her alone in nothing but her bra and panties nearly did me in. She was out before I left her bedside and I stood and watched her sleep for far longer than I should have. Not kissing her was becoming increasingly difficult. The only thing that helped was not being face to face with her when we fucked. I knew I should just come clean and tell her how I felt. I was almost positive she would reciprocate my feelings.

Feelings. Something I'd kept out of every equation for so long. Melissa was the closest I'd let a woman get to me and that was just because of how long I'd known her. Cassidy was filling a void in me I didn't know existed and I still couldn't wrap my brain around the fact that I'd let her in. She'd seen and accepted parts of me that I never wanted to reveal to anyone.

Love. Unconditional love.

Cassidy had handed over her body to me, with me not remembering her, and I knew her heart was there in the mix, though she denied it. It was more than silly wifely duties. She could've easily let me go and discarded me after the accident. I was used to people using me for what they needed and walking away with no qualms. Cassidy was different. She was mine and in the process she'd made me hers.

It was September and I woke in a cold sweat that night, like so many nights before. The dream ran rampant in my head again. This time

I had heard her voice or my imagination was playing tricks on me. It was Cassidy in my dreams and we were in her bed and it wasn't the bed at the club. We were saying and doing things unfamiliar to me, but probably normal for any regular couple. We were kissing, cuddling and whispering secrets to one another. She wore a necklace, but I couldn't make out what the charm was. I had to try to remember. These had to be memories. And if they weren't, they were things my body craved, wanted, needed, and desired. I had to let her know.

Having spoken to Annie about Cassidy having my DOM card, Annie filled me in. Apparently during our time apart Annie and I had concocted a plan for me to be Cassidy's DOM. The plot was complicated, but just validated my feelings for her. I had been willing to go to extremes then to have her and now—still not remembering her—I was willing to do the same.

That morning, with my DOM email open, I emailed her.

> Dear Cassidy,
> I hope this email finds you well.
> Annie gave me your name and
> mentioned that you might be
> looking for a new DOM. I won't
> go into any details unless I hear
> back from you.
>
> ~Master B

Only a few hours passed before I got a response.

> Master B,
> Thank you for your interest.
> However, I regret to inform you
> That I am deeply in love with
> my current DOM and I'm collared
> to him in every way imaginable.
>
> ~Cassidy

I had the answer I needed. I took her to the club that night and knew exactly what I had planned. It wasn't until I had her tied up and *blindfolded* that I had regretted taking her to the club.

Home. I wanted to take her home. My heart nearly burst at her words and she thought it was all pretend. I loved her and had fallen for her weeks earlier. I think I knew the night of the carnival and it had taken me by surprise. I knew I wanted her, had to have her, and demanded it be the only way I knew how; as my sub.

Once we made it home that night, after our debauchery in the rain, and I was lying in that big bed with her, limbs tangled and hands caressing, did I finally get it. *She* was my home, my anchor, my north star. She fell asleep in my arms and my brain flashed white as my vision left me.

I was lying on the table as Styx dug his needle into my back. "Why an anchor?"

"It's simple, really. She's been mine and it's time that I become hers. We're having a baby."

"Wow. Congrats man. I'm happy for you."

"Thanks. Me too."

The flash of white dissipated and my vision returned. I blinked rapidly as my eyes adjusted to the dark room. She rolled over as I pulled her back tight against my chest. Holy shit. I finally really, truly remembered something. I'd seen the tattoo in the mirror a few days after being home from the hospital and was surprised. I didn't ask her or anyone else about it, figuring it wasn't that important. Then, it happened again.

We were sitting on the couch downstairs and I was removing her boots and asking her about tattoos. I spotted the anchor on her ankle and she told me about Holly's tattoo. The conversation happened in warp speed and soon we were fucking on the couch.

It stopped and I was so exhausted that I couldn't keep my eyes open any longer. I fell asleep wondering what the sudden cause for these small memories coming back was. It had to be her.

twenty-three
Dedication

~ JAMES ~

IT WAS THE END OF SEPTEMBER and the night of the dedication ceremony for the art studio. Cassidy still had no idea. She just knew that I wanted to take her out and I asked her to wear a dress. I'd kept the couple of memories that I'd remembered to myself. I didn't want to get anyone's hopes up and no other memories had come back to me since that night. The only thing that was eating at me was that necklace I kept seeing in my dreams. I still couldn't make out what the charm was, except that it was black.

Earlier in the week Delaney, Smith and I had been at the penthouse at the hotel picking up all the artwork. I stood in the middle of what had apparently been my bedroom and looked around. No memory came back to me. I still had a few miscellaneous items there, but didn't think anything of it. I'd also been distracted from looking further when Cassidy called me on my cell.

"What did you do?"

"Excuse me?" I grew nervous, not sure what she was referring too. I had too many plans in motion and there was no telling what one she may have found out about.

"Did you pay off my student loans?" She sighed when I didn't respond. "I just got a letter saying everything has been paid in full. James?"

"Yes. I paid them off."

"You can't just do that."

"Why not?"

Groaning, "You're so frustrating. They were my loans to pay off."

"Cassidy, what's mine is yours. I have the money and it's silly to pay all that interest when I can more than cover the expense." When she didn't respond I said, "If you're that worried about it, you can work off the debt." I could hardly contain my laughter.

"Excuse me"

"We can come up with a payment plan that involves bondage and blow jobs."

"Oh. My. God. You are so frustrating. Goodbye."

"I love you. I'll be home soon!"

Smiling at the memory, I waited downstairs and heard her heels click on the stairs. She walked into the living room and looked stunning. She was wearing a black cocktail dress and her hair was pulled to the side. She'd gone all out. Her phone buzzed and she pulled it out of her clutch and checked the text message.

"Melissa just landed in Atlanta."

"And why is she there, again?" I knew Paul was there, but that didn't make sense.

"Cecily. She's made a few trips down there to see Cecily. Lena went a couple times, too, but not this time." She looked up to me and saw the question in my eyes. Laughing, "No. Lena had a crush on Paul, but that's it. She's dating Ryan."

"I wasn't thinking about Lena."

"Melissa…and Paul? Umm…no."

"If you say so." She put the phone back in her clutch as I escorted her to the door. "We'll be late."

"Yes, you keep saying that. And are you going to tell me yet where we're headed?"

"Nope." I walked her to the truck and when she slid in I handed her a blindfold.

"Really?"

"Yup." I watched her put it on and then walked to my side of the truck. "So, the house is coming along."

"The house?" She looked to me and tried lifting her head so she could sneak a peek out of the corner of the blindfold.

"Stop peeking! Yes, the house."

"Oh, I. I guess I wasn't sure if you were still working on it."

"Of course I am. Though, I'm not sure when it'll be finished. I'd like us to sit down and go over everything, since I don't remember anything you wanted. All I have is the drawings to go over."

"You still want to live out there. I mean, with everything, I didn't know if that had always been a dream of yours or not."

I grabbed her hand and brought it to my lips. "Yes. I want to live out there. I've lived in the chaos of the city long enough."

"It's a long commute…for us both."

"Well, it's a good thing we're both in charge and can make our own hours." She laughed. "And, that's what home offices are for. Speaking of work. How's the masquerade and auction planning going?"

"Good. Lena has taken over the masquerade and I'm handling the auction. I'm just not ready to hand everything over to her. She's capable, I'm just having control issues." I chuckled at that. "Don't laugh! Your Aunt Bev is making poor Lena crazy."

"Oh, how so?"

"She's changed the color scheme and we had to send out notices to all the guests. Apparently she's insisting on everyone wearing black or white only. It's ridiculous."

I smiled knowingly and agreed with her, "That takes all the fun out of it. My guess is everyone will wear black."

"Exactly. I love black, don't get me wrong, but I'm going to miss seeing all the purples and reds that are usually present."

"I'm sure everything will be fine. Don't stress about it." We drove for a few more minutes and I pulled into the parking lot. "We're here. Ahh, don't take it off. Not yet."

I parked and saw everyone there. Dad, Cal, Jane, Smith, Delaney, Lena, Ryan, and a few more people, including Cassidy's father, Dave. The renovation had turned out beautifully. News reporters would arrive soon and I thanked the heavens that the story hadn't been spilled yet. I helped her out of the truck and walked her to the center of the parking lot. Everyone was quiet as they circled around behind us.

"Ok. You ready."

Nodding her head, she said, "Yes!"

I took a deep breath and removed her blindfold. I still didn't remember what had happened, but I'd read the news stories and everyone had filled me in with their side of the story. I knew it would be hard for her to be there again, where Holly had died, but I hoped she'd be able to move past it with all our friends and family there.

Her eyes adjusted as she blinked a few times. I saw the emotion wash over her as it registered where we were. "I, why are we here? Why did you bring me here?"

I held her hand and put my other one on her back. "We're all here. Take a look."

She looked behind her and saw everyone there. She was confused as Cal walked over and said, "Look at the sign, Cass."

I watched as she hesitated. Cal took her other hand as her eyes looked at the small sign over the back door. The big one out front was even better. Her eyes scanned the sign. I knew what it said because I'd looked at it a million times.

Her voice was barely a whisper when she asked, "I, who did this?"

Oh, God. Maybe I'd misjudged. It hadn't been my plan, well, it was mine, but I didn't remember it. Delaney and Smith had to fill me in and I thought it was a great idea. "I'm sorry. I thought…"

She looked at me as she choked out, "Don't be sorry." She looked back to the sign. "Halos and Wings Art Studio." Then she read the line below, "In memory of Eva Benedict and Holly Madison." She released Cal's hand and placed it over her chest. "I, um, I'm speechless. Did you do this?"

I squeezed her hand and nodded. "I wanted to turn something that was bad into something good." Before I could go into more detail, she threw her arms around my neck. "I hope its ok."

Whispering into my ear, "Ok? It's amazing. I can't believe you did this."

"I had to."

"When did you do this?"

"Apparently I started planning back in May or June. Smith and Delaney helped." Pulling away, she looked to everyone who was there and blushed. She linked our hands and thanked everyone for coming. "Come on. I want to show you the inside before the reporters get here."

We walked in the back door and down the hallway. Where the bar had once been was now a counter and some shelves filled with pottery to paint. At another end of the room easels lined the wall with various blank canvases and at the other end were a few long tables where you could paint the pottery.

"Oh my, God. It's amazing." It was then that she spotted the art work on the walls. "James!"

"Another secret even I forgot about. Apparently I bought all of these before I took you to that gallery in June." She smacked my arm, "Hey! I don't remember."

"You're lucky you don't." She laughed as we looked around for a while longer.

Soon it was time for the official dedication out front. She stood by me, a smile on her face as the reporters flashed their cameras and I made a small speech. Any profit from the studio would go to the charity my mother had established, years prior for the local foster kids, and all of those donations would be made in Holly's name.

When we were getting in the truck to head home, I had a nagging feeling that I was forgetting something. I walked around to my side, after closing her door, and stopped near the tailgate and pinched my brows together as the flash of white happened again.

I was looking at a painting of Cassidy and then I was holding a necklace in my hands. The memories were separate but my brain had thrown them together in a jumbled mess. I closed the lid on the necklace and placed it in a drawer. The penthouse.

I had to go to the penthouse. I climbed in the truck, "Hey, I need to make a stop at…" There was a tap on my window and I rolled it down. Smith and Delaney invited us for a nightcap at the hotel bar. Perfect timing. "Yeah, I was headed that way. Sounds like a plan."

Cassidy tilted her head at me, "What are you up to?" I just shrugged my shoulders and she didn't press the issue. I had a massive headache and hoped that I would find what I was looking for at the penthouse.

We walked into The Benedict and I sent the three of them to the bar. "I'll be down in a few minutes." Cassidy glared at me and I assured her, "Promise, I'll be right back."

I got on the elevator and headed upstairs. When the bell chimed for my floor and I stepped out, I looked down the hall to the only other room that occupied my floor. Another memory paralyzed me.

She walked toward me in an olive green and black dress with a filigree mask on. I'd know her anywhere. I was outside myself as I watched the exchange we had. I watched as we stepped into the elevator.

Then the flash was gone. Shit. I stumbled to the penthouse headed toward the stairs.

I looked to the kitchen counter and remembered the first time I brought her here. I handed her water and then I led her up the stairs. I followed myself and her as they walked into the bedroom. I helped her take her dress off and then her heels and she fell over on top of me. We were laughing on the floor and then I was lying next to her and woke to find her gone.

It ceased again as I looked around for the painting. It wasn't there. I staggered to the other bedroom and found nothing. DAMMIT! I searched through my workout room and then headed back to the bedroom. I started turning the place upside down. Drawers were emptied to the floor. Where was it?

"James?" I was aware that it was Smith, but I didn't have time. "What are you doing? Did you lose something?"

"Go away!" Talking to myself, more than him I shouted, "Where the fuck is that necklace?"

I walked into the large closet and started turning over drawers in there and emptying the shelves. My hands shook when I found the two velvet boxes, each different in color and size. I opened the one that was clearly a ring box and my grandmother's ring stared back at me.

"Jimmy, I raised you smarter than that. She wants a ring."

"Mom, I'm not getting her a ring. Besides, I wouldn't have a clue to what she'd want."

"What about grandma's ring?"

"That was your engagement ring. I'm not taking your ring. Please drop it mom."

"Dude, are you ok? Where'd you just go?" He looked at the ring, but didn't comment as I closed the lid and handed it to him.

"Keep that safe for me." He just nodded and put it in his pocket. I opened the other box and looked at a black diamond charm in the shape of a blackbird. "Blackbird." I dropped to my knees.

Smith hunched down with me, probably worried I was having a stroke. "James, talk to me. What's going on?"

"I remember." Gripping his arm I pleaded with him. "Get Cassidy. Now!"

He nodded, "Ok, but you're not dying, right?"

I smirked, "No, I'm not dying. Please, get her now. It's important and don't fucking show her that ring or tell her I remember!"

~ CASSIDY ~

DELANEY AND I WERE SIPPING on our drinks when Smith decided to go see what was taking James so long. I was eager to get James home and show him my appreciation for everything he'd done for me, when he hadn't owed me anything. I still couldn't wrap my mind around everything he'd done. Delaney and Smith needed to be thanked, too.

"Thank you, Delaney."

"For what?"

I rolled my eyes at her and smiled. "For everything. You've really become a great friend to me. After everything that's happened over the past, well, year almost, I just can't thank you enough."

"It's been my pleasure. I'm really glad that we're friends." We clanked our glasses and took a drink. "So, how's it going with James?"

I blushed as usual, "Great. I'm so happy. With the amnesia, I just thought there was no way he'd let me in, but, he's almost more open with me now than he was before. It's weird."

"Not weird. He's been through a lot of turmoil over the last year, you too. I think the amnesia may have been a good thing. He was able to get to know you without all the baggage hanging over you two."

I nodded my head, "Yeah, I guess you could be right."

Snickering she boasted, "I'm always right!"

It was then that I saw Smith rushing to the table. James wasn't behind him and I immediately grew worried. I stood and asked him what was wrong before he had a chance to say anything.

"I think he's ok, but he needs you."

Grabbing my purse I spit out, "You think. What does that mean? Is he in the penthouse?"

Smith simply nodded as I ran to the elevator. He and Delaney were close behind and it was a good thing because I didn't have my keycard with me. Throwing the door open for me, I strode past Smith into the penthouse and looked to him. He pointed to the stairs. I ran up and headed straight for the bedroom. It looked like the place had been ransacked.

"James? Where are you?"

"Cassidy!"

I found him sitting on the floor of his huge walk-in closet. What the hell was he doing in there? It had been torn apart as well and I wondered if he'd found the place in that condition or if he'd done it himself. Kneeling down next to him, I placed my hands on his knee. His legs were bent and his hair hid his face from my view.

"James, please talk to me. You're scaring me."

"Why didn't you tell me?"

It was like someone stuck a dagger in me. Why hadn't I told him what? I racked my brain. The only thing we'd never discussed was the baby. I sighed as I tried to form words.

"Little bird." He finally lifted his head and his eyes met mine. Had he been crying? God, it was worse than I thought. "That's not your name, Blackbird. Why didn't you tell me?"

"I didn't want to pressure you." Wait. The hypothetical dagger left my chest as I asked, "How, why, did you just call me Blackbird?"

"That's your name isn't it?"

Before I could say anything more, he dangled the necklace in front of me. I thought it had been long gone and it seemed that James had it all along. My voice cracked as I asked, "Where, how did you get this?"

"I found it on the ground that day at the hospital after Dan tried abducting you. The chain was broken and I took it in to get fixed. Then I blew everything to shit."

"You've had it all this time?"

"Yes. Waiting for the right time to give it back to you." I didn't know what to say. I listened as he carried on. "I've been remembering things, little things. When we left the art studio tonight, I had a flash of the necklace here at the penthouse. I had to come and find it."

"You're remembering things?"

His hands grabbed my waist and pulled me closer to him. I was on my knees as we both held the others face. He tucked some hair behind my ear and said, "Not things, *everything*, Blackbird."

I shook my head in disbelief. "Please don't tease me."

"I don't tease." He cupped my face as I clutched his shoulders. "Always." He looked in my eyes, "Only." He kissed my lips, "Forever."

Together we whispered, "You."

His lips met mine and we took our time. Gently, he nipped my bottom lip between his teeth as my hands threaded through his hair. I licked at his open mouth as he pulled me onto his lap. There was a knock on the closet entrance and I groaned as I dropped my head to his shoulder.

"I'm going to assume everything's good here. I don't need to call paramedics or anything?"

James growled and looked past me. "Only for yourself if you don't get the fuck out of here."

"Aye, aye captain. It's nice to have you back." James picked up something and threw it at Smith as I chuckled. Smith and Delaney left us to our long overdue reunion on the closet floor of the penthouse.

"How long have you been remembering?"

He looked to me and rolled his eyes. "Does it fucking matter?" I tried not to smile at his tone as he demanded, "Fucking kiss me, wife."

~ JAMES ~

EVERY SINGLE MEMORY I'd lost came rushing back. My head was pounding with the information overload. Weeks and months of torture were finally over. She'd stood by my side, without falter, the entire time. She'd bent her own will to my whims as I made her my slave. I was a dick. I knew that she'd done it knowing it was probably the only way she'd get to me. She'd been right. The closer we became, the more frequent the dreams and glimpses of my lost memory had become.

We were sitting on the floor of the closet, her straddling my lap. My headache was starting to subside and Smith had just left. "Fucking kiss me, wife."

"I will, soon enough. How much do you remember of that day?"

I pulled her to my chest and said softly, "I remember seeing his car fly off that bridge and plummet into the water. I think my heart stopped. I remember telling Paul that no matter what, he had to get you to shore." I sighed deeply, burying my nose into her hair. I'd almost lost her, again. Then I remembered seeing the flash of white that went off in the car. I pushed her back so I could see her face. "I got your phone call, I heard everything you said." She wiped at her tears as I asked, "Did he try to shoot you?"

"No, well, yes, but I shot him first."

"Jesus Christ. You'll be lucky if I ever let you out of my sight again."

She trailed her soft finger down my scar and kissed my closed eyes, "I'm not going anywhere." She wrapped her arms around my neck and said, "About that kiss…I have one condition."

"What's that?"

"Take me home, no detours this time."

Groaning, I pulled the keys out of my pocket and informed her, "You should drive. My head is thrashing."

"Should we call a doctor?"

Smiling at her, I pushed her off my lap and said, "It's nothing a good pounding can't cure."

She shook her head and said, "It's time you pay up on your lost poker bet."

Shit. How did I tell her I'd really won the game that night? Delaney knew the truth, but I was pretty sure her loyalties now lay with Cassidy and not me and was surprised she hadn't revealed the truth to her. "Blackbird, let me love you first. I've missed you."

She started to speak and then didn't. As we walked out of the closet, another gift box caught my eye. Releasing her hand, I picked it up, remembering what it was. She looked to me and I handed it to her.

"Here, sit down." I moved her to the edge of the bed and told her to open it.

Hesitantly she opened it up. When she removed the lid and saw the contents, she pressed her lips together and struggled to hold back the emotion.

"I bought these the day I came back from the cabin, before…"

She nodded, "They're so tiny." She held up the baby booties, then the hat and the bib. She placed everything back in the box and replaced the lid. "Thank you. You know, your mom said something to me the day before she died." I was speechless as she continued speaking, "She said that you'd be so happy about the baby, like she knew. I wasn't even pregnant yet, I don't think."

I wiped her tears before pulling her to me. "I want a family with you, Blackbird. I never thought I'd say those words to anyone."

Whimpering into my neck, she reciprocated. "I want a family, too. It's just…"

Stroking her hair, "What is it?"

"I'm scared. What if I can't get pregnant?"

"Hey, you said the doctors said it shouldn't be a problem."

"I know, but, what if…"

"Shh, stop worrying about the 'what ifs'. I want a family with you, when you're ready." She nodded into my neck and asked that I be patient with her.

Holding hands, we walked out of the bedroom and down the stairs. She drove us home and once we were inside, I threw her over my shoulder like I'd done so many times before. I carried her up the stairs and knew we'd triumphed. I loved her more than life itself. She was the only thing in my life, which had once been full of debauchery, that mattered.

I walked into the bedroom and kicked the door shut behind me. Memories from before and after the accident swarmed my brain and I was thankful she insisted we go home. The penthouse was home for many memories, but the townhouse was our home. I let her slide down my front and smiled wickedly at her.

I pulled out my phone and silenced it before docking it to the speakers and putting on my 'Cassidy' playlist. I'd found the list after Smith gave me my new phone. I'd added several songs in the past few weeks and now that I remembered everything, all my song choices made sense. Some I'd even taken from her playlist for the club.

I played the song that I had added during my time away at the cabin. I spent those days sobering up and in daily sessions with Dr. Pratt. I knew then I could never let her go and all I wanted was to give her my love. *Give Me Love* by Ed Sheeran began playing as she walked around the room tempting me by the sway of her hips.

"I thought you said no sappy songs."

Closing the distance between us, I snagged her wrist and yanked her body to mine. "It's not that sappy. Give me love, Cassidy. Let me love you."

I didn't wait for her answer, simply feathered my goatee over her lips, cheeks, and neck. Her breathing increased as she gripped my arms and pulled at my suit jacket. I shrugged it off as she worked the buttons of my shirt. Before she had it fully open, she yanked it out of my pants and I pulled it over my head. I bent down and ran my hands up her stockings and as I reached her knees, my hands traveled under her dress to the hem of the stockings. She was wearing a garter belt.

"You're wearing the garter belt. You know what that does to me."

She just smiled as my lips met hers. She glided her tongue into my mouth with such fervor that I groaned. I cupped her face and pulled my lips away as I asked where the zipper was. She turned around and I found the small clasp and zipper that kept the dress closed. Slowly, I pulled it down as her ivory skin met my eyes. I spotted the back closure to her bra and took note that it was also one I'd purchased for her. I pulled her back as I bit on her neck, pushing her hair to the other side. Sliding the dress over each shoulder, I guided it over her hips. Once I heard the fabric hit the floor, I stood up and took in the sight of her. All white skin, black lace, and red hair. She was a sight to be seen.

Slowly, she turned around and closed the distance between us. I wanted to take things slow, but she was making it difficult. That memory of that morning in the dining room at the penthouse, all those weeks ago, came to mind. We had been frenzied and I didn't want that for us, not then anyway.

Like she read my mind she chanted, "Slow and hard, James."

I showed her my smile that I knew she couldn't resist and pushed her back against the bed. She leaned up on her elbows as she watched me undress. I left my briefs on and climbed on top of her fully intending to make her beg.

"*It Was Always You.*" Another Maroon 5 song that spoke to my heart, which was her.

"Another sappy song. I'm beginning to wonder about you, Mr. Benedict."

"Only the sappiest for you." She smiled sweetly as I lowered my lips to her.

I began kissing every inch of exposed skin, savoring every moment. Her skin was beginning to tremble and every caress produced a shudder or a moan of pleasure from her. Kneeling between her knees, I detached her garters from the stockings and pulled the belt off her body leaving the stockings. Her panties were next and I locked my eyes with hers as I pulled them down.

"James. Don't make me beg."

Grinning, "But you know how I love to hear you begging."

I reached for her hand and pulled her to a seated position. On my knees and still between her legs she cupped my erection as her lips moved over my torso. Her other hand moved up the back of my leg and into the hem of my underwear. Squeezing my cheek and digging her nails in, I growled as I reached for the hooks of her bra. Once it was unhooked, she shrugged it off and threw it to the floor. Leaning over her, she fell back to the bed as I took a nipple into my mouth. I sucked and nipped at it until she cried out, my other hand teasing her mound.

I kissed down to her navel until I reached the damp sweetness that was wholly her. Her clit was starting to swell when I took it in my mouth and worked my tongue over it. I loved watching her hips and thighs flex as she sought more pressure. She was seeking penetration and I knew it as she pressed harder into my face. I worked my briefs off then cupped her ass in my hands as she became more disoriented. When she panted my name, I pulled away and knelt between her legs.

"Cassidy, look at me." Those eyes of hers were magnetic. She searched for my face in the darkness and met my eyes. "I love you, Blackbird."

Panting and trying to smile, she replied, "I love you, too."

Lowering myself over her, my tip prodded her entrance. I kissed her lips, both our eyes open and slid into her. She was warm, wet, tight, and eager to meet my every thrust. Her walls quivered around me as they accommodated me and as it slowed, I pulled back out and right back in. Arching her back, she exposed her neck to me as I lowered my lips and began leaving my mark just below her ear. Her hands frantically searched for something to hang on to and I knew what she craved. My hands captured her wrists and pinned them to the bed on either side of her head.

I ground my hips against her as I asked, "Is that what you wanted?"

Sliding in again and a little deeper she whimpered my name. "James! Yes, please don't let go." She used the strength of my arms to her advantage and arched up into me further, rubbing every part of herself against me.

Repeating her movements, in rhythm to my own body, she became more feverish. "I won't let go. I'm never letting go of us."

Her eyes met mine and the wall of ecstasy glazed over them. She was about to come. I focused all my movement on her, my own release pushed aside. "H, harder." Her legs were trembling as they tried desperately to cling to my waist. "OH! Yes, right there."

The stillness settled over her—a telltale sign she was ready—and with my next thrust, she screamed my name as her release took over. My body took over as I drove her harder into the mattress, freeing her wrists she wrapped her arms around my neck as I succumbed to my own climax.

A few hours later and orgasms later, she was lying on my back and tracing the anchor tattoo with her fingers. I told her everything about when and why I'd gotten it. She fell asleep like that and I delicately rolled over as she burrowed into my side. I slept better that night than I had in months, if not years.

twenty four

Forever

~ JAMES ~

IT WAS BACK, EVERYTHING. A COUPLE weeks had passed since that night when everything came rushing back to me. I had just finished a meeting with Cal and Jane. They were taking the leap and starting the process to build their house. Paul was helping them with the design, though he was still in Atlanta. I hadn't admitted it to anyone, but I missed him. I had some things to ask him and hoped he'd be receptive.

After making that call I headed to the parking garage. The conversation had gone better than I anticipated. He agreed and I hoped it was the first step to getting him back to Michigan. Though, given the cold front we were entering, I wouldn't want to leave Atlanta either if I was him.

Cassidy was working late, or so she'd said. When I pulled in the drive, her car was in the garage. I was looking forward to another weekend with her. We didn't have plans and I planned on keeping her in bed all weekend, if I could. I'd chain her to the bed if I needed to and I knew she wouldn't object.

Chessa greeted me at the door as I set down my things. I picked her up and asked her, "Where's your, Momma?" I set her down and she darted up the stairs.

The music became louder as I made my way to our room. When I walked in, she was wearing her glasses, a white blouse that was unbuttoned, that black bra I loved fully exposed, black skirt, and knee high boots. Those had to be new. Shit! She looked like a naughty librarian. I adjusted myself as I took in the scene in front of me. She had candles lit, curtains closed, and the light off.

Her hair was up in a tight pony and she held a crop in her hand. I approached her and she put up her finger. "Not so fast Mr. Benedict." I stopped, eager to see what she'd do next. "Don't move."

Turning to her iPod, she scrolled through the playlist, hit a couple buttons, and then hit play. I shook my head at her and her choice of music. She was demented and I loved it. They were coming in concert and she'd already purchased tickets. *Whore* by In This Moment began blaring. She shooed Chessa out the door and closed it. We'd been pretty vanilla and boring the last week or so and it was evident she missed the spice.

"I have plans for you." She walked a circle around me, trailing her crop over my suit.

"Is that so? Since when are you in charge here?"

"You made the comment that I could, or was it should, be a switch." She turned in a small circle, took a bow and said, "Tada!"

"Cassidy…"

"Ah, ah, ah. Tonight, it's Mistress." She narrowed her eyes at me as she smacked the crop against her boot.

"Mistress." I closed the distance between us. Her boots added several inches to her height and she was nearly eye to eye with me. "What did you have in mind?"

"You, naked, NOW."

Once I was disrobed, she told me to get on the bed. Sitting on the edge, she placed her spiked boot between my legs, dangerously close to my package. Gently, she pressed the heel into my thigh and told me to remove her boot. I found the zipper and trailed my fingers down the exposed flesh as I released the zipper, repeating the action on her other foot. Her eyes traveled to my growing erection and she smiled wickedly.

"Roll over."

I laid back and rolled to my stomach. She climbed up my body and sat down on my bare ass. My rigid cock was pressed into the bed and it was almost uncomfortable. Her hand reached back between my thighs and grazed my balls.

"Shit."

I felt the smack of the crop on my shoulder as she barked, "I didn't give you permission to talk."

She was trying so hard and I found it amusing and hot. She'd definitely be wearing that outfit more often. She spent some time dragging her nails up and down my back, ass, and legs before she rolled me over. Showing me the leather cuffs I looked to her eyes knowing what she was asking. I trusted her and I wanted to give her what she wanted. I spread my arms up to the headboard and she strapped me in.

My cock was erect and lying against my belly. She left my legs free and began undressing. When she was completely nude, only her glasses on, she climbed on to the bed and stood above me. She began caressing herself as she stared into my eyes.

"Do you want to touch me, slave?"

"You know I do."

Her hand traveled to her clit before she slipped her finger inside. Pulling it back out, she brought it to her lips and asked, "Do you want to taste me?" I groaned as she smiled. She dropped down and kissed my lips. "Can you taste me or do you need more?"

Growling I demanded, "More."

She straddled my face and lowered herself to within inches of my hungry mouth. When her lips met with mine, I slowly stroked my tongue over her and sucked on her clit. She easily lost herself in the sensations, gripping the headboard with one hand and my hair with the other.

I thought she'd ride me till she came when she abruptly peeled herself off my face. Sliding down my body, my cock was in her mouth before I knew what was happening. She sucked, licked, fucked, stroked, and blew my cock until I was seconds from blowing my load and she stopped.

"Not yet."

"Cass...Mistress."

She smiled at me and brought her face within inches of mine. "Begging for more? I like when you beg. You should do it more often." I groaned, seeking the warmth of her pussy knowing it was only inches from my dick. "I love you, slave."

"I love you, Mistress."

She clutched my cock and slid down my length, hard. She quivered from the force of it and began rocking back and forth. I bucked my hips as my hands pulled on the cuffs.

"God, I love fucking you, James. But I need something else from you."

"Anything, what is it?" I pressed up into her again.

"Admit that *you* won the poker game." My eyes bulged as she snickered. She knew and tied me up anyway. "And that you *wanted* me to tie you up."

"I admit it."

Her hands released one wrist, her face just above mine as her body still rocked against me. Just before she released my other hand she switched on me. I saw it in her eyes.

"Make me your whore." My hand was free.

I fucked her mouth with my tongue as I flipped her to her back and drove into her. Getting on my knees, I pressed her legs together as I lifted them in the air causing her to moan. When she came, her face was pressed against the mattress as my hand held her hip and the other fingered her ass. As her climax ended, I grabbed the lube and pulled out of her.

Slowly, I entered her ass. When I was fully embedded in her, I pulled her hair back and kissed her mouth. "Only *my* whore."

"Only yours."

IT WAS THE morning of the Masquerade and it happened to fall on Halloween that year. I was a nervous wreck and trying to hide it. We were headed to the penthouse so we could get ready there. All my plans had fallen into place and she was none the wiser.

I sat down with Lena, Aunt Bev, Cal, and Jane. Aunt Bev looked at me, "Are you sure James? It's a lot of pressure to put on her, especially when you still don't have your memory back." Jane agreed with her.

"She's my wife and I told her I'm not going anywhere. This is how I intend to prove it."

"If I can interject." We all looked to Cal. He and I had become friends

and I sensed there had been some tension between us at some point. "You two have proven over and over again that you love each other; memory or not. Take it from me; Cass is a sucker for grand gestures. This is just that. She'll love it and she won't say no."

A weight was lifted from me after he said that. Jane then agreed with Cal, "He's right, James. I think it's a lovely idea. I'm just partial to these things happening behind closed doors, but I think we all know that." We all chuckled at the travesty that was Cal's first proposal. Before we could all start thinking about the horrible events that immediately followed said proposal, Lena had an idea.

"Why don't we request everyone to wear black, or dark formal colors?"

"I want her in a wedding dress. She deserves that moment."

We all began to brainstorm ideas and eventually settled on the one we thought best.

"Are you ok? You look stressed." She reached over and ran her hand over my thigh.

I smiled, "Nah, I'm good. Just house stuff."

"Ok. Anything I can help with?" Her phone then started chiming and I insisted she deal with work things.

After hours of final preparation in the ball room, she made her way back up to the penthouse. She was in the shower when Lena showed up to do her hair.

"Everyone's here. We're all set. She didn't freak out about the dress?"

I shook my head. "No, I told her not to worry about it."

Lena giggled, "I wish I could've seen the look on her face when she saw it wasn't the black dress, but a white one instead. Your idea to have Frida duplicate the black one in white was brilliant."

"Thanks."

"James? Is Lena here yet?"

I winked at Lena and shouted up the stairs, "Yup, she just got here. Listen. There's a problem with the house so I need to go make some phone calls. Enjoy your girl time. I'll see you down there."

"Ok."

I looked to Lena and threatened her, "Don't you dare let anything slip!"

"Stop worrying about me. Let me go get your bride ready."

~ CASSIDY ~

I STOOD IN FRONT OF THE mirror as Lena put the finishing touches on her hair. I heard Delaney yell up the stairs and told them we were in the bedroom. Delaney and Jane came walking into the bedroom, both wearing dark red ball gowns that matched. I looked at both of them and they laughed.

Jane said, "Apparently we have the same taste."

"And you don't follow instructions. That's not black or white. Your mom is going to have my head."

"Oh, don't worry about her. I'll handle her."

I rolled my eyes and looked at the white ball gown that hung on the door. Delaney took a few pictures as I told her to knock it off. "It's bad enough I'll probably stick out like a sore thumb."

"Why would you stick out like a sore thumb? That dress is gorgeous."

I groaned, "Yeah and its white. Everyone else is going to be in black or RED. You guys suck." I turned to Lena and asked, "Where's your dress? Did you go with the black one?"

"Umm."

"Lena!"

"It's red, too."

Before I could freak out, Delaney handed me a glass of champagne. I didn't question where it came from and quickly downed it. Lena got a phone call and seemed panicked. She assured me that everything was fine, but that I was needed in the ball room immediately.

We got my dress on and Delaney offered to come with me. I told Lena to take her time getting her dress on. Jane stayed back with Lena to help her with the zipper. The lobby was eerily quiet as the elevator doors opened. Guests should've been arriving in droves and I voiced my concern to Delaney.

"Don't worry. They'll be here."

The caterer ran over to me and started talking in circles about one of the dinner entrees and I made my way to the kitchen with him. Several minutes later I walked back to the hallway to find Delaney gone. Loud music was blaring from the ballroom and it wasn't what I'd discussed with the DJ at all. I barreled through the ball room doors and made it about fifteen feet into the room before I became paralyzed.

Marry You by Bruno Mars was blaring overhead. What the hell was going on? I spotted my Dad, what was he doing here? He'd told me that he and Lisa couldn't make it. Next to him were my uncle and some cousins of mine. My heart started racing as I looked around in a panic. Cal walked up to me, kissed my cheek, and handed me a red peony and walked away without saying a word. Then Smith did the same and then Jackson, my father-in-law.

My eyes found him in the middle of the room. His hair was down and he looked amazing in his tuxedo. He was all alone and my father walked over to me and handed me another large red peony. He placed his hand on the small of my back and kissed my cheek.

"I think James has something he wants to ask you."

Before I could say anything, he gently pushed me toward James. I stood there for a moment and looked around the room. I knew what this was; at least I thought I knew. He had turned the masquerade into a wedding reception for us. His hand reached for mine as I slowly approached him.

"James, how did you do this?"

He shook his head, "Can't you just be quiet and let me talk?" I pressed my lips together as I held back a chuckle. "I didn't give you the wedding you deserved, the ring or the proposal. I'm sorry for that. Will you dance with me?"

"Of course."

He wrapped his arms around me as *Marry Me* by Jason Derulo began playing. We were the only ones dancing and it felt how a first dance should feel. I noticed a photographer taking pictures, a videographer filming and friends flashing their own cameras. I would never forget that moment. Pulling back I looked into his eyes.

Whispering, "Always, only, forever, you."

He kissed me and said, "Only you."

I chuckled as he spun me around and pulled me back tight against him and sang the last few lines of the song to me. When the song ended, silence filled the room. I looked around nervously and then saw as he pulled a small box out of his pocket and got down on one knee.

"Oh, James." My hand covered my mouth and then my chest as I fingered my blackbird necklace.

He opened the box and a gorgeous vintage engagement ring stared at me. "I'm pretty sure I fell in love with you the first time I saw you sitting in my bar. I fell again when you walked into my office last October. I fell yet again at the carnival. You've stuck by my side when I deserved it the least. I can't live without you. You're my sun and stars, my heart and soul, my forever. Only you, Cassidy Arianna Benedict, will you marry me, again?"

"Yes, of course I will." He slipped the ring on my finger and it fit perfectly.

A large applause filled the room around us, but I was solely focused on him. He stood and molded his lips to mine before yelling, "She said yes!" Giggling at him, he kissed me again. When our lips separated he said, "Judge Mathis is here. He's waiting."

"What?"

"We're getting married. I picked your bridesmaids," he pointed to Jane, Delaney, and Lena who were all wearing matching red dresses, "I hope that's ok."

I shook my head at all three of them. "You guys are unbelievable." Looking back to James I said, "Its perfect."

"The chapel is setup outside. I'm sorry it's so cold, I wasn't expecting it."

"Stop. It's perfect."

Stepping into the hallway, the guests were all directed to the outdoor chapel. My father and bridesmaids hovered around me as I began scolding them all. "Who are the groomsmen?"

Before they could answer, I saw Paul with Cal and Smith. They were also wearing matching tuxedos. I stepped away from them and toward Paul. He smiled and we hugged. I couldn't believe he was there, let alone a groomsman.

"You didn't have to do this."

He shook his head, "I was honored to be asked. Everything is how it's supposed to be." He hugged me again and then Lena asked me who I wanted the girls to walk down the aisle with.

I looked at the six people in front of me and knew how it had to be. "I assume Smith is the best man," he nodded, "then Delaney is with him. Clearly Jane and Cal are together, which leaves you with Paul."

Lena nodded and I hoped it wasn't uncomfortable for her. I knew she'd had a terrible crush on him at one point and even paid him a visit in Atlanta which hadn't gone so well. She'd told me in confidence just a few weeks ago and told me when we were discussing her relationship with Ryan. She and Ryan had been dating for a few months so I figured it was no longer a big deal. Then the music started and Lena and Paul walked down the aisle, then Cal and Jane, followed by Delaney and Smith.

"You ready for this kiddo?" I smiled at my Dad.

"Yes! Besides, we're already married, so it's kind of a done deal."

"You look beautiful." I looked down at the dress and knew that James must've had a hand in that, too.

"Thank you. I'm very lucky to have so many amazing men in my life. Without you and Cal and now James, I don't know where I'd be."

"Let's not worry about that." He took a deep breath as the doors opened and the music changed.

"Oh, I love this song."

James must've picked it. It was on my JB3 playlist and I absolutely loved the song. *How Long Will I Love You* by Ellie Goulding began to serenade me as everyone stood, awaiting my entrance. I spotted him at the altar smiling back at me and my heart melted. That incredible man, flawed he may have been, but he loved me perfectly. Over and over again he proved to me he was willing to do anything to show me he loved me. All the hurt we'd caused each other had been worth it. Because without it, we wouldn't have been where we were.

My dad whispered, "Last chance. Say the word and we can run."

I laughed out loud and turned to my dad, "Not a chance."

The End

Playlist for Letting Go of Us

What Do I Have to Do? by Stabbing Westward
Letters From The Sky by Civil Twilight
I Kissed a Girl by Katy Perry
There's a Rumor by The August Empire
Coconut by Harry Nilsson
Look at You by Big & Rich
Sometime Around Midnight by The Airborne Toxic Event
End of Me by A Day To Remember
Wherever You Will Go by The Calling
Stay by Thirty Seconds To Mars
Break by Rebecca Roubion
Summer by Calvin Harris
Take Me Home by Cash Cash
Eyes On Fire by Blue Foundation
Sleeping With A Friend by Neon Trees
Boom Clab by Charli XCX
Best Night Ever by Gloriana
Miracle by Foo Fighters
I Won't Give Up by Jason Mraz
Come Get It Bea by Pharrell Williams
Water's Edge by Seven Mary Three
Just Give Me a Reason by P!nk, Nate Ruess
Over You by Ingrid Michaelson, A Great Big World

Desire by Meg Myers
Cosmic Love by Florence + The Machine
Give Me Love by Ed Sheeran
It Was Always You by Maroon 5
Whore by In This Moment
Marry You by Bruno Mars
Marry Me by Jason Derulo
How Long Will I Love You by Ellie Goulding

More from J.M. Witt

The Anchored Hearts Series
Letting Go (Vol. 1)
Hiding Away (Vol. 1.5)
Letting Go of You (Vol. 2)
Fading Away (Vol. 2.5)
Letting Go of Us (Vol. 3)

The Blind Vows Series
Trust, Honor, Love: (Vol. 1)
Body, Heart, Soul: (Vol. 2)

Woodland Creek Series
Mina's Revenge

KinkyFodder Chronicles
My Secret Submission: (1)
My Secret Possession: (2)

About the Author

Residing in Metro Detroit, International Bestselling Erotic Author J. M. started writing poetry and short stories as a young girl. Rediscovering her love of reading, after having her fourth child, she started writing again. She also works full time as an Office Manager for a large landscaping company.

Letting Go, her first publication, was released in December 2013 and 10th novel was published in January 2017.

She enjoys music, time with friends, sarcasm, concerts, spending time with her children and husband, traveling, and getting lost in a good book.

And if you ask nicely, she might show you her flogger and let you sample it.

You can find her at
www.jmwittbooks.com
Twitter # wittymomauthor
www.facebook.com/jmwittbooks

Official playlists for all her books are on
Spotify & YouTube

www.ingramcontent.com/pod-product-compliance
Lightning Source LLC
Chambersburg PA
CBHW030641260626
47157CB00007B/2440